North Hope Cove

Penny Doyle Douglas

for Gina

One

The car was at least a quarter-mile off the road; on his way out, he'd rearrange some brush to disguise whatever evidence left as he'd driven into the woods. Walking straight away from the car should take him back to the road's edge; he'd been careful not to steer more than necessary, driving straight into the forest. His cell phone was left behind, in the back of a bureau drawer with the battery removed so it would not be immediately found—if it ever was—and he'd dressed in his favorite jeans and boots. His note was written to a man nearly three years dead, so he burned it in the car's ashtray just after signing it. All that remained was to wait for dawn. Justin lit a cigarette. By the time he finished smoking it, there should be just enough daylight to set out.

Gabriel,

You know how I never liked to make promises. The only one I ever kept was almost the only one I ever made, and that was my promise to be yours and love you until death us do part. I only agreed to that second promise you asked for because death was so close it tickled the hairs on my arms. And I felt so guilty. Because taking care of you was hard. And I shouldn't have minded but sometimes (too many times, too much) I did mind. Watching you get worse every day and knowing it would never be better again, that I would never have you the same way I used to, was a slow-motion torture for me. And of course that's selfish. Because it was you that had the pain, and the sickness, and a lot of years stolen away—and it was me who survived. I'd have traded with you, you know. Right? You know.

So I promised to keep the house open because you loved it, and you were dying, and I loved you. But I never loved the house like you did. You know that, too. It wasn't me who welcomed the guests and sat up nights in the parlor talking to them, learning about their lives, the places they'd been. I wasn't the one who got up in the dark early morning to fix their coffee. I wasn't the one they wrote letters to, after they'd gone, saying thank you for a wonderful stay, meeting you was a pleasure. I'm not you, and I can't do all you did. I can't do it, even for you.

    No one will find me, and I never wrote anything or made any arrangements. I'd like to think the house will become a ruin, and some day burn or fall down, back to the land, like a ghost. I hate to think of someone else inside it, who couldn't ever love it as much as you did, and whose voice would be different, floating up every morning from downstairs, with a different laugh.

    It got bad for me, and then it got a little better, but then it got even worse, and it's never gotten better again. If it weren't for Lia sometimes making me, I wouldn't even get out of bed most days. And so I've failed at yet another thing, and failed you, and that's worst of all. I shouldn't have promised.

    I love you, Gabriel. I miss you. But loving you isn't enough, and missing you is too much. Maybe I'll see you when I get there.

    Your loving husband,
    Justin

By the time Justin squashed the cigarette's filter into the ashes of his note, the sky was lighter, violet and gray, rust-gold at the lower edge. He took his last seven cigarettes, the plastic lighter rattling inside the pack, and left his wallet on the driver's seat. No one would find him; he doubted anyone would look. But in case they did, there'd be no question. Even the high school dropouts populating the town's six-man police force would be able to connect the dots from the abandoned house to the abandoned car to his abandoned body. Just for fun, he tossed the keys under the driver's seat before closing the door. Make them work a little; they'd probably be grateful for something to do.

    He'd done pretty well driving straight in, or so he thought, but after fifteen minutes walking, he still hadn't come to the road. He took a piss on a tree, and lit another smoke, turned in a slow circle, looking for a clue. He couldn't see the car anymore, and listened for traffic noise, even though chances were almost zero; unsurprisingly, he heard only an occasional bird calling out a notice that it had survived the night, then one or two others congratulating it and confirming they'd made it through, too. A little ways off to his left was a small clearing carpeted with fallen needles and mucky leaves, and he picked up the trail of tire impressions and a few broken saplings, away from where he'd just come, that would lead him out of the woods onto the road. He knew the way from there.

The cigarette and the creeping dawn stoked up a craving for coffee, and Justin licked his teeth. Gabriel had always poured him a thermos-full to take along any time he got in the car to go into the city, somewhere noisy enough to drown out his thoughts. If he didn't make Justin a sandwich, he opened his wallet and gave him whatever was in there, *in the case you get hungry*. One of Gabriel's many rituals, another way he played host, always taking care of things, assuring everyone's comfort.

In five minutes, Justin was at the forest's edge. It took him even less effort than he'd imagined to camouflage the spot where he'd driven off the road. The ground was mostly hard packed dirt and scrubby non-grass, with no tracks he could see, and then just some bent-over tall grass at the border of the woods. He kicked it a bit, found a long, three-pronged branch with needles still attached, and dragged it out from a few yards behind the tree line. Looking at it from the blacktop, he didn't think anyone passing would look twice. And in all the previous times he'd come to check things out, he'd never seen another car, truck, or person; that particular corner of the national park was not a place most people would include in their itinerary. There were no campgrounds, no ranger huts, not even hiking or snowmobile trails. In a week or two it would be snowing, anyway, and that would take care of hiding anything his own eyes hadn't caught.

He took a final drag and flicked the cigarette butt to the ground ahead of him, crushed it underfoot when he caught up to it a few strides later, and kept walking. His sweater and t-shirt were not enough, and his upper arms burst out in goose pimples beneath the inadequate layers. His beloved old Doc Martens boots that had been in his life longer than anything or anyone—even Gabriel—sounded a reassuring, steady crunch-and-thud as he walked between the faded white line and the edge of the pavement. In about an hour, he'd be there. In an hour and a half, he'd be gone.

By the time the land started to slope upward, a long, unsteep hike to the top of the cliff, Justin was perspiring from the warmth of the low autumn sun and the exertion of his walk, even though he'd taken it slow. There came a visible bend in the road, and he had learned during previous visits to the site to veer right instead of following the pavement, continuing on scrubby grass. Despite the lack of blazes on the tree trunks or a trough worn through the fallen leaves, the way seemed obvious. Not so much because of anything visible—aside from a slight incline the woods looked the same there as anywhere—but a particular feeling settled low in his chest as he continued his steady-paced trudge upward, heavy and light at the same time, and it seemed to lead him, so he followed it.

The sense of hollow doom that had spurred Justin to drive into the woods the previous night was hardly new to him. He'd first sunk into himself as a kid, maybe eleven because he was in fifth grade for sure, and his teacher repeatedly nagged him to stop staring—out the window, or at the top of his desk, or at nothing—and his grades dropped, and nothing seemed as much fun anymore. It got better in the spring and through that summer, but the fog came and went, for years. By the time he left high school—early, got an equivalency degree and started working—he had already been hospitalized twice, only a few days each, and was put on a parade of medications with mild to hideous side effects but no discernible primary effect. He worked for a while, driving auto parts around for the mechanics at a string of car dealerships, living for free at his father's place while his dad was out working on lobster and crab boats for weeks at a time, and Justin managed to save enough money to go to the noisy places he'd always longed for—New Orleans, Miami, Atlantic City—riding buses, washing dishes, delivering pizzas, sleeping where he could.

For nearly two years, he'd been a vagabond, borderline punk, too hip to be homeless despite having no home. He landed in Boston, rented a mattress on the floor of a walk-in closet in an overcrowded student house, and passed a stinking, humid summer mostly lying down. That October he spent a week weighing the pros and cons of walking into traffic versus walking in front of a train, and ultimately walked into an emergency room instead. He spent three weeks in the psych ward. By the time he went back to the house for his backpack, his housemates had already rented out his room.

He'd been better for a long time, found a cheaper room farther north of the city, got another job driving, put six thousand miles on his car in three months. He met Gabriel while delivering mufflers and fan belts; Gabriel was a salesman but was too genuine and too kind, and so was reliably the lowest-grossing salesman of the month, every month. His apartment was small and neat, and he said hello to the neighbors, chatted with the checker at the grocery store, asked the old ladies having coffee together every day at Donny's Doughnuts when they were going to let him take them out dancing. Justin wasn't sure what to make of him at first; gregarious and with his slippery Brazilian-Portuguese accent, his charismatic machismo, so that Justin felt crowded, sometimes, just standing within a few feet of him. But of course he was gorgeous and charming, and for reasons Justin never fully figured out, Gabriel sought out his company. Flirty chitchat at the car lot turned into Gabriel cooking him dinner, kissing his neck, inviting him to move in. The fast flow of their relationship was a thrilling comfort, and Justin let himself be carried along. In less than a year they'd given each other pet names, promises, and gold rings, rented a bigger place together, talked casually about the future.

It was easy for Justin not to get out of bed, when they both wished to spend every minute they could there, together. By the time they found their balance, less desperate and more devoted, Justin was already swimming back up from it. At some point he'd stopped going to work, but Gabriel was pleased to have him there to fuss over, buying him shoes and cooking their dinners, and neither of them ever mentioned it.

It was the change in the quality of early morning sunlight that let Justin know he'd reached the top of the cliff, even more than the way the sloping ground leveled out. The forest was still thick, though there were more rocks—wide swaths that covered the ground, boulders, and little caves gray squirrels bounded in and out of—and the former stillness of the cool autumn air had given way to an assertive breeze that gusted and calmed but never really stopped. He bore left of each object in his path—large stone, tree, fallen branch—and eventually emerged onto the cliff top, the bumpy ground more stone than scrub. The sky was clean and the sun bright yellow-white above the gray of the ocean. A wide, mostly-flat boulder made a good enough stool, and Justin sat, lit a cigarette, waited for the sweat to evaporate off his forehead. The horizon was close but very wide.

Below and about a quarter-mile distant was the lighthouse, and a couple of small square buildings just inland of it which Justin figured for storage sheds, possibly even an abandoned cottage. Lighthouses were all computerized and automated, and he couldn't imagine even the most reclusive hermit would want to live so far out of town, so completely alone. It was a half-hour drive just to the edge of Parker Village, and another ten minutes to what passed for the center of town. Between Parker and the lighthouse, there was nothing.

The cigarette was good, and the quiet. He was glad it wasn't raining though he didn't think it would have stopped him; it definitely would have made his hike from his hidden car a lot less pleasant. His legs stretched ahead of him, ankles crossed, and he rocked them back and forth in a wide arc, watching the scuffed toes of his boots nearly touch the ground at each side. As he held the cigarette loosely between his first two fingers, his thumb worried the inner surface of his wedding ring; there'd been no wedding, but they called each other husband, and eventually there were legal papers that were nearly as good as. As close as they could get, anyway. Justin was sure his dad would have punched him in the face, had he known. Justin imagined him out on the boat just visible north of the cliff; he was as likely there as anywhere. Justin didn't keep track of him and they rarely spoke. His mom was under a flat marker in a cemetery down near Portland, beside her parents and brother.

Smoked down to the filter, the cigarette was flicked away onto the rocks, and Justin regained his feet, coughed and then sucked the deepest breath he could manage, pressing his shoulders down and back as he blew it out again. It was time. He picked a path to the edge, and began walking toward the cliff head, scouting out the best spot.

Two

Daniel awoke in the dark and found his way around the foot of his bed to where the alarm clock sat atop the low dresser. Once the alarm was silenced, he switched on the radio to get the news out of Augusta; there was only mild static, which meant little to no wind. He knew where to find the lamp, clicked it on, keeping his eyes shut until after he'd adjusted to the brightness through closed lids. The Lady Black Bears had won the home opener of the university's hockey season against New Hampshire, but the men had lost in both hockey and basketball. The expected high temperature inland would be in the mid-fifties, lower at the shore. Daniel gave his beard a thorough scratch, and right down his neck onto his chest. The green digits glowed 5:13. Another victim of suicide had been discovered at North Hope Cove the previous day. Daniel shut off the radio before the announcer said the name.

Feeding the wood stove and stoking it up, Daniel grinned a good morning to the dogs, who stretched and trotted over to be scratched around the ears, then immediately returned to their side-by-side beds to wait out the hour or so before Daniel set out their breakfasts. He couldn't blame them; never did. Once the fire had caught, Daniel warmed his hands, and started the coffee, dressed, all the rote preparations for the routine of his workday.

The previous afternoon had brought the swarm of activity and frowning people that always followed the discovery of a body among the rocks at the cliff's foot. The dogs had alerted Daniel near two o'clock, barking and pacing until he left the workbench where he'd been building up the worn teeth on some gears by soldering on fresh metal. On emerging from the shed, Daniel watched both dogs set off at a trot toward the base of the cliff, and stopped in the cottage to retrieve his cell phone, scrolling to the number that would ring a phone on one of the two desks in the police station down in Parker

Village. Within an hour emergency vehicles rolled up to the light station, parking carefully distant, near where Daniel parked his truck. The intruders knew to leave the grass around the cottage as undisturbed as possible, mindful that a man's home and property—even when it technically belonged to the National Parks Department—was not to be trod upon carelessly. As nothing could be done to save the poor soul, there was no urgency that might warrant trampling the land.

While the police and local newspaper photographer did their work, snapping photos from more angles than could possibly be necessary given the obvious conclusion—that another fed-up, broken-hearted person had flung himself off North Hope Cove's slate-gray cliff onto the rocks below—Daniel made coffee, dug deep in the back of a low cupboard for a half-full plastic bag of foam cups he kept for just such occasions, then set out a bowl of sugar and a glass measuring cup he filled with milk. The gathered crowd of cops, ambulance medics, newspaper reporter and photographer, and funeral home personnel would amble into the cottage in their twos and threes, careful to wipe their boots on the mat outside the front door, standing closer than normal due to the smallness of the kitchen, talking in low voices.

Later they learned he'd left his phone, wallet, and a sealed letter addressed to "Marie" in a plastic zipper-bag on the cliff top leaning upright against a rock, and Laura from the funeral home tucked it carefully into her big cloth shoulder bag. His name was Henry Block; fifty-seven years of age; from Thurston, some fifteen miles west of Parker. The state trooper who'd showed up when he heard the radio chatter about something going on up at North Hope stood just outside the cottage's front door to phone the wife. Daniel offered a plate of shortbread cookies and a bowl of black-pepper-dusted cashews, and stayed out of the way.

Breakfast was a bowl of oatmeal with a small apple grated into it; a slice of buttered rye toast; and a fried egg with ketchup; followed immediately by the day's first smoke and second cup of coffee, at the little round table facing the kitchen window. Outside, it was still dark, nothing yet to see, but the sweep of the lantern passed at regular intervals, changing the opacity of the reflections in the window panes. Daniel's pace was steady but not hurried; the sun wouldn't rush to rise just because he ate fast, so he didn't eat fast. The dogs huffed occasional sighs, sounding put-upon.

Once the body had been cleared off the rocks, and all that there was to be found—the shoes that had come off, the bag of identification left behind—gathered and toted away; once everyone had been offered coffee and traded the sort of gentle, small-talk gossip that passed for conversation, Daniel shook their hands, nodded, frowned, told them to drive safe. As he dumped the dregs from the cups, returned most of the cookies to the tin, and ran a damp cloth across the surface of the kitchen table, his hands shook. He felt a familiar, uncomfortable flutter in his gut, replaying the previous few hours in his head to be sure he hadn't said anything crass, hadn't laughed inappropriately, hadn't neglected anything that needed doing as host of the party. The dogs gave him space, and he smoked. Shortly he'd return to the shed to place tools on the pegboard, within thick black outlines showing where each belonged, but first Daniel had sat in his armchair and invited the dogs to rest their chins on his knees, petted their heads and talked to them about nothing much at all, until his gut settled and hands became steady.

Done with his breakfast, Daniel washed and dried his dishes and coffee cup, put them away with their mates—only three of everything: plates, bowls, forks, glasses—and fed the dogs, who by then were underfoot, ingratiating themselves to him, well aware of daily rituals. By the time that was done, he was ready to trade his slippers for the work boots left overnight in a plastic tray by the front door to dry.

It wasn't the fact of the dead man that made Daniel shaky and unsettled; a dead man demanded nothing, and his needs were very few. Witness him. Make a phone call. Set the dogs to guard duty, keeping the gulls away. It was just another routine—though one Daniel undertook only a few times each year—and routine suited him. It was the onslaught of company that burdened him, despite the fact they needed nothing and demanded very little, themselves—only answers to benign questions about how well Daniel's truck was running, conjecture about the upcoming week's weather, acknowledging that winter would soon be upon them, wondering whether he had enough books to keep himself entertained. But Daniel had come to the light station specifically for a quiet life of useful work. The disruption of six or eight visitors all at once was difficult for him to bear, and once they'd gone he often spent nearly as long as the visit had lasted worrying about whether he'd failed them somehow, in the time between their arrival and the completion of their true task: retrieving the body from the rocks and driving it away.

He'd been ten years at the station, and the faces from the village were almost all the same ones as ever, and though no one ever brought it up anymore, naturally they knew that—yes—he was *that* Daniel Howard, the lone survivor. Whatever else they thought about him they kept to themselves, and perhaps they forgave him, or even sympathized, because who could know what they might have done in Daniel's shoes? He was lucky to be alive, or so everyone said, and it might even be true. But he had failed that day, when he was needed. It was better for him to be where he'd ended up. Necessary, but apart.

Daniel loosened the latch on the dogs' door and they let themselves out through it, and shortly he went up the gravel path in the ooze of first light, out to the tower, the lantern drawing its off-white arc across the ground and through the shimmering last bit of fog over the water. By the time he climbed the stairs, the sun would be almost up—enough time for him to make inspections, listen for errant creaks or catches in the gears, any change in the pitch of the motor that moved them. In true, irrevocable daylight, he would switch off the lamp.

National Parks had sent a letter informing Daniel of a hearing, with a public-comment period leading up to it. They were going to automate the light. Given his seniority and his *particular personal history, to which this office is sensitive*, Daniel was invited to apply for a new post elsewhere. There were no openings at any of the fourteen remaining manned light stations. Daniel had stared at the letter, rereading, trying to absorb it, while his dinner went cold on the table in front of him.

His previous post—forever ago, when he was still the person he used to be—had been at the education center in the Abenaki National Forest. Despite having no background in forest science or education, through a series of staff changes and budget cuts and budget influxes and the passage of just enough time that somehow he ended up the senior staff member in his unit after less than three years, Daniel had been in charge of running all the programs for elementary school-aged visitors to the park. In the summer, day trips from area summer camps once or twice a week, and during the school year, student field trips. He would greet the groups—after a while he'd found the jokes that worked, and had a running patter that kept the kids mostly checked-in, at least long enough for him to impart to them that wandering off could get them lost and possibly eaten by a bear (more likely trampled by a moose, but kids liked the idea of a gory death by bear-mauling, so he maintained the little white lie for the sake of drama)—and then guided them through the science center. Sometimes there was time for the mini ropes course, or an easy hike past eagles' nests, carefully crossing a brook on stones arranged to look as if they might have landed flat-side up and not too far apart by some work of nature.

The kids that day were little ones, and of course no matter who they had been it would have been tragic, but the fact they were five- and six-year-olds made it downright grotesque. Fourteen of them, eight boys and six girls. Two teachers, both women, both younger than Daniel, one wearing a wedding ring, the other a little flirty with him. Sitting at the long maple-slab table on the low pine benches in two straight rows, Daniel in the middle on one side, passing around square patches of pelts—there were claws in the fox one; that always got them squealing in delighted disgust—and in those few chaotic seconds required to register what was happening, Daniel leapt to his feet, grabbing at little shoulders and hands, getting a fingertipful of fine hair. The sudden upward jump sent his head into the bottom edge of a cabinet that should have been relocated ages before, and Daniel hit the floor. By the time he came around, it was over. His ears rang but not loud enough to muffle the drowning sound of bubbling throats. Two soft moans. Then sirens. Later, he learned he had probably only been unconscious about four minutes.

Four minutes. Fourteen little ones and two women younger than him. And the madman, of course, who did not count. And because he'd laid on the floor for four minutes looking dead, Daniel became the lone survivor, and his survival became the great failing of his life. He'd attended all the memorials, sometimes two a day, which was something he knew but could not remember having done, whether from the blow to his head or some other compassionate trick of his brain, he was not sure. No matter. It was the least he could do. People held his hands, put their arms around him, told him they were glad he'd made it, though Daniel could not imagine why. After those were over he fell apart for a while, and still no one blamed him. He let his therapist talk to the higher-ups at Parks, and when he was ready to go back to work they offered him North Hope Cove, a job no one wanted—not even the man he would replace, who spent three days with him, almost wordless as he offered minimal training in what needed doing, and how, and when, before driving away in an old jeep, leaving Daniel to it. Daniel regarded acceptance of the post as the best decision he'd ever made.

The sun was up. The lantern looked and sounded fine, so he switched it off and waited for it to slow to a stop. Lined up along the edge of the floor were three spray bottles of vinegar and a stack of folded rags; he took what he needed and went to work cleaning the glass.

Three

"Don't think I don't see you over there," Daniel accused, casting a sideways glance. "One eye open. You don't fool me. *Just once* you could take a turn at this, and let a man sleep." Both brown eyes at last came open, and Daniel *tsk*ed at the utterly unbothered expression on his face. "Useless mutts, the pair of you," he muttered, grinning. "You too, lady, don't think you're off the hook." The blue eyes remained closed and she rolled her dappled head, demonstrating for Daniel how deeply asleep she was. Daniel shut the stove's door and moved around the little table and its mismatched wood chairs to start his coffee. Waiting there by the kitchen window for it to brew, Daniel peered beyond his own reflection, into the pre-dawn darkness. The lightening sky's few remaining stars were dull, their usual white sparkle faded to pale gray. Daybreak was still an hour off, but as was its habit, the sun dropped hints of its arrival well in advance.

Once he started fixing his breakfast in earnest—toasting bread and slicing salami, frying an egg in just a little butter—the dogs put on a show of having been woken by the noise and came to investigate, tails wagging, shaking the sleep-creases out of their shaggy coats. He tugged their ears, scratched their chins, freed the latch on the dog door so they could run down to warn roosting seagulls off the stone wall at the bottom of the yard.

Once he'd eaten his egg and washed his dishes, fed the dogs, dressed and made the bed, Daniel left his slippers by the kitchen door and stepped into his boots. The dogs checked in with him briefly as he traversed the crushed-stone path to the tower, then bounded off again to manage the gulls.

On his way up the twisting slate stairs Daniel carried a dustpan and whisk-broom, swept each step ahead of him, and emptied the debris into a wastebasket just outside the lantern room. He circled the room in the shadow of the lamp, coin-sized dollops of light chasing him around as the optics turned just above the level of his head. There was nothing of note in plain sight. Sometimes birds got in—one rather determined cliff swallow had built three nests under the eaves in a month's time and Daniel had removed each one with care, checking for eggs, finding none, and sweeping the floor of the fallen twigs and long strips of grass—but just then there was nothing to find but the gears, his stack of folded rags, and bottles of vinegar. On the eastern-facing window was an old marker, a narrow vertical strip of metal gone green with age, crossed near the top by a horizontal mark: *Sun Must Be At Least This High*, he often thought. The bottom edge of the orange-white sun was just then brushing the mark, so he threw the switch to snuff the light, the rotor slowing, its pitch changing, until at last it would settle and stop. Once it had, Daniel took up a cloth and went to work polishing the lenses.

An hour later he was out behind the cottage, weeding a little in his vegetable garden, the first autumn harvest nearly ready to be brought indoors. When he'd finished the gardening, he threw balls for the dogs along an alley of green scrub-grass between the cottage and the cliff that rose up and around like a stoop-shouldered man curling an arm to embrace the cove. Daniel pitched as hard as he could, the shepherds dashing hell-for-leather after their neon-bright rubber balls, then trotting back to redeposit them in a basket by the fence.

After twenty minutes or so, Daniel warned them their time was nearly up so they'd better make it good, then threw one more for each of them. But as the dogs reached the area where both balls had likely rolled to rest, they charged straight past, rushing on to where the rocks started—a treacherous collection of jagged boulders, some rough and impressive, the size of refrigerators, tractor tires, or holiday turkeys, all of them spilled out over a carpet of gravel sharp and small as arrowheads—and both dogs stopped directly beneath the highest point of the cliff. Each dog barked once to alert him, then sank onto their bellies with their heads held high, noses pointed into the cliff's shadow.

"Not again," Daniel said to no one. "Not today. Crissakes, it's not even Christmas."

He jogged to catch them up and sure enough, there was movement atop the cliff, distinctly that of some person languidly pacing back and forth. Daniel knew no magic words—he'd said many different things in the past; about half had worked—but one phrase had worked twice, and that would have to serve as evidence it was the right thing to say.

"Please don't jump!" he bellowed upward through cupped hands. The dogs came to sit by his feet, looking up to him, at attention as they awaited further orders.

The figure—tallish, rectangular, probably a man—stopped pacing, but as he was backlit by the sun, it was impossible to make out any detail of his features or age. Daniel shielded his squinting eyes.

He heard a deep voice, three meaningless syllables that came on a breeze and landed off to his right, then echoed around the cove.

"Don't!" Daniel urged in reply to whatever had been said. "Don't! Jump!" His shoulders were taut beneath the cabled wool of his sweater, and he felt a terrible, familiar desperation pricking at the edges of his awareness. What else could he say?

The man spoke again, a sort of staccato muttering that may not even have been a reply. But he didn't jump.

"Here, dogs." They knew the stern tone and got to their feet, poised for action. "Away to me," he ordered, and swung his arm in an arc that echoed the shape of the cliff. "Go get'im. Away!"

Off they shot, knowing the correct route to take around the spill of cruel rocks to make their loping, scrambling way up the slope. It seemed forever—Daniel waiting there in the scrub—while his mutts obeyed his command and their instincts to bring a straggler back into the fold.

The man went briefly out of sight before again drifting close to the edge with his hand raised near his head; Daniel tensed. The dogs barked a storm, and the man stepped out of view. Daniel whistled them back, followed it with a call of, "Come by! Dogs, come by!" He waited, gaze tracking anxiously between the precipice—still empty for now, a good sign—and the spot on the slope where the dogs should soon come into view. Daniel walked up to meet them, aware that the imperative at the moment was just to get the guy off the edge; everything that came afterward was just paperwork.

Not soon enough, the dogs crashed into view, running half-circles around the man, beside and behind him, showing him the way to sea level.

"I think your dogs are herding me," the man said, sounding surprisingly cheerful given where they'd found him.

"They sure are," Daniel agreed. The distance closed—yard by yard—until Daniel finally got a good look at him—improbably handsome, with narrow brown eyes beneath thick eyebrows, and waves of dark hair, dressed in faded black jeans and a wide-necked black sweater too big for him. Inexplicably, Daniel was suddenly self-conscious of his own very worn but necessary work boots, mud-spotted jeans, and clichéd fisherman's sweater. He ran his hands down his thighs, wiping off any residual dog slobber from his palms.

The man's hand drifted up for Daniel to shake. He did not smile. "Justin Strongbow," he said. "Sorry to bother you."

"I'm Daniel Howard." Daniel gestured first at the red-and-white dog and added, "That's Tugboat. And this is Maggie the Cat." He scratched the blue-eyed dog beneath her chin. "Tugger and Mags. Nothing formal here." Daniel crouched down to pet and scratch them, gave them praise. "Good work, you brutes. Nice job."

"Yuh, thank you both," Justin said, his accent giving him away as a native of the area, and he smiled at last—only at the dogs, and only for an instant.

"Home time," Daniel ordered, and the dogs trotted away toward the cottage. Turning to Justin he said, "Get nervous any time I see someone up there. Thanks for coming down."

"Your dogs didn't give me much choice," Justin replied with a shrug. "Sorry for trespassing; I didn't know lighthouses were still manned. I figured they'd all be automated by now. Like everything." He gestured, indicating the rest of the world.

Daniel motioned with his head for Justin to accompany him back toward the cottage, and they fell in side by side. "Actually, most of them are," Daniel replied. "This one's a little national park all its own, about two hundred acres and only me stationed here. They just haven't gotten around to automating it." He cleared his throat, thinking of the letter he'd received that the department was suddenly planning to do just that. "It's not a life most people would choose, but I guess I'm a special breed."

Justin looked across at him, and he might have been frowning, but it was hard to say, given the way his eyebrows naturally slanted down toward his nose. After a beat of silence, Justin abruptly drew back and his hands went up in front of his chest as he exclaimed, "Oh!" Daniel startled at the sudden movement, but quickly recovered. "I'm not a *suicide*," Justin intoned. Daniel raised his eyebrows. "You thought I was up there to jump."

"Most are, when they're standing at the edge like that," Daniel explained.

"No, no. Just out for a hike."

Daniel stole another look at Justin. His boots were more suited to a rock star than a mountaineer, surely, and the bulge of a cigarette pack was visible in his hip pocket. Nothing in his pale complexion indicated a man who regularly spent time outdoors, either, and while the cliff was not terrifically challenging, it didn't have marked trails. Then again, a local guy might know it would be a more peaceful trail to walk than some other, more popular hiking spots.

"Most people wouldn't come all the way out here to hike," Daniel ventured.

Justin's first reply was a skeptical hum. "Well, the fewer people the better is kind of one of my mottoes."

Daniel harrumphed a knowing, humorless laugh. "Oh, yeah? We've got that in common." They'd reached the gate; the dogs had pushed it open and left it for them. "Well if I haven't saved your life, at least let me give you a cup of coffee? Maybe the nickel tour?"

The lighthouse was not a particularly pretty one, and though the light station was not on an island, it was still quite isolated—the nearest town, Parker Village, just over fifteen miles away—and Daniel did not get busloads of tourists the way some keepers did. A few times each summer some old geezer with a checklist would drive up, then leave his wife waiting in the car while Daniel followed him up the twisting stair to the lamp room. Most days, though, he saw no one. Twice a month he drove the dogs into town in a semi-reliable pickup truck, checked his mail, and stocked up on groceries. He'd have lunch in the diner, one bottle of beer, chat with the old guys who were always there, while Tug and Mags waited outside. By the time he resumed the driver's seat, he was exhausted from smiling, making small talk, the lightly-panicked sensation that at any moment anyone could come from anywhere and demand even more of his energy.

Despite the heavy boots he wore, Justin's steps sounded lightly on the gravel walkway. Inside, Daniel stirred up the stove and fed it another log while Justin stood by door and unself-consciously eyed up the place. In the parlor: a worn chesterfield sofa with soft-cornered wood feet, a badly chipped coffee table in front of it, and Daniel's armchair with its good reading light standing by. An undersized but sturdy wood desk and a basic, black plastic rolling chair. The dogs' beds, of course. A dock for Daniel's phone and tablet, with speakers for his music and podcasts. On the kitchen side of the room, the round table and its pair of mismatched chairs, shrunk-down versions of the usual appliances—stove, oven, fridge—a wide soapstone sink that must have come from somewhere else once upon a time, and the coffeemaker on the counter. Daniel did his laundry by hand in a tub out back, hung it on a line to dry.

Every inch of bare wall, floor to ceiling, bore wood-plank shelves groaning with books. The lighthouse keeper's library was a sanity-saving tradition, and Daniel had inherited a starter one of about two dozen books, only a handful salvageable from the persistent damp, and had since built it up with his own finds. In the Parker Village post office was a labeled cardboard box where the locals left their discards for him; it filled up every two or three months and Daniel took it, returning the box empty the following week. Aside from the utterly random titles that had come his way over the years, he particularly collected stories about suicides, and two shelves over the desk were dedicated to them.

"Make yourself comfortable, have a seat," Daniel encouraged, and crossed to the kitchen to start a fresh pot of coffee. He arranged mismatched cups and saucers, spoons. "Milk and sugar?"

"Thanks." Justin, instead of sitting, scanned the spines of Daniel's books with his hands tucked into the hip pockets of his jeans like a student looking closely at paintings in a gallery, subverting the temptation to touch. "You've read all these?" he asked.

"Most of them. Some of the required ones I couldn't swallow all at once, so I set them aside to go back to later—Homer, James Joyce, the Bible—but anything less intense, I've passed through." By then just enough coffee had dripped down into the pot for him to pour two mugs, so Daniel fixed them up and crossed the room, offering one to Justin. The dogs looked up lazily from their beds with half-open eyes just in case Daniel had a cookie to share, immediately went back to dozing when they saw he did not.

"Thank you." Justin threaded his thumb through the handle, gripping the body of the mug in his fist. "Why just you?"

"Sorry?"

"You said it's just you here, manning the lighthouse."

"Oh. I used to work at Abenaki." They stood at angles to each other, an arm's reach apart. "With the kids coming in on school trips." Daniel waited for his response to register: his name that had been so long in the news, the phrase *The Abenaki Tragedy* that had been repeated so often it lost most of the heft it should have carried.

"Oh," Justin said suddenly, and his mouth closed tight for a minute while he looked closer at Daniel's face. "You're—"

"Yeah."

"*That* Daniel Howard."

"Unfortunately, yeah."

They were quiet a moment, drawing still-too-hot coffee from their mugs, Justin looking at the books, the ceiling, and the dogs, and Daniel looking at Justin.

"Don't get many visitors," Daniel said. "A third of them suicides, which brings a bunch of people but only for a few hours. You said you came to hike here because it's quiet—you know the area pretty well?"

"Mm," Justin's expression warmed, almost—but not quite—smiling. "I used to come up here pretty often."

"Not lately?"

"Things change."

Daniel nodded; the reply was the kind that might have been designed to invite further inquiry, but Justin's tone and body language absolutely did not, so Daniel left it.

Justin's eyebrows rose. "How many is not many?"

"Visitors?"

"Suicides."

"Three in the last sixteen months? Only one successful."

"That's a weird phrase," Justin mused. "*Successful* suicide."

"Suppose it depends on your perspective."

"You mentioned maybe giving me a tour?" Justin redirected, and set his half-full coffee cup atop the writing desk.

"Sure, of course." Daniel swept his hands a bit, indicating. "So this is the cottage. Built in the mid-1930s when the previous one burned down after a lightning strike." Daniel led them toward the door and the dogs alerted, but when they weren't invited along for the walk they drooped down again to finish their naps. Daniel circled the exterior of the cottage, pointed out his laundry tub and vegetable garden, the shed where he kept his tools and did his tinkering on the gears and whatnot, as needed. Everything in sight with even a hint of metal on it had to be wiped down with dry rags at least once a day to get the sea off, or it would be a pile of rust in no time.

"In the old days the keeper would have lived here alone, though his family might have stayed during the summer—any kids would have been delivered into town—often the wife, too—for school during the rest of the year. Back when the lamps were real wicks with real flames, it was endless work to keep them going, and if a fog came in the keeper might stay in the tower until it lifted, sending specific signals at regular intervals for hours at a time."

"How's it powered?" Justin asked, as they approached the light tower, crunching along another gravel path, narrow enough that they were mindful not to touch shoulders or elbows as they went.

"Solar, with back-up generators in case of failure. All I have to do is throw a switch twice a day. A second one—if there's weather—for the fog bell."

"Bell? Really?" Justin was incredulous.

"It's a romantic holdover to call it a fog bell; nowadays it's a recording of a fog horn," Daniel admitted, and Justin yelped a little laugh. "You laugh, but it's loud as hell and twice as annoying. I have ear muffs. The dogs, too.

"Anyway, you can see a mark there," Daniel pointed partway up the tower, to a bright blue X painted on the side about eighteen feet over their heads. "That's from high water, 1897. The keeper managed to keep the lamp lit, had to stay up there two days and nights until the ocean subsided. In the middle of his log book, at what should have been dawn on the second day, he wrote down the Last Rites for himself."

"That's awesome," Justin enthused.

"I gotta admit I agree, even though it's morbid." Inside the tower, Daniel let Justin climb the steps ahead of him, both men sliding their hands up along the coiled-metal cable that served as a handrail. Daniel continued his speech, and keeping his breath was a surprising challenge—he'd mounted the narrow stairway countless times, but he'd never had to carry on a conversation while he did it. "The first landing we'll come to, there's a door to the watch room. We can pass it by for now, head all the way up to the lamp—that's the real money shot."

Justin made an amused-sounding noise—not quite a laugh—his footfalls coming heavier, trudging, the longer they climbed. "When was it built?" he managed, sounding breathless.

"1815. The electric lamp came in during the early 1940s, and the solar upgrade shortly before I came—I've been here almost ten years, now."

"Long time for a lonely life," Justin commented, and the air went taut with recognition of comment's intimacy. Daniel cleared his throat.

"Lonesome, I'd say, more than lonely."

"Ah." Justin signaled understanding and agreement both in the single syllable.

"Here we are," Daniel announced, decisive. "Step to your right; there's room enough for us both, but barely."

Inside the lamp room, Daniel explained the gear box that spun the massive, glass optic around the lamp—even opened up the metal door so Justin could see the motor—and the array of lenses, and Justin's comments made it seem he actually found it at least slightly interesting. The space around the lantern was barely wider than a man's body, so they stood side by side, with a sturdy wood lattice over their heads making a ceiling of sorts, allowing diamantes of mid-morning sunlight to shower the walls and floor, their clothing and faces. Daniel pointed out the marks on the windows that let him know the time was right to light or douse the lantern.

"That only helps on clear days like today, of course," he clarified. "In weather, the light stays on throughout. Some days I'll run up and down the steps five or six times, if it's lively."

"Seems like this could all be pretty easily automated," Justin noted casually.

"Yeah, it could," Daniel agreed. "But then what use would there be for a man who needs to be busy and have routines, and can't tolerate unexpected noise or too much company?" His tone was mild, even amused, but Justin pinched his lips shut between his teeth and tilted his head to look up through the lattice. Daniel took pity and drew down a hinged door so Justin could have a look at part of the optic array. "Should I light it?" he grinned.

"Can you? Even in clear weather?"

"Put it in the log as maintenance. Sometimes I have to spin it in daylight, to reach the lenses for cleaning or repairs."

"Yes, then. Please."

Daniel threw the switch and the engine rattled, belts and gears humming to life. With only a brief creak, the optic began to turn, and the scattered coins of sunlight shimmered and shifted. Justin watched through the open trap door, his eyes scanning, lips parting in a smile.

"It's a hell of a thing," he said at last, sounding truly impressed. Daniel crossed his arms in front of his chest to contain its puffing up a bit. Another moment passed and Justin said, "Don't know why, but I thought it would be noisier."

"It's not so bad, no," Daniel agreed. He reached to power it down and its rotation devolved. Daniel fixed the trap door back in place with a sturdy click of its latch. "This came loose and hit me, once," he reported. "Lucky it was just my shoulder; I'm sure it would have knocked me out."

"The dogs would come find you," Justin guessed, and Daniel started down the steps, Justin trailing him.

"Punchline, they can't—or won't—climb stairs," Daniel grinned. "Once, the tide came so far up the waves were breaking just twenty yards or so from the house, so I decided we should climb the tower, and I had to carry them. Two trips up and down, and a lot of their size is fur, but even still, they're not exactly lightweights."

Justin let out a quiet but gratifying chuckle, and Daniel shouldered open the watch room door. Inside was a small wooden cabinet full of tools, plastic crates of emergency rations and bottled water, an old radio set, and a narrow metal-framed bed made up in precise, almost-military style, with extra blankets folded and stacked beneath on the smoothly polished wood floor. There were shallow, high windows nearly all the way around.

"In the old days, the keepers would stay up here during weather, minding the lamp; I haven't had much use for it except for that one flood I mentioned. But just in case," Daniel shrugged. Justin walked the border with the same interested but careful manner he'd displayed since examining Daniel's books in the cottage's parlor, making small movements and keeping his hands still and close, as if he were afraid of breaking something. He stopped to gaze out a window, at the cliff-face. Daniel fidgeted with the open latches on the front of the tool cabinet.

"Thanks," Justin said, still staring out at the rocks.

"No trouble," Daniel said. "Don't get many chances to give the tour. Hope my patter was all right."

"Y'know, actually I *am* a suicide," Justin said, punctuating it with a single downward nod of his head. "But I guess not today."

Daniel was dumbstruck, dropped his hands by his sides and stared at Justin's back. He opened his mouth, then closed it again.

"Like I said, I thought all lighthouses were unmanned—should have done more research—and I don't want to be found." He turned suddenly, and Daniel couldn't interpret the look on his face, only that it was utterly without despair, or even embarrassment.

"At all?"

"Better that way, I think, for anyone that might miss me. Not that I think anyone *will* miss me. There's really no one left to." He turned his palms up and let them drift—*nothing to be done about it*—and shook his head. His expression changed, and his tone. "Which is your favorite?" he asked, then clarified, "Your books about suicide."

Daniel's neck flushed hot beneath the edge of his beard; he felt caught out. Not that it was a secret; the collection was purposely shelved together, at eye level, though he found it remarkable that in a few brief minutes perusing the spines, Justin had made the connection.

"I actually was reminded of one story, when you first came down the hill," Daniel said, an automatic spill that surprised him. It seemed a time for naked confession, and he thought it would have been unfair of him to hide his shame when Justin had already unzipped himself and so freely showed Daniel his bones. "A drowned man washes up in a village where no one has ever planted flowers, and the men go off in search of someone to claim him while the women clean and dress him and comb his hair and fall in love with him. Because he's so handsome."

Justin cast his eyes at the floor briefly, then passed Daniel a glance that invited him to finish.

"No one claims him so they decide to give him their kind of funeral, dumping his body into the sea from the cliff's edge. But first they make up a family tree so the whole village become his kin. The men get pissed off at the women because they won't let him go, keep piling up all these little trinkets on top of his body, but at last they give him to the sea, and once he's gone, they rebuild their houses and paint them bright colors, and plant flowers on the cliff so sailors going by will notice their village, and know it was the drowned man's home."

"Why would they care if the sailors knew that?"

"Because once he belonged to them, everything was different."

Justin let go a quick, quiet hum and looked thoughtful. Daniel shrugged, "Anyway, it's a good story. Though it doesn't technically say the he drowned on purpose, that's how I've always read it. I suppose he may have just been a fisherman or sailor washed overboard in a storm."

"Maybe both," Justin suggested. "A guy who was suicidal but hadn't gotten around to it yet."

Daniel tipped and lightly shook his head, indicating he knew anything was possible.

"Didn't want anyone to think he was a slacker," Justin added, warming a bit to his addition to the story. "Wanted to leave everyone with a good impression of him, not some jerk who jumped into the ocean just to avoid pulling up the lobster pots."

Daniel suddenly realized it was probably insufficient not to take action in the face of Justin's admission he'd come to the light station to jump from the cliff. Maybe call the Parker Village police, or that retired nurse; she'd know what steps to take, who to contact to direct Justin toward help. Daniel reckoned he should know some of that himself, and wondered why after all his years, eight foiled suicides and six "successful" ones later, it had never occurred to him that perhaps there should be an actual procedure in place.

"Should I maybe call—"

Justin took one long step forward, gripped Daniel's sweater-sleeve in his fist, the other hand catching the back of his neck, and pressed a crashing, intrusive kiss against Daniel's slack lips. For a panicked second, Daniel held hands against Justin's chest, defending himself against the sudden approach. Justin made a mournful noise and in that instant an aching grief washed through Daniel, rushing inward from just beneath the surface his skin, pinching his guts and heart, weakening his knees so much he thought he may not be able to trust them. And all at once instead of pushing, he pulled, the thin knit of Justin's shapeless sweater bunching between his fingers and thumbs, and instead of having kisses pressed upon him, Daniel kissed—licking back, catching Justin's lips between his own. He felt Justin uncoiling, tight-gripped fingers falling loose, breath softening.

Justin stepped back just as suddenly as he had come, covered his mouth with one hand, avoiding Daniel's gaze, and wiped his lips with his fingers.

"I'm sorry," he said haltingly. "That was."

"No."

"*Ridiculous.*"

"It's fine."

Justin shook his head, sighed, near-laughing.

"Really, it's fine," Daniel told him. There was a long silence. The sun had risen to an angle that put the room at the edge of too much warmth. Daniel thought to suggest they descend; perhaps he'd invite Justin to stay for lunch before he went away. And come to think of it, how had he gotten there in the first place? But instead of saying any of that, or anything at all, Daniel closed the space between them and took Justin's face in his hands and kissed him.

There was desperation in it, tight-clinging, like drowning men grasping at the offered hand. Daniel steered them back to sit on the little bed, teeth clacking uncomfortably, knees in the way, the angles all wrong. He tucked his face into the stretched-out neck of Justin's t-shirt, rubbed his lips along the gritty stubble on his throat. Justin's hand rubbed rough against the front of Daniel's jeans and he had no room to open his legs, to push back, though he needed it more just then than he needed his breath. No one had kissed him, touched him—wanted him—in so, so long. Forever long. He'd made himself forget, somehow, that it really *was* a lonely life, and now the loneliness was undammed and Daniel held on for fear the rush of it would wash them both out to sea.

He was sweaty beneath his clothes; the room was hot and so were they. Justin's neck was sturdy even though his throat looked painfully vulnerable, and his hand at Daniel's bicep clutched, digging in urgently. His hand between Daniel's legs was not gentle, and Daniel couldn't be sure which of them the motion was meant to please. Daniel groaned into Justin's open mouth and ran fingertips over the front of his sweater, found the edges of his pectoral muscles and then the rumpled softness of his nipple, firming tight beneath Daniel's touch.

There was an uncomfortable twinge in the back of his waist and he raised his knee onto the mattress, adjusting the angle. Justin went for Daniel's fly, and his dark-eyed stare was more naked than any expanse of half-dressed skin. Daniel felt shamed by it; he was not up to the challenge of such an expression.

"You don't have to—"

"Please."

Justin's back bent, everything awkward, but his mouth was hot, deep, and Daniel shuddered, forgave himself in advance that he wouldn't—couldn't—last. He touched the back of Justin's bowed head, let his fingers ride the waves of the neck in motion. Daniel's own neck bent until his head sank back to touch the wall, and he felt splinters catching in his hair. Justin tight-gripped the waistband of Daniel's jeans, the fabric bunched around the leather belt, and he hummed, another layer of sensation. Daniel squeezed the back of his neck, a warning, and pinched his eyes shut, let the wash of wave after rushing wave tumble him, disorienting, destroying his sense of which was the way to drown, and which the way to the shore.

Justin uncurled himself partway, just the leading edge of upright. Daniel drew him into a bitter kiss he tried to reject, but Daniel persisted, stealing the shame out of it to keep for himself. After a few fumbling moments, Justin had dropped his hand into his own lap, and Daniel rested his palm there on Justin's wrist, touched his fingers, and Justin nuzzled lips and nose into Daniel's beard. His spine curved, closing down, and Daniel whispered against his temple, *yes*, only that, eliciting from Justin a sad-sounding whimper that rolled and spread into an open, low moan. As he began to subside, Daniel put arms around him, held him hard and close, and Justin collapsed into the embrace, heavy and hot, breath stale with leftover kisses as he sighed it away.

They reassembled themselves, amid an exchange of bashful, baffled glances, then descended the stairs, the air noticeably cooler as they returned to sea level. The dogs raced behind the house, chasing each other, warning the gulls away with quick yaps. Daniel and Justin stood watching them for a minute or two.

"I'm sorry to have bothered you," Justin apologized once more. "I should leave you in peace." His tone indicated he meant all three of them— Daniel and the dogs—had been discomfited by his unexpected visit to the light station.

Daniel crossed his arms and brushed aside a stone with the edge of his boot. "Let me at least feed you lunch," he offered. "It's a long way back to town."

"I," Justin said, but it ended in a shake of his head.

Daniel met his eyes. Dark, liquid brown. Glassy with expectation and some awful, long-lived thing Daniel recognized as his own.

"You should stay," Daniel said, with finality but also a touch of surprise. He cleared his throat. "I mean. You could stay, if you want. I'm driving into Parker tomorrow anyway, if you need a ride."

"My car isn't far away," Justin replied, and he shook a cigarette loose from his pack, then extended his hand, offering one to Daniel.

"Got my own, thanks." He let Justin light his smoke, and they stood for another quiet minute, just smoking and looking everywhere but at each other. After his third drag, Daniel asked, "You're all right?" He didn't want to intrude on a man's peace, or his plan, but he still had the nagging idea in the back of his brain that he should probably be offering something that amounted to actual help.

"For now," Justin said, and nodded quickly several times, pursing his lips together. All at once his posture shifted upward, and he seemed to stretch his spine, looking toward the road. "A walk to clear my head," he offered. "Or whatever. I'll get out of your way."

"It's no trouble."

"Thank your dogs again for me." Justin parked the cigarette in the corner of his mouth and offered his hand; Daniel shook it once, then let it go. "Keep up the good work."

"Haven't had a ship run aground yet," Daniel replied, and raised his foot, crossing ankle over calf, dipping down to crush out his half-smoked cigarette on the sole of his boot. "Take care of yourself."

"You, too."

And with that, Justin walked away, his path tracing the edge of the road. Daniel watched his back for a minute or so, then turned toward the cottage and went inside to fix his lunch. By the time he'd finished building himself a sandwich, Justin had rounded the bend in the road and was gone from Daniel's sight.

Four

Daniel lost some of his sleep for a few nights after the encounter with Justin, who'd come to the cliff to kill himself and instead wound up in an awkward, groping tangle with Daniel on the watch room's narrow bed. Most of it was because being kissed—being touched at all—was something Daniel had not had in a very long time, and though certainly he'd always had urges, and managed them as needed with internet pornography, memory, and imagination, his appetite was significantly stoked up by having had even those few minutes with an actual human man. He replayed it, eyes closed, in the utter dark of his windowless bedroom, and did as he must, perhaps half a dozen times over the course of those first few nights (and days; there was work to be done, but not every single minute was scheduled). He smoothed some of the edges of reality—in his mind their teeth did not click unpleasantly together mid-kiss, and he was able to hold out longer—but the hurried surprise of the whole thing had a certain appeal, as well, and the urgent, sad sounds that had occasionally punctured the too-warm air became especially precious memories, and made him wonder.

But it wasn't as if all he did was jack off to the memory of the sad-faced stranger he'd talked off the edge with two not-at-all-clever words—*don't jump*—because in the light of day, he often questioned the wisdom of letting a suicidal man simply walk off down the road. As he carried out his day's work, tinkering in the shed, tending to the last of his vegetable garden, Daniel told himself stories about Justin Strongbow, about who he was and where he had begun and where he might have ended up once he left Daniel's sight. Maybe he hadn't really come to the cliff to jump, only felt the weird pull of it once he'd hiked up there; Daniel, himself, had sometimes felt that bizarre tingle behind his forehead and in the back of his shoulders. There was something about high places that made even a healthy person entertain thoughts of what it might be like to fly from them, or to fall. Or maybe Justin had been in the grip of a dramatic moment, but once he got there, would have shaken it off, recognizing he was not that bad off—another sensation with which Daniel was familiar. He'd sometimes idly imagined driving his car off the road into a tree, or swimming out into the ocean until he was too far and too exhausted to ever return to shore, or tallied up pills, but even in the moment he doubted his own level of commitment. Surely the fact Justin had allowed Daniel to show him the lantern, had engaged with him in conversation and then sprung a surprise blow job on him must mean Justin had not truly reached the end of his line. Looking back on it, Daniel reckoned Justin had been rather easy to dissuade.

But then again, he'd mentioned more than once his assumption the station was unmanned, and that he was unlikely to be found. So perhaps it was only that Daniel had wrecked his plan, and Justin had walked away recalibrating, conjuring fresh ideas for a way to off himself and leave his body undiscoverable. Daniel found himself distracted by these impossible-to-prove theories about who Justin was, and why he'd showed up there, and where he might have gone when he left. Somehow after ten years of solitude and work to be done, and never a single minute spent worrying about anyone but himself and the dogs, two hours with a handsome stranger had rattled Daniel into a state of significant distraction.

The next Friday was his day to drive into town. First, the post office to get his mail, a few envelopes from National Parks that clenched his jaw; some magazines; and the usual pile of junk—sweepstakes come-ons and tool catalogs—but nothing personal. There were too few books in the box to warrant his claiming them; he'd wait to see if the collection grew by end of the month. Next stop, the barber's chair for his bi-monthly trim. The barber himself was an old guy with one of those faces that made it seem he could be ninety or sixty, but either way he was no youngster; his wife and her sister styled women's hair in the shop's other two chairs. Daniel enjoyed listening to the ladies gossiping because he rarely knew who they were discussing, and most of the news was good—babies, weddings, whose grandson went into the service and whose son just came back from a deployment still in one piece—overall harmless background noise that made him feel part of the village without actually having to be.

"How's the truck runnin'?" the barber—John Senior, he was always called—asked him as soon as he'd fixed the cape around Daniel's neck.

"Good. Good," Daniel said amiably. "Had the guy at Dealey's do a ring job couple months back and it's as good as any twenty year old Chevy is ever going to be."

"The father or the sons?"

"Not sure."

"When it's Some Guy and Sons, always go for the father!" John Senior shook the plastic comb for emphasis. "The kids are still learning."

"What, forever?" Daniel grinned.

"May as well be. The father always has two dozen more years' experience, no matter what."

"You make a good point," Daniel allowed, and as the barber set to his work, he was happy enough to let the conversation die. The wife was sitting in the stylist's chair she normally stood behind, tapping carefully at the screen of a smart phone she held as if it were slimy, then raised it to her ear.

"Pat? It's Christine. Did you hear anything about Annie's visit at the doctor's? God love her."

Daniel picked at the edges of his thumbnails with the tips of his pointer-fingers, hands on his thighs beneath the cape. After a few more minutes in which he and the barber exchanged no conversation, Daniel crumpled his face into what he imagined looked like a thought had just occurred to him, and that it likely wasn't even important.

"You know a guy named Strongbow, by any chance?"

"What now?" John Senior frowned. "Yeah, I know some of the family. Mark. His parents were Hap and Marla. He's a lobsterman, does some crab fishing, too."

Daniel did some math in his head, reckoned the couple might be of John Senior and his wife Christine's generation, and that Mark could be Justin's father or uncle.

"Mark had a son, maybe?" he ventured. "Justin Strongbow?"

By this time, Christine had ended her nosy phone call and turned in her chair a bit. "Oh, Justin! That poor thing. Moody like his father—so serious, even when he was little. But his mother. . ." she shook her head sadly. Daniel glanced at her in the mirrors, not wanting to risk a bad outcome as the scissors flicked and snipped in John Senior's hand. "Remember her, John? Meaghan Lucas."

"Who were her parents?"

"Bill and Sarah Lucas from out on Long Range Road."

"Oh, right. She was trouble."

Daniel's eyes widened quizzically, and Christine shifted in her seat as if settling into the story. "She and Mark had Justin young—they both left high school. He went out on the boats. She didn't know what to do with that baby. No one could tell her anything, though; teenagers are like that."

Daniel nodded.

"She left him here, there, and everywhere while she went for days at a time out to Orono, by the college, of course she wanted to be around young people. Some of them when they have babies young, they know it's time to grow up, but Meaghan was the type wants to stay a kid, be around other kids. And she was alone most of the time, with Mark out fishing, and there was no money." Christine frowned exaggeratedly, nearly pouting out her bottom lip, and she lowered her voice as if taking Daniel into her confidence. "She got into the drugs. Went off who knows where. The baby went to foster care, the one grandmother, the other grandmother, and then the state was going to put him for adoption. But the father's half Passamaquoddy so the tribe got involved, at least long enough that by the time it was all sorted out Justin wasn't a baby anymore, and they never did find him a place to belong. The grandparents, and Mark when he wasn't out fishing, but really that poor boy never had a chance. He was a handful as a teenager—moody like his father and always running off like his mum but who can really blame him, the way his life was."

Christine shook her head and drew a heavy breath she sighed out in a dramatic gust. "God love him. Once he was grown he left Parker and I don't know where he went. I thought maybe to college but I don't know with what money, and I don't know if he really even finished high school. Just looking around for something. Some people do that. Run away from a place because of how they feel. People do try to run from the things that break their hearts, don't they?"

Daniel held the breath he'd just taken in; she'd clearly forgotten he was *that Daniel Howard*. John Senior snorted a little. "You make it sound like a movie, Christine, crissakes."

"Anyways," she said pointedly, gaze directed at Daniel to be sure he was listening. "Eventually he came back. Not to Parker but close, out past Riverston, closer in to town, for the tourists. Opened an inn there, or a—whatsit—B and B. With a business partner, a Spanish guy from down Boston. Or, wherever he was really from, I guess he was living in Boston when Justin met him. Anyway, Justin ran that place with him and his wife for a *while*, five years? Maybe longer. I heard the partner died a couple years ago, but Justin must still be running it because he never came back to Parker."

Daniel took this in—far more information than he'd ever imagined or hoped he would get just from asking if the barber knew Justin's family—and pressed his lips between his teeth a bit. John Senior flicked the comb through the hair above Daniel's forehead, walked a half-circle around the chair, and nodded solidly.

"How about a shave, Danny?" he offered as he reached for the cape's fastenings behind Daniel's neck.

"Not this time, thanks."

"Suit yourself or go naked," the barber said with a shrug, grinning a little at his own clichéd joke.

After settling up with John Senior, Daniel took himself to the diner for lunch, ordered his usual meal of a club sandwich, bowl of soup—that day it was a surprisingly good, creamy one identified on the chalkboard by the kitchen pass-through as "pumpkin biscuit soup of the day"—and a cup of coffee. He passed on dessert but bought a cherry pie to take with him. The waitress called him "Hon," as she always did, and he left her a tip of three-seventy-five on a bill of six-and-a-quarter, as he always did. By the time he'd finished another round of small talk, eye on the door, back to the wall, he was feeling prickly and it became increasingly more difficult to force a smile. Time to head out.

On the half-hour drive away from town, with the dogs stacked up for the best view out the passenger window, Daniel replayed the story the hairdresser had told—probably embellished, romanticized, or misunderstood, as such stories often were by people not directly involved in them—about Justin's rough life as a youngster, and his prodigal return to not-quite-Parker-Village. He tried to square the idea of a welcoming, affable innkeeper with the guy he'd met at the cliff's edge—scruffy and slender bordering scrawny, dressed all in rangy black, with well-loved, loose-laced rocker boots on his feet—and found it nearly impossible fitting the two together. And the business partner from Boston—Spanish, with a wife—who'd died and left Justin in charge. Daniel wondered if Christine had misunderstood the role Justin played in the enterprise; perhaps he was the gardener, or the cook. Where would a half-orphan who hadn't finished high school get the money—or the idea, for that matter—to move back to the northern coast of Maine and open a thing like a bed and breakfast? She must have got it wrong, somehow.

Not that it mattered, of course, as Daniel was unlikely to ever see Justin again. Which was just as well; the fluke of their encounter was good spank-bank material, but Daniel was not cut out for relationships of any kind, and definitely not with someone who clearly needed a lot of shoring up. It was almost fitting that the only person he'd had sex with in the past too-many years had done so only as an alternative to ending his life. Daniel must have laughed out loud; the dogs turned their heads and didn't look away until he told them to *nevermind*. Daniel was untrustworthy company in the best of circumstances; it fit perfectly that only someone would absolutely no risk of loss would dare approach him. It figured.

He silently wished the guy well. Whether that meant getting his head shrunk by a therapist, or getting pumped full of happy pills, or even hanging himself in a closet, Daniel was grateful enough for their few pleasant moments together to hope Justin had found whatever he was looking for. It would be nice, though, if he weren't dead.

Daniel's afternoons were spent on whatever tinkering he had going in the shed or the light tower, wiping the salt and damp off tools and fittings as he went. Tools were always hung on their pegboard or returned to their drawers; over the bench was an antique rack of tiny wooden drawers where Daniel sorted screws, bolts, washers, and nails. Rags went on pegs to dry if they were wet, got shoved into a covered plastic bucket if oil-soaked. He swept debris and occasional sawdust off the bench, then across the floor, then out the door. On clear days the sun was enough to work by—the shed had two south-facing windows—so he used the overhead fluorescents or the bench-top lamp only when truly necessary. Once the shed was buttoned up, he passed an hour or so on whatever random thing might need doing—fence repairs, painting the front door and shutters on the cottage, raking fallen leaves in autumn or mulching the flower beds in the spring—and, finally, whatever time remained before supper was his own.

There was a dock off the edge of the property where he kept a twenty-foot runabout to motor around in, sometimes dropping the anchor to fish a bit, or just surveying views of the coast he didn't get to see in the regular course of his days. The station had no beach to speak of—just a gravelly, gentle slope to the water's edge when the tide was out, and no walkable land at all when it was in—but now and then on the hottest days of late July and early August he would shed his clothes and do a low dive off the end of the dock, always emerged shocked and gasping; the water was never warm, even in the height of summer. He'd found over the years that a fifteen-minute swim was a bit like hitting a reset button on his entire being. The cold was an invigorating challenge, and using his muscles in unusual ways left him feeling exhausted and accomplished. In the end it was the weightless feeling, the pull of the waves, the otherworldly qualities of the sea that soothed him. Daniel was no flower child, not prone to romanticizing the ocean in the ways expected—nearly required—of someone who worked beside it day in and day out, but he was also not completely immune to its ability to inspire awe, to make him feel so tiny as to be merely elemental—a single-celled organism shoved along in a hurried rush of cold blood.

When there was nothing else that wanted doing, he might hike the dogs up the cliff, or down the road a bit, or into the woods, trusting that when he told them it was *home time*, they would manage to lead him out again. Over the years he'd had them, they had never let him down. In winter when the sun vanished early, he stoked up the fire in the stove, sometimes brewed another half-pot of coffee or boiled milk on the stovetop for hot chocolate, fixed himself a little plate of something—crackers or nuts or a sliced pear—and then sat in his armchair with whatever book he was reading, letting himself fall into the story, occasionally dozing if the day's exertions were exceptional.

When he'd first come to the station it had taken him weeks to establish his routines, beginning with obsessively minding the lantern, and only gradually adding in other necessary functions, of which there were far more than he'd ever dreamed. The previous keeper had stayed on for only a few days to impart what wisdom he had, but as Daniel likely should have expected, he was a man of few words and ready to move on with his life, so his guidance was minimal. By the time he drove off in a truck even older than the one Daniel was always tending in hopes it would hold out just one more season, Daniel felt confident only in his ability to flip the switches that lit and doused the lantern. Back then he'd had three different alarms set to remind him of every daily function: waking in the dark, dousing the lamp, checking the weather reports and maritime schedules, filling in the log book, maintaining the lantern and the buildings, and lighting the lamp at dusk. For the first few weeks the wood stove's fire went out at least twice a day and had to be re-laid and coaxed back to life; most of Daniel's nutrients were consumed while standing upright, by uncooked handfuls.

But he was a man who craved a reliable schedule, predictable outcomes, and few interruptions, so he made a mission of mandating routines. His system at last established, Daniel became immutable. The occasional wrench in the engine inserted by a suicidal interloper's unbidden appearance was something he'd learned to accept, the required trade-off for the only two things he'd wanted since that day when he so spectacularly failed every single soul reliant upon him: solitude and usefulness.

Though his daily routine may have appeared stiflingly rigid to many, if not most, people—there had not exactly been a line of folks ahead of him angling for assignment to the light station at North Hope Cove—in reality Daniel had created a gentle, tidal movement of days and weeks, months and seasons, that comforted him. Which made it all the more disconcerting that even three weeks after his brief encounter with Justin Strongbow, he still found himself wondering how Justin had fared after rounding the bend in the road. Daniel even went so far as to take his tablet computer to his armchair one afternoon, scanning through nearly a month's worth of obituaries. Finding nothing in them about a thirty-ish local man having "died suddenly"—the usual euphemism for suicides and overdoses—Daniel searched for local inns and hotels, wondering if he might find something enlightening. Just for curiosity's sake.

Frustratingly—intriguingly—one search result with its two lines of preview text showed that there was a bed and breakfast precisely where Christine the hairdresser had said Justin landed when he didn't come all the way back to Parker Village, but when Daniel clicked through to a website, there were only error messages. That the page no longer existed seemed strange given that the barber's wife had also indicated Justin must still be running the place after the death of his business partner. Daniel was not an expert, but he imagined anyone in the hospitality industry—especially in an area with a limited amount of tourism—would want a functioning website. He wondered about Justin's business acumen, and then whether perhaps Christine had been mistaken about the end of her story. Maybe the bed and breakfast had died along with the co-owner, in which case, Justin could be anywhere.

Daniel hummed, and then made a disgusted noise at himself. Mooning like a teenager over a man he'd known for two hours was at best an embarrassment. Despite the fact that a segment of the acquaintance had been carnal, it did not bear thinking about nearly a month later. The poor guy was probably dead, anyway; he'd seemed pretty determined, and the air around him was heavy and dim. And if he wasn't dead, well, no doubt someone with burdens like those Justin must carry had no need of a man like Daniel, who could bear them no better.

The dead website for the inn had a phone number still visible, though, in the preview text of the search result. Daniel left the browser tab open, promising himself that if in another week he was still wondering about Justin Strongbow and what his fate might be, he'd give the number a try, only to find out once and for all if the man was still alive. Not with any expectations. Just to see.

Five

Daniel stopped in the watch room for pliers and wire-snips on his climb up to the light one afternoon, and the angle of sunlight through the windows, the too-warm tinge in the air, gave him a memory so vibrant his shoulders shivered a little. In the middle distance was the spot where Justin had stood, handsome and serious, just before he rushed at Daniel and caught him around the back of the neck. Daniel felt the same urgent flicker of panic, remembering it, though the thought of his hands flat against Justin's chest— half-heartedly resistant, holding him at bay—while Justin kissed his mouth open and shoved in the tip of his tongue wore a new glaze of excitement. His shoulders collapsed on a near-laugh of a sigh and he threw his gaze upward. *Get over it, man; you're driving yourself crazy.* And anyway, there was work to be done.

A few of the switches were sticky and hesitant; Daniel made a mental note to bring up some spray-lubricant the next morning. He snipped the frayed ends of a metal coil he knew would not electrocute him—but which had recently pulled a loop of yarn from his sweater sleeve—and bent the wires together, tucking the whole thing back in place once the threat was eliminated. He scanned the ocean to the horizon, noted some fair weather clouds up high, passing in front of the already-visible moon, and noted the height of the sun before switching on the light. He watched it turn for three revolutions before descending the spiraling stairs, stopped in the watch room to return his tools to their proper places.

Supper was a pair of undersized pork chops started in a skillet on the little cooktop, then finished in the oven while he boiled a handful of egg noodles he'd later flatter with butter and cheese, tossing in frozen peas at the end to put something green on his plate. The dogs had to be told twice they were sitting too close, and were ultimately banished to the parlor, where they sat with their ears up and their muscles taut, staring at him.

Once the dishes were drying in the rack, the kitchen table wiped clean and his chair pushed in beneath it, Daniel liberated a can of beer from the fridge and cracked it open on his way to his armchair. Before taking his seat, though, he changed course and stepped across to the little writing desk and the shelf of suicide-stories just above it. He found a slender volume with a turquoise-blue spine and brought it with him to the chair, set the beer can on the side table, twisting until it faced the right way, and slipped a cigarette from the pack that lived there. He lit it and shook out the match, which he dropped into the oversized clam shell he used as an ashtray. Holding the butt end of the cigarette between his teeth, he shuffled through the pages to find the story he wanted. It was the one he had recounted to Justin, about the handsome drowned man who inspired a whole village to claim him as family and then proclaim him to the world.

It was largely as he remembered—he'd read it more than once, but not recently—though he had forgotten one melancholy line about the villagers releasing the drowned man's body to the sea without any weights attached to anchor it, so that he could return to them if he ever wished to. While reading, Daniel occasionally lifted his cigarette to his mouth pinched between finger and thumb, took quick, hard drags then held in the smoke. Of course the final lines of the story were the big payoff, with its not-so-subtle moral about beauty in tragic circumstances, and how the tiny community rewrote its own story because it had been touched by this interloper without a story of his own, but Daniel lingered with the idea that even as the villagers went through the rituals they had designed to mark their acceptance of the end of a life, they had given themselves a little crack for hope to get in. The drowned man had disrupted their lives and burdened them, but in the end they released him through a door left open to welcome him back. There was something there about letting go, and about compassion—even skirting the edges of forgiveness—that Daniel could feel but not fully articulate.

He thought about Justin, and how he'd just let him stride off down the road like it was any other day and he was any other visitor—not that Daniel had visitors—and wondered if he should have said something to indicate he would welcome Justin back. He lay the book aside and carefully arranged the cigarette on the edge of the clamshell ashtray, took up his beer can and almost drained it. Belched. Tugger slept on but Maggie turned her head away from him as if offended by his deplorable lack of manners.

"Beg pardon."

Daniel had lately wondered how it might be having another person around. Not all the time, of course. But there was the sofa that he never sat on just waiting for someone to take up a place on it. He imagined someone upright at the end of it just around the bend from his own favoured chair, sharing the reading lamp and the ashtray. Or sitting at the far end with his legs stretched across the seat, ankles crossed, boots abandoned on the floor. And there was an extra chair at the kitchen table, with a decent view out the window. The bed was wide and comfortable, and though his had been the only body in it, Daniel flipped and turned the mattress every six months, so it ought to be evenly worn. The cottage was built for a family—though not a big one—and there were a few extra of everything. And he couldn't kid himself it was some unnamed, faceless anyone he imagined in all those places; it was dark-eyed, stubble-cheeked Justin Strongbow, who may or may not own a bed and breakfast out past Riverston, and who may or may not wish to ever see Daniel again. And who may or may not, for that matter, still be alive.

Before he could talk himself out of it, Daniel found the phone number for the inn with the dead website, and tapped it into his cell phone. He picked up the end of his cigarette and ashed it, then quickly dragged, all in the short space between hitting the *Call* icon and hearing the first ring. On the fourth ring, the call connected, and a recorded male voice with a slippery accent said, "Thank you for calling Blue Moon Bed and Breakfast. We apologize that we are not able to receive your call at the moment. Please leave a message and we will get back to you within twenty-four hours. Enjoy today!" The last line was delivered in a tone of such genuine friendliness, Daniel found the fact of being ordered around easy to forgive. He considered whether to leave a message, but since what he wanted to ask was not, "Is Justin there?" but rather, "Is Justin alive?" he decided it was better not to, and ended the call.

After one last pull on his cigarette, he squashed it out, emptied the last few swigs of beer into the sink before crushing the can and tossing it in the garbage under the kitchen sink. It was time to button up the house for the night.

"Time to go out, dogs," he said, and they uncomplainingly roused themselves from their beds by the woodstove and trotted through the dog door while Daniel put away the now-dry dishes and hung the towel from its hook on a drawer front. By the time the dogs returned he was stirring up the last of the fire, and Tugger nudged beneath his hand, looking for Daniel to stroke his ears a bit, which he happily did. Maggie made him work for it, lying curled in a near-perfect circle but keeping her head up until Daniel bent down to give her chin a scratch.

"It's lucky you're so pretty," he told her.

He crossed back to latch the dog door shut for the night, then clicked off the overhead light in the kitchen and the parlor lamps, at last making his way into the little bedroom just a bit wider than the bed, with only a narrow alley at its foot between it and the dresser. It was windowless, to keep the light from the tower out, and once the door was shut and the lights off, the utter blackness was otherworldly. A digital clock glowed from the far edge of the room, but otherwise there were no landmarks aside from what his body remembered and what he could feel—or bump—in the dark.

He wiped the bathroom sink dry and set down the toilet lid, then climbed in under the stack of blankets so heavy it reminded him of the lead apron used during dental X-rays and took up his bedside book, though his mind drifted to another thing pressing down on him—a response, composed so far only in his mind, to a letter about the impending automation of his light station. After only a few paragraphs of reading, he laid aside the book and turned out the lamp.

Dear Commissioner Levy,

I have been employed as the lighthouse keeper at North Hope Cove near Parker Village, Maine, for the past nine years, and previous to that was Director of Education at Abenaki National Forest. I write to. . . ask. No. *Implore?* That was like forceful pleading, wasn't it? Less desperate than begging but still urgent. *I write to implore you to reconsider*—could he reconsider? What were the chances it had been the commissioner's decision? He probably didn't even know about it. One postage-stamp sized park with a not-very-glamorous lighthouse was probably nobody's major priority, given that now the Parks Department was dealing with things like armed ranchers taking over picnic areas for whatever conspiracy-theory-spawned, live-free-or-die idea they felt needed defending.

I write to implore you to. Nope. *I write to direct your attention to the fact that the North Hope light is scheduled to be automated and my job eliminated.* Yours truly, Daniel Howard, a whiner and a jackass. *and the job of lighthouse keeper eliminated. As you may be aware, I accepted the assignment to North Hope Cove because*

That was where he got tangled up for good. Of course Daniel had grown to appreciate the light for the marvel that it was, and for its usefulness, and its rarity, and maybe someone with more poetry in them could have sold the idea of keeping the light just as it was based on that argument alone. But what Daniel wanted—needed—to get across was that his job at the light station was required for his continued survival. And even if someday he decided to rejoin polite society, there was a purpose to the North Hope light station that could potentially soothe some other tortured soul. Just as surely as there were very few normal people who would want to be posted to North Hope, there also must be more than a few for whom it would be a needed refuge. He didn't want to say it was a sort of therapy, or an escape—it was work; *always* it was work—but it offered something unique. Shutting it would shuffle Daniel off into something as yet unknown, but given his seniority and the trauma of that awful day at Abenaki, he would likely get his pick of assignments upon his eviction. He'd get by. But what about the next guy? Where would that guy go if the light didn't need him?

He wanted to write a letter because he'd been given notice about the Public Comment period, and knew that his comment was likely to be the only one. He also did not want to have to haul himself down to Portland to testify at the hearing. So he needed to write a hell of a letter. Daniel wasn't bad with words; he should be able to do it. But every time he started—even just in his head—it trailed off into a tangled heap he couldn't pick apart enough to show someone who didn't already understand it the way he did. There was just so much, and while Daniel was willing to credit himself being pretty good with words, he was pretty bad with feelings. And though he hadn't thought about them much until the closure notice arrived, it turned out Daniel had a lot of feelings about the lighthouse.

Dear Commissioner Pencil-neck,
Don't fuck with my lighthouse. You don't even know.
Most sincerely yours,
Daniel Howard (yes, that Daniel Howard)

Down by the dock, Daniel restacked stones to shore up part of the rock wall that was leaning. He couldn't ever seem to get them exactly where they belonged—anyway, who the hell was he to attempt improvements on something that had stood there for three hundred years?—and he'd already crushed the first knuckle of one finger. The dogs started up barking, neither playing nor doing anti-gull duty, but tenser, short and sharp and loud. His first instinct was to look toward the cliff, but they were nowhere near it, and anyway their cliff-related alerts were all silent body gestures, not barking. He called out a loud, "Hey, dogs!" to summon them, but they kept on barking and did not sound as if they were coming closer, so he got off his knees, stepped over the wall, and started toward the other side of the cottage.

"Hey, quiet. What's the matter?" he called out, and something in his stomach clenched slightly, and he walked faster, with longer strides, and eventually broke into a jog. "Maggie! Tugboat! Come by, dogs!" Just as he was about to let himself run, his balance shifted sharply and a lightning show of jagged pains burst along the outside of his foot and ankle, even partway up his calf. The stiff leather shank of his boot dug uncomfortably into his inner ankle and the hand that broke his fall scraped painfully across scrubby grass dirty with pebbles.

He cursed and groaned through clenched teeth, rearranging himself on one knee. The dogs continued carrying on, urging Daniel to investigate, but when he got to his feet the turned ankle was an agony to walk on. He limped toward the house, huffing hard breath through his nostrils, grunting, and he cursed each time he put weight on the ankle. "Dogs!" he shouted again, and the pain made him sound furious. "Come by!"

Maggie at last came rushing toward him, barking to alert him as if he hadn't heard her, met his gaze then immediately turned around to lead him. As Daniel limped on, she kept up the circuit—rushing away from him, then charging at him, then away again—while Tugboat barked a storm up by the front of the cottage, out of Daniel's view.

"If one of you dug that fucking hole I stepped in, I'm going to skin you," he threatened. "Fuck me, that hurts."

At last he rounded the corner and found Tugger with his head down and his hair standing out all over, barking his head off in the direction of the woods just across their road. Maggie yipped at Daniel and bounded excitedly between him and something he couldn't make out, though as he followed he began to hear high-pitched beeping at irregular, overlapping intervals. Ten or so yards into the woods, there was a fallen nest and a surrounding spill of hatchling birds.

"You're kidding me," Daniel sighed accusingly. "So what's *his* problem?" He cast a glance toward Tugger, then followed his line of sight. At first Daniel saw nothing, but after a few seconds, there was a low, smooth motion through the brush, probably a lynx or a bobcat. Daniel sighed again, and scanned overhead for sign of the mother bird. "All right, Maggie, good dog," he praised, though grudgingly, then much more firmly gave a bark of his own. "Quiet!" She stopped barking but her posture remained tense. Cutting the dogs' racket in half helped not very much at all.

Daniel found the likely spot where the nest had been, a crotch in the tree just over his head that still had a few twigs caught in it. He stretched his arms overhead to see if he could reach it, and he could, but just barely; his fingertips just brushed it, raining dirt and twigs onto his shoulder. Just the thought of the round trip to the shed and back for the old wooden ladder made his twisted ankle throb in protest.

"Look, fellas, I don't think we can solve this one. Circle of life." He shrugged. "I just. . ."

All at once there was a major commotion in the area where he'd seen the big cat, and Tugger bounded into the trees, giving chase. Maggie took off toward the house, then cut across to run down the road a ways, and barked to let Daniel know there was a car coming, which would explain the cat getting spooked enough to run off without its meal. The mother bird suddenly swooped overhead, warning Daniel loudly to back away from her babies.

"It's fucking chaos!" he cursed, and left the nestlings there on the ground while he hobbled out of the woods. He figured some poor misguided soul was incredibly lost, as no one ever purposefully landed at North Hope Cove unless Daniel had summoned them to take custody of a cliff-jumper.

The car that appeared was small and bright-colored, eventually revealing itself as metallic orange and egg-shaped. Daniel stood by the road's edge, hands on his hips, with a weird sense of anticipatory dread. Had he missed the hearing and someone from Parks was coming to escort him off the property?

"Hush, Maggie," he scolded, and she obeyed, and Tugger trotted out of the woods looking satisfied that he'd run off the cat. "Who's this, you think?"

The car pulled up and parked, but Daniel couldn't see past the sun's glare off the windshield. He and the dogs waited with tight shoulders and alert expressions. The driver's door swung open and a dark figure stepped out.

He waved. "Hey there." He pointed at his chin. "Justin Strongbow. Remember me?"

Six

Daniel was stunned. The dogs were jolly and rushed to meet Justin halfway as he walked up the last bit of road.

"Yeah, I remember you," Daniel managed, foretting his injured ankle just long enough to try to take a single, fully-weighted step, and stumbled a bit for his trouble. He gestured. "Turned my ankle just now."

"That sucks. Pretty bad?" Justin leaned to give the dogs sound thumps on their sides, and they sniffed around his hands and boots.

"Yeah, actually," Daniel admitted. "I think it might be."

"Broken?"

"No, but definitely sprained."

Justin had reached him by then and so Daniel offered his hand to shake.

"Need a ride into Parker?"

"I don't think so, no. I've got first aid supplies. Just wrap it up, ice it." Daniel was about to ask what brought Justin out to the cove, but Tugboat started up snarl-barking again, and took off into the woods. Maggie followed, though quietly. "Christ," Daniel cursed. "Leave it, dogs!" The dogs ignored him, which was unusual enough behavior that he suspected they were not going to settle until he solved the problem of the fallen nest. He glanced back to find the mother bird frantically trying to build a new one. The babies were still peeping frantically for help.

"What's up with them?" Justin asked, looking after the dogs.

Daniel explained, including the part about stepping in a hole as he jogged to find out what the commotion was, and that if he found out one of the dogs had dug it, he was going to toss them off the dock. He finished up by getting as near as he dared to the nest, even as the mother bird threatened to dive-bomb his head.

"You think it's a bobcat?" Justin asked, looking more tantalized than afraid.

"Probably a Canada lynx; I see them around here pretty regularly, but I've only ever seen one bobcat, and that was a couple years ago." He motioned up at the tree branch over his head. "I didn't think I could walk back and forth to the shed to get the ladder, or climb it. But maybe you could—"

"Yeah, give me a boost up and I'll do it." Justin crouched down and began to gently scoop up the hatchlings one by one, cradling the nest in his other hand.

"I was thinking you could get the ladder," Daniel said.

"Nah, just boost me up."

Daniel couldn't imagine being able to get back to his feet if he took a knee, so he merely bent at the waist, clasping his hands together to make a step. He felt Justin's hand on the back of his shoulder as he set his boot into the stirrup of Daniel's hands.

"You good?"

"Yeah, go ahead."

Daniel braced himself as Justin stepped up into his clasped palms, though as suspected, he was hardly a heavyweight. Justin steadied himself with his free hand against the tree trunk, and carefully lifted the nest back into place.

"Hang on," he said. "I just want to make sure it won't fall as soon as I let go."

Daniel grunted affirmation, and within a few seconds, Justin's hands landed on his shoulders and he jumped to the ground. Daniel rubbed his palms together while the two of them stood side by side, looking up at the nest. The mother bird landed on the branch above, then hopped down to the edge of the nest. It didn't budge.

"Nice work," Daniel said, with an appreciative head tilt.

"You, too." Justin grinned; his teeth were small and crowded and the color of cigarette paper. It was a hell of a charming smile. "What about the lynx? Will it just crawl up there to get them anyway? Cats can climb, right?"

Daniel hopped a bit, shifting around to look for the dogs. "They can, but a Canada lynx hunts mostly on the ground, and there's still plenty of food— winter's not fully set in yet—so it's probably not hungry enough to bother."

Justin nodded. "Ah, that's good. And the dogs are all right?"

"No worries about them," Daniel assured.

"You have a gun, anyway, if the cat comes back," Justin prompted.

Daniel shook his head, solidly, just once, and frowned. "Nope," he corrected. "No gun."

"What, really? Out here in the woods alone and no gun?"

"I'm supposed to," Daniel admitted. "Had to do the training and all, ranger stations are supposed to have them—and technically this is a ranger station—but it's. . ." he cleared his throat, shrugged. "Just not my thing."

Justin made a little *ain't-that-something* noise and shrugged, then mercifully circled back to talking about the dogs. "That's pretty crazy, that they'd protect those birds like that," Justin said.

"I'd like to think they're that compassionate and noble," Daniel replied, "But it's probably more about their territory. They're making it known that if anyone was going to eat those birds, it would be them. Or possibly me. But definitely not some wild cat, coming here from Away. Mostly it just turned out to be a pain in my ass," he added, then corrected himself, "Or—my ankle."

"Where's your first aid kit? Should I grab it for you?"

"In the house. I can walk." In fact, he dreaded the thought, but he wasn't going to sit on the ground wrapping his foot. The idea of pulling off his boot made him cringe; it was sure to hurt like hell.

"You want to lean on me or something?" Justin extended his elbow.

The prospect of leaning on Justin seemed equal parts necessary and humiliating, so Daniel naturally erred on the side of pride. "No, thanks. I'm good." He started to limp toward the cottage, gritting his teeth to stop himself groaning, and Justin walked slowly alongside him.

"Won't be easy climbing all those stairs later," Justin commented, and Daniel couldn't stifle that particular groan.

"No, it won't," he agreed, and unlatched the gate at the end of the gravel walk. "Shit."

"Is the only switch the one you showed me? Up at the top?"

"Yeah, but now I'm seeing why it might not be a terrible idea to have a backup at sea level." Once they were inside, Daniel went straight for his armchair. "In the kitchen there, bottom cabinet on the far left, is the first aid kit," he said, "Could you?"

"Yeah, sure, no problem." Justin collected the kit while Daniel started to untie his boots, loosening the laces far more than he normally would have, making extra space. As soon as the shank of the boot relaxed, blood rushed into his ankle and it throbbed; the boot itself had been semi-effectively compressing the injury.

"Jeezus," he cursed, and sucked his teeth.

"You have ice packs or something?" Justin asked, setting the big plastic chest on the coffee table in front of Daniel's chair, and flicking open the latches. It accordianed open, showing stepped shelves of bins like a fishing tackle box. Justin shifted a few things in the deepest part of the kit and lifted out a plastic packet he tore open at the corner. "It's one of those break-and-shake ones," he said, and whacked the blue gel-filled packet against the heel of his hand a few times, then began massaging it. Daniel, meanwhile, bit his lips and started to ease off his boot, letting fly a string of curses as he peeled away his sock.

"Oh, shit," he muttered. The outside of his ankle was fat with fluid and already the blood was pooling below the point of the injury, blooming a black-purple bruise.

"Man, that's a beauty," Justin agreed, with a grim sort of half-smile. He passed the ice pack. "Put that on while I find a bandage."

"There might even be a sleeve thing in there," Daniel told him, setting his foot up on the coffee table and leaning to lay the ice pack on it, bending it to conform. "More like a brace than one of those long elastic bandages. I know there's a wrist one, and maybe one for a knee."

"You have your pick," Justin told him, holding up a soft, sock-like ankle brace in one hand, and roll of beige bandage in the other.

"Maybe wrap it for now, and then the brace after the swelling goes down some."

Justin tossed him the bandage roll and left the brace on the coffee table, then started packing up the kit.

"There's some ibuprofen in the bathroom, top shelf of the cabinet," Daniel said. "Can I trouble you to grab me a couple—or four?"

Justin returned the first aid kit to its place, moving comfortably around the cottage as if he were at his ease there, opened cabinets until he found drinking glasses and ran the faucet to fill one, then crossed to the bathroom for the pills. From inside, he called, "If you're taking a bunch, you'll want to eat something."

It was nearing lunch time. Looked like Daniel was having a guest. "I can make us some sandwiches," Daniel replied. "I might have some chips. I'm due to make my run into Parker in a few days so supplies are a little low right now."

Justin emerged and set the glass of water and bottle of pills on the table beside Daniel; he had to lean across him to reach, and Daniel sat back as far as he could. They exchanged the small smiles required when one man invaded another's space, to signal no attempt to attack or colonize.

"I can fix it," Justin told him, and there came another round of cabinet-opening, drawer-pulling, and fridge-searching as he tried to locate the makings of a midday meal. "OK if I make coffee?" he asked.

"Love some," Daniel told him. By then he was securing the bandage in place, and slid his bunched-up sock halfway up his foot, just to cover his toes. He reached for the plastic bottle of pills, thumbed the cap that he never bothered to twist, as there were no children around to protect from poisoning themselves. As he shook the pills into his palm, it finally dawned on him to wonder precisely why Justin had driven up just when he had, without warning or invitation. He cast a glance toward the kitchen, at Justin's back as he worked at the counter beside the sink.

Daniel swallowed four pills and two huge gulps of cool water, then asked, "So what brings you out here?" After a half-second, he added, "If you don't mind me asking."

A hearty shrug of the shoulders from Justin. "I felt like driving, and so I drove a while, and then I was driving up Route 18, and then I was here."

"There are other places to go, off 18," Daniel said.

There was a pause while Justin lifted sandwiches onto plates, and tore open a bag of kettle-cooked potato chips he'd found in the breadbox with the marble rye. "I didn't mean to bother you," he said apologetically. "But I wanted to. . . I don't know. . ." another shrug, and judging by his actions it seemed to Daniel he should have turned around by then, a plate in each hand, but he kept fiddling, giving Daniel his back.

Just then the dogs came trotting through the dog door, and their tails started wagging, and they seemed not to know who to greet first; no matter Daniel's opinions of unexpected company, Tugger and Mags were obviously delighted by it. They ran in a tumble between Justin in the kitchen and Daniel in the armchair, until Daniel said, "Places, please," and they went to their beds.

"Wow, they really listen," Justin commented, at last turning away from the counter and crossing the room with the lunch. He set both plates on the coffee table, then returned to the kitchen and found the coffee mugs in the second cabinet he tried, filled them both with fresh coffee.

"They're pure shepherd," Daniel told him. "They like to be given orders, and jobs to do. Right now their job is to chill out."

"How do you take it?"

"Just black."

More opening and closing of doors until Justin found a one-pound bag of sugar inside a zippered plastic bag to keep the damp out of it, then three drawers slid out and in before he found a spoon. At least the milk was in the obvious place. Daniel leaned up and claimed a plate, set it on the arm of the chair and waited for Justin to join him.

Justin settled in the middle of the sofa, reached to set a mug on the side table within Daniel's reach.

"You've had them a long time?" Justin asked, and bit off the corner of a triangular half of the sandwich, which Daniel discovered was deli-sliced, rare roast beef and Swiss cheese, slathered with grainy German mustard.

"Just over four years," Daniel said. "There's a guy out by Keyes with a farm and a herd of sheep; they make cheese from the milk. He had a big litter of pups but only wanted a couple for himself, to train as herding dogs. He put an ad online and I went and picked out these two."

"Brother and sister. That's cool."

"When I started teaching them commands, I used the ones sheepdogs are taught, because I figured they might have heard them while they were puppies. And maybe there's some—I don't know—embedded genetic memory or something." Daniel shrugged, smiling at the dogs. "Yeah, I'm talking about you," he teased them.

"What are the commands?" Justin asked.

Daniel explained the basics: *come round* and *away to me*, directing them clockwise or counter-clockwise around the flock, to steer it, were ones he used to get them to run to his right or left. He used *come by* to summon them back to him. Of course, they knew all the other basics—sit, stay, down, and to go to their places—and when he wanted them in the cottage he told them it was *home time*.

"So no wonder they all but pushed me down the hill that day," Justin said.

Daniel had begun to wonder if they were ever going to acknowledge the last and only time they'd seen each other. "Yeah, they do that," he started, but before he could say more, Justin interrupted.

"Do you think you'll need crutches?"

He hadn't considered it. "Don't know. I guess it will depend how it feels to walk on it, now that it's taped up."

"It's not going to fit back in your boot, I bet," Justin asserted, and as his plate was empty, he picked it up and brought it to the kitchen, where he left it to sit on the counter by the sink among the open bread- and chips-bags, the knife sticking out of the mustard jar, and the paper and plastic wrappings from the cold cuts and cheese in disarray. All of it together gave Daniel an itchy urge to get up and straighten it. "Doubt if they'd have crutches in Parker Village," Justin said, returning to the sofa and picking up his coffee mug. "Probably have to drive all the way into Calais for that, to a Pharm-Mart or something."

Daniel laughed a bit. "I don't know that I'll be driving anywhere for a while."

"Oh, damn. That's true," Justin agreed, glancing at Daniel's elevated right foot in its crumpled sock and bandage.

"There's a whole room at the back of the shed full of random old junk; I'll rummage around in there."

"Or order some online," Justin suggested.

"It would just get delivered to the Parker post office," Daniel corrected him.

"Someone could bring it out here to you. I could."

Daniel looked at him, and their eyes caught then quickly tore away again.

"Thanks." A second of silence, then Daniel blurted, "Why are you here?"

Justin brushed his hand against his mouth and sat back a bit.

"I don't mind," Daniel assured him. "It's only that no one ever just shows up. Or if they do, they aren't inclined to drive up and say hello."

Justin clutched one fist in the other. The cuffs of his pullover sweatshirt were faded to dark gray and stretched to shapelessness. "It was good that time," he said plainly, not looking at Daniel. "I mean, it was weird. And kind of awful. Not my best day."

Daniel answered with quiet agreement, "No."

"No, it wasn't good, or—?"

"Not your best day."

Daniel studied Justin: dark waves of hair that looked uncombed but not truly dirty, a few days' stubble on his upper lip and chin, his narrow nose and thick eyebrows all just as Daniel had remembered them. Daniel took note of his hands, compact and soft-looking, with clean fingernails. His knuckles smoothed and wrinkled as he squeezed and released his fist. Justin at last met his gaze.

"I mean," he said, and even shrugged a little. "I thought it was good. I thought you were. . ."

Daniel raised his eyebrows, prompting Justin to continue.

"I liked the tour, and that you turned on the light in the daytime."

Daniel felt himself smile, felt a strange sort of bashful pride rise up in his chest, and he told himself it was because Justin appreciated the light.

"And I liked the story you told me—about the drowned man and the villagers."

Daniel wished Justin was sitting where he'd lately imagined him—on the near end of the sofa, just in reach there by the arm of his chair—but Justin was planted wide-kneed in the center of the sofa, and he crossed his arms protectively across his belly, tucking his hands in at his sides. There was too much space between them to close pseudo-accidentally, so Daniel could deny his intention if it turned out he'd misjudged something. Easing his ankle off the coffee table and setting his foot to the floor, Daniel leaned up, set his elbow on the chair-arm and dropped his head sideways against his palm, scratching fingers through the hair behind his ear.

"Yeah," he said, wanting to put a compassionate end to Justin's foundering recollections of their earlier meeting. "It was good."

Justin smiled again, showing his teeth a little. "Sorry again about—"

"S'all right," Daniel said immediately, and waved it off, playing along with this newly prevailing narrative—that it had all been a sad, messy moment of weakness; just a dying man looking for comfort and a lonesome man giving in to his long-shelved need for human touch. "We can forget it."

On an exhale that might have been a sigh of relief, Justin said, "OK. Yeah, OK." They both nodded, and their postures loosened, and their eyes did not meet.

Just then the dogs raised their heads, ears up, and an instant later there came a wide, rumbling boom that shook the air. The hairs on Daniel's arms bristled.

"Shit," he muttered. "Storm isn't supposed to hit us until tomorrow." He got to his feet and half-hopped to the kitchen. He leaned on the edge of the sink with both hands and craned his neck to look south through the ocean-facing window. A clear demarcation line separated the pale blue of the overhead sky from an adjacent smear of near-black cloud. Just then a fork of lighting split the cloud, and Daniel tensely awaited the thunder's report. "The leading edge is about seven miles off. I'll have to look at the map to see how big it is."

"It was raining a little in Six Rivers when I left there," Justin volunteered, in a tone that signaled a desire to be helpful.

Daniel limped back to his writing desk and woke his laptop, stood leaning over the back of the desk chair as he steered to the relevant forecasts.

"When was that?"

"About ten-fifteen?"

"Moving pretty slow, then. That's good. It'll give me time to climb the stairs." He squinted at the screen. The storm was a monster, with a wide center full of heavy rain, lighting strikes showing up from edge to edge, but—he'd estimated correctly—it was not fast-moving. Likely it would be over them within the hour, and it might linger there until midnight, maybe longer. Another lengthy rumble of thunder. The dogs jumped to their feet, wandering around, itchy. Maggie went for the water dish, and Tug stood at Daniel's side, flicking his tail.

"You think you can make it up there?" Justin asked, and he moved to the front door to look outside.

"I have to."

"Yeah, but." He let whatever else he might have said die. "I'll go look in the shed for you," he volunteered.

"Do you mind?"

He shook his head and hummed in the negative.

"You'll see the door to the back room. I don't think I've seen crutches in there, but there might be a cane?"

"I'll see what I see," Justin said, and vanished through the front door, pulling it shut behind him.

Daniel made an entry in the electronic log; the Coast Guard and National Weather Service would be able to see that he was aware of the approaching storm and would change the light's pattern appropriately, within the hour or when the storm encroached on the cove, whichever came first. He re-checked the shipping schedule and the sailing plans of whatever fishing boats were out. Pleasure boats were possible in his neck of the woods, too, but nothing outside the spare usual was in the books. The most challenging part of dealing with this particular bout of weather would be getting himself up the tower to the lantern. Once Justin had come back from the shed, Daniel would thank him for the help and encourage him to get on the road and into Parker Village before the storm was over them; parts of the road from Route 18 to the cove would turn muddy and treacherous—especially for a compact car without all-wheel-drive—and Justin would be safer the farther he was from North Hope, even driving into the storm.

As Daniel hobbled around gathering his slicker and hat, contemplating whether to bother with the heavy, water-tight boots or stick with his regular ones, it did occur to him that he felt a bit of disappointment over Justin's arrival at the station resulting from an aimless drive, and that he'd apologized for their previous encounter. Daniel could imagine the afternoon having played out differently, particularly if Justin had sat within easy catching distance. But despite having enjoyed the conversation, it seemed Justin regretted the sex, so Daniel must let it go.

Anyway, there was the weather to contend with.

He packed his rain gear into an army-surplus backpack big enough for a weeklong trek in the woods, which Daniel knew from experience, having camped and hiked for at least that long—several times, with only the pack, a map, and a compass—in the Abenaki forest before the place had been ruined for him.

It would be easier to hunker down overnight in the watch room than to aim for multiple trips up and down the tower, so he packed water and food—with no real emergency at hand, he wouldn't have to use up any of the tower's supplies—as well as his tablet and phone, and the book he'd lately been reading, which he pulled off the night stand.

"Out," he told the dogs, figuring they were unlikely to get another chance for a pretty long while, and they obeyed, following each other through the dog door.

Justin returned carrying a tall, ornately carved wooden stick.

"I found this wizard's staff," he said, gesturing to it with exaggerated, jokey reverence. "If it doesn't help you walk at least you can bring some trees to life."

Daniel smiled widely and took it from him, setting its end on the floor with a satisfying thud. About a third of the way down was an obvious hand grip, with gentle curves and flares that fit his palm and curled fingers comfortably. "One of the old fellas must have made this for walking the land," he ventured. "It might help, I guess."

"Makes you look cool," Justin grinned at him. "That mountain man vibe. Rugged."

Daniel felt his face betraying him with curled lips and raised eyebrows. "Oh, yeah?" He struck a pose, felt stupid, let it go.

"I closed up the shed," Justin said, a quick return to the business at hand that made Daniel feel even stupider for having flirted back at what felt like a pretty transparent pass at him. "What else can I do?" Justin looked around the room. They both spoke at once.

"You should head out of here."

"I'll carry up your pack. Oh." He already had his hand on the straps of the backpack, which he released, and jammed his hands into the pass-through pocket on the front of his hoodie. Daniel could make out the edges of Justin's phone moving as he flipped it over and over inside the pocket.

Daniel hurried to add, "The road washes out sometimes, between here and 18. If you wait much longer you could get stranded for the rest of the day—maybe all night." He employed the walking stick as he picked up his left-behind lunch plate and their coffee cups, stacking them to carry to the kitchen.

Justin shrugged but didn't smile. "I have nowhere to be, and it seems like you could use the help." He took the plate with the mugs balanced on it from Daniel, and brought it quickly to the sink. "But if I'm in your way, you know, it's cool, I get it."

Daniel scratched his chin, digging three fingers into his beard, then dragged his hand along the disturbed whiskers to smooth them back into place. It occurred to him that in nearly ten years at the station, this unexpected visit from Justin was now, at nearly three hours, the longest he'd ever had a guest. He glanced at the counter top, still littered with the makings of their lunch. "What a mess," he said, and Justin looked startled, glancing at the counter as if snapping out of a dream. He picked up the metal cap for the mustard, pulled out the knife from the jar and scraped it clean on the edge, then stuck the knife-blade between his lips and pulled it out again to catch whatever remained.

Daniel unplugged his laptop from the wall and wound up the cord, tucked it into his pack as Justin continued straightening the kitchen.

"I don't mind the company." Daniel decided it even as he said the words. "I just wanted to warn you that if you *were* heading back, better to get while the getting's good."

Justin stuffed two potato chips in his mouth and crunched loudly as he folded over the top of the bag, returning it to the bread box beside the fridge.

"Hanging out in a lighthouse during a big storm sounds pretty damn cool," he said. "I won't get in the way."

"Yeah, no," Daniel said, waving it away. "Really I can probably use a hand."

"Good, then."

Daniel had latched the dog door, and as Justin followed him out, pulling the front door shut, he asked, "Should I lock this?"

"I never do," Daniel told him. "No point; there's never anyone around, and I doubt a bear could work the knob. Just leave it."

The fire was stoked up and the dogs got an early meal, so they were content. Justin shouldered the pack and followed Daniel up the stairs even though it must have been frustrating to follow him, easing his way up so slowly, setting both feet on each tread before stepping up to the next, with aid from both the carved walking stick and the metal-cable railing. When they were about a quarter of the way up, Justin idly asked, "Where do you piss, though?"

"Off the side!" Daniel enthused. "There's a catwalk around the lantern room, for cleaning the windows. Just be careful you're sure which way the wind is blowing." They shared a hearty laugh over this before Daniel added, "If you have to take a shit, though, you do it in a bag."

"That's worse than camping," Justin said, with a shake of his head.

Once they reached the lantern room, Daniel leaned on the stick as he walked while Justin tried to stay out of his way—not succeeding very well given the close quarters. The sky was by then more gray than blue, and the rain had begun—fat drops thudding on the windows—with its attendant lightning flashes and low, grumbling thunder.

"I'm setting the signal for inland storm conditions," Daniel explained. "To let boats know they shouldn't approach; landing in this cove in a storm is especially dangerous—low visibility, and a lot of rocks." He opened the metal door of the secondary switch panel and swung it out of the way so Justin could see. "These notations here," he indicated a column of tape strips with smudged ink symbols on them. "Describe what pattern each switch is programmed to run—adjusting the speed of the lamp's rotation, and the size of the apertures. In the old days, with the wicks, the keeper would have used different mirrors and covers, lit and doused the lamp to various timings. And the oily smoke meant cleaning the windows pretty much constantly. It was a much harder job then, compared to what I do now."

"I couldn't do it," Justin offered, and somehow Daniel knew he meant it was his own fairly easy job Justin was asserting was beyond his ken, but played dumb.

"Nor me. Back then the keeper would have an assistant or two rotating in and out of service—so he'd have had days off now and then."

"When's the last time you had a day off?" Justin asked, and Daniel snapped the panel's door into place, then leaned back and up to watch the light.

"I think the longest I've been away from the station is about ten hours, once when the truck needed a repair and the part had to be driven up from Portland."

"I used to do that—driving auto parts to garages—when I first left high school."

"Yeah?" Daniel replied casually. "What do you do now?"

"Not much," Justin admitted jokily, then redirected. "So you've never spent a night away since you got here?"

"No. Not that I've got anywhere else to be."

"Holidays? Visiting family? Or a good date that didn't end?"

Daniel laughed out loud at the last part. "No dates. No family."

"Too bad."

"It's fine," Daniel shrugged. He pointed to the stairs. "It's a little warmer in the watch room, and there's places to sit."

"Sure. Lead on, Hop-Along." Justin grinned devilishly at his own lame joke.

In the watch room, Daniel switched on the lights as the sky dimmed, a combined effect of the approaching storm clouds and autumn's early dusk creeping in. Justin took up a spot by a window, and Daniel arranged a tiny space heater, setting it to run at its lowest setting just to take the edge off the cold, then set to unpacking the supplies from his backpack.

"You should put your foot up," Justin told him.

"Soon as this is done," was Daniel's brush-off. "Sit down if you want, there's a couple of folding chairs there." He gestured to the space beside a small table, where two wooden chairs stood waiting. Justin unfolded them both, tucking them under the edges of the table, kitty-corner to each other rather than across, and sat on the edge of the bed with his elbows on his thighs, watching Daniel unpack. Daniel avoided looking at him, trying to tamp down memories of the last time he'd seen Justin sitting just there, bent and folded, clutching at Daniel's clothes. He felt a rolling hollow in his belly, like the barrel of a wave, then the chop as it collapsed.

He pulled out the plastic bottle of ibuprofen from the pack, tossing it up so it rolled in the air before landing back in his palm, then set it on top of the tool chest. The last thing he pulled from the bag was a bottle of bourbon.

Justin made a knowing sound when he saw it, and grinned. His smiles were rare, Daniel had come to notice, which made them seem more genuine. Daniel felt rewarded by them, as if he had scored points each time one came around.

"Not much else to do," Daniel told him. "It's a big storm, but the conditions are unlikely to change much, so if it weren't for this ankle I wouldn't even stay up here. Just keep an eye on conditions and run up if I needed to. But. Better safe than sorry. So." He offered a smile of his own, conspiratorial. "Let's have a drink."

"Brown liquor," Justin said ominously.

"Used to get me in a lot of fights," Daniel confirmed, and he turned one of the folding chairs, not needing to move it much, sat, and arranged his foot on the edge of the bed.

"Here," Justin said, quickly folding the bed's pillow in half, and Daniel lifted his leg so Justin could tuck it beneath his ankle. "So you're that guy at the bar I would always avoid," he sly-grinned. "I've never been in a fight; I'd always ghost as soon as it smelled like trouble."

"Aw, you're not a man 'til you've been in a fight," Daniel chided.

"That's ridiculous." Justin shook a cigarette loose from his pack and then slipped out a plastic lighter tucked inside it. He extended his hand, offering Daniel a smoke; which he declined with a frowning shake of his head, but went into his shirt pocket and fished out his own pack. Justin smirked, "Next you'll tell me I have to smoke cigars and join the army."

"Sorry if I've offended your boyish sensibility," Daniel joked, smiling around the cigarette between his teeth as he struck a match. "What are you, thirty? You should have been in twenty fights by now."

"Thirty-three."

"Twenty-two then."

"How many have you been in?" Justin challenged. He stood up from his seat on the bed and looked around for an ashtray. Finding none, he brought over a half-finished plastic bottle of water and set it on the floor within reach of them both.

Daniel took a leisurely drag on his cigarette and squinted, thinking it through.

"Two?" he answered at last. Justin looked stunned, then they both broke out laughing.

"You're full of shit," Justin accused.

"Nah."

"In bars, you said?"

"Once in a bar, once outside a bar. Anyway," Daniel spun the cap off the bourbon bottle and leaned a bit to pass it over. "Here. We'll be fighting in no time."

"Sure." Justin sniffed, half-grinning. He downed a swig, grimaced and let out a whoosh of breath, passed the bottle back.

Daniel took a deep slug, rolled it in his mouth before swallowing. It stung the whole way down, then spread like an ooze of lava through his belly. He drank again—it went down easier the second time—and handed it back. Justin held it half-balanced on his knee.

"So I have to make a confession," Daniel ventured, telling himself the bourbon made him brave. "A few weeks after I last saw you, I started asking around about you, down in Parker."

Justin's eyebrows rose a bit, widening his dark eyes. "Oh, yeah? What are they saying about me down in Parker?"

"The barber and the hairdresser—that old couple—they knew more about your parents, I think. Said you had it pretty rough as a kid."

A scoffing laugh from Justin, then, "Yeah. Pretty rough."

"Your dad's a fisherman?" Daniel asked, leading with the most innocent part of the tale he'd heard.

Justin nodded and hummed in the affirmative.

"Still?"

"He's a first mate now; not as much work out on the decks. His back's pretty bad. Sits in the captain's chair when the captain's in his bunk, I guess."

"Ever been out on a fishing boat?"

"A couple times. Not my kind of work. Which is too bad because they make good money, and if you don't have a heroin habit you can even hang onto it for a couple months." Justin took a series of small swigs of the bourbon and passed it back to Daniel, then lifted the plastic water bottle and ashed his cigarette into it. "You must have done some fishing," he ventured.

"I haven't been out on boats much, actually. Just the runaround I've got down at the dock."

"Seems like a lighthouse keeper would be all about sailing."

"Nope. I like the land. The forest. When I started at Parks I wanted to get to Shenandoah, on the Appalachian Trail. Maybe up to Alaska. Real wilderness, forests. I was never an ocean person; I like the mountains. When you're out in the woods it feels like it could just go on forever, like you could get lost in it, be part of it. The coast feels like the opposite of that. It's the end of the world."

"The ocean's another world," Justin offered, and his voice was soft-edged; Daniel held onto the bottle another minute, hoping to avoid a shamble up to the catwalk, to vomit off the side, before night had even fully fallen.

"Not a world I want to explore," Daniel replied. "I've grown to appreciate it, but it's pretty easy for me to turn my back on it when I don't need to pay attention."

"I like the beach," Justin said thoughtfully, gaze fixed somewhere beyond Daniel, as if looking back over his memory. Daniel tried to imagine artsy, black-clad Justin on a beach, could only picture him more or less as he was: tight black jeans and a punk rocker's unlaced boots, though he could just about imagine him in a t-shirt—a black one, though. Justin went on. "I love Old Portsmouth Beach."

"That's not a beach," Daniel corrected. "That's a carnival."

Old Portsmouth, about two hours south of North Hope, was the only coastal beach in Maine with a boardwalk full of bars, souvenir stands, ice cream shops, and video game arcades, and it did, in fact have several carnival rides, including an old wooden roller coaster and a huge ferris wheel. It was a garish, clown-suited mockery of a beach, strewn with trash and sunburned children vomiting cotton candy into the sand. Twice a year it hosted motorcycle rallies, and the rest of the time it was overrun with tourists and teenagers.

"I like busy places," Justin said. "I like noise and a lot of people around who don't want anything from me."

Daniel shuddered over another swallow, and Justin reached for the bottle. Their fingers touched, though they hadn't before. Daniel dropped the butt of his cigarette into the water bottle and gave it a swish for good measure. He made a mental note to check the expiration dates on all the fire extinguishers in the tower, the cottage, and the shed.

"A place like that is a kind of hell to me," Daniel said.

Justin shrugged, and didn't argue. "What else did they say about me?" he prompted.

"That it's pretty sad you got to age thirty-three without taking a punch," Daniel grinned. Justin rolled his eyes. "They said kind of a lot of things. More than they probably should. You know how people run their mouths." He flicked his hand open and closed, mimicking a working jaw, then waved it. "I don't know." He left it for a few moments, then said, "They mentioned you owned a hotel?"

Justin nodded. "I sure did. Still do. It's not a hotel, though, it's a house. A big house, but just a house. Over in Six Rivers—you know where that is?"

Daniel nodded and hummed.

Justin took a hard slug of the bourbon and Daniel watched his Adam's apple bob as he swallowed. "I inherited it."

"They mentioned you had a partner who died," Daniel said.

Justin looked surprised. "Did they? God, they really knew it all, then, I guess. I barely remember those people! What are their names?"

"John Senior, and the wife is Christine."

"Oh, yeah. They knew my dad's ma. Nosy old cusses."

Daniel saw no point holding back—it wasn't him that had given away Justin's whole life story, all he'd done was ask if they knew anybody named Strongbow and it had just poured out at him—so he said, "She said you had a business partner—and he had a wife?—and he died, but they thought you must still be running the place since you never moved back to Parker."

Justin's eyebrows rumpled toward each other in the middle. "That's what they said? Business partner?"

"She said he was from Boston."

Justin let go a small, bitter laugh, and Daniel leaned in to reclaim the bourbon from him, as Justin looked agitated and likely to kill the last of it. "He was my *partner*," Justin said, with emphasis on the word. "He was my husband."

Now it was Daniel's turn to raise his eyebrows, widen his eyes. "Oh, jeez. I'm sorry."

"Thanks."

"No, I don't think they knew that. She said he had a wife, though?"

"His niece, from Brazil, Lia. But his sister was much older than him so Lia's closer to his age, I think she's forty-one or –two. She's the inn's housekeeper."

"What was his name?" Daniel prompted, not sure what else he should be saying.

"Gabriel. Pereira."

"How did he. . .was he ill? He can't have been very old."

"He was forty-six when he died. Pancreatic cancer."

"I'm sorry," Daniel said again.

"Thanks. Anyway, so. Yes, I own a house in Six Rivers but I don't run it as an inn anymore. That was Gabriel's thing; he loved everything about it. He enjoyed meeting people, talking to them about where they were from or where they'd been. He was a really good host; the guests all loved him."

Daniel gave him a little smile.

"I promised him I'd keep it. Lia still makes the beds and dusts the bookcases, video-calls with her sisters and watches Brazilian soap operas on her phone all the rest of the time. I moved into one of the guest rooms. I keep saying I'll open it next season, next season. . .but it's never—" he shook his head, looking angry at himself. "Maybe in the spring." He tilted his head to catch Daniel's eye. "See? I can't let it go, and I can't—" he cut himself off with a shrug. "I'm talking too much."

"Brown liquor," Daniel said, and held out his hands, shaking his head.

"Brown fucking liquor."

"Well," Daniel said, sensing the need for a change in the air. "I need to go piss off the side." He got to his feet, mostly-hopped to where he'd propped the walking stick by the watch room's door. "While I'm up there I can check the reports and switch the signal if I need to. Then we can eat something, if you want; I brought up the rest of those chips, and most of a chicken I had in the fridge, in pieces."

Justin nodded acknowledgement and bit his thumbnail.

"You can go down to the cottage if you want," Daniel offered from the doorway. "Not always easy to be in such close quarters. If you need some space."

"Thanks."

"Front door's unlocked," Daniel reminded him, and began his hobble up to the lantern room.

In addition to his injury slowing him, Daniel took his time after ducking back in from the rain, circled the light, pulled up the latest weather forecasts and maritime schedules on his phone. He would not expect any boats within sight of the tower until after dawn, and the worst of the storm was passing over them just at that hour, its center about ten miles east off the coast. Another three to five hours and they should be in the clear. He decided to leave the storm signal running despite the reports there'd be no ships, just for safety's sake. By the time he was negotiating the last few stairs before the landing outside the watch room, nearly a half hour had passed, and he half-wondered if he would find Justin had gone—down to the cottage, or beyond—in order to relieve the pressure created by close quarters and conversation about topics more personal than bar fights and favorite places.

"All right?"

"Fine," Daniel smiled. "The eye's passing over us now. Few hours to go."

Justin had found all the food Daniel brought up from the kitchen, and set it out on the little table in two portions; he'd made plates out of the foil wrappings. There were pieces of cold chicken, its previously-crisp skin gone flabby from a day in the fridge; a pile of potato chips for each of them; and two mandarins apiece, a pair of which Justin had peeled, segmented, and fanned out artistically beside the rest of the meal. As Daniel moved to pull his chair out from under the table where Justin had placed it, Justin snapped open two plastic bottles of water and set them in place.

"Looks good enough to eat," Daniel commented.

"With our fingers, though," was Justin's apologetic-sounding reply.

"I didn't think of forks and knives. I don't usually have company to impress."

"Don't worry about it." Justin sank his teeth into the fat end of a drumstick. Once he'd half-chewed to make space for his tongue, he asked, "You cooked this?"

"Who else?" Daniel shrugged.

"It's good."

"Thanks." Daniel licked the oily pad of his thumb. "You arranged it pretty nicely."

"Old habits. I used to do the food at the B and B when I wasn't—um—whenever I could."

"Oh?" A gentle sound, inviting him to say more if he wished, or to move on to something else. Daniel had the impression there was a lot Justin wasn't saying; he kept catching himself, leaving sentences half-finished. It was not an unfamiliar sensation to Daniel—often when people learned he was *yes, that Daniel Howard,* they would stop mid-thought, afraid of saying something thoughtless or of reminding him of his failure that day.

Justin busied himself rearranging his food, staring down at it with a concerned expression. "When I get depressed I stay up too late, and then I can't get up early." He cut a glance at Daniel as he added, "The guests want breakfast from seven to ten whether you went to bed at four a.m. or not."

"Right."

Justin shrugged and went back to eating, brushing it away. "After we eat, then what? How do you pass the time when you're up here?"

"Usually I read, but that would be pretty rude of me. There's a deck of cards."

"I don't know any card games but War."

"And all I can remember are about sixteen variations on Solitaire," Daniel grinned. "Turn out the lights to eliminate the glare, and watch the lightning show. The light gets in the way sometimes when it comes around, but I forgive it."

Justin made a comically suspicious face. "Are you in love with the light?" he demanded.

The laugh that boomed forth from Daniel surprised even him. "I am," he said, nodding his entire upper body. "You're right, I am in love with the light. I'm married to it. It owns me." He laughed again. "Hundred percent."

They were finished with the food and cleaned up by licking fingers and swiping hands on the legs of their jeans. Justin grabbed the half-bottle of bourbon he'd set at the wall-edge of the table out of their way, spun the cap off, and took a big swig. Offering it to Daniel, he got to his feet and rolled his neck, turning his head in a figure-eight. He slipped his fingers backward through his hair and Daniel could see—just for a second—that his hairline rose at the temples. Taking a giant step backward that put him nearly halfway across the tiny room, Justin said, "So teach me what it's like to be in a fight."

"What?" Daniel swallowed the liquor, slightly mellower for having been opened earlier and because his prior consumption had somewhat softened his senses.

"Nothing crazy," Justin assured, showing his palms. He wore a narrow gold band on one finger; Daniel hadn't noticed it before, but knowing Justin was widowed made it noticeably poignant. "Just show me how to throw a punch. I promise I won't knock you out."

Daniel scoffed. "Have you noticed you're half my size? There's no chance of you knocking me out."

"OK, then, let's go. Pass the time. Come on."

"I'm playing hurt, though, remember," Daniel said as he lifted himself off the chair. He stood firm on his good foot, just resting his toes and the ball of the other foot on the floor to keep his balance without putting real weight on his sprained ankle. "Have you seriously never punched anyone? How about a punching bag?"

Justin shook his head. He stood slightly sideways, left foot in front, and held his balled fists in front of his chest, knuckles facing the ceiling and elbows toward the floor. "I might have punched a pillow a couple times."

It was Daniel's turn to shake his head, pityingly. "First of all, tuck your thumbs down or you'll jam the knuckle when the punch lands." He demonstrated, and Justin bent his thumbs farther, nestling them down nearer where they belonged. "Now, make this part flat as you can." He tapped the backs of his own folded fingers between the joints. "You might need to loosen your fingers first to set it up. Here." He took a half-hop closer to Justin and grasped his wrist; Justin let him readjust the set of his fingers. "Righty or lefty?"

"I'm left-handed."

"Well then first, switch up your stance. Arms and legs move in opposition to keep you in balance—just like walking—so if you're throwing a left, you want your right foot a little in front."

Justin did as he was told. Daniel took hold of his left hand instead, and set his fingers in place. "Now firm it up by squeezing, but not to curl your fingers. Try to squeeze them together, as close to each other as you can get them."

Justin looked at his fist, tried for it, and made an amused sound.

"OK, so," Daniel began, turning his own body a little, and squaring up both fists in front of his chest. "A good old-fashioned punch in the face is always satisfying, and if you have a decent jab, you can put a guy down by going right for the nose."

Justin threw a tiny jab at the air between them.

"But in reality, it's hard to land that, especially if you're a novice. And even more especially if you're drunk. So in a bar fight, you're safer going for body blows. Get some weight behind them, use both fists for a one-two, and the torso is obviously a much bigger target so you're more likely to land a punch."

Daniel demonstrated a one-two combination of a roundhouse-right followed by a left-handed uppercut, nowhere near Justin's torso, only giving him the idea. Then he threw two quick jabs, right-left, straight out from the center of his chest.

"Here, step in a bit. OK. So. Imagine I just made a joke about fucking your mother or spilled a beer on your shoe or whatever—"

"Called me a cocksucking faggot," Justin prompted, his eyebrows drawing down into a frown.

"All right, whatever gets you going," Daniel allowed. "Try to throw two jabs right at my midsection, halfway between my belt and my nipples." He held the edges of his palms against his torso to illustrate the space he described.

Justin made the motions, a quick left-right combination, but stopped well short of making contact.

"Nice. This time go for it."

"Nah."

"I mean, not like to knock me down, but like you'd punch a guy on the arm as a joke."

Justin's expression displayed that particular brand of half-drunk concentration so common to men who'd been sharing a bottle of bourbon over a couple hours' time, and Daniel imagined his own might be similar, as he was far from intoxicated but had definitely rounded off most of his sharp edges with liberal internal application of middle-shelf whiskey.

There was a flash of lightning then, and a quick crack of thunder, and Daniel cut a glance toward the windows, which was the exact moment Justin chose to throw his punches. With ample warning, Daniel would have tensed his muscles to brace himself, but as it was, he let go a matched set of "oof" sounds and bent forward a little, arms crossing in front of his waist.

"Sorry. I thought you were ready." Justin sounded sincerely sheepish but also couldn't repress his smile.

"No worries," Daniel assured him. He hopped a bit to settle himself. "So, boxing is one thing, but if we're being honest, in a street fight you're going to be sloppy. So just get a fistful of a guy's shirt and try to get in as many as you can, aiming for his head and face, like so." Daniel didn't actually grab Justin by the shirtfront, but instead laid a hand on his shoulder, then mimed punching him repeatedly from up high; Justin didn't flinch; but his eyes narrowed and his shoulder was taut under Daniel's grip.

"OK, but," Justin said as Daniel backed away from him. He licked his lips. There was another clap of thunder, followed by a smaller one, and their echoes. "I want to. . ."

Daniel understood him, and turned to offer his shoulder. "Go ahead."

"Can I?"

"Sure, go for it."

Justin's mouth tightened into a pinch, and he dropped his eyebrows. His lips twitched in a circle.

"Come on, lady," Daniel goaded, smiling around it, but Justin made a low growling sound and punched him high on his flexed arm, immediately pushing his fist into his other hand, rubbing away the shock of it. Justin's smile broke wide, looking pleased with himself. "Not bad," Daniel told him. "Here." He held up both hands in front of his chest. "I can take a couple more."

Justin's expression became serious again, and he jabbed a few times—probably not as hard as he could hit, but not entirely pulling his punches, either. Daniel's hands stung and he had to brace them hard to absorb the blows, sinking into his knees to maintain his balance.

"More?"

"Sure. A couple. Try an uppercut." He adjusted his hands and Justin punched up once, drew back, shook his head. Daniel sensed what he wanted and returned his palms to where they'd been, in front of his chest. Lightning behind clouds momentarily whitened the view out the windows, and thunder shook the floor under his shoeless, bandaged foot. Daniel lowered his voice. "What are you gonna do, pussy? Fight me? Go suck a dick, bitch."

Justin charged forward, punching his left hand into Daniel's right again and again, both of them grunting in time with it. "Fuck," Justin growled, "You." "Fuck. You. Fuck. Y—"

He aimed wrong, or Daniel's hand slipped, or both, but whatever the cause the result was that Justin landed a heavy shot to Daniel's chest, below his collarbone on the meat of his pectoral muscle, and knocked him off balance. He twisted and hobbled just enough to land on his back, diagonally on the narrow bed, and Justin fell forward over him, his knee planted between Daniel's thighs, on one elbow and one hand, a little breathless, his face just far enough from Daniel's to see each other clearly.

Daniel stared up at Justin's dark eyes, his flaring nostrils, lips slightly apart, and Justin met the gaze fearlessly. Daniel snaked a hand up to clasp the back of Justin's neck and held him, as he lifted his head off the mattress to meet him partway.

Justin held firm. "I don't—" he said quickly, and shifted so his forearm was across Daniel's chest, keeping him pinned long enough to say in a rough whisper, "I don't want to be nice to you." His expression sought permission.

"All right."

Daniel nodded tightly, once, and after a second's pause to scan his face, Justin thrust a hand up under his chin, beneath his beard dangerously close to his throat, and held him. They pulled each other into a rough kiss, meeting force with force, thunder and lightning and something even darker than the edges of the sky clashing and reverberating. Daniel gathered a fistful of Justin's hair and pulled him close, their teeth scraping unpleasantly before Justin forced Daniel's mouth wider, pushing in his tongue.

A quick drop and shove of Justin's thigh caught Daniel's thickening prick beneath a scrape of his clothes, and Daniel's pelvis rolled up to meet him. A stubble-speckled blade of jaw hovered just in reach, so Daniel leaned up and caught it in his teeth. Justin bucked, gasped, dug his fingers hard into Daniel's bicep, wriggling and pressing to leave bruises. They met in another harsh kiss and Daniel clawed up and under Justin's sweatshirt, another layer of t-shirt beneath, dragged the edges of his fingernails upward until he found a pleasingly thick nipple in among the hair of Justin's chest, and gave it a series of rhythmic pinches in time with the grind of their hips. Justin released a deep whine, caught Daniel's lip between his teeth, then licked into his mouth again. He made a significant, selfish shift of his lower body, and rocked hard against Daniel, humming through tight-bitten lips.

An urgent surge swept Daniel's gut, and he held Justin close around the back, rocking both their bodies sideways and over, until he could slither down to his knees on the floor, biting at Justin's thighs through the sturdy fabric of his jeans, and pressing his knees apart. He slid his palm down along the jeans' fly, and Justin's hands followed the motion, unzipping and shoving down. Daniel got two handfuls of fabric and tugged until they were all the way past his calves, catching on the tops of his boots. Black boxer briefs showed the tantalizing outline of Justin's hard cock, pointing up and to his right, a darker damp spot near the crown. With one hand scratching fingers in Daniel's beard, Justin traced his own shape with the fingers of the other, then rolled himself up to sit. Daniel leaned in and mouthed at his balls through the knit cloth of his briefs.

Justin cursed, and Daniel roared hot breath through Justin's boxers onto his balls, then tried to get his fingers around Justin's cock, couldn't quite, slid and dragged, and they both moaned. Justin raised his ass off the mattress and shoved the underwear down, the waistband catching on his cockhead, and Daniel hurried to help get them out of the way. Justin's cock was thick, its crown purple-pink and slick-looking all over, and the hair around its base was dark, thick, and made Daniel growl. He licked his lips, gathered saliva, and wound his tongue in a spiral around the head of Justin's prick before sliding down and back, down further, wanting him deep, wanting his mouth and throat filled up. Justin grabbed at his shoulder, his neck, the back of his head, and slid his hips forward on the bed, groaning loud on every outstroke.

Wanting to shake him apart, have him, make him rumble like thunder, Daniel clutched at Justin's thigh, and his buttock, thrust his hand up the length of his chest to find his nipple and pinch, all the while licking, sucking, breathless, moaning, until Justin gripped his shoulder and gave it a push, making high warning sounds through tight-bitten lips. Daniel clawed at him, pinned him, pulled him closer, and had him, heard him cursing in a voice with more gravel in it than it had before, licked and swallowed, sucked until Justin shuddered, shivered, and started to collapse.

The room lit up in strobing blue-white and there sounded a cracking report of thunder, then its echo off the cliff, as Justin persuaded Daniel back onto the narrow mattress, hovered over him half-dressed and panting, his tongue flicking out to wet dry lips, biting his lip while Daniel opened his pants and shoved them down toward his knees. His sprained ankle throbbed in time with the rush of blood from his pounding heart, would not be forgotten even in a moment of distracting desperation. He leaned up and opened his mouth against Justin's neck, the hollow softness of his throat just below the stubbled jaw, and Justin ducked and swerved to claim a rough, messy kiss. They both hummed, and Justin licked his palm and fingers, reached between them to take Daniel in hand.

Justin's hand was soft and small, squeezing and pulling—twisting— ungentle—his eyes electric with want. Daniel slid his hands up Justin's bare back beneath his clothes, to feel his shoulder blades jutting as he supported his weight, working Daniel's prick with urgent strokes. Daniel dragged curved fingers downward, to cup Justin's ass and knead the flesh, soft and hard, the thick muscle beneath, spreading and squeezing, pulling Justin closer. Distracted, Justin slowed his hand, his body rippling a shudder of orgasmic aftershock, and Daniel squeezed harder, dug his fingers in, and let go a scolding noise that reminded Justin where to focus.

It took barely any time for Daniel to ease his way up to the edge, and he held himself there as long as he could, breathing hard across dry lips, and cranked his hips upward to counter Justin's motions. Justin leaned low, humming in his ear, then biting at it, placed sucking, teeth-scraping kisses down the side of Daniel's throat. Daniel caught the glimmer of a pale lightning shock through half-closed eyes. A crack and rumble that lingered, and the irresistible pull toward the edge he finally flung himself over, the quick jagged shock of warmth firing outward from his center along every nerve to the tips of his grasping fingers, the ache of his injured ankle. He was suddenly aware of wet cooling on his low belly, a different sort of dampness tickling the hair at his temples and the skin of his thighs where they touched Justin's.

Justin lowered his weight off his arm, onto Daniel's chest, and there were more rough kisses that devolved into sucking—biting and pulling—scraping of teeth against soft skin. Eventually Justin dropped away to the inside of the mattress, lying with his back to the watch room's rough-hewn wood wall. Lightning. Rolling thunder. The storm was moving north, losing intensity as it went; soon enough, it would be calm. The two moved to rearrange their clothes, and Daniel crossed the little room for the bottle of pain relievers while Justin lit two cigarettes. Daniel had the distinct feeling each was waiting for the other to speak first. He chased three pills with water from a plastic bottle, then traded the bottle to Justin in exchange for the lit cigarette.

Leaving Justin the bed, where he was stretched on his back with his jeans pulled up but still unfastened, his boot-clad feet crossed at the ankle, one arm tucked behind his head while he looked ceilingward, Daniel resumed a seat on one of the wooden folding chairs, elbows on splayed knees. He moved a plastic ashtray from the floor behind the head of the bed, and set it on the mattress's edge in easy reach for both of them. There was a faint flicker of lightning, then after a few seconds, a muffled boom. The storm was moving faster as it went farther north, running toward the sea, though its passage over the jut of land where the light station was situated had weakened it a bit, sapped some of its energy, so that now it was not only quicker but lighter, too, with less to say for itself.

The overhead light was horrible and harsh, suddenly offensive to Daniel's eyes. He switched on a camping lantern that hung above the little table, and moved to kill the fluorescent. The sudden absence of its low buzzing was noticeable, creating a different quality of silence between the two men. As Daniel resumed his seat on the wooden chair, Justin gave a loud exhale, forcing a stream of white-gray smoke upward and away.

"The last time I left here," he said quietly, "I drove straight to University Hospital. They kept me for a week."

Daniel waited without saying anything.

"I'm as sick as Gabriel was. Just in a different way. And I know eventually it's going to kill me." He took a deep drag, held the smoke while he ashed the tip of his cigarette, then let it go in a drawn-out, gentle exhale.

"Right now I'm pretty good—tweaked the meds, and I do all the things that have helped stave it off before. It's like being in remission—but it never lasts."

He turned his head toward Daniel for the first time since he'd started speaking, and Daniel gave a small nod of understanding.

"Sounds dramatic, I know," Justin said, with a self-deprecating twist of his lips.

"No," Daniel replied instantly.

"Hm." Justin finished the smoke and tamped the butt end in the ashtray before abandoning it. "It was hard," he said. "Really hard, taking care of him. Watching him just. . .fade. He got so weak. He had a lot of pain."

Daniel hummed acknowledgement.

Justin swung himself up to sitting, not facing Daniel, slightly slumped. "I wouldn't wish it on anyone," he said, indicating not only that his husband's end-of-life suffering had been unbearable, but that Justin's suffering had been, too.

"Yeah," Daniel said, and brought the ashtray to the little dining table to smother the last of his own cigarette.

"This is good, though," Justin said, and their eyes met. Justin looked expectant, perhaps a little wary.

"It is," Daniel agreed.

"Just. You know." Justin shrugged. "In a week or a month, I don't know."

"OK."

Justin smiled lightly, and got to his feet. He glanced toward the door and his grin changed to a less charged one. "I guess I have to go piss off the side?" he ventured.

"Best to go with a buddy the first time," Daniel told him, and he leaned on Justin's elbow instead of taking the walking stick, and started the slow hobble up the stairs to the lantern room, leading the way.

Seven

Daniel limped around the kitchen fixing breakfast for two—more than doubling everything, in case Justin liked a bigger breakfast than Daniel did— and the dogs took themselves outside. He had woken to the alarm set on his phone, his chest close to Justin's back in the narrow bed. As he rose, silencing the musical tone, Justin had let go a questioning sleep-grunt, his outline just visible in the darkness.

"Time's it?"

"Not yet six. Stay and sleep."

After smoking their final cigarettes of the night, lingering in the open door of the lantern room with the storm easing to light rain just beyond the windows, they'd returned to the watch room and finished the bourbon, not talking much. The bottle emptied, Justin kicked off his boots and stretched out on his side facing the wall. Daniel sat to remove his own single boot, ducked beneath the bed for one of the heavy wool blankets stored there and shook it loose of its folds, then twisted and stretched to drape it over both of them, lining himself up along the mattress behind Justin, with one hand tucked beneath the pillow they had to share, and the other resting on his own hip. It was far from comfortable, but Daniel figured it would do. After a few still, silent moments, Justin reached back in search of his hand, drew it around in front of his chest, cradled it back-to-palm in his own hand. Daniel accepted the invitation and moved closer—belly to low back, thigh to thigh—and nuzzled into the waves of Justin's hair; Justin exhaled an almost-hum. Daniel had earlier joked that Justin was half his size, which of course was an exaggeration, but he was slightly built and at least a few inches shorter than Daniel; they fit together perfectly. Daniel fell asleep to the feel of Justin's ribcage rising and falling beneath his arm.

Daniel had not bothered to descend the tower immediately on waking, knowing by the time he'd hopped and tiptoed his way down, he'd have to head up again to be in time for dawn, to switch off the light. Instead, he had gone directly to the lantern room and busied himself sweeping the floor, wiping down surfaces with a cloth dampened with white vinegar, and squirting oily lubricant into door hinges, window latches, and other less-attended-to fixtures. After sunrise, he switched off the light and began his slow descent to sea level.

Opening the cottage's front door excited the dogs, who sprang up to greet him; clearly spending a night locked in while he was locked out had concerned them, and they sized him up, sniffing at his boots and hands. Only when they seemed satisfied he was in acceptable working order and had not traveled anywhere exotic did they indicate a need to go out, so Daniel unlatched the dog door.

"Bit of rain last night, dogs. No puddles. No mud." Daniel recognized it was a futile demand, but who knew when something might sink in with dogs. It was always worth trying.

As he made his final circuit of the kitchen, withdrawing the narrow milk carton from the fridge for Justin's coffee, Daniel caught sight through the west-facing window of a black-clad figure animatedly dashing back and forth to the dogs' basket full of balls, tossing them in every direction, rapid-fire, calling out words Daniel couldn't quite make out. For their parts, Tugger and Mags were leaping and racing, jubilant at the surprise of an unscheduled ballgame. Daniel stood a moment, watching. Justin smiled more in the minute or so Daniel watched than he had since the two had met—unguarded, wide smiles that sometimes might even have been laughter. The dogs looked pretty pleased, too, of course. After a couple more tosses and retrievals, Justin gave each dog a few pats around the head and face and started toward the cottage. Daniel returned to his work of preparing the morning meal.

The three came in together, though the dogs went toward the parlor while Justin worked his way around the kitchen table to the coffeemaker; Daniel had set out a mug for him and Justin filled it, then spooned in sugar and poured milk from the nearby carton. He stirred the coffee with the sugar spoon, left the spout of the milk carton unfolded, set the wet spoon down on the counter.

"I made enough," Daniel told him, gesturing at two plates with a short stack of pancakes on each, and four eggs cracked into the frying pan on the stove.

"Excellent," Justin said, and stood nearby watching as Daniel flipped the eggs one by one. Soon they were settled at the table, passing salt and pepper shakers, each using his own knife to scratch pats of butter off the stick on its plastic dish. "How's the ankle?"

"Unwrapped it to have a look; it's bruised to hell but the swelling's gone down some," Daniel reported. "Luckily I don't have anything that desperately needs doing today; I'll try to put it up and keep ice on it."

"If you need a ride into Parker, I have to pass through on my way back to the house," Justin offered.

"Thanks, I have what I need. Maybe it'll be healed up enough for my drive in next week." Daniel stalled for time, chewing a mouthful of pancakes longer than strictly necessary, while he decided what to say next. At last he landed on, "So you've got work to do at your place, then."

Justin shrugged. "Not really. But my meds are there."

"Oh," Daniel said quickly, indicating Justin need not elaborate, leaving him room to choose. "Right."

Justin shrugged, half-smiling. "They're working for now; I figure I should get while the getting's good."

"I took some anti-anxiety meds for a while after Abenaki," Daniel said. "Talk therapy, bereavement groups, all that shit."

"Any of it help?"

"Some. Enough that it was worth trying everything to find the things that did."

Justin sat back from his empty plate and cradled his coffee mug in his hands. "But now you're fixed?"

Daniel laughed darkly, looking at his fork as he swirled the last bite of his pancakes through a trail of maple syrup, cleaning the plate. "Not possible. But the crisis passed, and I'm learning to live with it."

"Still learning?" Justin asked.

"Yep."

"Good luck with it, then."

Daniel looked across at Justin's dark eyes studying him—not making him feel picked apart, only carefully read. Daniel gave him a small smile, and downed the last of his coffee.

"Can I do anything before I go? Any heavy lifting? Maybe you want a dance lesson. I'm pretty good."

Laughing at the joke, Daniel replied, "Thanks. I think I'm OK. Rain check on the dancing, though."

They pushed back from the table and Daniel stacked the dishes, needing just a half-step between the table and sink, where he lowered them in and fought against the urge to start filling it with hot water and suds, to wash and dry them right away, as was his routine. He pushed in both the dining chairs.

"Gotta hit the head, then hit the road," Justin said, gesturing toward the bathroom door, then disappearing behind it. Daniel wet a rag and wiped down the table top, then reached into the back of a low cupboard for a tall, green-metal thermos bottle he filled with coffee. He dumped in a few spoonfuls of sugar—the sugar spoon had a dry beige ring in its bowl from Justin having stirred his coffee with it—and poured in about a half-cup of milk, swirled the bottle to blend it all together, then twisted on the lid. He lit a pair of cigarettes, left one in an ashtray he set in the empty center of the kitchen table, and set the thermos beside it.

"This for me?" Justin asked when he returned, pinching the cigarette's filter between finger and thumb and raising it to his lips. He let it dangle from the corner of his mouth while he patted his pockets. He pulled out his phone and stroked the screen with one finger. "Dead," he announced. "Charge it in the car. I was gonna ask you to put your number in."

"Oh, ah," Daniel said, fumbling in his jeans' pocket for his own cell phone.

"Maybe check on you in a few days, see how the wizard staff's working out."

"Cool," Daniel replied. "Well, give me yours and I'll put it in my phone."

Justin looked chagrined. "I don't know it. Here, got a pen?"

Daniel went into his kitchen junk drawer—pens, scissors, rubber bands, transparent tape, each in its own compartment—and fished out a slim permanent marker he passed over. Justin pushed up his sleeve, revealing his dark-haired forearm, then offering up its pale underside. With the cigarette once again parked between his teeth, he said, "What's yours?" The pen hovered above the inside of his wrist. There were crosshatch scars there; some skinny and white, others thick-purple and wormy. Daniel looked down at the phone in his hand, tapped his way to his contact list and recited his number as if he was reading it. Justin scrawled it in inch-high numerals across his skin. He tossed the pen on the table, plucked his smoke from his mouth and blew across the ink to dry it before sliding his sleeve back into place.

Daniel wanted to say something about Justin following through on the promise to call, but bit it back, lest he come across as overbearing. The previous night they'd pretty much agreed their relationship should amount to shared bourbon and rough sex; to make any more demands—even jokingly—seemed to Daniel a dangerous prospect. No expectations, no lingering goodbyes. All for the best; Daniel had work he needed to do.

As if the move was choreographed, they both started toward the door, and Daniel stopped short to grab the thermos. He held it out for Justin to take.

"One for the road," he said.

Justin's smile broke wide and unguarded. He cradled the thermos in both hands, stared at it a moment. "Thanks," he said. "S'nice." His voice had a different, softer quality to it than any Daniel had heard from him before. He tucked it under his arm. "You don't have to walk me to my car," he said, glancing at Daniel's wrapped ankle with his sock pulled halfway up his foot. The dogs, sensing leavetaking behavior, wove their way around Daniel's feet, looking up expectantly with wagging tails.

"I guess you can probably find your way," Daniel admitted. They stood on the border of the kitchen and the parlor for an awkward few seconds before Justin made a sudden step forward, holding his cigarette out of the way in one hand and gripping Daniel above the elbow with the other. His face tilted up as he pressed a kiss against Daniel's mouth, brief and chaste, then drew quickly away.

"Take care of yourself," Justin said, then gave each dog a quick pat on the back. "And you guys take care, too."

With that, he let himself out, raised his eyebrows at Daniel as he backed out the door, and was gone. After another minute or so, the dogs' ears perked up at Justin's little orange car starting up, the crunch of tires on the gravelly dirt of the road as he made a wide turn, and then the fading engine noise as he drove away.

"What do we make of all that?" Daniel asked the dogs, looking from Tugboat's brown eyes to Maggie's blue ones. After a silent moment, he shrugged and added, "Yeah, me neither." He set his phone in its dock, selected a playlist of the music of his youth, and limped to the kitchen to finish washing the dishes. Two forks, two knives, two mugs. A pair of mismatched plates. The sugar spoon. When he went to return the milk carton to the fridge, he could feel it was nearly empty, two days ahead of schedule.

Dear Daniel Howard,

Please be advised that National Parks has accepted a proposal from Nashua Automation Engineering, Inc. to undertake necessary conversions as required to automate the lighthouse at North Hope Cove Station. As such, Nashua Automation Engineering, Inc. will send an engineering team to survey the property and buildings before submitting its final plans to this office. Please make all Parks buildings, land, and assets available for the team's inspection. Potential dates are weather permitting, and are listed below.

Sincerely,

Leslie Rhodes

Junior Director

Northeast Region Physical Plant, US Dept. of National Parks

TXT from [617-555-7913]: Hey there Hopalong. Text me a list and I'll bring you groceries tomorrow.

It had been five days since Justin drove away with Daniel's thermos full of coffee. Just as Daniel was readying himself to make the afternoon's slow climb up the tower on his improving but still sore ankle, his phone chirped to life, startling him. He so rarely got text messages or calls he'd forgotten the sound of the notification beep. He grinned at it.

You don't have to.

TXT from [617-555-7913]: Bourbon for sure. Dog food? If they get too hungry, they'll eat you. And right now you're easy to catch.

Daniel laughed out loud at that, and Maggie gave him a look from across the room. Daniel held up the phone and pointed to it, mouthing, *It's him.*

Headed up to switch on the light. If I think of anything I can't live without for a week I'll get back to you in a minute.

TXT from [617-555-7913]: I found a book of rules for card games in our parlor. I'll bring it.

Daniel typed, *Bring condoms, too,* but immediately backspaced to delete it.

Does it have strip poker in there? Cheesy as hell, but better.

TXT from [617-555-7913]: Four different versions.

Yes, bring it.

TXT from [617-555-7913] OK, text your supply list and I'll see you tomorrow.

Daniel contemplated sending one of those sideways smiles, wanted to punch his own face for it. Instead he left it at, *Will do,* and swiped and tapped to add the number to his contacts list. *Justin Strongbow, 617-555-7913.* There were choices beneath it with radio buttons to tap: Family, Personal, Business. Daniel frowned. "What, no choice for Guy Who Drives Over An Hour To Jack Me Off While I Bite Him, For Some Reason I Can't Understand, Because It's Not As If I'm Exactly A Prize And He's Pretty Cute And Could

Probably Find A Normal Person Closer To Home?" He tapped the button beside Business, and then clicked away from the texting app to make a final check of the overnight weather forecast.

Half-gallon whole milk, 5lb bag potatoes, ground beef, doz eggs, bread (not white), shortbread cookies in red/black package, oranges

Daniel's thumbs hovered above the screen for a moment before he moved the cursor to add *condoms* between the ground beef and eggs. He was only a third of the way down the stairs from the lantern room when he heard the phone signaling Justin's reply; he decided to save it until he got back inside the cottage, inexplicably half-worried that he might have overstepped somehow, speaking—well, texting—so plainly, when up to then it had been more their style to talk obliquely around things. If nothing else, it would be stupid of him to run Justin off just then given that he really did need the milk and bread.

Once he was back inside, on a pulled-out kitchen chair unlacing his boots to put them away for the night, he finally ventured to check the message.

TXT from Justin Strongbow: Now you're talking, big man. I fkn love those shortbread cookies!

Eight

In ten years at the light station, it was never so difficult for Daniel to leave his bed in the morning as it became after he started sharing it with Justin.

As promised, Justin had arrived mid-afternoon just under a week after that stormy night in the watch room, with the last half of a cigarette in the corner of his mouth and two armloads of plastic grocery bags. He'd brought more than what Daniel had requested, not just the eggs and potatoes, but two kinds of pretzels, two pounds of bacon, cherry jam, cinnamon-sugar breakfast cereal, and a brown cardboard box full of day-old pastry. There was a twelve-pack of cheap beer, a bottle of bourbon to replace the one they'd shared during his previous visit, and five DVD movies marked *5 for $20*. He dropped the bags on the kitchen table and counter, and Daniel instantly unpacked everything and put it in its place (though he had no designated spots for plastic-bagged cold cereal or bakery seconds, requiring improvisation). Justin crouched down for greeting-sniffs from the dogs.

"They're grateful for company other than mine," Daniel told him.

"Nah." Justin dismissed it and let Maggie knock him down to sit so she could stand with her two front paws on his thigh while he scratched her chest and chin.

"It seems to be going around," Daniel added, speaking into the upper cabinet with his back to the parlor.

There was a moment of silence pregnant with the possibility of Justin returning the flirtation, but Justin only clambered to his feet and brushed dog hair from his palms, asking, "So, what needs doing?"

Daniel carried on putting away the last of the groceries, then cracked open a can of beer for each of them. He passed one over and they bared their teeth at each other; Justin's eyes were bright but his expressions were difficult for Daniel to decipher. Daniel swallowed, then said, "I've been putting off raking up the leaves from the yard, in hopes the wind would do the work for me, but it's been pretty calm all week." In fact, the previous week's nor'easter had stripped the last of the leaves from the trees at the woods' edge and in the cottage's back and side yards, then tossed them in soggy drifts against the wood fences, where they had stayed since the storm.

Justin nodded decisively. "All right then. Let's get to it."

They spent a few hours at it—only finished the front yard—hefting rakes-full of fallen leaves into wheelbarrows Justin then pushed several yards into the woods and dumped. Daniel still hobbled on his ankle, and it ached more the longer he stood and walked, but he was able to stay mostly in place, loading the barrows and doing some of the raking, while Justin made the round-trips. They didn't talk much, only now and then about the work at hand; passing the hours in companionable quiet, sinking into the rhythm of the work. By the end Justin's hands were blistered in several places but he didn't complain, only pierced them with a safety pin sterilized by the flame of his cigarette lighter, and then covered them with small, beige bandages.

As dusk drew on, Justin trailed Daniel to the tower without invitation, even started up the stairs ahead of him. "You don't have to walk all the way up," Justin offered. "Just stay in shouting distance and tell me which switch to flip." He'd bounded up ahead, and his voice echoed down the tower stairs. "All right, four switches here, which is it?"

Daniel continued his limp up the stairs; he would not be able to rest unless he'd seen the switch properly set with his own eyes, but he was willing to play along in the meantime. "The yellow one on the right."

There was a second's pause, then Justin replied, "None of these is yellow."

Shaking his head, Daniel mounted the next step—good foot first, then set the bad one beside it so it wouldn't have to bear his weight—and hollered up, "On the right. Far right."

"Nope," Justin said. "Far right, OK, fine. But it's not yellow."

"There's a yellow—" Daniel began, and picked up his pace; he was only a dozen or so steps from the landing. "Never mind, I'm almost there. It's got a yellow ring around it, sort of."

"I'm switching on the far right one. . .There it goes."

Two more steps, across the short landing, and Daniel hopped in through the lantern room's narrow doorway. He stood beside Justin, leaned across to point at the switch panel. "Look. Just here. There's yellow here in the. . ." He looked, squinted, ducked his head closer. "The fuck?"

There were four switches. Three were single width—very like light switches everywhere in the world, the heavy-duty ones used in public buildings that gave a satisfying thump as they locked into place—and one double-width, a plastic bar across, attached to two metal spokes. Plastic backing lined the switchbox, and behind each switch it was a different color: black, blue, red. . .and behind the far right, industrial switch, green.

"That some kind of color-blindness?" Justin asked. "None of them are yellow."

Daniel frowned. "I'm not colorblind. I just." He raised his hands helplessly. "I picture it in my head and it's yellow. I always think of it as the yellow switch." He flicked open the door to the secondary panel, the one he'd shown to Justin on their last visit up, with pre-programmed settings for different weather conditions assigned to different switches. The backing plate was metal inside the panel, painted black, with a yellow stripe down the middle between the two columns of switches. "Jeezus, that's weird," Daniel cursed, and flipped it shut again. The turning lantern made sparkling, coin-sized shadows shimmer on the walls. "I would have sworn."

Justin shrugged. "One of those things. My husband and I once got into an argument about whether the guest room doors opened into the rooms, or out into the halls," he offered. "I was right; they opened in."

Daniel, meanwhile, was scanning the circumference of the lantern room, looking at every surface and curve as if seeing it for the first time, checking for anything else he'd been misperceiving for the best part of a decade. He'd never had another soul around to correct him or argue. He felt strangely untethered—even checked himself to see if he was swaying. Justin fumbled with a pack of cigarettes, a fresh one, finding the end of the plastic string and unzipping the wrapper, pulling the top off and crumpling it into his pocket. He tapped the pack against the heel of his hand, three times, hard.

"You want a smoke?"

"Thanks."

Once he'd lit one, Daniel pinched it and dragged deep, leaning his back against the wall, listening to the motor hum. Justin gazed out the window toward the ocean, the faded-silver gray of the evening sky just hovering over the horizon as the sun finished its fall into the sea. It was a meaningless mistake; Daniel knew every switch and the wires and fuses behind them, as well, and it shouldn't matter that the picture in his head was ever-so-slightly askew. But Justin had just showed him something—right in front of him, every day for years—that Daniel had never seen. He cut a glance down and sideways, studied the switches again.

"Weird," he said out loud.

"That's what my high school bully used to say," Justin deadpanned, and Daniel couldn't help but smile.

"Not you."

"Yeah, well."

"Getting cold up here. Hungry?" Daniel asked, pressing himself up away from the wall.

Daniel fried steaks in a skillet with butter and ribbons of onion drizzled with honey to turn them nearly black, sweet as burnt caramel. He made a pot of mashed potatoes, and steamed the final harvest of yellow squash from his vegetable patch. They washed down the meal with two beers each and then Justin scrubbed the dishes while Daniel dried and put them away. By seven o'clock, Daniel's day was done; he took off his boots and sat with his foot up on the coffee table while Justin sank into the middle of the sofa.

"Now what?" he asked.

"Usually I read, sometimes watch something on the laptop. I'm asleep by nine-thirty or so, most nights."

"Really? That early?" Justin looked incredulous.

"I get up before dawn."

"I couldn't do it," Justin said, with an impressed sort of headshake. "I'm a night person."

"What do you do with your evenings?" Daniel asked him.

He shrugged. "Dick around online. Watch TV."

"Worth staying up late for," Daniel said, lightly joking.

"Yuh, not really," Justin agreed. "If I didn't have the house, I'd live in a city; then I could go out at night and do stuff. Not much to do in Six Rivers. They roll up the sidewalks at eight."

"If you're not running the inn," Daniel said, "do you have to stay there? Couldn't you sell it?"

Justin's mouth crumpled. "I made a promise."

"Yeah."

They were quiet for a few long moments. Finally, Justin sat forward with his elbows on his knees and looked sparkling-eyed at Daniel. "So, but, what if you had someone over, in the evening."

"Hm?" Daniel played along.

"Cute guy, maybe, likes your—you know—this mountain man vibe you've got going. With the beard and the flannel shirt."

"Cute artsy guy, you mean? One of these dressed-in-black ones, walking around in his tight black jeans like his thighs don't half-kill me with lust?"

"Mm," Justin agreed, and slid closer to the end of the sofa, touched Daniel's hand and stroked fingertips up the back of his wrist, dipping under the cuff of his sleeve. "If you had a cute guy over who was constantly getting half-hard, thinking about all the ways he wants you to fuck him—"

Daniel made a sudden move to catch Justin's wrist in his fist.

"You'd probably want to sit and read a book, and then go to sleep early."

Daniel pulled Justin's hand—the heel of his hand, the one he'd smacked with the cigarette pack earlier—to his mouth, and gave a sucking, biting kiss, teeth feeling for bone, licking up the soft inside of his forearm until the pushed-back sleeve of his sweatshirt blocked the way. Justin planted his knee between Daniel's thighs and his fingers dug into the back of Daniel's neck, the tight muscle of his shoulder, kneading and pinching, humming hot beside Daniel's ear.

More deep, growling kisses, and hands sliding under the edges of each other's shirts, teeth dragging against each other's throats, and Daniel let his legs fall open so Justin could work a knee between Daniel's thighs, a threat of pain that made Daniel gasp a groan and pinch hard at Justin's nipples beneath his sweatshirt. It occurred to him they'd only had sex mostly dressed, and though he could feel that Justin was slight, with an enticingly hairy chest and belly, he wanted to see more, touch everywhere—those thighs that had, in fact, caused him no small amount of distraction; the ass he'd followed up the tower stairs, watching it move with each step.

"Bedroom," he managed to rumble between rough kisses. "Take off your clothes." It came out like an order, and Justin sucked his teeth.

"Take off yours. I want to bite you all over."

Three nights like the first one, their lips chapped raw, both wearing a constellation of fingertip-shaped bruises, and the smell under the sheets was of musk and sweat. Each morning as Daniel's alarm sounded, they both stirred, stretching and turning over. Justin's hand grasped his thigh, then quickly relaxed back into sleep, and Daniel lingered to stroke his arm or back, dip his nose into the hair behind Justin's neck, and it was all he could do to drag himself away from the temptation to go on stroking until it turned to clutching, pinching, and pinning him down.

Justin let out grumpy noises and sometimes made one last reach for him as Daniel unfolded himself from the warm cocoon of the bed, only truly dropping back to sleep when it became obvious Daniel was up and out for good. Daniel liked to steal a glance at him in the ambient light that oozed in when he opened the door of the pitch-dark, windowless bedroom; Justin's waves of hair spilled over his face like fine black net.

Justin slept on through Daniel's heating up the cottage and letting the dogs out, cooking breakfast—he covered Justin's plate with foil and set it in the oven to keep warm—even most of Daniel dressing in the narrow space between the bed and the bureau. Daniel had already made his slow descent from the tower by the time he caught sight of Justin on the front step, hugging himself against the cold, smoking a cigarette.

"Thanks for leaving me breakfast," he called across the yard.

"Sure," Daniel smiled back.

It was Justin's third morning at the station, and despite the fact of him trailing a wake of untidy left-behinds—never-rinsed coffee mugs, doors standing open, cigarettes still faintly burning in the ashtrays—Daniel was grateful for his help with necessary work, and found he just generally enjoyed having Justin around. It was the first time he'd ever even considered sharing the space with another soul. Justin's was an undemanding kind of company; he seemed as content as Daniel to work—or read, or eat—in near-silence when silence seemed necessary, and conversation, when it came, always came easy. And of course there was the sex, which they'd had several times in the few preceding days, expending aggression and frustrated energy. Daniel always finished feeling used up and exhausted, a sensation he'd always sought by filling his days with work, unfailingly grateful to surrender to it at the end of each day, his body falling into sleep as heavy and fast as one sailing off the cliff.

He opened the gate in the little white fence to let himself into the yard, noticed Justin was wearing only his socks on the cold stone of the front stair. They stepped inside the cottage and Justin crushed out the stub of his cigarette in the plastic ashtray by the armchair, sank down onto the end of the sofa and reached for his boots, tossed messily beneath the coffee table.

"Have to go back today," he said to the floor, and Daniel felt a weight of disappointment sink from his shoulders downward.

"Do you?" was all he said in reply.

"Date with the headshrinker."

"Ah." Daniel warmed his hands in the radiant warmth from the top of the wood stove.

"Need to do a pharmacy run, pay my phone bill, put gas in my car. And my dad's boat was supposed to come in yesterday so I'll see if he's around to say hi to."

"Out fishing?"

"Cod and crabs. He'll have a bunch of money; maybe I can get to him before he's gambled it all and can trick him into paying his rent ahead a few months."

Daniel laughed. "You get along OK with him?"

"I guess." Having gotten his boots on, Justin began gathering his things and packing them into his battered black and gray messenger bag—some clothes he'd left on the bedroom floor, a green toothbrush, amber-plastic prescription bottles, a battery-powered beard trimmer—the secret to his perpetual three-day stubble. "Maybe we'll get a beer and throw darts or something he likes; that'll leave him smiling." Daniel went into the kitchen and searched for the thermos bottle, to fill it with coffee for Justin to take with him.

"What a thoughtful son you are," Daniel joked mildly.

"It's this thing I do," Justin told him from behind the mostly-closed bathroom door. "With people who might miss me when I'm gone. I want them to have a good memory of hanging out with me, or, like, if I talk to my grandma on the phone I always tell her I love her." There came the sound of the toilet seat and lid dropping into place, and the flush, then Justin emerged into the parlor. "I don't want anyone to worry it was their fault, or have our last conversation be something ugly."

Daniel fixed the coffee and twisted the cap into place on the bottle's neck. "Considerate of you," he commented.

"Yeah, or just kind of OCD or something. If I argue with my dad, I have to come back later and fix it. It bugs me until I do."

"What does the headshrinker say about it?" Daniel asked, smiling a bit.

Justin laughed. "That I need to forgive myself for the way some things went with Gabriel just before he died. That no matter what I do to create nice memories, people who love me will still grieve for me." He rolled his eyes a bit. "All the expected things. She's pretty good with the meds—listens to what I say about how they're working, and side effects, and works with me on adjustments—but she is definitely not willing to admit I'm terminal."

Justin scanned a row of spines on one of the overstuffed bookshelves, placed his index finger on the top edge of a book and pulled, catching it as it fell. Daniel handed him the thermos of coffee, and Justin's face went soft around a smile. "Thanks. Borrowing this." He waved the book a bit. "Now I'll have to come back," he said, gesturing with the book and the bottle at once.

"I'm counting on it."

There was a pause and they both looked away. "I'll say bye to the dogs on my way."

Daniel checked his watch. "They're probably wondering where I am."

Sure enough, Tugger and Mags were nosing around their basket of fetch-balls, pacing impatiently, and when the two men emerged onto the gravel walkway outside the front door, Tugboat let out a single, sharp bark to reprimand Daniel for dawdling when they had a schedule to keep.

"Bye, guys. I'll see you around," Justin called. He turned his head toward Daniel. "Take care, on that ankle. Another fall and next time you might not make it back to the cottage. Get eaten by the mountain lion."

"It was a lynx," Daniel grinned.

"Or the gulls. Peck you to death."

"What a cheerful thought," Daniel said, and as Justin's hands were full with his bag, the coffee, and the book—a collection of witty essays about world travel on the cheap—he pulled open the driver's door of Justin's little orange car.

"I'm a ray of sunshine," Justin told him, tossing the bag and book across to the passenger seat.

"Oh, yeah. You're wicked sunny," Daniel agreed. He wanted to ask when Justin thought he might be back, but instead took a step back from the car. "Drive safe. You got snow tires on this thing yet?" He looked; Justin did not have snow tires.

"I have my husband's truck, for the snow," he said. "An old Suburban. Tire chains. Plow. The whole thing."

"This one fits you better," Daniel mused. "Anyway, see you later." He reached out and squeezed Justin's upper arm, just that, but Justin took it for a cue to lean in and kiss him, briefly and close-mouthed. He stepped closer, and kissed deeper, with one hand on Daniel's chest and the other behind his waist.

"Don't use all the condoms before I see you again," Justin warned, and Daniel was taken aback to hear something from him that sounded so near the edge of jealousy. Of course it was a joke—they both knew perfectly well that Daniel had no one else, and hadn't for a very long time—but it also felt a bit like Justin was staking a claim to him; Daniel found he didn't mind.

"That kiss was pretty nice," Daniel commented, and tilted his head, narrowing his eyes at Justin.

Justin caught his meaning and said, "Fuck you," and punched him on the arm, smiling all the while.

"OK, then," Daniel nodded, and once Justin had slid into the driver's seat, Daniel shoved the door shut and stepped away. An unpleasant final exchange meant Justin would have to come back at least once more; Daniel was among those chosen few who were likely to miss him after he'd gone.

Nine

TXT from Justin Strongbow: I miss Maggie and Tugboat.

    Not me though.

    TXT from Justin Strongbow: No, not you.

    Got all your errands done?

    TXT from Justin Strongbow: Toss them in the truck and meet me in Parker for supper.

    The light.

    TXT from Justin Strongbow: After the light. Good weather all week; the light will turn whether you're there or not.

Daniel thought it over. He had an instant, thrill-ride reaction in his belly to Justin suggesting they get together, but he hadn't ever spent an evening away from the lighthouse. The thirty-minute drive back from Parker would probably be enough time for him to beat any storm his weather forecast apps might warn him of, but it felt like an unnecessary risk, going all that way just for supper.

    You're welcome anytime. Tug and Mags like you visiting.

    TXT from Justin Strongbow: Not you though.

    No, not me.

There was a pause; he worried for a second Justin might not be getting the joke.

    TXT from Justin Strongbow: Just to recap—I asked you on a date and you told me the dogs like me.

    I don't know how to do a date. It felt perhaps too confessional, and Daniel deleted it. Instead he just typed, *Date?*, and sent it.

    TXT from Justin Strongbow: As much as dinner at The Coffee Pot can be thought of as a date, yes. Eating together, out.

Daniel twisted his fingers into his beard, tugged at a few whiskers near the corner of his lip. Naturally, it seemed a simple request, but Justin didn't yet realize how difficult time spent "out" was for Daniel to abide. How exhausted it always left him. How sometimes a person just calling hello from across the street when he wasn't expecting it could set his heart thumping so hard and fast he worried he was having a coronary. That the second he stepped out of his truck in Parker, he began counting down the minutes left until he could return to the safe silence of the light station. Justin had hinted at lots of his own. . .*stuff*. . .and though Daniel had admitted to being *yes, that Daniel Howard*, and that he needed the light for its isolation and routine, there was a definite imbalance between the two men when it came to confession. It hardly seemed like a text message was the right way to try explaining it all, though.

You brought those DVDs last time and we haven't watched them yet. Would that be a date?

TXT from Justin Strongbow: Borderline.

Daniel thought it over. *It's just that I've never been so far from the lighthouse after dark.*

TXT from Justin Strongbow: I get it. Will you think about it, though?

Eating and talking with you? Sure.

TXT from Justin Strongbow: Out.

Yes, out. I will think about it.

TXT from Justin Stongbow: Here comes Lia to yell at me in Portuguese and vacuum around me. I'll talk to you soon.

Why does she yell? Does she not now you're a ray of sunshine?

TXT from Justin Strongbow: Missed that memo, I guess. Or it was in English and she couldn't read it. I'm being ordered out of my room like a child.

Where will you go?

TXT from Justin Strongbow: Might drive out to Orono and sit in a coffee shop with this book I borrowed. Talk to you soon.

Three days passed with no word from Justin, and on the fourth day—just as Daniel was settling into his armchair with his book after a few hours' tinkering in the shed—he appeared.

The dogs went trotting out to meet him before Daniel even heard the approaching car's engine or the crunch of its tires. Daniel's ankle still ached and he kept it bandaged most of the day, but he could get his boots on and off without wincing, and had returned the carved walking stick to the back of the shed. Though Daniel hadn't asked for anything when last they'd spoken, Justin arrived carrying grocery bags. He wore a black wool pea coat over his usual slim black jeans and the same stretched-out-of-shape black sweater from the first time they met. His backpack, slung over one shoulder, looked stuffed full, and Daniel wondered if perhaps he intended to stay a while, and felt pleased at the prospect.

"Hey, Sunny," Daniel greeted him, folding his arms across his chest—inadequate protection from the November cold—as he waited for Justin to cross the yard.

Justin smiled in a way that looked half-pleased and half-embarrassed. "Hey, you. Brought beer and bagels."

"Perfect," Daniel grinned, taking the bags from him and leading him into the cottage. Mags was bouncing around Justin's feet while Tugboat loped along just behind, trying to look like he didn't care one way or the other, his wagging tail giving him away. "I told you they'd be pleased to see you." He set the bags on the kitchen table.

"They totally are. Makes a man feel like a king."

"Why do you think I have them around?"

"And what about you? Happy to see me? Or is that a giant wizard staff in your—hey, no wizard staff."

"Don't need it anymore. Put it back out in the shed."

Justin frowned theatrically. "I think I'll miss it."

"Another thing you're welcome to visit any time."

"Missed these dogs," Justin said, and gave them what they'd been waiting for, crouching down to scratch and pat them. He dropped his backpack on the floor by the armchair while he was down there. "Missed the sound of the ocean. Missed that dark bedroom."

"And me?" Daniel ventured, raising an eyebrow at him.

"Missed you, too," Justin said, so plain and simple it took the wind right out of Daniel and he stopped halfway to the fridge with a little bucket of cream cheese before regaining himself. "Missed you at the diner the other night."

"You went without me?"

"It was the meatloaf special."

"Can't blame you, then."

Justin took off his coat and left it in a heap on the floor, then unzipped the smaller front pocket of his pack and removed the book he'd borrowed. Instead of returning it to the bookshelf, he set it on the coffee table.

"I have to come clean and tell you I was reading some stuff about Abenaki the other night," Justin told him, shifting to curl himself in Daniel's armchair, shaking loose a cigarette from his pack and striking a match he then waved until it went out. "Not in a tabloid way or anything."

"OK."

"Sorry that happened to you," he said.

"Thanks."

"Glad you survived."

"Thanks. People used to say that to me a lot. Or that I was lucky to have survived, lucky to be alive." Daniel lit his own smoke, stood leaning back against the edge of the kitchen counter while he took his first drag. Justin's legs were drawn up close, his knees visible above the chair's arm.

"You didn't feel lucky, though?" Justin prompted, sounding as if he already knew the answer.

"No, I felt like a failure. I *was* a failure." The distance between them, the objects between them, seemed necessary but still inadequate. It wasn't something Daniel had discussed with anyone except the therapist he'd been ordered to meet with six times before National Parks would let him come back to work, as part of his short-term disability leave of absence "compensation." The woman had been compassionate and seemed to know her way around trauma and grief, though not his particular kind, but every second Daniel spent talking about the massacre—thinking about it—in that early aftermath had been torturous. "I went to so many funerals. Their parents looked me in the eyes and told me they were glad I was alive, but of course every one of them was wondering why I didn't save their kid."

Justin bit his thumb, and nodded. Daniel braced himself for Justin to contradict him—*you don't know that; you couldn't have saved them; you really are lucky to be alive*—but he kept quiet and listened.

"I read the guy had been living in the forest for a while, doing that survivalist thing?"

"He was."

"Did you know he was out there, before?"

Daniel sucked hard on his cigarette, and shook his head. "None of the rangers ever saw his camp. None of the visitors ever reported coming across it. But when they finally found it, it seemed like he'd probably been living out there for months. Probably moved every couple, few weeks."

"Crazy asshole," Justin scoffed. "What the fuck was he so mad about?"

Daniel only shrugged a little and shook his head. "This time of year kind of sucks for me. When the leaves start turning, it reminds me of what the forest looked like then. I'll be so glad in a couple weeks when it starts to feel more like winter and less like fall."

"Still?"

"Not as bad as it used to be, but anniversaries are always a mind-fuck. Bad anniversaries, I mean."

Justin nodded, twisted in his chair to stub out his cigarette in the ashtray on the side table. "My husband died just after New Year's. So Christmas, New Year's, all that's wrecked now. And then the winter just goes on forever, and you never see the sun again until May, and that sure doesn't help."

"No," Daniel agreed.

"I mean, I've always been depressed; sometimes it gets me for a long time, months and months," Justin stretched his arms over his head and leaned back into it. "It's not like there's anything new under the nonexistent sun. But losing him put me down in it for a long time. Really bad. And the anniversaries, like you said. Bad anniversaries."

Daniel wondered if knowing his bad anniversary was only a few months ahead of him had contributed to Justin's decision to go to the cliff, that day they'd met. If he'd been one of those weirdly-named "successful" suicides, he wouldn't have had to face another reminder of his loss.

"You still wear your ring," Daniel observed.

Justin looked at it. "I don't know if I've ever been happy, but when I was with him, it was as close as I ever got."

"He was a good guy?" Daniel knew the answer, just as Justin had when he'd asked Daniel's feelings about being the sole survivor.

"Really good. Better than I deserved." Justin's expression changed, a snap-out-of-it moment, and he grinned. "But I was younger and hotter than he probably deserved, so it balanced out."

Daniel laughed and used the kitchen faucet to put out the butt of his cigarette, then tossed it in the trash. "Hotter than I deserve."

"Not so young anymore though."

"I doubt you'll get many complaints," Daniel said slyly. "Definitely none from me."

"How long 'til you have to switch on the light?"

Daniel drew out his phone and quickly checked what time the sun would set. "Well over an hour."

Justin said nothing, only started for the bedroom, tugging at his sleeves to begin shedding his sweater as he went.

That night they lay naked under the weight of the quilts, in the golden light of the antique bedside lamp, face to face with their heads resting on their hands. Daniel lay his fingertips lightly one by one onto the spots of bruises he'd left earlier on the front of Justin's shoulder, like slotting pieces of a puzzle together, then let his fingers slide a drift downward over his chest, through the dark hair covering his pectorals, to brush the top edge of his belly. At last, Daniel's hand come to rest cupped loosely around Justin's forearm.

"How long will you stay?" he asked.

"Few days, I thought." Justin reached to flick aside a stray lock of hair at Daniel's temple, smoothing it in the right direction. "Is that OK?"

"Definitely OK," Daniel smiled.

"Is it. . ." Justin began, and frowned a bit. "It's OK that it's rough," he said tentatively, in a tone that begged confirmation.

"Sure," Daniel replied. "I'm enjoying it."

"How long had it been since you had sex with someone?" Justin asked, sounding curious and nonjudgmental. "Almost two years for me."

"I don't want to calculate it; it's too depressing," Daniel told him. "Much longer than two years, though. I tried dating a little, but I always made them come to me because of the light, and I guess I'm not compelling enough for that to be sustainable, because no one came by more than a couple times before they made excuses and stopped."

"I'm plenty compelled," Justin smiled at him, and stroked the side of his face, his beard, down his neck to rest his hand in the hollow of Daniel's shoulder.

"Thank whatever for that!" Daniel exhaled in a near-laugh. "Anyway, it was the only thing that made me feel lonely, when otherwise I was content."

"What, sex?"

"Connection to people," Daniel said, his voice quieting. He reached to draw up the blankets closer around his shoulders. "And the expectations. . .It was too much pressure and it freaked me out to have someone relying on me. I don't have it to give." Justin's eyes were closed, and Daniel pulled him closer with a hand on his low back. "I'm not the guy to trust with your life, obviously."

Justin nestled his head beneath Daniel's chin, his hands curled meditatively between their two chests. "I don't have enough life left to worry about trusting anyone with it."

"I'd call that a pretty good match," Daniel whispered, and he let his fingers wander around in the half-long curls of Justin's dark hair. Justin hummed and pressed a soft, quick kiss against Daniel's chest just below his collarbone. Daniel murmured, "Going to sleep?"

"Mm."

Daniel leaned away just long enough to click off the lamp, plunging them into heavy darkness. Justin's head nodded gently, just a bit, to comfort himself to sleep. Daniel held him tighter, arms around his naked shoulders, and whispered over his softly rocking head, "That's good."

Ten

The first snow finally fell in early December. On his last three-day visit to the light station, Justin had helped Daniel attach the snow plow to the front of his truck, and though Daniel had become adept over the previous several winters at doing it unassisted, he admitted to himself alone that it really was easier with an extra pair of hands. With Justin directing him from outside the truck, he'd lined up the harness on the first try. The snow started just before dawn—or so Daniel assumed given there was already a dusting on the ground by the time he unlatched the dog door—and came down soft and steady until just after dark. It was an inland storm, small and without bluster, didn't chop up the waves or shove the tide up the shore toward the cottage. As Daniel cleared the snow from the walkway and front step that evening after switching on the light, he wished Justin was there to share the snug fire, or to recline side by side in Daniel's bed watching one of the marked-down supermarket DVDs.

Still coming down out there? Looks like it's stopping here.

TXT from Justin Strongbow: Stopped a couple hours ago, I think. You got a lot?

Maybe five inches.

TXT from Justin Strongbow: There's a joke there I won't make.

We know better.

TXT from Justin Strongbow: Lia's decorating the house for Christmas. The lawn guys I should have cancelled three years ago came and put lights on all the trees and bushes.

It must look nice. When you come next time we'll go find pine boughs to make a wreath.

TXT from Justin Strongbow: Do you do a tree in the house? Give presents to the dogs?

A little one. Some little ones.

TXT from Justin Strongbow: Do they have socks to hang by the wood stove?

I'm pleading the Fifth on grounds of it's embarrassing.

TXT from Justin Strongbow: In love with the light, AND you think those dogs are people. OMG, are they your children?

They're my tenants.

TXT from Justin Strongbow: Meatloaf special tomorrow night at the diner. Can I take you on a date?

Will you come home with me after?

TXT from Justin Strongbow: Yes.

Then yes.

Daniel had checked the forecasts at least three times in the last hour before switching on the light; mid-twenties and clear, waxing moon about half, no precipitation or fog for the coming few days. Having reassured himself that the light would—as Justin had said—turn whether or not he was there, he focused on the other worrisome prospect ahead of him: a few hours in Parker Village, acting normal.

He shaved around the edges, smoothing his neck and sharpening the upper border of his beard; trimmed his mustache with tiny scissors; then worked softening balm through his whiskers, in plenty of time for its scent to fade down from potentially offensive levels. A plastic comb pulled through hair just shy of needing a trim, his gingery, light-brown bangs lying soft to the side, mostly covering the deep worry-lines that crossed his forehead. He even dragged his fingertips along his eyebrows to tame them a bit.

His best clothes were the same as all his others: jeans in various washes and states of repair, long johns and plain white undershirts, t-shirts for the summer, a couple of thermal Henleys, and a pile of plaid flannel button-downs. It was just the diner, of course, and it was Parker Village; Daniel imagined each man in Parker likely owned no more than one necktie and only wore it to funerals and possibly some weddings. For his part, Daniel owned not even one. He chose a newer, clean pair of medium-blue jeans and a black leather belt with a simple matte-silver buckle; a black thermal shirt free of stains or moth-holes; and over that a green and black plaid shirt, tucked in. There was only the small bathroom mirror for reference, but he thought he looked all right. A dozen and a half wall push-ups before he donned his parka. A cigarette to calm him on the drive into Parker.

Justin was already there when Daniel arrived, stomping snow from his boots on the thick black mat in the vestibule. Justin smiled and waved him over to a booth in the corner. Daniel surveyed the place with a sweeping gaze as he walked: three guys at the counter, a young couple in a booth at the opposite end of the room from where Justin sat. The cook visible beyond the pass-through to the kitchen, and two servers, both women, fiftyish, Betty Jane the blonde one, and Linda the skinny one. Daniel shrugged off his parka and hung it on the hook at the edge of the booth; Justin's coat was crumpled beside him on the burgundy-vinyl bench seat. Daniel slid in across from him, putting his back to the room. Justin's hair was pushed up away from his forehead and fell in neat waves, long sharp sideburns visible along the back edge of his jaw. He was wearing a close-fitting black pullover sweater with a graphic of white vampire teeth, open-mouthed, dripping red blood. There was a double-loop of leather cord around his neck with a bunch of plain silver metal rings resting in the notch at the base of his throat.

"You look handsome," Justin said quietly.

"So do you."

Daniel stole a glance over his left shoulder at the three men at the counter, Betty Jane bustling behind it. He caught Linda in his peripheral vision as she approached with glasses of water, two straws with half the paper wrappers still attached.

"Hi guys, how you doin'?" she smiled at them. "Special tonight is meatloaf with mushroom gravy, comes with mashed potatoes or rice pilaf, and mixed vegetables. Soup's chicken noodle. Do you know what you'd like or should I come back in a minute?"

They both ordered the special, declined the soup, asked for colas to go with it. Daniel watched her walk away, turned just a bit further in his seat to see the door behind him. The young woman at the other end of the room let out a whoop of laughter, and her date snickered in response. Daniel's upper back hurt.

"Look," Justin said, drawing Daniel's attention back where it belonged. Justin held out his phone, scrolling photos of his house, the former B and B, lit up at night with white lights on the shrubs in front of the foundation, and in the few small trees visible in the wide front lawn coated with fresh snow. There was a spotlight aimed at the front door, painted traditional, Colonial red and decorated with a red- and gold-ribboned pine wreath.

"It looks nice," Daniel said. "Is it just the house? Does it have a barn or anything?"

"Yeah, there's a garage for four cars, and a barn. There's a sort of shed thing, too, way out back. The barn's like a function hall, for weddings. But right now it's just storage." Justin pointed to the far right window on the second floor. "This is my room."

There came the jingle of bells from the exterior entry door, then low male voices. Daniel turned to look. Three men who appeared to be just barely out of their teens—two wearing caps bearing the name and logo of a fishing boat called the *Downeast Queen*— came tumbling through the door, laughing at some joke that had already gone by. They dragged chairs out from beneath one of the central formica-topped tables and continued their conversation, too loud for the room, oblivious to other patrons. Daniel rubbed three fingertips hard across his lips and turned back to Justin, his jaw clenched tight, scrubbing the palm of one hand slowly but firmly up and down the leg of his jeans, beneath the table.

"Scallop boats are coming in," Justin commented. "My dad said."

Daniel nodded. Justin's phone lay face down on the tabletop.

"They're making huge hauls, he told me." Justin lowered his voice. "Those guys probably have more money in their pockets right now than they've had in their whole lives put together."

"I'm in the wrong line of work."

"Me, too," Justin smiled.

Daniel could hear Linda telling the guys the specials, and they replied with smart-ass, sarcastic questions, making each other laugh. One asked if he could have a pizza delivered to the diner. Another said he had a rack of beers in his truck and wondered if he could bring it in. The waitress had seen it all, and clearly knew how to handle them, but Daniel was listening for any change in tone, any harsh word or casual insult. Drunken young men could turn on a dime, he knew. Punches could start flying. Or worse. He leaned his chin on one hand, kept the young fishermen in his peripheral vision.

"You all right?" Justin asked.

"Sorry, yeah." Daniel refocused. "I remember you said you're living in one of the guest rooms? I thought those places had attached owners' apartments."

"It does. It was that thing you always hear about not being able to spend time in the rooms you shared with someone who's not there anymore. His stuff everywhere, memories, all that. I tried a couple of times to start sorting stuff, but it was—just—paralyzing. I would open a drawer and stare at it, maybe take out a few things and put them somewhere else—on a bed, or a table—and then I had to sit down. Or lie down and sleep." Justin brushed Daniel's knee with his knuckles. "I didn't get very far. Just made a mess."

"There wasn't anyone to help you?"

"Just his niece, but she only barely tolerated me while he was alive. I keep paying her even though there's hardly anything for her to do—she sends the money back to her family in Brazil—but we're not close. I don't know enough Portuguese to have a real conversation with her, so I don't even know if she still has a valid visa, or if she ever plans to go back to Brazil, or what. I promised Gabriel I'd keep the house, and Lia just comes with it."

"What if you want to sell it someday?" Daniel asked.

Justin threw his hands apart, with an exaggerated *beats-me* expression on his face. "I kind of want to, just to find out what Lia would do. I honestly have no idea what she's thinking. Three years she's been living in her little room downstairs, dusting and vacuuming for no more than an hour a day, video-calling with her sisters the rest of the time. Twice a week to church, and every couple months she goes on an overnight bus trip to a casino in Bangor."

"Maybe you should stop paying her," Daniel suggested, without malice; it wasn't for him to judge.

"When the money runs out, I figure," Justin replied, taking the comment in stride. "Once the bills are paid, there's still plenty every month to pay her so I just kept doing it. It's not like I need it."

Linda brought their dinner plates and glasses of soda on a tray she balanced on one hand while serving from the other. As she set down the last of it, a cacophony of braying laughter from the fishermen made Daniel's shoulders twitch.

"You guys let me know if you need anything else," Linda said, and was about to move away.

"Can we get a pecan pie to take, and the check as soon as it's ready," Justin told her.

"Sure, hon. Enjoy, and I'll be back in a couple minutes."

Justin thanked her and pressed the side of his fork through the corner of a hunk of meatloaf.

"In a rush?" Daniel asked.

Justin swallowed, made a casual wave of his fork. "You're edgy," he said. "Not in a good way."

Daniel's gut sank with humiliation at having his anxiety so easily read.

"We'll get out of here," Justin said easily. "No biggie. You could have said."

"No," Daniel said, half protest against the suggestion they leave, half denial of his own ability to express aloud how completely his nerves were wrecked by any time spent in public, let alone with his back to a room containing unpredictably loud, semi-drunk men. It was too much for him to keep track of, and it was draining his energy at a rapid pace.

"It's cool. I get it."

Daniel felt his eyebrows rise; he held his knife and fork in white-knuckled hands but didn't touch his food. "Do you?"

"I guess not totally, but it doesn't take a headshrinker to see what's going on. Sorry I was so pushy about coming out."

Daniel started pushing his food around on the plate, even took a half-bite, just to have somewhere to focus his gaze other than at Justin's face. His neck and ears felt hot. "I wanted to. It's fine. I mean. Not 'fine.' It's a date."

"So's a DVD at your place," Justin said casually.

"You said that was borderline."

"I'm stupid sometimes."

"Nah."

Linda brought them a white box tied with red and white baker's twine, and laid the check face down on the edge of the table. "Whenever you're ready. How is everything?"

"Very good, thanks," Daniel managed, and even smiled at her.

"All right, good then." She gave Daniel's shoulder a quick pat. "I can't remember ever seeing you here except at lunch."

"First time for everything," Daniel replied.

A sudden, jangly bang of a fist landing hard on the table behind them, making the flatware jump, and the young men spoke in raised voices.

Daniel started, immediately followed by a muttered, "Fuck." Justin leaned to look past Daniel's shoulder.

"You start breaking up the place, heads'll roll," Linda scolded the fishermen good-naturedly.

"They're just talking," Justin said to Daniel. "Telling a story or something." He turned the check over, reached into his wallet, and laid two twenties on top of it. "Should I ask her for a go-box?"

"No, let's finish," Daniel said. Justin was already halfway through his meal, and Daniel had little appetite but thought he could manage the few minutes it might take Justin to finish eating.

"I know it probably doesn't help for me to say it, but everything's cool."

Daniel only nodded, staring at his plate.

"And so are you." Justin leaned, ducking his head. Daniel cut his gaze upward to meet Justin's. "It's fine," he said, emphatic but soft. "Just means I get to go home with you sooner." He grinned mischief and winked.

"Sorry."

"Nope."

They shoveled up the last few forkfuls of their dinners, and Justin took a long pull on the straw in his soda even as he slid out of the booth. They shrugged into their coats and Justin picked up the pie by the criss-crossed twine.

"G'night, guys. Take care," Linda called, and Betty Jane echoed her.

Once outside, Daniel sucked a lungful of still, cold air, and walked several quick paces away from the door while reaching into his coat pocket for his cigarettes.

"I'll follow you?" Justin volunteered, easing up beside him, then sidestepping back and forth to keep warm.

"Sure. Or go ahead. I want to stand here a smoke a minute."

"Naw, I'll wait." Justin took a few strides to the driver's door of an old, dark-gray Suburban and opened it just long enough to set the pastry box on the seat inside it, emerged from it feeling inside his pea coat for his own pack of smokes. They leaned their backs against the side of Daniel's truck-bed, exhaling cigarette smoke and puffs of their own frozen breath.

"Sorry again."

"S'all right," Justin replied with a shrug, and his tone was such that Daniel believed it really was all right with him, though it didn't make him feel any less embarrassed by his distracted jumpiness during their meal. Daniel held his cigarette between his teeth long enough to zip the front of his parka.

After another few silent minutes, side by side smoking under the blue-orange light that hung over the little parking lot, Daniel smirked and grumbled, "And that's *after* a bunch of therapy."

Justin laughed a little and leaned sideways until his shoulder bumped briefly against Daniel's bicep.

"Hey, man," Justin joked back at him, "you're lucky to be alive."

Daniel let out a gruff chuckle and flicked the butt end of his cigarette into the middle of the lot, watching it arc up and then roll when it landed, still glowing orange at the end. "Come home with me," he demanded.

"Thought you'd never ask."

Eleven

Daniel lingered in the tower after powering down the light, cleaning lenses with a chamois, then using sprays of white vinegar and a mini-squeegee on the windows. The air was cold, but there wasn't much breeze and the sun through the glass warmed him enough that he shed his coat and shoved the sleeves of his sweater and the thermal shirt beneath it up toward his elbows. He'd left Justin naked and asleep in his bed, left breakfast in the oven for him to find. He was two-thirds of the way around the lantern room with a rag tucked in his back pocket and the chamois in his hand when he heard an echoey, "Hello up there!" from somewhere far down the stairs. "Should I come up?"

"No, I'm on my way down," Daniel lied, and set aside his cleaning supplies before plucking his coat off a hook in the wall and beginning his descent, fast as he could manage on his still slightly-tender ankle.

"Thanks for feeding me," Justin said, as Daniel landed on the granite slab at sea level, and slipped easily into Daniel's offered embrace. They exchanged a few kisses, and Justin's face lit soft with a grin as they leaned away to look at each other. He gave a stagey shiver of his shoulders and pressed closer against Daniel's body. "Freezing. Come inside and throw me around a little—warm me up." His tone was gravelly and his lips curled up with teasing .

Daniel hummed frustration. "Work," was all he said. "I need to cut some brush to widen the path from the bottom of the cliff to the top; it's going to take me at least a few days and there's storms forecast to come in by Tuesday morning."

"I'll help," Justin told him. "We can start right after." He took a big step back and pulled Daniel by the hand, walking backward down the path toward the cottage. "It can wait a half-hour." Daniel let himself be pulled, couldn't help but wolf-smile, looking Justin up and down, ill-dressed for the weather in just his jeans and a t-shirt with one of Daniel's red watch-plaid flannel shirts open over it for a jacket. If ever there had been a more perfect geometry than the triangle formed from Justin's shoulders down to his narrow hips, Daniel didn't care to know. "Maybe an hour," Justin corrected himself.

Within a quarter of the stolen hour, Justin was on his knees, fingers curled over the top of the bed's antique wooden headboard, back, neck, and head bowed due to Daniel's grip on a fistful of hair as Daniel thudded into him, eliciting loud, crying groans on every one and of Justin's exhalations. Daniel watched his prick disappear between the pink-mottled mounds of Justin's ass, biting his lip, savoring the rough slide and clutching heat of Justin's body around him. His grip on Justin's left hip was firm, fingers curled and clenching. He adjusted his knees to change the angle, and Justin's tone changed from groaning to whining, gasping, and Daniel knew he'd found the spot, drove relentlessly against it, his own fire stoked up at the thrill of giving Justin such pleasure that he made frantic pulls at his own cock, whimpering and wriggling and urging *yes. . .ohmygodyes. . .Daniel. Daniel. Yes. Daniel.*

On the other side of the closed door, one of the dogs barked, and Justin groan-laughed, and Daniel growled, held him, fucked. Fucked. *Fuck yes you feel so good come for me come for me I'm coming. . .*fucked and fucked and collapsed forward and howled. Justin shuddered beneath him, his slender body going jagged beneath Daniel's grabbing fingers, palms sliding over his back, pinching his thighs, pinning him in place with Daniel deep inside him as the last shocks subsided, both of them shivering and panting out curses.

They parted, gasping, and found clean places on the mattress to lie, hips and shoulders at odd angles, breath heavy and loud as they settled. Daniel peeled off the condom, knotted it, dropped it into the small metal can beneath the bedside table. His set one hand palm-down on Justin's thigh just below the deep crease where it met his torso. He let his fingertips roam until he was tickling crinkly hair with a gentle rocking motion of his hand.

"The dogs thought we were killing each other," Justin said with obvious amusement in his voice.

"Not yet," Daniel replied, grinning.

"Should I try to be quieter?"

"Don't fucking dare." Daniel rolled up onto his side, sliding a finger-splayed palm over Justin's body from belly to shoulder. "I love your noise." There was a red mark on his throat from Daniel's scraping teeth, and Daniel brushed his fingertip over it. "Pass me a smoke, Sunny, I need to get to work."

"I'm coming."

"Nah, you don't have to."

"I like it." Justin lit two cigarettes from his own pack and passed one to Daniel, who rolled onto his back once more. They lay side by side, blowing smoke at the ceiling. "I may as well be useful as well as ornamental."

"I'd say you're recreational," Daniel mused, grinning.

"You could use a little R and R after all this time with nothing but work," Justin commented.

Daniel was, in fact, unsettled by how distracted he could become with Justin there. Distracted by Justin. When they weren't fucking, they worked—side by side or at least nearby, not talking much except when necessary to get things done right and on time—or Daniel cooked and they ate, or Justin played with the dogs, or they walked along the shore's rocky edge, or out into the woods. Daniel knew every inch of the land as well as he knew his own hands, but somehow when Justin was standing on it in his black clothes, with the wind tossing his wild hair across his intense brown eyes, the entire landscape changed. There was a mad fluttering in Daniel's gut sometimes when Justin called to him across the yard; his presence was equal parts enlivening and invasive, a rose blooming amid the dead winter thorns. All wrong. Shocking. Delightful.

They spent the afternoon with gas-powered trimmers and handheld saws, widening the path, and only got about twenty yards into it. Justin worked hard but slow, leaving one task half-finished to walk three paces and start a fresh one, then returning to finish the first, beginning a third, making minor mistakes and having to divert to the tool shed, or switching from manual to powered and back again. Eventually, he got it done, but Daniel marveled at his inefficiency. Justin reminded him of himself, ten years before, scrambling to establish the systems of his days. The difference was Justin seemed perfectly at ease with his scattershot methods, and never stopped to wonder if there was a better way. Daniel, for his part, prepared for his work by gathering tools and supplies, began at the start, and steadied on through the logical progression of steps to the end. Cleaning up after himself, returning things to their homes clean, oiled, sharpened and ready for their next tasks, was the final step of Daniel's every process. Justin's was a cigarette and a self-congratulatory smile.

"Maybe if you let it grow over, there'd be less incentive to climb it," Justin suggested, as they wheeled the tools out of the woods in the wheelbarrow they'd used to move the brush from the path's edge into the forest.

"I did try that once; it just made it harder for me, and the dogs." Daniel told him. "There was one I could hear talking on her cell phone to her mother, talking about coming home that weekend for a family party. Two minutes later, I was already too late. If the path had been clearer—"

"Maybe not," Justin interrupted, sounding protective and compassionate—more the former than the latter—not the dismissive reflex Daniel had come to hate.

Daniel nodded, shrugged his shoulders a bit. "Maybe not," he agreed. "But either way, I'd rather it be cleared."

Justin hummed acquiescence. "What's next, boss?" he grinned. Daniel glanced at his watch, and at the sky, which was clear sliver-blue, with high wisps of white cloud overland.

They put away the tools, Daniel wiping the saw blades with a rag and tipping gasoline from a plastic canister into the trimmers' small tanks before Justin set them in their places. "Just time for something to eat before I head up the tower."

Justin ducked his head, sniffed, made a comical face. "I'm gonna take a shower. You work a man too hard."

"And you love it," Daniel fired back, grinning.

Justin snarled and snapped his teeth. On their walk back to the cottage, Maggie trotted out to meet them, then walked at Justin's side. Daniel felt another strange blend of feelings: pleased that his mutts seemed to have grown as accustomed to Justin's intrusions as he had, and liked him; and perhaps just a little jealous that Mags had chosen to walk at Justin's heel when normally she'd be walking at Daniel's.

"We're going to end up in a weird jealousy triangle thing," Justin commented, as if reading Daniel's thoughts. "I can't resist the blue eyes."

"Hers, or mine?"

"Neither one."

Daniel's neck felt hot, and he tugged at a patch of whiskers in his beard. Mags went into the house ahead of them and staked out a spot on the sofa where she knew Justin would eventually land, so that she could rest her chin on his knee and get her head scratched. They scraped mud from their boots and Daniel went straight to the kitchen, reclaiming unwashed-but-not-dirty drinking glasses left over from lunchtime from inside the sink and filling them with cold water.

"I have to go back tomorrow morning," Justin said. "For my therapist. Meds check."

"OK." Daniel passed him a glass of water and they both gulped gratefully.

"Wish I didn't have to go," Justin said into the bottom of his glass, just before draining it.

"Me too. But you'll come back." Daniel ducked into the fridge, rummaged until he found plastic-wrapped salami; he drew out a stack of slices and used his free hand to shake a slice of bread from the bag, folded them together and shoved in a thick bite. He gestured with what was left and made a questioning noise.

"I'm good," Justin declined. He opened the front of the stove and poked at the logs, stirring up some hidden fire.

"Can I come out and see the house some time? I'm curious. I imagine your bedroom wall having posters." Daniel made a face like he couldn't believe it himself. Justin laughed.

"Sorry to disappoint you. But sure, anytime. Come with me in the morning and then we can drive back together in time for the light."

Daniel found himself inordinately pleased that Justin was concerned about the light. He went on chewing for a moment and Justin must have taken his pause for reticence, adding, "Or if you don't want me back right away, you can come out whenever."

"No, I do," Daniel replied quickly, with an urgent desire to repair Justin's bruised feelings. "I want you back. Right away." He pointed to the sofa. "And so does Mags, I bet."

Justin leaned across the coffee table and ran his fingers over the back of her neck.

"So, yeah, if the weather looks like it's going to hold tomorrow, let's do it." They exchanged smiles across the room though Justin moved to erase his with a drag of his hand across his mouth, and Daniel turned to busy himself tying up the bread bag and returning the loaf to its rolltop box.

"Any of that pie left for after supper?" Justin asked, and worked his black sweater up over his head, pulling his t-shirt with it, crumpled both and tossed them into the bedroom through the open door. He lifted one ankle onto his opposite knee to peel off his sock, checking his balance with one hand on the bathroom door jamb.

"One piece I'll fight you for," Daniel replied. He got another glass of water and drank it a bit slower than the first.

"Can I buy it off you?"

"With what money?"

"Don't have any money," Justin admitted with a half-smile. He slow-scratched his fingertips through the hair of his chest.

Daniel raised his eyebrows and licked his lips. "Mm. Good."

"So did you grow up in Maine? Not around here, or I'd have known you," Justin ventured, driving twenty miles over the speed limit along the mostly empty rolls and twists of Route 18 toward Parker Village, one hand on the steering wheel while the other ashed his cigarette through the cracked-open window.

"Massachusetts."

"What part?"

"Around Everett."

"I know kind of where that is," Justin offered. "I lived in Boston for a couple of years—Union Square in Somerville, and Allston for a while. One of the rich suburbs?"

Daniel snorted a laugh. "No. I moved around a lot, but just in those couple of towns near there that are all pretty much the same—working people, a lot of immigrants."

Justin hummed acknowledgement. "I got moved, too, just between my grandmothers and my dad mostly." Daniel felt guilty, suddenly, for having already heard at least the village-gossip version of Justin's childhood. He turned to look out the passenger window of Justin's truck, at the passing trees. Justin went on to add, "My mom was really young when she had me, like sixteen. She partied a lot. Pretty soon the state took me away from her and gave me to my dad, but he was kind of a knucklehead, too. Not a partier or whatever, but he was a kid, too, and the only job he could get was fishing, so he was away a lot and my grandmothers babysat me."

"Sisters and brothers?" Daniel asked.

"None I know. I guess my mom had two more kids when I was like ten or twelve, but she was living in Florida by then and they got adopted down there."

Daniel made a noise of understanding. "I was in foster care," he said. "That's why I moved a lot. Back and forth to my mom a bunch of times, foster homes, a couple of group homes. I was kind of a pain in the ass."

"Your mom did drugs?"

"No. She had some mental issues, and she had a couple of boyfriends who beat her up. That's why they took us, because she wouldn't get rid of the boyfriends."

"What about your dad?"

"He broke my arm when I was two, so he wasn't allowed to see us except at the social worker's office. He only ever showed up a couple of times, then they stopped bringing us because he wasn't going to show up anyway."

"You have sisters and brothers?" Justin asked through teeth clamped around the butt of a fresh cigarette he was lighting one-handed while he steered.

"Two brothers. One's in and out of prison; last I heard he was in on a third-strike for armed robbery or something. The other one was the baby; he got adopted by his first foster parents and when we were still kids they moved to Arizona. Talk to him a couple times a year. He's married; they have two kids, girls. I met the wife at his wedding, a couple months before Abenaki."

"How many foster homes were you in?"

"Two during elementary school. Then I was in a group home for a year because I was stealing and getting into fights and stuff. I was a pretty pissed-off kid."

"Well, you would be."

"I guess. Went back to my second foster parents but I couldn't get along with the dad, so then it was back to another group home for like six months, until the end of the school year. The last foster mom I stayed with from the time I was thirteen until I finished high school."

"She was a good one?"

"An awesome lady. She still sends me emails every couple of months, invites me for holidays and stuff."

"Do you ever go?"

"I used to." Daniel shrugged and let his gaze drift. Justin waited him out, dragging on his cigarette and exhaling out the corner of his mouth, toward the open edge of the window. "It's just too much. I mean, I have to stay for the light, but even if I didn't have the light, I don't think I could."

"Holidays are pretty high-key," Justin replied, and Daniel could sense Justin understood why he stayed away. "Ever invited her up to see the lighthouse?"

"Never thought of it."

He actually hadn't, and so wondered why he hadn't. His foster mom, Laura, really was an awesome lady—she took in a lot of teenagers and provided a good balance of structure, high expectations, encouragement, and practical life skills—and Daniel wouldn't have minded seeing her again. She'd kept him on track in high school, helped him apply to college, and kept her home open to him after he was technically on his own. He did a quick mental calculation and figured she must be about seventy.

"You should invite her. People think lighthouses are really cool, and plus she'd probably want to see that you turned out good."

"Did I?" Daniel asked, smiling, glancing over at Justin.

"You're all right."

They were through Parker Village by then—Route 18 was its main street, straight down the middle of town—and out the other side, approaching Six Rivers.

"We have like a half-hour before I have to go to my appointment. Do you want to go to the house first?"

"Whatever you think."

"May as well stop; we can grab a coffee at least."

Daniel looped back a bit in their conversation. "When did you live in Boston?"

"I was like twenty."

Daniel did the math in his head. "I was already working at Abenaki by then."

"Do you miss it?"

Daniel hadn't really considered. "It's hard to say. I guess I was pretty happy there, before. But obviously my memory's tainted by how it ended. Even the word, Abenaki—it used to mean the forest, the park, which is a great park that I really loved—but now it means the shooting. The Abenaki Tragedy, The Abenaki Horror, The Abenaki Massacre." Daniel pinched a fingerful of whiskers and tugged absently at it. "After a whole life of shit, I got a couple of really good years. I wonder what the rest of that guy's life would have been like."

"You feel that different," Justin commented.

"Oh, yeah. That guy died with those kids and their teachers. I'm someone else."

"Better or worse?"

Daniel glanced over at Justin's profile as he drove. "You sound like my old therapist. That's exactly the kind of thing she would have asked me."

"Well I've heard enough of that kind of stuff from my own shrinks to know the lingo."

"Just different. The memory of it is Technicolor hell. Knowing how badly I failed weighs a fuck-ton, and I'll be carrying it around on my back forever. The way it rewired me isn't my favorite."

"They can treat some of that post-traumatic stuff," Justin offered.

"Some," Daniel agreed, only half-believing. "I think there are just things you never recover from. Coping is an option, but every day you wake up and you're not sure if you'll be able to; it never goes away, but it changes. It makes new rules every day."

After a moment, Justin said, "I know."

Daniel put a hand on Justin's thigh and gave a gentle squeeze. "I know."

Twelve

The Blue Moon Bed and Breakfast Inn was an old Colonial-style house, a big blue square with the front door centered between pairs of windows, and five more windows straight across the second story. A wooden plaque near one corner proclaimed it, "Home of Jean-Jacques Tremblay, Shipwright," and boasted a date of 1762. The barn Justin had described was visible just behind it, and the place was decorated for the holidays with a massive pine wreath on the front door, as Daniel had seen in photos on Justin's phone. Smaller versions of the beribboned wreath hung in the middle of each window. Justin pulled around behind the house to a parking area with space for a dozen cars, though the only other vehicles visible were his little orange egg-car and a small SUV the same color as the pavement.

"It's bigger than I thought," Daniel commented as they emerged from the truck. There was quite a bit of land behind it, gently sloping away from the house in all directions, bordered by woods. Though far from isolated, the inn was tucked away from its neighbors in a way that gave a sense of privacy, an escape from everyday life. A nice place for a few nights' vacation, Daniel thought.

"Six guest rooms and the owners' apartment, plus an in-law suite for Lia."

"It's a nice spot," Daniel offered. Justin gestured for him to go up the wood stairs to a large but unfurnished deck, through sliding glass doors to a dining room open to the parlor, its sofa and chairs clustered around a massive stone fireplace. Justin barely looked around as they passed through the rooms to the entry foyer, where they hung their coats on a tall rack by the front door. None of the lamps or overhead lights were on, and though the day was clear and bright, the angle of the sun and the surrounding forest contributed a blanket of cold gloom.

"So that's the breakfast room and parlor," Justin said. "Kitchen at the back. Over here's another room with the TV and books." Daniel could see some of the second parlor through its doorway; Justin had already started up the stairs—pale wood with a red and blue carpet runner—so Daniel followed, feeling concerned about his boots dirtying the rugs.

"It's a really nice house," Daniel said, true admiration in it, despite how limp it probably sounded. Framed photos lined the staircase wall, mostly landscapes and scenery, a few of Justin and a sleek-looking, tanned man who must be his late husband. Daniel wanted to linger, but it felt invasive so he didn't slow down, only took in whatever he could on the way past, as if he might learn something about Justin he'd yet to know.

"I should use more of it," Justin replied, though his tone made it clear he was unconvinced of the idea. "This is my room, here," he said, and turned the knob on one of the thick wood doors, pushing it open and standing aside for Daniel to pass.

The room was not terribly big, and the ceiling was low. Dark gray walls, the wood trim around the windows painted silvery off-white. There was a door in one corner leading to the bathroom, a squatty wooden armoire that could easily be as old as the house itself, and a television set atop a low dresser. The bed was unmade, pillows at crazy angles and blankets turned back in a diagonal lump, tugged loose from the corners. Black clothes were scattered in various piles on the floor, and a laptop computer sat open but sleeping on the nightstand. From just inside the doorway, Daniel quickly spotted six abandoned coffee mugs and two overflowing ashtrays. A small trash can in one corner overflowed with paper cups and the plastic wrappers from gas station cuisine. The whole place smelled of stale cigarettes and a faint whiff of sour perspiration.

"Comfy," Daniel smirked.

"I'm a slob, I know. But it's my cave, I can mess it up how I want."

"Of course. When you bring guys over, I guess you have your choice of clean rooms to take them to," Daniel teased, with the frightening thrill in his throat that Justin might agree.

"You're the first man that's been in this house in three years," Justin replied. "Unless Lia's up to something I don't know about. Some guy from her church, maybe."

Daniel was surprised at the relief he felt knowing Justin had no one else but him. Justin claimed a pack of cigarettes off the nightstand and checked the bedside clock while he lit it.

"I have to go in a couple minutes, but you can hang out if you want. Meds check is only a five minute thing, ten minute drive each way, so I'll be back in half an hour."

"All right."

"Here, come down and we'll get some coffee."

When they entered the semi-industrial kitchen, with its massive six-burner stove and long wooden work-island, they met a woman with graying brown hair pulled back from her forehead and hanging loose down the back, to her shoulders.

"Lia, como vai?" Justin said, going straight for the coffee maker and then to the sink to fill its carafe.

"No *smoke*, Shustin," she scolded, but she smiled and the tone was of someone more amused by his incorrigibility than annoyed at his disregard for the surroundings.

"Sorry." He tipped his head toward Daniel. "Meu amigo, Daniel Howard."

"Hi, nice to meet you." Daniel offered his hand and she shook it gently.

"My cousin, Lia Costa," Justin added, and started the coffeemaker. A row of white mugs hung from hooks under the upper cabinets and Justin liberated two. "Você quer coffee, Lia?"

There came an upbeat trill of music and Lia lifted a phone from the pocket of her cardigan. She answered, waved off Justin's offer, and drifted out of the kitchen, chatting away in Portuguese.

"You speak Portuguese?"

"Not really, just a little. Gabriel's English was really good so I only learned what I picked up from him and Lia talking. She probably understands more English than she'll use with me, but who knows. Gabriel used to say she was half shy, half stubborn about it."

"She likes you, though," Daniel said, and Justin liberated the coffee pot halfway through the cycle, in a hurry to fill their mugs.

Justin shrugged. "We get along all right."

"When she told you not to smoke she looked at you like a mom in a TV show—that irrepressible scamp, what's he up to now?"

Justin laughed. "You're seeing things," he said. "I have to get out of here or I'll be late. There's food in the fridge, probably, and you can hang out down here—you saw where the TV is—or in my room. I won't be gone too long." He patted his pockets.

"All good," Daniel assured him, and Justin leaned up against his chest and hip, hands resting at Daniel's waist. Daniel moistened his lips a little and they kissed.

"No *smoke*, Don-yell," Justin intoned, mimicking Lia's scold as well as her accent, narrowing his eyes and frowning.

"Yes, I can see that rule is hard and fast," Daniel replied, and gave him another quick kiss before Justin drew away. "I'll smoke outside."

Once Justin had gone—taking his coffee mug to the car; Daniel hoped he would not have to brake suddenly—Daniel stood in the kitchen with his cup for a few more sips, opened a couple of cabinets and the refrigerator, which held equal portions of healthy food and complete junk; Daniel could easily imagine which belonged to Lia and which to Justin. He made a slow stroll through the dining room with its large, central table and two smaller, round tables Daniel assumed must have been put to use when the inn was at full capacity. The parlor was inviting, almost stereotypically New England in its décor: a watch-plaid throw draped over the sofa's back and a brass pineapple propped on the fireplace mantel. But the furniture was soft and billowy, inviting a guest to kick off shoes and curl up by the fire.

The second parlor was smaller, with similarly comfortable furniture and a big television set mounted to one wall. The bookshelves held paperbacks in several languages, and countless coffee-table books of photographs with varied themes—high end automobiles, international cityscapes, wild animals and birds of northern Maine (of course), and Brazil's neon-bright Carnival celebrations—plus a row of guest books. Daniel slid one free and opened it at random.

Gabriel and Justin,

Thank you for being such gracious hosts during our long weekend "leaf-peeping"! Your home is so lovely and we enjoyed our conversations with you over breakfast and in the evenings—is there anything Gabriel doesn't know about? Thank you for the insider info about the best lookout spots. We hope to return again next year.

Best,

Mike and Alyssa Ferragamo

Marblehead, MA

He flipped a few pages and read another entry.

What a wonderful time we spent at Blue Moon! We can't thank you enough for all you did to make our daughter's wedding special. The barn was so beautifully decorated, the tables set so perfectly, I teared up when I walked in on Saturday morning! The meals were wonderful and you made us feel your home was ours for the weekend—I know how our family can take over a place but you were just delightful company and so helpful with everything we needed, from dealing with the vendors to finding a roll of white ribbon at the last moment! Thank you both, Gabriel and Justin, from the bottom of our hearts. Love from the Flahertys—Marianne, Tom, Kayleigh, Dylan, and TJ, and from the new Mr. and Mrs. Carter and Olivia Bannon!

Daniel slid the book back into place; the wedding talk reminded him of the photo-wall beside the stairs and he started up, stopping a couple of times to see everything in more detail. There were photos of landscapes sufficiently exotic he assumed they must be of Gabriel's home country of Brazil, and some more obviously local, of docked lobster boats and wooden covered bridges. There was one of Justin, only identifiable by his shape and posture, the thick waves of his hair, leaning against the side of the inn's barn, with the glow of a cigarette visible in the hand hanging by his side. Another was an obvious family photo of about two dozen people of all ages dressed similarly in white shirts and dresses, surrounding a very elderly man enthroned on a plastic lawn chair.

Near the top of the stairs a black frame held three small photos in vertical arrangement. The first was of Justin, wearing a tailored black dress shirt and deep-red, patterned necktie, smoothing the lapels on a black jacket worn by Gabriel, who had dark hair longer on top, and angular features. The second was of two hands stacked together, wearing new gold rings; and the third was of the two sharing a kiss on the city hall steps, both smiling more than puckering up, their hands clasped together by their sides. Daniel scanned all three, and returned to the first one, taken from an angle that suggested an unguarded moment—a stolen photo—of two men anticipating the ceremony that would start a life together. Justin looked amused, maybe even bashful, as if he'd just been paid a compliment and wished to deflect it despite his pleasure at it. He was gorgeous. Daniel was a little jealous of Gabriel having got to see him looking that way—having made him look that way—and of the two in a moment so full of hope and promise.

Daniel, broken, skating the thin edge of failing to cope, needing the excuse of required work to get him out of bed and moving forward every day, would never know that feeling—that everything was about to change for the better, and that anything was possible. He knew too well that *anything* truly was possible, including an angry man with a gun taking sixteen lives away from the world in under ten minutes, and wrecking a man's peace for as long as he lived. It was possible for a man whose relative youth still offered every opportunity at happiness to climb desperate onto a cliff-top one morning, intent on throwing himself off it, to end his own suffering. Any horrible thing was possible. What a life.

Daniel moved on, up the stairs to the landing, where he glanced through open doors into guest rooms made up in traditional fashion, with fluffy white bedding and potted plants standing in their corners. One shut door was too tempting to pass by, and he tried the knob, expecting it to be locked. The door opened and Daniel took a single step inside it.

The little living room was overpowered by a hospital bed, its back bent up, facing a window looking out over the fear of the property. A nearby table was littered with the kinds of sick-tending supplies normally associated with a hospital rather than a home: liver-shaped plastic tubs, foil packets of alcohol swabs, cheap socks with rubber grips on their soles, a spiral notebook folded back with writing all over the page—notes made of when and how bad, how little sleep, how much medicine, pain rated on a one-to-five scale—and plastic-lidded paper cups bearing logos of convenience stores and donut shops.

Rumpled blankets and a flat pillow lay on the nearby sofa; someone had made a bed of it. The kitchen, visible over a half-wall with a bar top covered in paperwork—open and still-sealed mail, semi-organized files—and a potted cactus with a plasticky-looking yellow ribbon tied around it. There was a pizza box by the sink, and an uncorked wine bottle. The whole place looked as if it had been abandoned in a hurry, and never returned to. Daniel stepped out, pulling the door shut with a quiet click. He needed a cigarette.

Making his way out to the back deck, Daniel bombed a smoke from the pack and lit it, took a deep, slow drag that heated and tightened his chest. He scratched his beard with his thumbnail, and descended the wooden stairs, walking across the back lawn toward the barn. It was closed up, no windows in the wide sliding doors to peek into, so he circled around behind, skirting the edge of the woods, pacing out the land. Blue jays shrieked at each other somewhere nearby, and he could hear running water; there must be a brook somewhere just out of sight, in the forest.

Weren't they a pair, Daniel thought bitterly, all cracked-edged and easily spooked and fragile. Daniel had a deep urge to enfold Justin in a bear hug, hold him close and too tight, kiss him breathless to tell him Daniel got it, understood him. That they fit.

He was down to his last few drags and had walked quite far from the house, to the lower edge of the backyard, by the time Justin's little orange car came into view. He started toward it and Justin came to meet him halfway, the two finishing the walk to the house side by side.

"Everything good?," Daniel asked, polite rather than prying.

"Good enough for now. She gave me homework!" He sounded outraged.

"They do that sometimes. I think it's optional, but can't we all use the extra credit?"

Justin grinned and grabbed for his hand, dragged him quicker toward the house.

"Hey, careful; my ankle's not a hundred percent yet."

"It's good for you. Come on, we're going to my room."

Soon enough, they were wrestling on Justin's unmade bed, plucking and dragging at each other's clothes, then pinching and biting at each other's newly-bared skin. Justin groaned encouragements every time Daniel put hands on him, pulled at Daniel's wrists and shoved Daniel's legs with his knees, until Daniel was on top of him, face to face, grinding their pricks together, pausing every few strokes to lean down and grab a kiss. Justin licked into Daniel's mouth, scraped fingernails down his triceps, and across his pecs, making Daniel grunt in time with his rocking hips, Justin's legs wrapped around his thighs tight enough to lift his ass off the bed, countering Daniel's movements.

"Mm. . .fuck. . ."

"So good. Here."

Daniel planted a knee, wrapped arms around Justin's back and rolled them over so Justin was straddling him, and with one work-rough hand, Daniel caught up both their cocks. Justin arched his back and shuddered, pinching his own nipples, pushing fingertips through the hair of his chest, then doing the same to Daniel.

"Harder."

"Faster."

Daniel pulled, squeezing, rolling his wrist, and Justin, hovering above, planted hands on his shoulders, curling his back with his head hanging so the tips of his hair brushed Daniel's nose and forehead, and bit back a shout as he came, cursing, across Daniel's quivering belly. Daniel encouraged him, his own need rising, and after a single shivering sigh, Justin swung one leg over to kneel beside Daniel and his mouth—hot—still gasping—slid around Daniel's prick. He began to hum and moan in time, using his hand to make up the difference, and Daniel jutted up between his lips, his hand on Justin's hip, ass, thigh, gripping wherever he could. Scratching.

"Mm, look."

Daniel lifted his head and watched Justin pumping with his fist, swirling the tip of his tongue around the crown of Daniel's prick, and he clutched the bed sheets in his fists as he came, spilling in hot pulses against Justin's nimble lips, and over his still-sliding hand. Justin looked self-satisfied and hot-flushed as he drew away, up onto his knees on the mattress, bouncing Daniel gently as he reached for a discarded t-shirt and wiped away the mess from both of them, then vanished into the bathroom where Daniel could hear the faucet run. In a moment, Justin returned with a semi-clean-looking glass of water he gulped from and then offered to Daniel while he reclaimed his clothes from the floor and stepped into his jeans.

"That was fun," Daniel commented, feeling very much that he was stating the obvious.

"I'll say." They exchanged wide, soft smiles. Justin dropped Daniel's t-shirt and sweater onto the mattress beside his thigh, then his jeans with the belt still in the loops; the buckle jangled as he moved them.

"When did you figure out you like it rough?" Daniel asked, and he liberated his cigarette pack from his jeans' hip pocket, found a book of matches on the nightstand. He sat up against the headboard and a few bent pillows, pulled the sheet and a blanket up to his waist.

"When I went at you that way and you went along with it," Justin shrugged. He pulled a couple of shirts over his head, layering up against the cold, and lit his own smoke.

"What, really?"

"Something wrong with it?"

"No. It's fun." Daniel exhaled and looked around for an ashtray. Justin passed him a half-full one and Daniel balanced it on his thigh. "I just said," he pointed out. "Wasn't like that with your husband, then."

Justin picked apart his hair, scrutinizing his reflection in a mirror over the dresser. "Nope. Can we go back to the cove now?"

"Sure, whenever you're ready. Do you need to pack a bag?" Daniel studied Justin, cutting his eyes away whenever Justin looked back at him, as he began to pick up random items of clothing off the floor, sniff them, and either throw them in a small pile on the bed or reject them back to the floor. Justin was frowning significantly, his eyes narrow. After a moment, Daniel redirected, stubbing out his cigarette and moving to fold the clothes Justin had heaped on the mattress. "I like the pictures on the stairs, there, coming up. That one of you by the barn. And the one of the moose peeking out through the trees. Was that out here in your woods?"

"I forget. I think so." He went into the bathroom and Daniel heard the steady splash as he peed. "No, it was in Vermont. Before we found this place. We were looking at another inn, stayed there two nights. That's when I saw the moose."

"You're the photographer, then?"

Justin emerged from the bathroom, buttoning his jeans. "Used to. My camera broke and I never replaced it."

"They're expensive," Daniel said.

"I just never got around to it."

"You took that family picture, too? With all the white clothes?"

"No; I never met his family except Lia. They're very religious. That was around the time we got together; he went for his grandfather's ninetieth birthday a couple months after we met. The ones that knew he was gay either cut him off or pretended it wasn't true. I wasn't welcome."

"Did any of them come to your wedding?"

"No."

"Your dad? Your grandparents?"

"My grandparents are old-fashioned; I never told them. I've only got one grandmother left now, anyway. My dad pretends not to know; I go along to keep the peace. It's also why I don't see him that often. It bums me out too much to have to pretend. Does your family know about you?"

"There's really only my younger brother, and we barely know each other. When we talk he's too busy telling me about his kids to ask me about myself, and I don't volunteer anything."

Justin stopped moving, stood still with a different, deeper frown creeping across his face. "It's really weird we found each other."

Daniel stopped folding the zip-front hoodie in his hands, let it settle on his still naked lap. "I guess it is," he agreed. "The world's smaller than we like to think, though."

Justin stepped forward and put his hands against the sides of Daniel's face, tilted it up so they were looking at each other. "I wouldn't wish it on my worst enemy," he said quietly, and raised his eyebrows, seeking Daniel's acknowledgement that he understood.

After a few long seconds in which Justin's eyes searched his own, Daniel nodded sympathy for him, if not agreement. An admission that he'd let himself step inside the apartment—that he'd seen the hospital bed and the intensive paperwork of serious illness: schedules and notes and piles of bills to be paid—crowded up against the back of his lips, and he almost let himself say it, but gave in to cowardice and some degree of shame, and swallowed it back. Instead, he said quietly, "Let's get back to the light."

Thirteen

Dear Daniel Howard,

This notice is a reminder of the public hearing regarding automation of the lighthouse at North Hope Cove, Maine. As the current lighthouse keeper at the site, your input is invaluable, and you are urged to appear and testify. The date, time, and location of the hearing are contained in the enclosed memorandum. You will be allotted forty-five minutes to offer a statement, which will be entered in the official record. The panel hearing testimony will include the regional and local National Parks directors for the relevant area; two members of the United States Senate's Working Group on Conservation and Maintenance of Public Lands, including Maine senator Anne Ogilvie; a representative from Nashua Automation Engineering, Inc.; and two residents of Hope County.

    Sincerely,

    Leslie Rhodes

    Junior Director

    Northeast Region Physical Plant, US Dept. of National Parks

"You're going to this thing, right?" Justin asked, tapping the letter Daniel had left on the edge of his writing desk. "The thing about the light? In Portland."

"I don't know." Daniel was sitting in his chair with a book in hand, in his sock-feet as they'd only partially re-dressed themselves upon rising from Daniel's bed after sex-instead-of-lunch. Justin had a last look at the letter and took his spot in the middle of the sofa. He set down a big bowl of chips and a smaller one of salsa he'd shaken from a bottle—something he must think passed for a midday meal. They both reached in, dipped chips, and crunched away.

"You have to," Justin said, his voice gently urgent.

"I think they'll do what they want, no matter what I—or anyone—says about it. It's the government. I wouldn't be surprised if the entire reason for inviting me is just so they can point to it later, in the record of the hearing or whatever, and use whatever I have to say as proof of how open they were to other alternatives. But they can't have any real intention of changing course, just because one loser with post-traumatic anxiety is worried he won't be able to get another job."

"But if you don't, wouldn't you wonder if you should have? It can't hurt."

"It won't help," Daniel insisted. "I've been thinking of sending a letter. They can enter it in the record, or set it to music, or set it on fire—whatever they do it will come out the same. I don't want to have to spend a day driving to Portland and back, in a place I've never been, with people I don't know and can't trust, just to have them shut me down anyway. I'd rather spend the day here working."

"I think you should go. I'll go with you."

Daniel reached over and touched Justin's knee. "It's nice of you to say that."

"I will. I'll drive, if you want. Or whatever you need."

Daniel smiled at him. "Thanks. I'd kiss you but I've got jalapeno and garlic breath."

"Me, too. Go for it," Justin grinned at him, and leaned in to receive a mostly-chaste kiss.

"Did I hear your phone going off while we were in there?" Daniel said, tipping his chin toward the bedroom.

Justin agreed he had, and crossed to the kitchen table to reclaim it. Daniel went on eating chips and returned to his reading. After a few minutes spent swiping and staring at his phone, Justin returned to the sofa. The dogs came trotting in from outside, sniffed around the coffee table and were shooed away; Tugboat went to retrieve his favorite chew toy from the corner of the kitchen, while Mags leapt up beside Justin on the sofa, begging to be petted and scratched. He obliged, with the phone still clutched in his other hand.

"So this woman emailed, and I guess left a voicemail," Justin said slowly, absently running his fingers through the fur at the back of Maggie's neck. "Saying she'd like to talk to me about buying the house."

Daniel felt his eyes widen. "Just out of nowhere?" he asked.

"Yeah. Well. Sort of. She and her partner stayed with us a couple of times. I remember them a little bit; they're from Rhode Island. She says they're ready for a career change and they're looking to buy a Bed and Breakfast up this way. When she saw the website's down she did some research and. . ." he waved his hand in the air; Daniel could fill in the rest fairly easily—in the internet age it wouldn't be hard for her to get the gist of the story from Gabriel's obituary, the fact of the inn extant but not doing business, confirmation Justin still owned it, even his cell number.

"Pretty forward of her," Daniel commented.

"They must really like the house," Justin replied, distractedly rolling his thumb up and down his phone's screen, already on to other things. "I'm sure there are plenty out there already up for sale, that she didn't need to come searching me out."

"So you'll think about it," Daniel said. He brushed his palms together to wipe away the salt left from the chips.

"Naw, I'll write back and tell her no." He didn't look away from his phone, only shook his head, mouth rumpling in a dismissive frown. They fell back into silence, each leaning forward now and then to dip a chip and noisily crunch it. Daniel carried on reading—a freshly-begun novel he knew nothing about except that the author was a favorite of his—and Justin went on fiddling with his phone, now and then dropping his hand to stroke Maggie's blue and white fur while he read. They had beer in bottles—two apiece—and eventually the salsa was gone and there were only crumbs left in the big bowl on the coffee table, and nearly two hours had passed in companionable quiet.

Daniel set a bookmark between the pages of his book—no chapter breaks, no wonder he'd stayed so long in it—and saw that Justin had turned his phone face down on his thigh, sunk lower on the sofa to rest his head on its back, and closed his eyes. He looked asleep except that his fingers stroked slowly through Maggie's fur. Daniel rose from the arm chair, stretched with a quiet sigh, then brushed a few fingertips over Justin's jeans-clad knee. Justin's lips curled up into a soft smile but otherwise he stayed as he was.

"Hey, Sunny. Heading up to switch on the light. You're staying?"

"Mm," Justin affirmed. "I'll wash dishes so we have some for supper."

"Sure you will," Daniel lightly teased, gathering up the bowls and empty bottles.

"Well, I'm not now, if you're going to be a dick about it," Justin said, still smiling, at last opening his eyes and lifting himself more or less upright. Maggie adjusted the angle of her head on his thigh.

Daniel set the bowls in the sink, plugged the drain and started the water running. Once he'd put the bottles in the bin to go to the dump, he added a squirt of liquid soap; steam rose off the surface of the water, reminding him the stove likely needed another log or two to get them by until bedtime.

"What's for supper, anyway?" Justin asked, tugging at his pullover sweatshirt here and there to draw it closer to his wrists and further from his throat.

Daniel ducked into the fridge, pulled out the drawers. "Sausage, peppers, and onions," he reported. Reaching into the freezer, he shifted its contents to free a round loaf of crusty bread twice-wrapped in plastic, which he set out to thaw on the counter near the stove. "There's some ice cream in here, too."

"Yes, please," Justin replied, and at last slithered out from under Maggie's head as he stood up from the sofa and stretched his arms overhead. He found the hook for the wood stove's door and pulled it open, then tossed in two small split logs from the pile nearby and shut it again.

Daniel shrugged into his parka. Before he zipped it up, he did a last check-in with the weather reports on his laptop, open on the desk. "Back in no time," he said. "Don't know about you, but I'm starving. I'll start cooking as soon as the light's lit." He stood and zipped the front of his coat. "Come on, dogs. Out you go," he directed, and both shepherds stood, shook off their dozes and stretched low and long, then followed Daniel out the door.

He stole a quick glance at Justin's back, heading into the bathroom, making special note of the tight fit of his jeans around his backside, and resolved to drag him to bed as soon as the dishes were done and the cottage buttoned up for the night.

"Be good," Justin told him casually, a smile audible in it.

The moon was already huge, the sky clear and cloudless, the air frigid but still, and Daniel left his hood down. Tugger and Mags had wandered down the sloping yard, along the strip of grass parallel to the upward-slanted path. The sun was low in the opposite side of the sky—nearly there. He climbed the stairs at a steady slow pace. In the lantern room, he lifted the switch into place and stood by, scanning the horizon as the motor revved up to speed and the lens array began to turn. Once satisfied with the steady hum and the fluid sweep of the beam, Daniel circled the light. He made cursory checks that all was right, all the while distracted by the promise of spicy cured meat and fried-to-wilted-death vegetables piled greasily into a folded slice of thready Italian bread. Though the reason for skipping a real meal—to tussle on top of the bedspread with Justin until they were both panting and sweaty—was valid, chips and salsa did not pass for lunch in his world, and Daniel was ravenous. At that moment, he would not have been able to honestly distinguish which he lusted for more: the slim-hipped hottie in his parlor, or his supper.

A glance out the window, and the sun was only a white sliver above the horizon. He looked for the dogs, didn't find them where he'd expected them to be—near the fence, by their basket of fetch-balls—and felt his nosebridge tighten with a frown as he swept a gaze over the land.

"Oh. . .come on. . ." he said to no one. The dogs were walking wide, jagged circles through the rockfall at the cliff base, barking now and then, trying to get his attention. He strained and squinted, but couldn't see much in the shadows and quickening darkness. He took his phone from his pocket and sent a text to Justin.

Looks like the dogs found something down by the cliff.

TXT from Justin Strongbow: Something?

Somebody. There's flashlights under the kitchen sink, can you bring one out?

TXT from Justin Strongbow: Meet you by the gate.

Justin brought two flashlights, obviously intent on accompanying Daniel on the grim errand. The collar of his pea coat was raised to cover his neck, emphasizing the angles of his face, and he had a black knit watch cap pulled down low on his forehead.

"You don't have to come," Daniel told him.

"It's all right," Justin replied with a slight shrug, then added, with something like hopefulness, "Maybe it's not, you know. Somebody."

Daniel gave a noncommittal hum. He knew his dogs; he'd trained them. He started down the hill and Justin followed, the two walking not quite side by side. As they got further from the house, the spilled glow of the lights near the front and back doors could no longer reach, and though the sky was clear and the moon bright, they employed the flashlights to save them another sprained ankle. Neither spoke.

Within a few minutes, they were picking their way through the rockfall, finding paths, once or twice having to hoist themselves and each other over waist-high boulders with spaces between wide enough for the dogs to slip through down low, but too narrow for a man to pass. Tugger was barking every few seconds, sharp declarative reports that echoed off the cliff wall.

"Good dog, Tugboat. Well done," Daniel praised him. "Quiet now. Good dog." The dog jumped in place, back and forth, in response, and did as he was told.

They took the long way around another boulder, and after rounding the curve came upon a broken body in a heap about ten yards ahead of them. Maggie trotted to them, circled around Daniel and headed back toward the spot, showing him the way. "Good dog, Mags." Daniel leaned to brush his fingertips over the top of her head as she made a second pass. He raised his voice a bit and said, "Home time. Good dogs." The two ran up to Daniel, checking in one last time, and he waved toward the house. "Go on," he told them, and they started back toward the house at a trot.

Justin had walked slightly ahead of him and was by then within a few feet of the body. He passed the beam of his flashlight over what looked no different from any other odd-shaped lump there in the rockfall—khaki trousers, marine-blue parka. A single shoe lay on its side, between Daniel and the body. Light hair, and not much of it; his face was turned away. Justin circled around.

"Don't know him," he said. "I don't know why I thought I might."

Daniel reached Justin's side, aimed his light and took a quick look. Eyes shut; face badly scraped—the side of it lying against the gravel clearly even worse. Legs and arms at every wrong angle. Silent. Dead.

"Small world," Daniel shrugged. "You might have."

"What do you do? I mean, what do you usually do?"

By now it was fully dark and the cliff blocked the moon so they stood in its long shadow; beyond the flashlight beams was utter dark all around. The blackness was disorienting; Daniel listened for the ocean, looked up toward the cottage for its lights, trying to place himself correctly. He felt weirdly light, as if he might drift up and hover. Focusing his light on the body, he took a long step backward as if in thought.

"Call the police in Parker. They usually come with an ambulance. Within an hour there'll be half a dozen people here. I just make them coffee and stay out of their way."

Justin reached into his jacket and pulled out his cigarette pack, tucked his flashlight under his arm while he lit it. "Smoke?" he asked, and extended the pack.

"Thanks, no, I have mine." Daniel shook his head as if woken from a dream, shoved into action, and he reached into his own coat for his cigarettes and phone. Once he'd set the cigarette between his lips, Justin reached to light it for him, and they steadied each other's hands for as long as it took. Daniel had an urge to shoo Justin away, fearful of contagion. Justin paced a bit, aiming his light at the ground, but did not move in the direction of the cottage. Daniel scrolled, dialed, waited. "Yeah, it's Daniel Howard out at the North Hope light. My dogs found a body, a suicide."

Once he'd finished the call, Daniel tilted back his head, blowing a dragon's breath at the sky. Inwardly, he shook, but his hands were steady. Justin had circled around, standing a few yards off shining his flashlight on the lost shoe.

"Can I move it?" he wondered.

"They usually take pictures," Daniel told him. "Better not to touch anything."

Justin hummed acquiescence. They stood apart, smoking, and Justin switched off his light. After another drag and long exhalation, Daniel did the same. The darkness was enveloping, even with the cottage's lights visible at the top of the yard. The ocean was calm, its waves washing rather than crashing, sounding tired and desolate.

"Shouldn't they have found him this morning?" Justin said after a while. Daniel heard Justin's boots crunching, disturbing the debris underfoot, brushing it around.

"It must have been while we were inside, after we came in for lunch."

"While we were fucking," Justin mused. "Reading books. Eating chips. Falling asleep on the couch."

"Yeah."

Daniel rarely indulged in wondering about what came before, when the body had been a person; it felt disrespectful for him to speculate. He left them their dignity by not imagining their weeping, pacing, making last phone calls or writing the notes some of them left on the cliff top. He could make out the shadowy lump in front of him on the ground that could have been just another rock, and suddenly envisioned the living man he'd been just that early afternoon—in his khakis and puffy winter jacket—how the breeze would have disturbed his thin, combed-over hair. How he might have had tears on his cheeks, or how he might have run—furious—maybe shouting— willing himself to be brave for once in his life, and just get it done. Daniel dipped his head and rubbed his eyebrow with the back of his knuckle, let out a hissing sound—the shadow of a curse.

"All right?" Justin asked, immediately reframed it with, "It's fucking cold."

"Yeah. Let's head in; they'll be here soon."

They started toward the cottage, shoulder to shoulder as much as they could be while navigating the rockfall, with lights trained ahead of them. The dogs came out to meet them as they entered the front gate. Before even reaching the front step, though, there came the swing of headlight beams across the little yard, and they reversed course to meet the occupants of the police department's white and black SUV.

The police deputy—a fiftyish, ex-military guy named Thibodeau—stepped out, offered his hand for Daniel to shake.

"Hey, Danny," he gruffed. "How's things?"

Justin crossed his arms over his chest, turned halfway away, snickering to hear Daniel called "Danny".

"Getting by," Daniel replied. He tipped his head. "Out on the rocks. Guy about sixty. I'll send the dogs out, they'll show you."

"I'll wait for the EMT rig; they're right behind me." The cop gave Justin a quick look. "Is that you? Mark Strongbow's kid?"

"Uh-huh. Justin." He offered his hand and the deputy shook it.

"I know your dad."

"What'd he do now?" Justin asked, and Thibodeau and Daniel both took it for a joke and started to laugh, but Justin's expression quashed it.

"No, nothing. We both went to Hope County High; he was a couple years behind me. What's he doing these days?"

"Still fishing," Justin replied.

The small talk devolved into corny jokes and Daniel tuned it out, keeping Thibodeau's holstered handgun in sight. He was aware even without seeing it that there was a shotgun mounted in the SUV, as well, and he crept slightly sideways toward the cottage. His gut roiled noisily.

The ambulance crunched up then, no lights or sirens, and Daniel stood in the path of the headlights and directed it to park as near the path as possible without digging tire-ruts into the scrubby lawn. Before the medics even opened their doors, another pickup arrived, driven by the most junior police officer of the handful working in Parker, who would photograph the scene and the body.

Once grim-faced greetings were exchanged, Daniel again offered to send the dogs out to lead them to the body, and it was agreed the cop with the camera would go with the medics and the dogs, while Deputy Thibodeau would climb the path to the cliff top to see if there was anything left behind—a backpack or wallet, or a note. More than once, there had been an oversized plastic zipper-bag containing the person's phone, ID, and last letter. Daniel had handled them, not minding much about whose face was on the driver's license, or whose name was on the envelope.

The deputy produced a flashlight even better than the ones Daniel stocked under his kitchen sink, and looked across the yard, toward the cliff.

"I'll walk up with you," Justin volunteered. The deputy and Daniel both replied at once.

"Thanks."

"You don't have to."

Justin gave Daniel a half-smile probably meant to reassure him. "Buddy system. No one should climb that hill alone after dark." He set a cigarette between his lips, then drew out knit gloves from one of his coat pockets and pulled them on. Daniel stepped closer to offer him a light. The deputy had moved away to converse with the others, but Justin dropped his voice anyway. "It's cool," he reassured. "You stay and make the coffee."

"It's all right," Daniel acquiesced, "But you know. Just let them do their jobs and go. I have to be in bed in like two hours."

"Oh, I know you do," Justin winked, and gently tossed an elbow against Daniel's midsection. "No big deal. I'm kind of curious." He shrugged, and exhaled a lungful of smoke up and away from them. "I'm creepy like that."

"Ready, then?" the deputy called, and Justin gave Daniel a last grin before drifting away.

"Oi, dogs!" In a few seconds, Tugger and Mags arrived, tails wagging, looking at him expectantly. "Go get 'im." He swept his arm in the direction he wanted them to go, and they joined up with the medics and police officer, trotting toward the area where the body lay. Within a few more seconds, Daniel was alone in front of the cottage, voices vaguely carrying toward him through the sharp air, beams of light bobbing away, becoming smaller and dimmer by the moment. He went inside.

There'd be nothing else needed from him but to sign his name to a statement Thibodeau would call him the next day during business hours to confirm the details of. He was so hungry. But it would be rude to be in the middle of fixing supper when they all returned, with not enough to offer them. He had only ever laid in supplies enough for himself—and now for Justin, too—and he couldn't stretch it into dinner for six. He'd wait; he and Justin could eat after they'd gone. It would be late by then, and almost certainly he'd go to bed with heartburn.

Daniel sat down on his armchair, still wearing his parka, boots planted on the floor, waiting stiff and upright. He fiddled with his phone, checking the time. One more perusal of the maritime schedules and the weather forecast, then his restlessness drove him pointlessly to the kitchen. He opened the fridge, and everything he saw made him feel vaguely sick. Daniel was beyond hungry; food was unappealing. He'd have to force himself to choke something down and may as well leave it until breakfast. Beginning to sweat beneath his coat, he shook it off and went to hang it, and on his way by, pulled open the door to have a look out beyond the yard. Shimmering flickers of light jigged around down in the rockfall. He drew out his phone from the breast pocket of his shirt.

Tell Thibodeau he was wearing khakis and a blue parka.

He shut the door against the cold and moved to stoke up the stove.

TXT from Justin Strongbow: To tell him apart from all the other guys lying around there? :-D

Daniel huffed a breath out his nostrils, tossed his phone through the open bedroom door onto the bed, and went to start a pot of coffee.

It was nearly eight when they brought the body up on the stretcher and slid it into the back of the ambulance. Justin was the first one in the door, the two cops trailing him. Their faces were high pink from the cold, and the junior deputy stomped his boots on the mat just outside before stepping in, which made Daniel glance down; Justin's and Thibodeau's boot-soles were snow-caked, and the floor around them glistened.

"Nothing up top," Thibodeau reported, and Daniel nodded, arms crossed over his chest. Justin unbuttoned his pea coat and threw it over the arm of Daniel's reading chair. "His wallet and a note were zipped up in his coat pocket. William Wicklund, from down Shelbyport. You know him?"

Daniel shook his head.

"Nah, us neither—that's a ways out." Thibodeau dismissed his own question with a wave of his hand.

"Coffee?" Daniel offered, feeling sick, ready for them to go. The pot sat empty on its warming plate; he'd forgotten to switch it on.

"Thanks, no. We'll get out of your hair."

Daniel felt a shiver of relief that quickly dissolved away in the acidic churn of his hunger, exhaustion, need to breathe. He felt skinned.

"Thanks for the call," Thibodeau finished, and offered his hand. Daniel shook it, his fingers tingling.

"Of course," he managed to reply.

"Need a ride into Parker?" the cop asked Justin then, and it was clear he had not yet figured out why Mark Strongbow's kid was out at North Hope Cove after dark, keeping company with the reclusive, touchy lighthouse keeper.

"Nope. Thanks anyway," was all Justin replied. He stared strangely at Daniel, who was sure he himself must be looking pretty strange.

Within a minute the cops had been swept off the front step and Daniel stood on the gravel path watching taillights recede into the night. The light turned and the sea swept in gentle shushes against the rocky shore. The cold got easily past his flannel and the thermal shirt beneath, creeping up and down Daniel's spine, raising goose bumps on his arms.

"I made you a sandwich."

Justin's own mouth was partially full, and he offered a folded-over and filled slice of the Italian bread. He gazed up the road. "They gone?"

"Mm," Daniel replied, and stepped in to take the offered sustenance. The smell of peanut butter hit his nose all wrong and he wanted to refuse but bit the thing nearly in half and fought to chew it and get it down. He'd been so hungry but had come out the other side. His head hurt. Justin stepped back, making room for him to enter the cottage. Daniel forced the last of the sandwich down. On the counter by the kitchen sink, the peanut butter jar stood uncovered, with a knife stuck in.

"What happens next?" Justin asked, and sank onto his usual spot in the middle of the sofa, shoving off his unlaced rock-star boots with the toes of his opposite feet. "To the guy, I mean?"

Daniel slid into his desk chair and clicked around to get to his log. "They take the body to University Hospital." *Lamp ON to standard pattern, 1655h.* "To the morgue there." *Sunset, 1659h.* "Usually the coroner will already be waiting." *1700h, dogs alerted in rockfall, cliffside.* "Contact the family I guess." *1705h, discovered body of male Caucasian, 60yrs approx, deceased. Authorities contacted; body removed 1945h.*

"Hope he left them smiling," Justin said, and dragged his hands backward through his hair. He shook his head. "Hey."

Daniel looked over at him. Justin flashed a smile rife with a promise of trouble.

"Rough me up a little; it'll make us feel better."

Daniel bit his lips. "Do we need to feel better?" he asked, and it was only as the words met the air that he realized they were heavier than he'd intended them to be.

Justin held his gaze a moment, went on holding it even as he twisted his head side to side and replied, "Nope."

The sugar finally hit his bloodstream, softening some of his nerves' sharp corners, though Daniel's appetite was far from satisfied by the hastily-made half-sandwich. Now it was late and Justin wanted him. He got up from his desk and latched the dog door, moved to the kitchen to withdraw the knife and spin the lid back on the peanut butter jar. He brushed crumbs into the sink with the side of his hand. As he reached to switch off the light overhead, Justin pressed up against his back, arms snaking around Daniel's middle, pulling up close against his back. He hummed a growl, wrapped a hand around Daniel's metal belt buckle and with the other clutched at Daniel's chest.

"Come on."

Daniel turned; Justin gave him room, and as soon as they were face to face clamped Daniel behind the neck and pressed a hot, hard kiss on him. Daniel's palms slid down Justin's back from the blades of his shoulders to his waist; he let himself be kissed, kissed back, held his breath. In time, Justin drew away, all flashing dark eyes and parted, flushed lips he licked to dry them. Daniel reached for his wrists and guided Justin's hands to his own chest, put them to rest. With fingertips, he traced the outer edges of Justin's forehead, brushing back the spiral, skinny locks of hair that had fallen across it. His thumbs rested against Justin's cheeks and jaw, tilting him just so—gently—and his lips brushed soft against Justin's. Their noses touched. Daniel fitted their lips together precisely, nobody's whiskers scratching the tender skin around the other's mouth, holding Justin just tight enough that he could still get away if he wished to.

Justin revved up to speed in scant seconds, catching Daniel's lower lip between his teeth and tugging, scraping. He reached down for Daniel's hip, and then inward, palming his crotch, grunting an urgent, low sound as he ducked to press his teeth against Daniel's throat. Daniel let himself be jostled, bitten, pushed back against the edge of the kitchen sink, but soon made a hushing noise and let his own sliding hands settle at Justin's elbows, persuading him to soften until Daniel claimed his wrists and finally the backs of his hands. He lifted one to brush his lips across the palm, and in a gentle trail down the soft-skinned thumb.

Justin's shoulders tightened and he leaned away, eyes narrow with flickering suspicion. Pulling Daniel toward him by fingers folded into the waist of his jeans just behind his belt buckle, Justin backed through the kitchen and past the stove to the bedroom. All his top layers—t-shirt, thin pullover sweater, and zip-front sweatshirt—he worked up and off in one crisscross yank, then flung them at the floor. Assuming a languid sprawl on the bed, leant back on one elbow, he gave Daniel a dirty, narrow-eyed look.

"See what you want?" He stroked one nipple in a slow, tight circle with the tip of his middle finger.

"I see you," Daniel assured him. Standing by the corner of the bed, Daniel worked open his shirt buttons and drew the tails out from the waist of his jeans, but didn't undress.

"Try and get it," Justin challenged. Next should come growling and grasping, a struggle to claim and deny each other, red and purple marks on legs and chests. Teeth and nails. Holding too tight, refusing to be held.

Daniel planted a knee by Justin's hip and ran a palm down his shoulder and the length of his finely-muscled arm. Caught up his fingers and tangled them with his own as he settled onto his hip. Once in reach, Justin attacked Daniel's neck and collarbone with bared teeth, tried to rearrange their clasped hands to catch Daniel's wrist.

Voice low and rough with demand, Justin muttered, "I wanna—"

"Shh. . ." Daniel's nose brushed Justin's forehead, burrowed into his hair. His thumb brushed a soft rhythm against the back of Justin's hand, and he littered kisses wherever they landed—Justin's temple and the top edge of his ear, the blade of his cheekbone and between his eyebrows. Justin lay taut beside him, unmoving. Pulling away.

Daniel released his hand to grasp his chin, steady his jaw for a kiss on the mouth, and as their lips met Justin clutched at Daniel's waist, clawing up his low back with urgent fingers. He kissed hard and Daniel fell away from it, met his eyes and waited. Justin's expression was full of suspicion.

"What's up with you?" he asked.

"Please. Just let me," was all Daniel could think to reply, and kissed him again, gentle but without hesitation, and Justin's hand slid around to press his chest, holding firm against any closer advance.

It went on for long moments, in waves. Daniel stayed soft, seeking depths in which to settle; Justin thrashed and beat against it, demanding the comfort of confrontation.

"This isn't—" Justin protested, as Daniel skated his lips across Justin's narrow chest, nipple to nipple, tongue flicking out here and there, lips closing down in soft-sucking kisses.

"I know," Daniel replied, "Another time." and guided Justin's hands onto his own shoulders and back, rolling his torso to feel the soft palms and fingertips pressed too hard against his skin.

Soon they were naked, skin rippling with chill bumps visible between the shadows each cast across the other as they moved, and Daniel's slow motion caresses and open-mouthed explorations were met with snarled noises of frustration, Justin pushing and pulling, grappling in an attempt to arrange Daniel into the old familiar shapes. Eventually Daniel submitted to Justin astride his hips, a deep grind and gritted teeth, both of them holding their breath until they had to let it go in loud gusts. When Justin's hand moved to half-circle his neck, Daniel caught it and kissed it, held it curled by his open mouth.

Another urgent, "Come *on*," from Justin, who dropped beside him, his expression tangled-up pleasure and something like annoyance. Daniel half-rolled to meet him, coiled an arm around his back to pull him close, kissed him and hushed him and reached between their bodies, slowing the pace. He nodded, nuzzling, quick-kissing between gusts of breath, Justin handling him in kind. They discovered neutral ground and rocked up to meet each other there, cold feet on each other's ankles, the motion of their bodies digging up the quilts.

In the gathering moments after, Daniel petted and kissed; Justin scratched and bit. His fingernails kneaded at Daniel's chest like cat's claws. He nipped at Daniel's shivering shoulder. Daniel used two fingers to stroke Justin's hair into place by his temple, drew the border of his cheek and jaw, and the valley down the side of his throat.

"Hey."

Justin's eyes were closed; he tipped his chin lazily upward to indicate wakefulness.

"Sunny."

Justin hummed and moved closer, for warmth.

"Look at me a minute," Daniel said, still quiet. He wished for more light on Justin's face, to see all his fine details.

Justin's lashes lifted and his eyes were black coins, wide open.

"When it comes to it," Daniel began, quiet but firm, "If it does. I need to be able to find you."

The black eyes closed, then opened, stared, then looked away. He stopped scratching, hand resting high on Daniel's chest. Daniel could feel his own heartbeat against its heel, and waited for the promise.

Instead, what came from Justin was a mild dismissal. "Nah. . ."

"I don't want you to be alone," Daniel insisted, and when he closed his eyes he saw a broken body at wrong angles on the rocks, not gray-haired, not in a blue parka. He envisioned empty, never-laced black boots scattered in different directions. He opened his eyes to find Justin studying his face. Daniel covered Justin's hand with his own, curled his fingers in to make space beside his own chest, held on. Waited.

"I can't promise."

"Please. I'm not asking you not to. Just please let me find you."

Another long pause; Justin shivered, his feet fidgety. Daniel shifted his grip, clasping tighter to his hand, conveying his intention.

At last, Justin nodded gently. "Yuh, OK. All right," he acquiesced, and nodded more, confirming it to himself. They kissed to seal it, and then Justin murmured. "You know you don't have to."

"I know."

"I've said before I wouldn't wish it on anyone."

"You did it for him, though," Daniel said.

"I wanted to."

"I want to, too."

"You don't know how bad it can get."

"No. And I don't know if I'm up to it. But I want to." Daniel kissed him. "I'll try like hell."

Fourteen

The bedroom in Daniel's cottage had quickly become Justin's favorite place. The bed was deep and heaped up with quilts and blankets, though every morning the tip of his nose was cold. At night Daniel was there, sturdy and close, with a heavy arm draped over Justin's waist as Daniel nosed up close behind him. He'd determined his favorite pillow, claimed his side of the mattress, grown used to being awakened at a terrible hour by the alarm Daniel crossed the room to silence; Justin hummed at him and curled into the warmth Daniel left behind in the bed, then dropped easily back to sleep. And the best part of all was the dark.

A warm, cozy bed in a windowless room felt like the thing Justin had been waiting all his life for. Whether he woke at six a.m. or noon it was always the same, inviting him to close his eyes and drift back down. It was a place custom-made for perfect sleep. He thought that if it wasn't for having to get up and piss, and once in a while eat something, he would happily stay forever, laze the day away with the quilts tucked around his shoulders, the pillow cradling the side of his face; spend the nights getting off with Daniel, then holding on or being held, until Daniel had to go out to the light. He would stay and stay, eventually die there, fall to dust and sift himself down into the filling of the mattress.

He dreamed. A glass elevator in a skyscraper that went up and up forever until its doors opened onto a Christmas tree farm. He barely noticed the shift from sleep to waking. Turned his head and knew by the feel of his hair against the pillowslip he was two days late for washing it. Stretched, ducked down and sniffed; his armpits were sour and dank, not that he cared. Found his phone in the dark, on the nightstand where he'd left it face down and nearly dead. It was late. Daniel's work day was already nearly over. They'd eat lunch and then read. Justin wondered whether it was too soon to cut a Christmas tree. He wanted to go back to sleep, arched his back and groaned into the stretch.

He lay back and let his eyes close, held his phone loosely against his chest, telling himself to get up and go. When he looked at the time again, a half-hour had passed, and he forced himself up and out, bare feet on the cold floor shocking him into the real world. He still needed to turn on the lamp to find his way to the door.

The cottage was empty, Daniel and the dogs off at their day's routines. The bathroom mirror confirmed Justin's hair was lank and oily, and that his beard was several days overgrown. His breakfast was in the oven and he ate it despite the fact everything on the plate was ruined by several hours at 200 degrees—fried eggs gone rubbery and stiff, bacon strips shrunken and tough as jerky, toast that snapped like crackers. The coffeemaker had switched off; Justin poured his half of the pot into a saucepan and set it on the stovetop to warm it. He left it too long; it boiled and turned bitter but he drank it, took the mug with him to the sofa with his cigarettes.

The dogs came wriggling in through the dog door, followed by a whoosh of frigid air before it fell shut again. Tugger headed for the water bowl but Maggie came straight to the sofa and lay her chin on Justin's knee. He greeted her and gave her head a generous scratch while she thumped her tail against the sofa and coffee table. Daniel arrived shortly after, his cheeks above the top edge of his beard flushed pink, huffing in the way of people just in from the very-cold. He gave Justin a grin as he stomped snow from his boots.

"Chilly!"

"Looks it. What were you doing?"

Daniel shed his coat and hung it on its usual wall peg, bent down to loosen his boot laces.

"Washed all the glass in the lantern room. That took about an hour and a half. Then did some time in the shed, tuning up the snow blower. Threw balls for the dogs."

Justin rose and stepped over the coffee table to get to him, laid hands on his neck to sample the cold as they kissed. Leaned in, tilting shoulders and hips, to get as close to Daniel as he could.

"Slept in," Daniel observed. "Is there more coffee?"

"I burnt it; I'll make more." Justin released him and moved to the kitchen. "The bed's too comfortable. Plus, I didn't fall asleep for a long time."

It was easier with his back turned so he scooped the grounds at half-speed, didn't turn the faucet up all the way so the pot took longer to fill.

"Yeah, I thought maybe you were still awake," Daniel commented. A beat, and the sound of Daniel sinking into his armchair. "All right?" He sounded so tentative.

Justin shrugged even as he said, "Sure." He wasn't sure, and thought he might regret the promise he'd made. He was still at angles over the quiet, reverent way Daniel had had him the previous night. All Justin's rules were bending into a blur. "You're hungry for lunch?"

Daniel let out a mild groan and Justin knew the sounds of him picking up his paperback from the side table, sliding his bookmark out and then in, further back. "I'll get up and make something in a few minutes. Thanks."

Justin finished with the coffee, turned to lean against the counter to wait for it to drip through. "You do a Christmas tree, you said? I was dreaming about them."

"Oh, yeah?" Daniel's eyebrows rose and he set the book in his lap while he flashed Justin a grin. "We could cut one in the next couple days. You're hanging around a while?"

"Headshrinker, day after next."

"Tomorrow then?"

"Awesome."

They had to walk quite a ways into the woods to find a tree that suited them; short-needled, higher than it was wide, tapering to a narrow top, just slightly taller than they were so it wouldn't bend at the ceiling. Their breath whooshed out in great swathes of steam, dragon-like, as they carried it back to the cottage, Daniel with his scarf lashed to the trunk to make a handle, Justin's hand wrapped around the narrowest part of the trunk near its top. The dogs trotted along beside them, Tugger looking proud of himself as if he'd felled the tree himself, Mags occasionally distracted by a squirrel or bird she chased for a few yards to show it who was in charge, then loping back to her place at Justin's right side.

Daniel went to the shed where he had a stand for the tree, while Justin waited in the front yard, smoking a cigarette and flexing fingers stiffened from curling around the tree's trunk. He scanned the seaward horizon, mostly bright blue with wispy, horizontal clouds far out over the ocean, then cast a glance back toward the shed to find Daniel on his way back carrying an old green-painted metal stand and a old-style wooden toolbox that resembled a basket. His walk was upright, purposeful; he was so thrillingly big and handsome and hairy-chested. A growl gathered low in Justin's belly, and he fed it hot smoke with a deep, last drag from his cigarette. Justin's first impressions of Daniel had been of a cautiously guarded man, confident in his abilities to make and do, but inept at—or at least unsure about—personal interaction. What a gutting-up it must have taken for him to solicit Justin's promise not to disappear. Justin blinked the wind out of his eyes.

They'd cut the tree down with a chainsaw, but Daniel used an old, sturdy-looking wood handled saw to take a fresh slice off the bottom of the tree's trunk, ensuring a clean cut so it could take up water. It took all four of their hands to get the stand attached by use of four long screws turned until they just penetrated the trunk. Together they lifted the tree upright and shook off the clinging snow, then carried it inside. It just barely fit between the end of the sofa and the bookshelf-covered wall by the bedroom door, and they'd estimated the height accurately—there were a few inches' clearance above its upright top branch.

"What do you put on it?" Justin asked.

"I have a box of stuff I bought a couple years ago. The usual."

Justin fished the empty hard pack from a pocket of his coat, set it high up in the branches, the crowning star. Daniel gave him a broad smile, half-laughed.

"That's about perfect," he said.

Once they'd trimmed the tree with colored lights and metallic-plastic balls, ropes of gold beads and slender glass icicles that looked so real Justin had to fight his urge to snap them in half, they sat back to admire their work, smoking cigarettes and giving the dogs a sharp talking-to any time their sniffing curiosity threatened to get out of hand. Daniel really did have stockings for the dogs; Justin hung them from the bookshelves with their hanging-loops tucked under the spines of thick hardback books.

Justin looked hard at the glowing tip of the cigarette between his fingers, watched the smoke streaming upward from it. "So," he said, never shifting his gaze, "You're my man now?" He could feel Daniel looking at him, and after a moment couldn't help but steal a glance. Daniel's smile was a soft small curve, and once their eyes met, he gave a subtle nod.

"And you're mine. That's how it works, I think. You probably remember better than I do."

"So now it's all soft kisses and whispering, and all that shit?"

"No," Daniel replied plainly. "Did you hate it?"

"No." Justin blew out smoke, then licked his lips. "You wanna wrestle?" He stubbed out the butt of the cigarette, leaned forward, grinning mischief.

Daniel's response was to grab him hard by the chin to turn his head into a rough kiss.

With a dirty smile, Daniel challenged, "What do you think?"

A cool, heavy hand stroked downward from his shoulder, and Daniel's low, crunchy voice said, "Time to wake up, Sunny." Justin felt the sleep sloughing off him, twisted to dig a fresh burrow closer to Daniel, curving around his back as he sat on the edge of the bed. "What time's your appointment? You should wake up." Justin thrust out his hand from beneath the blankets, searching for Daniel's thigh, to brush and squeeze. Daniel caught him and pulled Justin's hand to his mouth, kissed then gently bit the tip of his little finger.

Justin moaned a hum. "Lie down and sleep with me."

"Don't tempt me. Sooner you go, sooner you can come back."

Justin got his arms around Daniel, hung on with one hand behind his neck, and let his weight pull them both down. Daniel laughed his surrender, hands beneath the covers, cool and dry against Justin's bare skin. In no time they were sucking kisses onto each other's necks, and Justin relished the rub of Daniel's jeans against his naked legs, dug his hands up under Daniel's sweater and t-shirt to find the fuzz on his belly, quivering beneath his pinching, gliding fingers. Daniel finished him by hand, urging him on in a muttering voice, until Justin spurted across his fingers and onto his denim-clad thigh; Justin used the ruse of cleaning up his mess to duck and wriggle himself into place, opened Daniel's fly and licked wetly over the head of Daniel's prick until he gave up in kind, filling Justin's mouth with heat and salt, thick wet that Justin gulped down to get rid of it.

Wriggle-stretching until they were face to face, Justin felt spent and lazy, and allowed his eyes to close as he dug in his forehead below Daniel's bearded chin.

"Come on now," Daniel quietly urged, stroking Justin's arm as if he might let him out of it after all. "At least get up and have a smoke. Coffee." He tugged Justin's wrist, pulled on his fingers. "There's biscuits for breakfast, come on."

Justin groaned a final protest but let Daniel guide him up to sitting. Daniel found Justin's hoodie and longjohn pants on the floor and dropped them across his legs.

"Time's it?" Justin asked as he wrestled himself into the shirt.

"Quarter to eight. Will you make it?"

Justin hummed affirmation. He was sick of the headshrinker, the pharmacy runs, the morning meds. It was so much more pleasant to drag Daniel back to bed, read on the sofa, eat pie after supper. And of course there was the house. When he was in it, what choice did he have but to think about it? He'd meant to open it, season after season, but never had. Probably never would. His promise haunted him; his gut roiled resentment at Gabriel for having extracted it from him, knowing Justin, knowing the inn was Gabriel's dream alone and Justin had only been there out of love for his husband. Had Gabriel loved him as much, he'd never have trapped him in the house.

The smell of brown gravy warming on the stove—and his mouth's watery response to it—drove him out of bed to the kitchen at last, where Daniel was pouring them coffee and fixing Justin's plate: biscuits and gravy, sausage hash with two buttery fried eggs on top. Daniel kissed Justin's hair as he set the food down before him. He took his usual chair, drew out his phone from the breast pocket of his blue flannel shirt.

"Snow coming," he reported. "Heavy and steady for at least twelve hours, starting around noon."

Through a mouthful of sopping crumbs, Justin said, "I'll have to race it back here."

"You might," Daniel agreed. "Looks pretty ugly."

"Maybe we'll get stuck in the watch room again," Justin grinned, mugging mischief.

Daniel looked knowing, and replied, "I wouldn't mind."

The headshrinker wanted him to talk; Justin just wanted to get out. She said his affect was different, low-energy. He said he was tired—which was not a lie—but did not elaborate that he was always tired even after nine, eleven, thirteen hours' sleep. He did not tell her about the emails and texts from the woman who wanted to buy the house, because if he talked about them he'd have to stop ignoring them and do something. Think about it. Talk about it. Respond. He did not tell her about Daniel, now officially his man. He'd keep that card to play later, as evidence of his contentment, proof everything was fine and getting better. She asked him if things were coming up for him as they always did midwinter, about Gabriel at the end—did he feel more distance from it? Was it less affecting than last year? Justin did not want to admit he missed him less. He did not want to give up his grief, the dark velvet ditch in which he could wallow. She noticed he was impatient to leave, sensed he was distracted, would let him go if they weren't going to get any productive work done. Scheduled the next one—maybe it's a good idea to meet weekly until after the first of the year—and Justin mumbled half-apologies as he left.

Outside, the snow had started, coming down fast in huge puffy lumps, at an angle. He really would be racing the storm. His car slipped and floated disconcertingly as he drove to the inn; he'd have to take the Suburban back out to the cove, or else risk going off the road. Once inside, he stomped snow off his boots and left them by the glass doors in the dining room. In the kitchen an aroma of coffee lingered, and Lia's rice cooker steamed away on the counter. There was no sign of Lia, though, and the coffee carafe was in the sink, filled with suds. He'd stop at the Coffee Pot in Parker Village and grab a cup on his way back, maybe pick up a pie and some supper to take; with the storm, Daniel would surely rather tend the light than cook a meal. Justin half-hoped they might spend the night up the tower, passing time in the watch room, keeping eyes on the storm.

Once upstairs he stopped in the little laundry room and fished from his bag what clothes he had bothered to bring back, dropped them into an empty basket, lying to himself he'd get to it eventually. In his bedroom, his ashtrays and trash had been emptied but his bed remained rumpled and ripe. The bathroom sink was free of toothpaste blobs, and the toilet seat was down. He felt guilty rather than intruded upon, wished he'd remembered to lock his door to save Lia the work.

"Lia?" He hung out the bedroom door by one hand wrapped halfway around the jamb. "*Está nevando.* Do you need anything?" He waited for a reply but got none. A glance through the window lit a fire under him; he could barely see the barn through a thick haze of fast-falling snow. Near-empty pill bottles rattled in the bottom of his bag as he shoved in fresh underwear, socks, longjohns, and two black, hooded pullovers. He brushed his teeth and as he spit into the sink, planting fresh blobs of foam onto the clean surface of the basin, Lia called to him from the stairwell.

"Shustin, *você está em casa?*"

"Hang on, I'm coming out. I'm only here for a minute."

She had a plastic bag from the US Vets' thrift store out on Wood Road, and her hair glittered where the snow had melted onto it.

"You shouldn't drive in this. *Neve*. Dangerous. *Perigoso*." He shook his head at her, miming a steering wheel, and she waved him off with a scoffing expression.

"Letter for you," she told him. "Downstair."

"Thanks. I'll get it on my way out."

"No drive, Shustin," she scolded. "*Perigoso*."

"Nah, I'm OK."

"You amigo. Don-yell." She quirked up a wrinkly smile that made him prickle all over, thinking of Daniel, more than his friend.

Justin nodded, avoiding her gaze.

"Be happy," she told him. "He's good?"

He nodded again. "He's a good guy," he affirmed. "Too good for me, probably, but I'm not gonna point it out; he'll figure it out sooner or later."

She gave him another smile, then shook her finger at him. "No drive," she intoned. Justin only nodded, eye-rolling and shrugging right along with it, waving her away. He could drive in snow; he'd been doing it all his life.

Stopping at the pharmacy and for coffee, then on my way.

TXT from Daniel: Call me when you get on 18 and I'll start plowing my road.

Will do.

Daniel had old-fashioned manners, always trying to make Justin comfortable, make things easier for him. The thermos of coffee he always made sure Justin took with him as he drove away from the cove. The breakfast plates left to warm in the oven. Clearing the road even though Justin's truck had its own plow. He was undemanding but open to receive Justin's jokes, his complaints, the rough way he wanted him. It seemed all right with him that Justin was hibernating his way through the winter in Daniel's deep bed, in the welcoming darkness of his windowless bedroom. All of it made Justin hectic to get back to him, to shake Daniel in his grip, to kiss his lips raw amid Daniel's ginger-blond whiskers, to sit together not touching while they read, to help him chop and mend and tinker all around the light station.

Thinking about you.

TXT from Daniel: That so? Maggie's lying on the couch waiting for you. Misses you.

Not you, though?

TXT from Daniel: No, not me.

Justin smiled and started out of his room, being sure to lock the door to spare Lia any further sense of obligation about cleaning it up.

Outside, he tossed his bag across the interior of the Suburban, reached in to start it so it would warm up while he brushed off the snow. The key turned but nothing happened. Justin cursed and took the driver's seat, glanced at the ignition and tried again. Nothing.

Forty-five minutes later, he'd tried jump-starting the truck with his car, to no avail. He went into the house for soda, poured it over the connectors to burn the rust off them, and still had no luck. Either the battery was completely dead, or there was a connection problem in the engine and the thing would have to be towed into town for repair.

My fucking truck won't start. No luck with a jump.

Justin was annoyed at himself for never having put snow tires on his car; he didn't have chains to fit it, either. Lia had decent tires on her car but he couldn't borrow it and leave her stranded, not knowing when he'd be back.

TXT from Daniel: Bad battery?

That or the starter.

Justin shifted his bag from the passenger seat of the truck into the car, and got in, started it up.

I'll just take my car, go easy.

TXT from Daniel: Don't. It's crazy out there. Storm ends tonight. Come tomorrow when the roads are clear.

I'll be the only one on the road. No problem.

TXT from Daniel: Please don't.

Justin sat back and bit his lip.

I've been thinking all day about sex in the watch room, though.

TXT from Daniel: Ha! If that's what you want, we can do that any time. Stay where you are tonight.

What are you, worried about me skidding into a tree and then freezing to death?

TXT from Daniel: Well, no, I'M not worried, but Mags is pacing the floor.

Tell her I'll see her tomorrow, I guess.

TXT from Daniel: Be safe.

Justin hadn't lied to Lia, putting a shine on Daniel by saying he was too good. He really was a good man, and he understood Justin in a way no one— not even Gabriel, *especially* not Gabriel—really ever had. The mere fact Daniel accepted Justin as someone bound to die, hadn't tried to talk him out of it or brush it away as an over-dramatic play for attention, was proof he'd chosen the right man to spend the end of his life with. Daniel was so good, in fact, Justin sometimes even wished he wasn't dying.

Fifteen

By mid-afternoon, the storm had been blowing for over four hours—Daniel reckoned the snowfall at over an inch an hour—and his internet cable had sunk under the weight of heavy, sopping snow until it detached from the corner of the cottage. Thus reminded, he plugged in his phone and tablet to charge in case the electricity went, too, then gassed up the generator, and set out extra batteries for the radios and flashlights. There was an old-style, paper log book on the shelf over his desk, the last entry into which had been penned the previous March during a four-day blackout when his only light was from the tower, thanks to its government-funded, solar-powered generator. Daniel regretted his failure to warn Justin he could fall out of contact, though given Justin's dogged insistence he could drive through a blizzard on summer tires, Daniel figured he'd be on his way back to the cove as soon as the snow let up, overnight or early the following day. The cable going down wouldn't be a long enough silence for Justin to miss him, or to worry—Daniel's real fear was that Justin might assume he was being purposely ignored.

The dogs needed persuading when time came for the evening's last trip outside; Daniel backed down the walkway, calling to them in more and more coddling tones, until at last they picked their steps carefully into the yard and did as they must. He couldn't persuade them to stop inside the door and so had to chase them around the cottage with a rag to dry their paws, then swipe it with the toe of his boot over the many wet smears they'd left on the floor.

"Even Justin knows to wipe his feet," he scolded them. "And he's only been coming here a couple months." The two followed each other around the cottage, room to room, unsettled and bristly because of the storm, double- and triple-checking that all was as it should be. Daniel took a last look out the window to check on the light—still displaying its *No Safe Harbor* pattern—then lifted his dinner dishes from the drying rack and put them away, straightened the dish towel hanging from the oven door. As he latched he dog door, he allowed the dogs one more nervous round of the bath, bedroom, parlor, and kitchen, before finally huffing, "That's enough, now. Bed."

Once they settled on their pillows by the stove, he squatted down to pet and scratch them a while, eventually sinking from a crouch to a seat on the floor, enjoying the happy way they turned over and sighed under his hands, their paws folding limply, one last shake of their ears before resting their heads.

He checked his phone for texts, found none.

Hope to see you tomorrow. Going to bed now. Night.

Once he'd brushed his teeth, changed his clothes, and slid under the thick stack of quilts on his bed—the sheets freezing cold—he made a final check.

TXT from Justin: I'm going to have to get the truck towed to the shop.
If the roads are clear, I'll be out your way early as possible.
Sleep good.
x

Daniel dedicated most of the next day to clearing snow. He gave the snow blower some love, filling the gas tank and greasing the moving parts, before muttering a few hopeful words that it would start for him, and yanking the cord. He cleared a wide path from the front yard to his truck, shoveled around its tires, then threw the snow off the front and back walks, and the path to the light. Lunch was two sandwiches, three handfuls of chips, and a beer, then he was back at it, plowing an area large enough for both his and Justin's trucks to park and turn around, then continuing up his road. By the time he made it out to Route 18, and turned around for the final pass in the direction of the cove, he had only about forty minutes before the light must be attended.

Daniel lingered in the lantern room, watching the broken coins of light shimmer against the walls as the lamp turned, listening for anything unusual in the sound of the motor. Eventually he got out his phone and took a photo through the window of the cliff face, wind-driven snow stuck to it in diagonal slashes, looking like a badly frosted cake. He sent it to Justin.

This passes for pretty at the moment, I think.
Did you get the truck out to the garage?

Road's plowed and ready when you are.

Daniel wondered if he sounded needy, was so out of practice with these kinds of interactions—*"You're my man now?"*—that he couldn't even gauge it. He was who he was, and after ten years alone at the light station, he didn't imagine it would even be possible for him to be any other way, at least not convincingly or for very long. He'd just be honest—maybe only say every third or fourth thing that came to mind, just in case—and let it lay wherever it fell.

He was already turning over breaded chicken cutlets in a skillet coated with shimmering oil by the time he heard the notification sound from his phone.

TXT from Justin: The guy over there is tied up with plowing jobs, said he can get out here tomorrow.

By the time I heard from him I was already too lazy to make it out your way.

No one's plowed us out, either. Nice time for the truck to go. :-/

Daniel removed his chicken to a plate covered with a towel, and peeked in the oven to see if the frozen fries were the right color yet.

I can come out tomorrow and plow, if you need it.

Once he'd served himself supper and was partway through it, Justin replied.

TXT from Justin: You know I always need you to plow me.

;-D

Oh but you mean the snow???

Several thoughts crossed Daniel's mind all at once; he chose the least graphic one.

Can I call you in a little while? When I go to bed.

TXT from Justin: You better.

"You made it, eh?" Daniel smiled, walking out to meet him as he swung down from the seat of his truck.

"Naw, easy. Clear sailing all the way."

Daniel led the way to the side of the house where the cable line had fallen, pointed out the connectors. The line lay half-buried in the trench it had made for itself, between the house and the shed, sloping up from the ground to the nearest utility pole. Daniel left the man to his work, with an offer of coffee and an invitation to come inside and grab Daniel if he needed anything. Once the dogs had greeted the cable guy briefly, Daniel called them down the yard for a ballgame. Their distaste for the snow was not as great as their love for a fetch, so they romped through it, making trenches of their own, in crazy zig-zag patterns. The snow stuck in clumps to the hair of their legs and bellies.

The work was done in under an hour, and Daniel threw the guy a wave as he left. Checking the weather reports and maritime schedule on his laptop eased a creeping tension in his shoulders Daniel hadn't noticed was there. The paper log book was an interesting diversion, but he was glad to be able to type the morning's entry—a bit later than he normally would have, he'd saved it—and submit it online. Once he'd caught up on the world—news headlines, hockey scores, and an email from the Regional Director with a tentative date for the property inspectors—Daniel stripped and remade the bed with clean sheets. The previous night's call to Justin had been just as he'd hoped—dirty talk while they both jerked off, then some sighs and whispers about missing each other, *wish you were here so I could kiss you good night. . .but, so, good night. Sleep good.* It was past time for him to change the bed; they'd been sleeping and having sex in the same smelly sheets for weeks. A pair of Justin's thermal pants fell out onto the floor from where they'd been stuck between the mattress and quilts.

Gonna go into Parker to the laundromat. Can I come out your way?

Daniel brought his basket of laundry—topped with Justin's thermals— to leave by the door, then went into his desk drawer for a pad and pen to make a grocery and supply list.

TXT from Justin: Thought you did your wash in a bucket or something? Just bring it here. I'll let you do stuff to me while it washes.

Daniel laughed, and flushed hot with want. Lately that happened a lot; he'd always had urges, looked at porn, did what was necessary to ensure a decent night's sleep. But the burning surge in his gut and chest at the thought of being close to Justin was, if not entirely new, unfamiliar after many years of disuse.

Yeah? What kind of stuff?

TXT from Justin: Whatever you want. What DO you want?

Daniel sucked his teeth.

If we start up with this now, texting, I'll never make it out the door.

TXT from Justin: Come over then. Drive fast.

I'll drive like hell, as a matter of fact.

Forty minutes later, Daniel and his basket of laundry were crossing the town line into Six Rivers, though by all legal and safe standards it should have taken him closer to an hour.

Be there in ten minutes.

TXT from Justin: Don't text and drive. But hurry up.

What did Daniel want to do? Hold him and smooth his dark eyebrows into place. Feel his solid, narrow back pressed close to Daniel's chest, their hips hinged at the same point with Daniel's knee pushing between Justin's thighs. Touch him gently, teasing, everywhere, until his hips bumped up and back and he made frustrated sounds and reached behind to get a grip on Daniel's thigh or forearm. Smell the back of his neck. Kiss him there. Wrap arms around him, hands on his belly and chest to feel him breathing. Slick up and stroke him, not to make him shout but to feel him shiver and then soften, hear that delicious hum as he settled.

Within half an hour he was stripping off his socks, leaving them inside-out on the floor of Justin's steamy bathroom, then dropping his layers of work pants and long johns and stepping into the too-hot shower, kissing Justin through a smile of relief at just being near him. They went on kissing—biting—as they took each other in hand, the water too quickly rinsing away the suds they used to ease the way.

"Missed you," Daniel told him, licking beads of metallic-tasting warm water off Justin's temple, kissing it off his cheek.

"Mm, you too," Justin murmured, braced himself, hanging onto the shower door handle and Daniel's shoulder, bent impossibly, closed his eyes against the rivulets of water running into them and licked a flutter around the crown of Daniel's prick, then again, just that—after days apart—enough to set him off. Daniel's knees softened and his groan echoed; Justin leaned up hard against him, chest to chest, supporting him by pinning him backward against the wall. Daniel's hand curved around Justin's as he stroked himself light and quick. In no time, Justin was there, too, and they both shivered, and laughed satisfaction, kissing open-mouthed.

"You're coming back with me," Daniel asked without asking, as they did their own and each other's final soapy once-overs, trading places now and then, adjusting the showerhead to reach them both.

Justin turned off the water and dropped his hands backwards over his head, gathering the ends of his hair to squeeze out a small torrent, then opening the door to reach for towels folded in a basket on the floor near their discarded clothes. Daniel accepted a proffered one—clean, soft, hotel towels no doubt arranged there in the basket by Justin's cousin the housekeeper—and wrapped it around his waist.

From under the hood of another Justin replied, "I want to."

"Good."

Once they'd dressed and lit cigarettes they assumed their places on Justin's bed with pillows tucked behind their backs, legs extended with ankles crossed and the ashtray on the mattress between them.

"What do you want for Christmas?" Justin asked, cigarette between his teeth bobbing as he spoke, leaning to draw the wad of blankets over their bare feet.

Daniel shrugged. "Peace on earth, good will toward men? I don't know. Nothing. I'm getting the dogs some rawhides. Yogurt."

"You can get me a six-pack," Justin grinned.

"Easy enough," Daniel replied. "I knew there was something about you I liked."

"I'll get you some porn."

"Make me some," Daniel suggested.

"On my phone? Text it to you?"

"Yeah. Please."

"I'll get right on it."

Daniel nodded, and Justin leaned over to crush his cigarette butt in the ashtray, nuzzled in to press a kiss against the side of Daniel's throat. Stretching upright once more, twisting shoulders to stretch his spine, he said, "I haven't told my shrink about you."

Daniel looked at him, raised his eyebrows. "No?"

"She thinks I'm depressed."

Daniel thought the same, but kept his mouth shut. Justin rose from the bed and got busy gathering clothes to take to the light station. He went through his usual sorting ritual of shaking and sniffing, dumping some into a pile on the floor and the select few onto the foot of the bed. Daniel wondered why, with a laundry room not a dozen steps from his bedroom door, Justin hadn't washed anything in the intervening weeks, but supposed anyone not required to do his laundry in a tub outdoors likely took such convenience for granted.

Without elaborating further on his therapist's opinions of his emotional state, Justin said, "I got a letter from that woman. Well, from a lawyer. An offer to buy the house—or—the business. Fourteen pages."

"That's a hell of a letter," Daniel commented, and put out his cigarette.

"A contract, really. Pretty fucking forward, I thought. I usually like having my asshole at least tickled a little before I bend over, you know?"

"Oh, I know," Daniel smirked. "Same here. What are you gonna do, y'think?"

"I don't know. Say no, I guess. I have to. I promised Gabriel I'd keep the house. Maybe I'll open it this year."

Daniel only nodded, as it was not his place to weigh in. Something occurred to him, and before he thought to rephrase it, he asked, "Where's he buried? Or—"

"Half his ashes I sent to his parents. The rest are downstairs, next to the fireplace." Justin shoved balled-up clothes into his bag, then glanced at his phone. "Time to head back?"

Daniel agreed, and rose to dress, begging a kiss from Justin as he passed—one which was readily granted. Daniel growled, grinning, and gave Justin's backside a rough grope before moving on.

They were nearly out the back door when Daniel paused, head tilted toward a not-quite-right noise somewhere to his left.

"You hear water running?"

Justin's face rumpled and he made for the kitchen's swinging door. Daniel dropped Justin's bag there by the sliders and trailed him; as his hand hit the door, pushing inward, he heard Justin groan, "Oh, man. . . Dammit!"

Water poured from the ceiling in a narrow but steady stream, and a shallow puddle had already spread itself across half the kitchen floor.

"Should I check upstairs?" Daniel offered instantly.

"Nah, it's the roof; there's nothing above this room. I knew it was probably ready to go but. . .fuck."

"Do you have a roof rake? Maybe we can get some of the snow off before it's all melted."

"I don't even know. Maybe in the shed behind the barn," he looked frantic and furious, opening and shutting cabinet doors. "Are there no fucking rags in here? Or a bucket? Jeezis. Lia! *Preciso de uma. . .fucking. . .tigela!* Lia!"

"Is it locked? The shed?"

"Yeah," Justin answered, and shoved an oversized ceramic mixing bowl under the leak, which splashed down over his forearms. "That last drawer on the right, there's a set of keys in it somewhere."

Daniel found the right drawer, and three keys on a plastic bottle-opening key chain. "You all right here?" he asked. "What can I do?"

"Yeah, no. Nothing. *Lia!*"

"Shush, shush," Lia scolded as she entered. "Ay, no."

149

"I need a bucket," Justin told her. "Towels and a mop." She bustled off, clicking her tongue.

"It's only water," Daniel said, trying to reassure Justin, who looked set to unravel. "It'll be all right."

"Yeah, I know," Justin grimaced, and threw a huge wad of paper towels down at the edge of the puddle. He muttered, "This fucking house," and shook his head, frowning, his expression frustrated and forlorn.

Outside, Daniel fitted the key into the shed's padlock and dragged the door open, blinking to adjust to the darkness inside. He found the usual gardening machines—lawn mower, chainsaw, seed-spreader, wheelbarrow— and a jumble of handles leaning up against the right-hand wall: rakes and spades, bulb planters, and a long-arm manual saw rusted beyond redemption. Four plastic snow shovels, but no roof rake. A wooden ladder hung from hooks in the roof beam, so Daniel liberated it, took the sturdiest-looking snow shovel, and carried both toward the house. He could see from outside roughly where the leak in the roof would be, aimed himself toward it, and leaned well over to start clearing the heavy, semi-melted snow, as far as he could reach without climbing onto the roof.

After a few minutes and about two square yards of progress, Justin emerged onto the wooden deck and said, "You have to go if you're going to get back in time for the light."

Daniel humphed agreement and hefted a shovel-load of snow over his shoulder. "You're coming," he reminded.

"I can't leave the mess," Justin said. "And I should get a guy out to patch it before we get another storm. The ceiling in there is like wet newspaper; I think it might fall in, and I'm not going to make Lia clean that up."

"I think Oggert Brothers does roofing," Daniel offered, and scraped one last clump of snow off the roof before starting to descend the ladder. "You know them?"

Justin scrubbed both his hands hard over his face and nodded into his palms. His shoulders were sloped. "I hate this kind of stuff," he said.

Daniel was torn. He glanced at the sky but was afraid to look at his wristwatch. "Fuck, Sunny, I'd stay if I could."

"It's all right. I still have to get the truck towed; I'll do it all at once and then come out by you. If they can come right away to do the patch, I'll be there tomorrow."

Daniel had by then mounted the wooden steps and put his arms around Justin, who was tight-wound and stiff, but after a moment he dropped his chin onto Daniel's shoulder and his back softened a bit as Daniel drew him close.

"It's just a hassle," Daniel reassured. "These things happen with old houses, all the time."

Justin nodded and drew back. "Really, you need to get on the road."

"Text me later, let me know how you make out."

"Yuh, I will."

Daniel rifled in his coat and pants pockets for phone, keys, and cigarettes. "All right. See you tomorrow, then."

Justin didn't walk him to his truck, only lingered on the deck and threw him a wave as Daniel rolled out of the parking area. An hour later Daniel was sprinting up the path to the tower, double-timed up the steps and made it to the switch just as the sun dipped below the mark on the window. As the optic began to spin, Daniel sank hard against the lantern room wall, breath heaving as he tried to catch it. His heart pounded, from the stress of the drive—racing the setting of the sun—and the exertion of taking the tower steps two at a time. Partly, too, from the near-terror of almost missing his deadline. He had but one thing in the world he absolutely must do, and never once in ten years had he failed to do it. Though he knew it was illogical to think so, he did feel the light needed him. He knew himself to be unworthy of trust from any person, but his light had always trusted him to keep the schedule, know the patterns, manage and repair. He'd almost missed it; the feeling was hateful. No more near-misses—and for what?—sex in the shower and a place to do his laundry indoors.

Daniel slapped his own face. "Handle it," he ordered himself, then went down to feed the dogs.

Justin did not text that night, or the next morning. Daniel had folded his basket of laundry and tucked his clothes into their drawers, cooked himself a frozen burger patty on a gluey supermarket roll and heated up baked beans from a can for his supper, then read for a while in his armchair. After breakfast and attending to the light, he threw balls for the dogs then combed the snow out of their coats. He spent nearly an hour assembling a soup in the crock of a slow-cooker and set it to simmer. He updated the log, ordered his phone to play him one of his old favorite albums, and resumed his place in his armchair with his book.

How'd you make out with the roofer? he texted at last, as it neared dusk. The cottage seemed more snug for the scents of bay and onion bubbling away in a bath of broth he'd brewed up from chicken carcasses a few weeks previous, and frozen in quantities suited to soup-for-one—or two—with leftovers to last a few days. He'd already switched on the light, then heated the oven to toast a loaf of crusty bread, and was ladling soup into a wide, shallow bowl by the time Justin at last sent a reply.

TXT from Justin: They're swamped; can't make it until tomorrow afternoon. The guys from the garage finally took the truck, though. Agreed with me it's probably the starter. So there goes $275.

Is the roof still leaking? Did you get it cleaned up?

TXT from Justin: It's fine. I just wish I was in bed with you. For days and days.

Daniel's chest twinged. It might be about sex, but he doubted it. Justin had lately been like a hibernating bear in the cave of Daniel's bedroom, reluctant to leave the shelter of the stacked quilts regardless of what enticements Daniel offered. He cast a glance at the sofa, where Maggie curled on the left cushion, a habit she'd picked up when her crush Justin chose the center cushion as his own favored seat; the Christmas tree stood by, crowned with the empty blue-and-white cigarette box Justin had placed among its topmost branches.

He had a sudden urge to ask Justin if he'd been taking his meds, though of course it was none of his business. Instead:

That sounds so good. I'll keep it warm for you til you come back. You never told me what you want for Christmas.

TXT from Justin: Do you know anyone I could hire to burn down the house? After a few long moments, he added, *Just kidding.* Then, *Lia made me supper so I'd better go down and eat some of it.*

Call me later, maybe.

After he'd cleaned up the kitchen, Daniel latched the dog door and doused all the lights, climbed into bed with yet another book, read for just a few minutes before he fell asleep. Justin never called.

A few days later, Daniel was hanging a bird feeder he'd assembled in slapdash, don't-really-know-what-I'm-doing fashion from scrap wood stored in a barrel in the shed, when he heard the unmistakable rumble of a diesel truck with a manual transmission coming up his road. Spurred to hurry, he twisted the hanging wire around a leafless maple branch, then backed down the ladder. The bag of seed leaned plumply against the tree's biggest visible root. Daniel squinted up the road until the truck came into view—an unfamiliar, dark green pickup with neither plow nor roof-mounted lights. The dogs raced out to investigate, and he gave a command to settle them down before either barked, then summoned them to his side. They came, though reluctantly, but kept eyes on the interloping vehicle.

Eventually the truck came to stop parked behind his own, and the National Parks logo on its door became visible when the driver slowly pushed it open. Two men emerged, waving and calling out greetings as Daniel met them in the middle, where they shook hands.

"Daniel Howard?"

"Course."

"I'm Ben Gideon from the regional office, deputy to Leslie Rhodes, who I think has written you a couple of times? This is Gil Halliday with Nashua Engineering." Halliday had a tape measure on his belt, three pens just visible in his shirt pocket beneath a fleece vest halfway zipped, and a metal clipboard, folded shut.

"All right," Daniel said, feeling snuck-up-on and suspicious. The dogs waited to be introduced, but were not, so only stayed at Daniel's side, alert to any further untoward behavior by the ambush visitors.

"Sorry to bother you, but Gil's up from New York and we thought since the weather was good we'd swing up here for a look, do some sketches and make a few notes."

Daniel's torso felt hollow and his fingers tingled; he shoved his hands into his pants' pockets in case they were trembling. "The hearings aren't until next month, I thought?"

"No, of course. Still negotiating, nothing's final," the deputy director said, falsely reassuring, sounding as if he didn't mind one way or the other what happened to the light station, but also as if he knew Daniel was to be handled with care. "But you never know, with the storms we've been having, and it's always good to have concrete info. Can't really get an exact sense of the place with just satellite photos and online maps."

Daniel nodded and flicked his gaze at the white-gray sky. "Well, can I get you some coffee? I was about to make a fresh pot."

Halliday stepped forward then, a guy in his late twenties with a careful haircut and leather oxfords that gave him up as someone from Away. Not to be trusted, in any case, and Daniel's hand itched in a different way, and he drew in a long breath through his nostrils.

"Just had some coffee in the car on the way out—up?—" Halliday glanced from Daniel to Gideon, looking for his audience reaction before finishing. "So, I'll pass on that, but I could use the men's room."

Daniel led them into the cottage, made a pot of coffee despite no one wanting it—including himself—just for something to occupy his shaking hands. Gideon busied himself with his phone, standing just inside the front door, as Daniel had not invited him to sit down. After a moment, Gideon asked distractedly, "So I guess we'll be seeing you up at the regional office? Gonna get a desk up there?"

Daniel's jaw ached, and he purposefully unclenched his teeth.

"Not that I know of," he said.

"No? Moving on, then."

Daniel shook his head, forcing a frown-smile. "Dunno. No one's talked to me. You've heard something?"

Gideon looked uncomfortable, faked his own smile. "Not at all. I know they wouldn't put you out of a job without a good effort to reassign you."

Daniel could hear what was left unsaid: you, *that Daniel Howard*, a special case.

Halliday rejoined them, picked up his metal clipboard from the edge of Daniel's desk and wrenched it open. "Coffee smells good," he commented.

Daniel's hand twitched toward the cupboard door to fetch down a mug before he remembered they were intruders, not guests, and caught himself. With arms crossed over his chest, he leaned back against the counter.

Halliday asked some questions about the generator, whether the power lines were reliable—lose power a lot in storms?—whether Daniel knew the age of the lamp's motor, if the solar panels were in good shape. Scribbling notes on his pad, he said to Gideon, "And the state will keep up maintenance on the road."

Daniel interjected, "The state doesn't maintain it; I do."

Halliday frowned. Gideon offered, "I'll have to double check whether there's a line item for that. May have to negotiate with the government, offer some incentive. Paving and snow removal?"

"Yeah, just the minimum, in case of an emergency repair." The two were speaking to each other as if Daniel wasn't there, and with each passing second he felt more and more as if he wasn't. Tugboat came and sat by his feet, looking up at him, slow-motion thumping his tail on the floor. Halliday said, "This building can house the batteries, maybe drop a wall here and have those on one side and the other for the inverter and controller. Hardwire it all here and run lines to the tower."

The idea of power cables dangling from the lighthouse made Daniel's stomach turn. They were talking about turning his cottage into a shed for an electrical transformer. He half-expected them to start yanking books off the shelves and flinging them to the floor, ripping doors off hinges, building their wall and trapping him in a corner.

"Gonna have to ask you guys to leave," Daniel said brusquely, probably too loud, and puffed himself up to full size.

They both turned toward him, twisting at the waists, blinking confusion.

"I live here."

One of them made a noise like, *ah*, and Daniel stepped around the kitchen table to open the door.

"It's not a building. It's my house. Tell Leslie Rhodes that if she wants to send people out here to plan the best way to fuck up the station, she needs an appointment."

"Hey, Dan." Gideon showed his palms, surrendering. "Didn't mean to bug you. Sorry, man."

"All right," Daniel replied, though he and the entire situation were far from it. "Take care." He stood with one hand on the doorknob, squeezing hard where they couldn't see. Maggie got down from the sofa and turned restless circles near the stove, while Tugboat stood bristling beside him, and showed his teeth. "Quiet, dog. Bed," he commanded, holding his voice purposely low. "Sorry you drove all the way up here," Daniel said, and his chest was heaving, he couldn't help it.

Gideon and Halliday started out the door, looking like they might offer to shake Daniel's hand, but as it was the one gripping the knob, he didn't offer it. With downcast faces and more muttered apologies, the two scuttled past him and out the door. Daniel stood on the stone step, lit a cigarette as he watched them climb into the pickup. Gideon made a sloppy three-point-turn, and finally drove away. Surely they'd be telling the story back at the office, that the guy up at the North Hope light station was a little off—pretty angry, with guard dogs and everything—and might give them problems. Of course, with his history, you can't blame the guy for being a little paranoid or whatever, but he's going to need to be handled.

Daniel stayed on his front step, staring up his road, for as long as it took him to smoke his cigarette. Pinching the very last of the butt-end, after one last squint-eyed scan of the road to reassure himself he was alone, Daniel went inside. For the first and only time, he locked the door.

Sixteen

Justin tilted his head toward the shore, and the mischief-filled expression on his face—upward-curved lips, raised-and-lowered brows above glinting eyes—made it easy for Daniel to go along. They stood at angles to each other on the pebbly strip that couldn't really be called a beach, and Justin squinted out over the calm roll of the water. It was late morning, and Justin had pulled up in his newly-repaired Suburban not a half hour earlier, announcing there was something he wanted to do.

"You're not gonna do it," Justin chided.

"I will if you will," Daniel told him, smirking, up for the challenge. No way he'd back down from the dare; there was his manhood to prop up. And a novel experience—a thing he'd never even thought to do—shared with Justin proved an irresistible proposition. He could see no valid argument against it.

Justin said nothing more, only reached inside his sweatshirt, arms in and out, and in no more than a minute both men were naked in the freezing sun, the soles of their feet pinpricked by gravel. The instant the last piece of clothing hit the beach, they both took off running—whooping wildly—then gasping and yelping—neither willing to be the last one in. Quickly hip-deep in the frigid ocean, they finally took the dive, side by side like dolphins, like harbor seals wriggling to propel themselves through ice water. Daniel's chest felt tight and narrow, blowing out breath he'd barely managed to suck up before his face hit the water. Four strong kicks and he aimed for the sky, shattering the surface with a shout and a full-body shudder.

He blinked saltwater from his eyes, spun himself, looking for Justin's dark head to appear nearby. He could barely feel his legs as he worked them, treading water, desperately wanting to start for the shore and get the hell out. He swam a few strokes, enough that his foot touched bottom in the troughs of the low waves. He searched again. The sun-sparkle on the surface tricked his eyes. He attempted a breath he could use to call out, but his chest wouldn't go and he coughed. Daniel circled, ears thrumming with a rush of blood as his heart beat even harder. What a stupid fucking idea this had been—the Atlantic ocean, off the coast of Maine. In December. Daniel at last sucked a full breath, was about to shout Justin's name.

"Fucking amazing, right?!"

Justin's head and shoulders bobbed up about ten yards farther out.

Relief dragged Daniel under, to rinse away the film of fear. Immediately upon rising, he started for shore. After a few strokes he turned to see Justin close behind him, just his upright head visible, a quick thrust forward, a backward hitch, another jut forward.

"How did you stay down so long?"

"You don't know it's cold until you're halfway out again."

"Not even a little bit true."

Justin had just about caught him, and Daniel's shoulders ached from drawing them up and in, trying to hide from the cold. Justin's lips were dusky indigo, pale around the edges. The two quick-ducked to grab their clothes as they sprinted, laughing curses, the whole way to the cottage. Tugger and Mags crowded them, looping crazily around their legs, as they crashed naked through the front door.

"Now what?" Daniel demanded. Their skin was pimpled with cold, their hair frost-crusted. Daniel licked salt off his lips, hugging himself by the wood stove.

"Shower?" Justin suggested, teeth chattering, vigorously massaging his upper arms.

"Bed," Daniel said, and they rushed to yank up the quilts, each wrapping himself in one and meeting in the middle to get close, both shivering hard. Daniel smiled as he wrapped Justin up in blankets and his arms, kissed his cheek just beneath his eye.

"What did you think?" Justin's chin still quivered.

"That was insane," Daniel replied with a shake of his head. "Thanks."

Justin looked pleased and shifted his calf between Daniel's ankles, nestling closer. "Told you it was awesome," he said.

"It was not awesome; it was horrible. But I'm glad I did it."

Justin nodded understanding. After a few moments lying close, the quilts soaking up the last of the water from their skin but doing little to warm them, Justin snaked a hand over Daniel's hip and pinched his thigh just below the crease of his backside, making Daniel jump and grunt with pain. Reflexively, he clamped a hand hard around Justin's jaw, deforming his mouth as he pulled Justin to him, kissing hard. They stayed in bed the rest of the morning, wore the quilts like togas when they eventually got up to find food, shared a steaming shower that battered their chests and backs, turned them mottled pink and made them sweat. By the time—hours later—that Daniel had to dress and make his climb to the lantern room, each of them wore a fresh layer of bruises beneath dried saliva, sticky smears of lubricant, and flaking dried cum.

Daniel updated the log: *Swam in ocean (37F), 0930 for about ten minutes. Spent remainder of day indoors attending to personal business. Light switched on at 1650; sunset 1703. A perfect day.*

Over a supper of tuna melts and the last of Daniel's slow-cooked soup, they caught each other up on the state of Chevy starters, patches on leaking roofs, and unexpected intrusions by federal employees and private contractors who had likely never stepped foot anywhere more rural than Central Park.

"You have to go to that hearing thing," Justin insisted. "You have to stay here."

"They're already talking about filling this house with equipment. They let a guy drive up here from New York to look at the tower and figure out how to wire it up like a fucking table lamp," Daniel replied grimly. "It's a done deal."

"Maybe not."

Daniel set his empty bowl on top of his crumb-covered plate and gave them a gentle shove away from himself, reaching into a breast pocket for his cigarette pack. "I mean, I'm pissed. But on top of it to have them standing not twenty feet away from me, talking about putting up a wall in my house, like I'm not even here. I fucking live here. You know?"

Justin nodded, chewing the last bite of his sandwich. "I'll be so bummed if I can't come here anymore."

Daniel lit two cigarettes, passed Justin one. They both leaned back in their chairs, Justin stretching his legs with his ankles crossed beneath the table, flexing and cracking his toes inside thick gray socks.

"I don't know what else to do," Daniel said at last.

Justin nodded again, mouth rumpled with sympathy.

"Not that it's any of my business, and tell me to fuck off about it if you want," he began, and flicked ash off his cigarette into the plastic ashtray on the table between them. "Do you have money? Like, could you get an apartment or whatever?"

Daniel shrugged. "Yeah, I'm fine on that." The truth was he had been getting the same salary for ten years, with next to nothing to spend it on, so his bank account was probably pretty flush. "Not enough to last forever, but I'm not broke. I'd have to get a job. I don't know what."

"They won't reassign you?"

"There's not going to be another thing like this. Where I can just do my thing in peace. I'd have to go back to the world." He thought about it a few minutes while they smoked, each staring at a different corner of the ceiling. "I can't imagine it. You remember that night in the diner? We had to leave because guys were talking loud." He shook his head at himself.

"You can come stay with me at the house," Justin said. "I'd leave you alone." He grinned, and Daniel couldn't help but return it.

"That's generous. But will the new owner-ladies go along with that?"

"Fuck that," Justin said, and crushed out his cigarette butt.

"You told them no?"

"No, but I had a fucking nervous breakdown about it while I was there," Justin told him. Daniel gave him a questioning look and Justin explained. "Sort of blew up at Lia, while we were dealing with the mess in the kitchen. In English, though, so who knows what she got out of it. But I was on my knees trying to soak up gallons of water with a handful of rags and I kind of lost it. Like, all I wanted to do was be here, and instead he stuck me with a broken truck and a broken house, and this contract I could just sign my name to and be free of it, but he made me promise to keep the fucking thing and I don't even know if I want it. I don't know if I ever wanted it. Probably not."

"You wanted to be with him," Daniel said, signaling his understanding. "People do things for the people they love."

Justin's expression changed from irritated to deflated. He got up from his chair and started moving their empty plates and bowls to the counter. "I know," he allowed.

"Swim in the ocean in December." Daniel shifted his gaze upward, raising his eyebrows to see out from beneath them. Justin caught the glance, held on for half a second, then turned back to busy himself with the clean-up.

"Have sex with no fight in it," he replied.

Daniel's chest felt hot and tingly in a way that was nothing like the panic he'd felt standing in the doorway ordering the deputy regional parks director and some frat boy from New York out of his house.

"He wouldn't want you to be miserable about it," Daniel suggested.

With a tone that invited no reply, Justin said only, "I promised him I'd keep it."

Justin ditched the last of the dishes on the counter top, and retreated to the sofa, where he lifted his feet onto the table. Scrolling and swiping at his phone, everything about him made it clear he was unwilling to further discuss the inn, his late husband, or people who may or may not be in love. He scratched Maggie's head when she leapt to curl up beside him.

"You traitorous ingrate," Daniel scolded her, shoving up his sleeves to wash the dishes.

"You weren't giving her what she needed, so she went elsewhere," Justin teased him. "She knows you're in love with the light."

"Right."

"Leave it and come sit."

"I can't; it'll drive me crazy."

Justin hummed and shrugged, went back to his phone.

Eventually Daniel did find his way to the parlor, sinking gratefully into his chair and setting one foot on top of the coffee table, stretching and turning until his toes brushed against Justin's. Justin grinned at his phone and Daniel reached for his book. After long minutes of quiet—the fire in the stove sounding a muffled pop now and then, and once Tugger shaking his head so his tags rattled—Justin went into the bathroom, semi-closing the door so Daniel overheard the splash of his piss hitting the water, then the flush, and perfunctory-at-best handwashing sounds.

"Got any first aid cream in here?"

"Antibiotic ointment," Daniel replied, "in the medicine cabinet. It's in a tube? Here." He rose from his chair and went to the bathroom to find it. "What's up?" He set the tiny cap on the back of the sink and held the tube poised to smear ointment from the tip.

Justin held out his right hand, palm-up. "Blister busted," he said, pointing to a raw pink spot just at the base of his middle finger. Daniel squeezed a dab of the yellow-clear jelly onto the spot and Justin spread it with his finger.

"Need to cover it?" It was an awkward spot for a bandage.

"Nah."

Daniel covered the tube and stuck it back in the cabinet. The bathroom light turned both of them bluish as they stood close together in front of the mirror. Daniel caught Justin's palm in his hand and looked hard. "You're getting calluses," he commented, tracing the pale bump of one beneath his ring finger.

"All the work you make me do around here," Justin smiled at him. "Raking leaves and chopping trees and putting the plow on your truck."

Daniel grinned and pulled Justin against the front of his hip by a hand in the small of his back. "I seem to remember the only things you touched were your cigarettes." He held up his own hand. "I've still got a scar on my knuckle from tearing it up when the pliers slipped."

Justin caught him and kissed his knuckles, sucking with the edges of his lips. He made cooing noises, pouted. "Poor you." He guided the recently kissed hand behind his waist, and without further prompting Daniel slid both hands over the stubbly fabric of stretchy-denim jeans to cup Justin's ass, kneading and pulling, drawing him even closer. Justin tipped his head, pressing open-mouthed into Daniel's neck just beneath the edge of his beard.

"Bed," Daniel murmured, rocking his head back so Justin chased his throat, kissed his ear lobe, lay his hands at the sides of Daniel's whiskered jaw to center his mouth in place. Justin hummed agreement and started backing out of the tiny bathroom, Daniel still clinging to him with hands on his backside, their knees and feet bumping as they went, clumsy, smiling into their kisses. In the end Justin struggled free and Daniel chased him in a U-turn around the stove and the dogs' beds into the bedroom, kicked the door mostly-shut behind them while Justin torpedoed onto his stomach on the bed, snapping on the small bedside lamp because they both liked to see.

Daniel followed close, hands and knees caging Justin beneath him, dipped down to playfully bite the back of his neck like an errant pup. Once freed, Justin wriggled over onto his back, pulling Daniel's face down to his own, kissing open-mouthed and deep, his tongue seeking all the textures and tastes of Daniel's mouth. Melting down onto him, Daniel fought a growling desire to crush Justin breathless beneath him. Justin released his jaw to reach down and center Daniel so their hipbones aligned, and shoved up hard against him, snaking a figure-eight grind through the layers of his jeans and Daniel's work pants.

They kissed and kissed, lingering there, Daniel happy to stay at it as long as Justin liked, because his lips were chapped rough and just wet enough, and the nimble tip of his tongue circled the tip of Daniel's, then licked in, and now and then Justin opened his lips to sigh, or to grunt with the effort of another deep hip-roll.

Daniel slid sideways, dragged at Justin's waist to turn him so they lay face to face, and Justin smiled with his eyes closed.

"Sunny."

Justin lifted his eyebrows but didn't look. His fingers wormed their way into the front of Daniel's waistband, crumpling up the hem of his thermal, tugging it up and out. His fingers on Daniel's belly were rough-tipped, with bitten nails and dry needles of cuticle prickling past his navel as Justin worked the shirt ever-upward.

Daniel kissed the corner of his mouth and leaned away again.

"Hey," he said. "Look here a sec."

Justin's dark eyes half-opened, and Daniel reached down to gather up one of his hands, drew it up between them.

"I'm glad you came back," Daniel told him.

"Course I came back," Justin replied with a frown. "I'd always rather be here."

"Seemed like maybe you were going to stay in Six Rivers a while, when you didn't come out the next day like you said." Daniel wanted to say more, that he had imagined Justin back in the gloom of his dark gray room at the inn, burrowing into his dirty sheets; sleeping his upside-down schedule; unwilling or unable to shower, dress, pack a bag, and drive the hour to the station. . .and what all that might add up to.

"Had some stuff to do. I'm not going anywhere now, for a while," Justin said, and squeezed Daniel's hand. "Don't worry." There was a quick pause, and he said mischievously, "So let's get down and dirty."

"I'm falling in love with you."

Daniel knew he had been falling since the first time they met—an unsmiling, stubble-faced man dressed all in black offering his hand for a shake as the dogs herded him down from the cliff top. All the time they spent sharing work Daniel would normally have done alone, in twice the time, had brought him a sense that—just maybe—everything he did from then on, didn't have to be done all on his own. Every rough shove and lingering bruise was evidence of fighting to get close to Justin, in whatever way Justin allowed. All their talk-around-the-edges shielded Daniel from the sharp tang of his particular terror—that although he had found a way to keep himself upright, he could not be trusted to hold up anyone else—but, really, what had ever been easy for either of them? And the distance to cover had gradually become so much smaller. Justin was *right there*, and the words were *right there*. And knowing from the start it could never be forever, to Daniel it felt like violent crime to waste another minute at arm's length. Maybe tying up together could keep them each from drifting. Saying it aloud wouldn't fix anything. It couldn't change anything. But it was the truth. And they didn't have much time.

Justin studied his face for a half-second, and his mouth turned up and down at the corner, thinking it over. Lifting himself to settle astride Daniel's thighs, Justin stripped off his top layers and flung them toward the floor. Daniel drew up his therma as high as it would go, inviting Justin to touch his chest, which he did, bracing himself on Daniel's pecs as he lowered down to kiss him once more, deep and slow, in wordless reply. Daniel ran work-rough fingers through the buttery waves of Justin's dark hair, smoothing it back behind his ears, holding his neck, letting himself be kissed. Justin drew away from their kiss and stretched full-length along the front of Daniel's body, resting his weight, and flashed another version of the amused, sad smirk from a few moments earlier. His eyes glittered, but he closed them, and lowered his mouth beside Daniel's ear, lips brushing skin and hair as he whispered.

"Don't."

Seventeen

Daniel woke before the alarm sounded, shut it off so Justin could sleep, then dressed in the dark and left him sprawled on his belly beneath twisted blankets, silent and soft.

After Justin's admonishment that Daniel should not love him, they'd kissed and clutched at each other, lay naked with hands on each other smoothing and petting rather than pinching and scratching. Justin had kissed unspoken words into his mouth, *This is good enough; isn't this enough?; just this—soft—the way you want it—and let's don't talk about it. Let it be. Let it be this. Just this. This is enough.* Side by side and face to face, they'd stroked each other, kissed until the loss of breath forced them apart, hummed affirmation and appreciation, then went on soothing each other with their callused fingers, and Daniel could have fought it but ultimately allowed sleep to wash over and pull him down while Justin drew curlicues in the hair of his chest with one swirling finger.

He hadn't said the things he'd wanted to, hadn't argued. *It's too late, it's done, you don't have to say the same, just let me.* As he fixed them breakfast he told himself he'd dreamed it. As he ate he promised himself he'd leave it alone and not push. Each day was enough to bite off, chew, and swallow—to ask any more from either of them was certainly too much. As he climbed the tower Daniel wondered what had come over him, to say such a thing to a dying man, and as he flipped the switch he forgave himself. He'd been alone so long he'd forgotten loneliness. Anyone in Daniel's situation would have felt the same. Said the same. Been overcome and lost his mind. Descending the steps he resolved to go back to the way things had been before he'd said it.

Fresh snow was falling—tiny, weightless flakes that threatened nothing much—as he let himself into the shed and resumed work on what he'd come to think of as his secret project. On returning the carved walking stick—his tree-animating wizard staff, according to Justin—a few weeks previous, he'd come across another bundle of long, straight dowels that upon closer inspection had revealed themselves as the base of a three-legged stand for an old telescope lying abandoned on the floor with hopelessly broken lenses. The tripod looked and felt ancient, but someone had made it with love, turning shapely curves into the legs and carefully hammering the brass fittings so the scars left behind seemed like purposeful decoration rather than mere haphazard damage.

Daniel spent the best part of two hours hand-sanding yellowed varnish off the surface of the wood, changing the grit of the papers as needed to dip into the coved hollows, brushing up over the swells. He figured it for a woodworking project of one of the previous keepers; his online research of telescope tripods had turned up only practical, sturdy examples—even handmade antique ones were all of similar, simple design using straight dowels, or mass-manufactured with minimal flash—so the one he'd come across was clearly something made beautifully and with precision as a way to pass the time, perhaps even to keep from going mad. It was built of maple and pine, both plentiful in the nearby woods, and Daniel intended to stain it in two shades, just enough to seal it up and make it pretty, to enhance rather than bury the beauty of the woodgrain. And so again, it had become a project to pass time when the keeper might otherwise be left—perhaps dangerously—to only his own thoughts.

Once he'd returned it to its place in the back room of the shed, filed the sandpaper in the wooden drawers of the work bench, and swept the benchtop as well as the floor, Daniel strolled back to the cottage, looking for a fresh cup of coffee and something to take the edge off until lunch—an apple or a folded-over sandwich.

"Hey, Sunny," he said cheerily to the half-open bedroom door. The dogs were nowhere around, but the fact of the door not fully closed indicated if Justin wasn't up and out of bed yet, at least he might be awake. Daniel went straight for the coffeemaker, which had by then shut itself off. He could see by the markings on the side of the carafe that Justin had poured a mug. His unwashed breakfast dishes were in the sink, the stove switched off after warming them. Daniel refilled the filter basket with half-again as many fresh grounds on top of the already soaked ones and filled the water reservoir, then set the pot back on the warming plate and switched the machine on.

His mind drifted to memories of the previous night, of Justin gentle and melancholy in his arms, of slow deep kisses that signified agreement that too much had been said, a silent consolation offered in place of more wrong words. Waiting as the coffee dripped, Daniel felt the pull of the dark bedroom, the lure of Justin's naked body and the way it would have heated the bedclothes, put a soft dip in the mattress that Daniel would automatically fall toward as soon as he lay down beside him. Licking his lips, Daniel pressed the door fully open, sought the familiar shape of Justin beneath the quilts, curled up with just his wild dark curls of hair visible, or sitting up against a pile of folded, mashed pillows with his knees drawn up beneath a tent of the sheets and blankets, fiddling with his phone.

But the bed was empty. The blankets were pulled up into place—imperfectly—but even the slight effort Justin had made toward straightening the bed after getting out of it was unusual. There were no puddles of discarded black clothing on the floor and his bag was leant upright against the front of the dresser. Daniel's stomach tightened even as he told himself it was about damn time some of his own habitual neatness had rubbed off on his frequent houseguest. He listened: no sound of his dogs barking. Heart lurching toward the cliff, Daniel adopted an artificially relaxed pace as he moved outside. A halt on the front step, and he glanced to his left to see Justin's Suburban parked beside his own truck. The ocean threw loud lobs at the shore—a constant, rolling roar that enveloped the station.

He whistled for the dogs, and put his hand on the gate while he listened for them barking in response, or their panting breath as they bounded toward him through the thick coating of snow on the ground. The seconds stretched on forever; each second that passed with no response placed the dogs farther from the cottage; Daniel mentally mapped landmarks. The fallen oak in the woods. The last National Parks sign on their road. Route 18. They couldn't be on the beach, and beyond that was only the freezing churn of the waves. They must be well beyond the shed, past the birch stand where he'd once encountered a mother black bear with her cubs. If they were up the hill, they were near the top. Or on it.

At last Daniel forced his gaze to the cliff. Steel gray and boldly displaying its every choppy crag, each wrinkle and blemish on its face thrown into sharp relief by the mid-morning light. Daniel marched at it, making furious calculations of time and energy required to negotiate the winding, upward trail as it meandered and switched its lazy way to the scrub-covered ledges crowning the cliff. He thought to whistle again, but if Tugger and Mags were up there, surely they'd have arrived at his side by now. It was curious to think they had gone so far they wouldn't have heard his whistle, or if they had, that they were still on their way home. With a few hundred yards ahead of him before he even reached the base of the trail, Daniel's ear was caught by the clack of shifting gravel, then the quick-fire thumps of running paws, and Tugboat materialized at his side, tongue showing in his open mouth, tipping his face up quizzically.

"Where've you been, mutt?" Daniel asked him, bending to give the dog's head a quick scrub of acknowledgement. He glanced back to trace Tugger's path across the rockfall. "Where's your sister? Where's Justin?"

The dog loped away toward the rocks, then circled back looking expectant and confused. Cold fingers of wind off the ocean dipped into the open neck of Daniel's coat, and he adjusted the collar, indulging a quick shudder. The unspoken words *go get'im* sat heavy on his tongue, but he couldn't spit them out, only squinted across the splay of boulders and gravel, seeking any misplaced shape amidst the familiar low skyline.

Maggie barked once, somewhere nearby, but Daniel couldn't pin it in place because of the wind and the echoes off the cliff face. "Where is he, Tug?" Daniel asked, in a tone that indicated his next words would be a command, and he followed it with a steadier-than-it-felt, "Go get'im. Go on, go get'im."

Tugger surprised him by running away from the rockfall, back toward their road and the woods. Daniel followed distantly, walking fast, not giving in to relief even as the craggy gravel receded behind him. The ocean thundered louder than ever. Tugboat raced into the forest, and Daniel lost sight of him. Starting to jog off the path, his boots were almost too heavy to lift. There were fresh footprints through the snow, alongside a random mess made by the dogs following in disorganized exuberance. If he'd just turned around—if he hadn't assumed the worst of the cliff—he would have seen them. Daniel chastized himself for having let the staticky noise of his rising panic drown out his common sense. With snow on the ground, looking for fresh footprints was a no-brainer. And yet his brain had been out-shouted by a body flooded with adrenaline—a clanging and familiar fight-or-flight dread—which made him too stupid to think.

"Hey. Good morning."

Justin. Smiling, with his knit watch cap pulled down to his eyebrows in front, and an empty coffee mug dangling by its handle from one hooked index finger. Daniel feared his knees might give out, so stood his ground waiting for Justin and Maggie to reach him.

"Did you know there's a graveyard out there?" Justin asked, looking close to delighted, completely at ease in a way that made Daniel ashamed at his own stupidity.

"Yep. Some of the keepers from the 1800s. I figure when it's my time, I'll walk out there and bury myself beside them," he half-joked, forced casual. "Not covered in snow yet?"

"I guess you would know," Justin corrected himself, looking quickly at his feet. "We were following a bobcat."

"Without a gun?" Daniel wondered, and the two fell into step as they trudged through the snow, the dogs following close, both panting the exertion of a hike in deep snow.

Justin laughed. "We weren't following that close. Anyhow, it took off pretty quick. We kept walking a little because I figured I could follow my tracks out, even if the woods swallowed me up."

Daniel left off reminding Justin it was a Canada lynx, aware Justin was purposely digging a friendly finger into his ribs, calling it by the wrong name.

"What were you doing out in the shed?" Justin asked, and their upper arms brushed together, then he sidestepped to bump Daniel a bit harder, grinning.

"Woodworking," Daniel shrugged. They circled around to the front of the cottage, and Daniel admonished the dogs to stay outside so he could clean them of snow before they entered the warm house, to leave dripping trails for at least the next hour. Justin crouched beside him on the step and they both patted and combed with their fingers, the dogs' tails wagging all the while. Daniel worked a golf-ball sized clump out of Tugboat's coat and tossed it. "Why'd you say don't fall in love with you?" he asked, and kept at his work, as if it were nothing much to ask, low-key chat while they brushed the dogs.

Justin froze for just long enough that Daniel noticed it, then resumed his very un-methodic picking through Maggie's fur. He sighed lightly. "The thing about falling in love is that when you finish falling, you land on the rocks. And then you're at the bottom, and it's a long climb back up to that feeling you had at the beginning, just stepping off the edge and starting to fall."

"You're a fucking poet," Daniel told him, not sniping, only breaking tension.

"I know, right?"

"Was it like that with your husband?" Daniel asked, looking for further explanation of why a man to whom he'd made such a tender confession would reject it so soundly, leaving Daniel feeling bruised and lonesome, even as they stripped each other down and sank warmly together until the warmth turned hot and they both burned in it—crying out—sighing relief.

"No. It's like that with you."

Justin met his gaze, and smiled, acknowledging the weight of it.

Daniel patted Tugboat's rump and both dogs went through the dog door while the men got their feet under them and Daniel turned the knob, stood by to let Justin go in ahead of him.

"Not that I wouldn't be like this," Justin said, as they shed their coats and hung them on the pegs inside the door. The cottage smelled welcomingly of recently-brewed coffee, and the dogs lapped noisily from the water bowls. Daniel stomped his boots free of snow on the mat, stood there waiting for what remained to melt and slide off the uppers before venturing further inside. Justin had stepped out of his own never-laced, not-warm-enough-for-winter ones, and set them on top of the wood stove before moving to pour them coffee. "But I think I would have been like this sooner. And it would have crept up instead of coming on so quick like it did."

Knowing it was stupid to say, Daniel offered, "You're smiling."

"Woke up feeling OK," Justin agreed, and handed Daniel a mug of black coffee filled higher than was entirely safe. "But now I want to lie down until tomorrow." Justin took his usual seat on the middle sofa cushion, knees wide to account for the length of his slim legs in the narrow space between the couch and the coffee table. "Like, really want to," he emphasized, and his shoulders sloped down on a sigh.

Daniel wrapped frozen fingers around his warm cup, blew across the surface, and decided his boots were good enough. He wiped the soles one final time and moved to his armchair.

"Do what you need to," Daniel told him. "Whatever you want."

"Come with me," Justin said, and usually it would have been accompanied by a dirty, knowing smirk, or a growl. But Justin only looked across at him a moment, then leaned forward to set down his mug, slid sideways to get closer, beckoned Daniel with body language to meet him in the middle, and they kissed, melting soft.

As they drew apart, just enough, Daniel said quietly, "It's not like I can go back and stop myself."

"I know."

"I wouldn't, anyway."

Justin smiled, and tilted his head, indicating their next destination. He murmured, "I know."

Eighteen

"Your hands are getting soft again."

Ten days and two snowstorms later, it was the early afternoon of Christmas day, and Daniel had granted himself a day free of work so he and Justin could spend the holiday together, as they liked. An hour after lunch, the way they liked to spend it was propped up on pillows in the bed whose sheets were scandalously fouled and well overdue for a trip to the laundromat in Parker Village, with Daniel's laptop nearby in case they ever got around to finishing the movie they'd started watching the previous night, but which had been serially placed on pause throughout the morning so that they could eat apple pie with thin slabs of cheddar cheese and whipped cream from a can, doze nestled up like folded-over bundles of freshly paired socks, and have sex of several different flavors.

Justin let his fingers dance between Daniel's, rearranging their hands without breaking them apart, so he could verify Daniel's observation about the texture of his palms.

"Is that your way of saying I haven't been working hard enough?" he joked, and feigned pulling away so that Daniel would grab hold of him and pull him back. Daniel obliged the obvious ruse, kissing the knuckles of Justin's first two fingers before settling their tangled hands back on his lap.

"Nah, I like it," Daniel assured him, and he did. He liked the contrast between his own hands—thick-fingered, with callused thumbs and endless scratches and scars—and Justin's smaller, more delicate ones. Even though his nails were bitten to the quick and the skin around them was always ragged, his palms and fingertips were smooth and soft, and the base of each hand was a pleasing, near-perfect square.

That morning, Justin had risen with Daniel, in the dark, and they made breakfast together of oatmeal and chunks of overripe banana cooked in cinnamon tea, sprinkled with brown sugar and chopped walnuts—a recipe Justin had perfected back when he was serving breakfast to guests at the Blue Moon Inn, and which had over the course of their acquaintance become a favorite of Daniel's. Because it was Christmas, they put Bailey's in their coffee, and clacked their mugs together and wished each other merriment before opening the dogs' gifts—rawhides and cups of blueberry yogurt; a jar of peanut butter Daniel insisted would be doled out in reasonable time but which Justin immediately jammed three fingers into and let Maggie and Tugboat lap up in no time flat; a new brush; and a bag of rubber squash balls. Thus appeased, they were sent back to their beds with plasticky, bacon-scented bones to keep them occupied.

Justin went into his bag, and from under a jumble of black sweaters and socks took a small, rectangular package wrapped in cartoonish paper, with a store-bought bow taped on. Daniel, who had not had a Christmas present from anyone in over ten years, found he could not disguise his reaction, eyes and nose prickling as he reached to receive it from Justin's hands. He was embarrassed at having to wipe away tears with the pads of his fingers, then run the cuff of his flannel sleeve across his nose. Justin made comforting noises and moved to sling his arms around Daniel's shoulders from behind, as Daniel sat on the floor while Justin was on the end of the sofa nearest the Christmas tree.

"So dumb," Daniel scolded himself. "Sorry."

"Now I wish I'd gotten you fifty presents. A hundred. When's your birthday?"

Daniel patted his hand and leaned to scrape his bearded jaw into the crook of Justin's elbow.

"Well, open it," Justin demanded.

It was a book, as Daniel had assumed from its shape and weight even before he'd begun peeling back the wrapping paper. Vintage 1950s, bound in woven red fabric gone beautifully soft at every corner. Daniel lifted it to his face and inhaled; it smelled of pipe tobacco and warm dust.

"I got it at the library book sale, not too long after I met you," Justin told him.

Daniel opened to the table of contents. The book was *Two-Handed Card Games: Fifty Variations for the Smallest Cards Parties.* Daniel remembered their first night sitting out a storm in the light tower watch room, how neither of them knew anything to do with the deck of cards but solitaire and kids' games.

"It's amazing," Daniel told him, and moved from the floor onto the sofa to offer a kiss. "Thank you, it's perfect."

His gift for Justin was under the bed; he'd wanted to put it under the tree but the dogs were too nosy and would have had it undone in no time. Daniel retrieved it and lay the awkward and not-so-neatly wrapped gift on the coffee table, then sat next to Justin on the sofa as he began picking at the knot in the ribbon.

"What is it?"

"You'll see in a minute."

The ribbon at last loose enough to slide off, Justin pressed a tear in the paper with his thumb and impatiently ripped it away in every direction to reveal the restored telescope stand Daniel had been refinishing for weeks. As Justin lifted it off the table and began to turn it over in his hands, Daniel caught the dubious expression and rescued him with, "It's a tripod. I don't know what kind of camera you like so I ordered a universal clamp; I can change it out for you if you'd rather have a different one."

"I know. It's really nice." He set the brass feet on the floor and examined the clamp at the top. "Did you make it? No, it's old."

"Refinished it. It was in the shed—used to be for a telescope. I know you said your camera broke, but."

"Thanks. It's great. I can't believe you fixed it up for me; it must have been a lot of work." Justin ran his fingers over the smooth finish of the wood; Daniel had stained and oiled it so the wood wouldn't be smothered in lacquer that might flake and would almost certainly discolor.

Now it was Daniel who felt a little doubtful. Why give Justin a gift for which he had no use? Someone who wanted to take photos would surely have had his camera fixed. He wondered if it seemed pushy, like Daniel was subtly telling Justin what he should do.

"I know it's not very practical; I'm sure modern ones are much lighter and probably easier to level. But the clamp has levels in it."

"I see," Justin rushed to reassure him. "Seriously, it's awesome." He grinned, and Daniel melted a little. "Now I have an excuse to buy that Nikon I've always wanted." Justin leaned close and offered a kiss, which Daniel gratefully accepted, letting his hand come to rest on Daniel's thigh. When they broke apart, Justin lay the tripod under the tree and glanced out the windows by the front door. "Sun's coming up?"

Daniel hummed confirmation and rose to stretch. "Back to bed for a while after I turn out the light?"

"If you're coming with me," was Justin's smiling reply.

And so after Daniel's climb to the lamp room, and the two of them throwing the new squash balls for the dogs—across the parking area and up the road, because the snow blanketing their usual spot had become so deep that Tugger and Mags were reluctant to venture into it—Daniel had watched Justin strip off his longjohns and hoodie, then peel off his socks and snuggle down into the bed, cursing the cold sheets even as he licked his bottom lip and held open one side of the covers, inviting Daniel to join him. What started out as playful, boys-will-be-boys tickling and pinching turned fiery-rough, and Daniel pinned Justin face-down, pressing across his shoulders with one forearm, fucking down into the slit of his arse and between his thighs, while Justin moaned urgent encouragement and did what he could to get himself off, one hand beneath his body, rubbing off against his fingers and the sheets. They finished panting, growling, and rearranged themselves for urgent, open-mouthed kisses that staked their claims on each other, each asserting his dominance in the ongoing fight, each declaring himself that round's winner.

As they lay together with tangled fingers, reeking of sex and feeling the glow of the holiday spirits they'd been generously pouring into their morning coffee, Daniel let his eyes close and dropped lower against the pillows. Justin insinuated himself under Daniel's arm, murmuring a satisfied sound as he dug his head into the hollow of Daniel's neck and shoulder. Daniel's thoughts drifted on gentle waves of post-orgasmic, deep winter sleepiness, envisioning Justin in the other kitchen chair while they ate their supper together—much earlier than Justin probably would have preferred—and in his languid sprawl on the center sofa cushion, with Maggie's head on his thigh and one of Daniel's books in his soft, square hand. The way his eyebrows drew down and together in the middle as he read, an almost-frown of concentration. Time spent side by side in companionable silence outdoors, working, walking the land.

A fresh flare of terror shattered through him as he waking-dreamed of Justin on the rocks. Justin washed up on the beach. Justin swinging by his stubble-rough neck from a tree at the woods' edge. Justin crumpled on the bathroom floor, with foam in the corners of his pale-blue lips. Daniel jolted—that hideous sensation of wheeling in air—and he must have gasped because Justin hushed him.

"Felt like you were falling?" he murmured, and turned his head to plant a kiss on Daniel's chest.

"Like you were," Daniel corrected, before he had the presence of mind to stop himself.

"Hmm?" Justin raised himself onto one elbow and looked concerned, perhaps suspicious. His dark eyes were narrow.

"Bad dream," Daniel told him, and shrugged. "Nevermind. I forget." He was certain Justin knew it for a lie, but was kind—didn't poke in any deeper—and mercifully changed the subject.

"Is there any more pie?" He waggled his eyebrows comically, eliciting a smile from Daniel. "I'm going to get some. You want any?"

"Nah, go ahead."

Justin rose and quickly stepped into his longjohn pants, dark gray thermal with holes where the elastic of the waistband had broken away from the fabric. He pulled on Daniel's green tartan shirt, open in front, looking like a kid in his dad's bathrobe. Probably for Daniel's benefit—planting seeds he'd later come back to reap—Justin adjusted himself with a fondling hand over the y-front of his thermals, gave Daniel a little wink, then vanished into the kitchen. Daniel lay down and pulled the blanket close to his chin, curling up with his knees near his chest.

It had never occurred to him to be troubled by how much they never discussed. Justin slept too much, seemed unmotivated to do much of anything, was clearly avoiding consideration of the offer to buy his inn—as if not thinking about it would somehow make the whole situation go away. Of course, that was none of Daniel's business, and Justin had more than once stated outright he felt obligated to keep the big house because of a promise he'd made to the dying man he'd loved, who'd loved the house whether Justin did or not. But Daniel couldn't help thinking Justin might be happier if he let the place go and moved on to whatever it was he actually wanted to do—if Justin even knew what that was. He'd married young, and went along with what his partner wanted; that was hardly unusual, lots of people let the rush of early love carry them away. But his husband was gone, and Justin was still young; if he didn't want to own an inn, Daniel thought it unfair he should bear the burden of one for thirty or forty years.

But it seemed Justin was resigned to holing up in his guest room with its en suite bath, as the house fell down around him, unused and unloved, while his late husband's middle-aged niece dusted the bric-a-brac and watched Brazilian television. It was not for Daniel to raise any objections. From the beginning there had been an understanding between them, that Justin's time was limited and that Daniel wouldn't struggle against it. Daniel stretched as long as his body would go, hands pressing the wooden headboard, heels over the edge of the mattress. If Justin could keep a promise to a dead man, Daniel should be able to keep promises to Justin—not to hold on too hard, not to dig in—and not let his sappy feelings put words in his mouth that Justin could *make a choice to stay alive, for me.* Being with Justin meant accepting he was terminal. Whatever time they had was what they had, and even if it was just another month, or just another day, it was a damn sight better than Daniel's previous ten years alone.

A sudden explosion from outside the bedroom, "Aw, for fuck's sake! Idiot!"

"Hey. Hey. What's up?" Daniel pulled on sweatpants and went to the kitchen, where he found Justin holding his phone in one hand while the other squeezed his temples with thumb and fingers.

"My dad got picked up in Portland for driving suspended, with two bottles of pills with someone else's name on them."

"Damn. He's in jail?"

"Mm. I'll have to go sign for his bail. What time is it?" Justin looked around for a wall clock despite the fact of the phone in his hand.

"It's Christmas," Daniel replied.

"No, I know. But the cashier's only open tomorrow eleven to three, and driving down in the morning I don't know if I can get to the bonds place and the courthouse in time. If I miss it, they won't let him out until Monday. So I should just drive tonight and stay down there, get in to the bail bondsman first thing, and get to court in time to get him out." He looked at the ceiling and forced his shoulders downward. "Fucking lecture him like a kid the whole way back."

"What's he doing in Portland?" Daniel asked, putting aside for the moment Justin's suggestion he would soon be leaving to make the four-hour drive.

"Came in from fishing like two weeks ago. Probably got off the boat with ten grand and already he doesn't have a thousand left to get himself out of jail. Fucking idiot. You see where I get it from." Justin smiled at his own joke.

"So you're going down tonight?"

"In a little bit, I guess," Justin said thoughtfully. His slice of pie on its plate sat waiting for him, and he sank into his usual chair, picked up his fork.

"Gotta stop in Six Rivers and get my car. I'd have to fill up the truck six times between here and Portland."

"Wish I could offer to go with you," Daniel said, and started a fresh pot of coffee, then ducked into the fridge to find something more like lunch than yet another slice of pie.

Justin laughed. "No, you fucking don't," he scoffed, "But I appreciate the gesture. You'd lose your mind in Portland."

"I've been to Portland," Daniel protested, with a grin.

"Really? When?" Justin demanded.

"I don't know. Right after college."

"OK. And that was when?"

"Like twelve years ago? Fourteen?"

"Like I say. But thanks for saying it, anyway." He shoveled in a mouthful of pie and whipped cream, chewed twice then talked around it. "If I get out of here around four, I can be in Portland by nine, I figure. No traffic today so I can put my foot down and make up a little time. We'll turn right around, and I'll be back late tomorrow night. Next day, noon, at the latest."

"Tell your dad I say he's an idiot. Fucking up Christmas."

"In my experience that's kind of what dads do," Justin shrugged. "My dad's brother stole all the presents from under my grandmother's tree one year. When I was about thirteen my dad and his girlfriend got into it, both drunk as fuck, and she bit his fingers so bad he had to have like a million tetanus shots."

"We're better off, I guess," Daniel said, and joined him at the table with a ham sandwich and a fresh bag of chips. "Just you and me and the dogs."

"Best Christmas I've had in a while," Justin confirmed. He swept his finger along his plate to wipe up the last smears of whipped cream and made a show of licking it off.

"Are you seriously making suggestive gestures at me on this holy day?"

"Wait. Was that not you rutting up between my legs earlier? On this holy day?" Justin's expression was exaggerated thoughtfulness, trying to place him.

"Damn fucking right it was," Daniel smiled at him, and pressed his knee against Justin's under the table.

"I need to get in the shower."

"Can I join you?"

"I think you better."

Just before dusk, Justin climbed into his truck and started it up—*rebuilt starter but it goes like an old one*—and Daniel passed him a thermos bottle full of coffee and a bag of sandwiches and apples.

"I'll text you when I stop," Justin told him. "Couple, three hours. You'll probably be asleep."

"Text me anyway. Drive safe. If you get tired—"

"Just close my eyes and sleep while I drive," Justin finished for him.

"Right. Or, you know. Pull over. But whatever works for you." Daniel started to step back, caught himself. "Oh, one more thing."

"What's that?"

Daniel pulled him by the back of his neck, kissed him hard and deep, until they couldn't breathe.

When they drew back, Justin let go a whooshing breath with a soft *whoof!*, sounding impressed. "That was something," he said, and pulled his shoulder belt across his chest, adjusted the heat vents.

"So maybe you'll miss me," Daniel told him.

"No worries about that," Justin grinned.

Daniel told him again to be safe, then pushed the driver's door shut and stepped back. He hugged himself against the cold, watched the truck back out and turn, gave Justin a last wave goodbye, and once the taillights faded from view, made his way to the tower to switch on the light.

TXT from Justin: My dad is an incredible idiot.

So you said. You got him out?

TXT from Justin: In the nick of time. Court was earlier than I thought so I was scrambling. Now we have to go get his truck out of the pound. Another couple hundred, probably. I'm just waiting for him to start hemming and hawing, getting ready to ask me to pay for it.

What does he spend his pay on?

TXT from Justin: Card games. The bar. He's wearing new boots.

Christmas present to himself.

TXT from Justin: He's really generous with himself.

So will you get back today/tonight?

TXT from Justin: I hope. We're finishing lunch and then we'll go to the impound lot.

Good luck.

The day was unusually warm—or if not actually warm, the air was very still and dry at the midday low-tide—so that morning after switching off the light, Daniel braved washing the bed sheets in the outdoor basin. He boiled three big pots of water on the stove, took one outside to mix with icy-cold spigot water, just warm enough so his hands didn't stiffen up and go numb. He dunked in the sheets and pillowslips one after the other, gave them a thorough squeeze and swirl in the tepid soapy water, then scrubbed them against the old Chevy grill he used as a washboard. The second two pots of hot water came out for the rinse, and his fingers turned pink as he wrung out the laundry with bare hands. He draped everything over the clothesline he'd run between the corner of the house and a small, decorative maple tree, and clipped it all in place with wooden clothes pins.

By the time Justin texted about his day at the bail bonds office and in court with his father, it was mid-afternoon and Daniel had already begun to doubt Justin would make it back to North Hope before Daniel went to bed that evening. The fact of another errand to ransom his dad's car made it seem nearly impossible. The door would be unlocked; if Justin made it back late he could let himself in.

Daniel filled the bird feeder he'd made, took the dogs for a tromp through the woods, got back just in time for the light. He lingered in the lantern room, letting the hum of the motor mildly hypnotize him while he looked out to sea, watching the tide creep its way up to shore. He took out his phone and snapped a picture, which failed to capture anything like what he saw, but which would have to do. He sent it to Justin.

Taking its time getting back here. Reminds me of someone I know.

It was cheesy, but felt less so than just texting, *I miss you.* The gnawing in his gut nudged him out of his reverie, and he descended back to sea level, pondering what to fix for his supper.

TXT from Justin: You're probably in bed already. Nodding at the wheel so I stopped here at the house to sleep. Up your way first thing tomorrow.

TXT from Justin: Fucking wired from all the running around and the shit with my dad. Wonder if he made it home? Can't sleep but shouldn't drive. Drinking bourbon! Wish I was curled up with my man.

TXT from Justin: Brown liquor, right? Gave up on sleeping for now. Watching old movie I think might be Casablanca? What are you dreaming about? You look cute asleep.

TXT from Justin: You look so cute asleep it made me think of you awake and naked and biting me so I jerked off and came so fucking hard.
Thinking about sucking you off.
And your fingers in my ass.

Miss you so much it's stupid.

Nothing's easy.

> *TXT from Justin: I hear birds outside. I'll just sleep a little and get on the road. Call and wake me up at like 9???*

Daniel woke up to the string of overnight texts from Justin, lingering over the dirty talk to the extent he ended up doing likewise, quick and efficient, careful not to make a mess of the fresh sheets, then eating breakfast fast so he'd get to the light on time. He'd decide at nine whether to actually put in a wake-up call; Justin probably needed a normal number of hours of sleep more than Daniel needed him there at the cottage. He chided himself for having become so needy for company after only a few months of knowing Justin, when for the previous ten years he'd done just fine with almost none. Justin was right about one thing: nothing's easy.

He was deeply engrossed in a post-apocalyptic novel in which the apocalypse wasn't due to a zombie outbreak or nuclear disaster, but rather the extinction of honey bees, when his phone chirped at him that he had received an email. Setting aside the novel was like waking from a dream, and he blinked hard to rouse himself back to reality as he swiped the phone's screen to life.

Hi Daniel,

First of all, I want to apologize for springing a visit on you the other day. I realized later that naturally you might feel put off and skittish about it. It was really foolish of me to just show up like that. So, my bad on that.

Given the calendar year is coming to a close, HQ is sending out notices about retirements coming up in the new year. There are a couple of pretty choice field posts opening up, and I'm sure if your lighthouse goes automated Parks would give you pick of the litter. You might have to ride a desk for a couple months to hang on to your seniority and all, but how does a California beach you can see Mexico from strike you? Or there's another one on the Appalachian Trail, out in West Virginia; I know you like the woods. Anyway, just wanted to clue you in. I've attached the list of posts coming open in the next six months in case you're interested in making a back-up plan.

Take care,

Ben Gideon

Deputy Director, Northeast

Daniel could not imagine himself on a beach in southern California, even for fun. He'd never been further west in his life than the White Mountains. The Appalachian Trail gig could be something tolerable, except that it probably meant dealing with a lot of people, given the popularity of hiking and the relief some of those hikers felt when they finally got to a ranger post and found someone to talk to or beg energy bars from. He scrolled the roughly three dozen listings, fewer than half of them field posts, and sucked a sharp breath when he noticed one of the jobs opening up was his old one at Abenaki. That there was no mention of it in the email must mean the deputy director was aware it could be a touchy subject—he may even have meant to remove it from the list and forgotten to do so—and with good reason. Daniel felt shivering-cold for a moment, and his face and fingers tingled.

He knew he should drop his head between his knees to reverse the rush of blood and prevent himself passing out but instead only went utterly still, with his phone loose in his hand on the arm of his chair, and closed his eyes. He counted to himself, trying to make his inhalations and exhalations expand to a count of four, but it was a struggle. Behind his closed eyes, he saw the small hands of the kids on either side of him at the table, all twitching to grab at the fox pelt or the snake's spine, barely restraining themselves. He saw the neon-yellow of their matching t-shirts, and the one teacher's slender pink hairband over the crown of her head, holding back straight, hay-colored hair.

And then there were the soft moans, and the horrid burbling noises, and the salt-and-copper stink in his nose. And Justin was there, slumped beside him with an open mouth, ruined with blood that covered him everywhere, much more than there should be, and Daniel reached for him but couldn't touch him.

He opened his eyes and still saw it—Justin torn apart, as if by the claws of a wild animal instead of sprayed with bullets—and leaned forward until his chest hit his thighs. He gripped the edge of the coffee table to stay steady; he feared tipping forward onto the floor. He went on counting, trying to breathe, heart pounding loud in his ears. Worst of all was the doom-like feeling crushing him, convincing him he was dying even though he knew he wasn't dying, but *christ* it felt like dying, he was dying, he was *dying*, in—two, three, four—hold—two, three, four—out—two, three, four—just let it end—two, three, four—Justin—two, three, four—dying. . .*dying*. . .

At last he got his breath to cooperate, and the sensation of impending disaster began to drain out of him. When he touched his face it was clammy so he wiped his hands up toward his hairline, clearing away the damp of perspiration. Daniel was utterly wrung out, felt like he'd sprinted a mile in the sand. Slowly, he lifted himself, felt the giddy rush of blood reversing direction and slumped down until his head touched the chair's back.

He hadn't even noticed the dogs sitting by, quiet but alert, and when he half-opened his eyes to look at them their tails started going, and Tug nosed at his hand until he petted the brown and white head. Maggie put her chin on his knee, and he gave her a scratch between the ears.

"Good dogs. Well done," he told them. "Been a while since we did that, eh?" He went on petting and scratching, connecting, and letting go of his panic. Within a few minutes he felt normal again, which was perhaps the strangest sensation of all. One minute: dying. The next minute: his armchair and his book nearby and his dogs making themselves known, like any other minute of any normal day.

TXT from Justin: OMG, I slept forever. Did you call? Anyway, getting moving. No worries. See you when you get here.

Nineteen

Daniel retreated to the safety of predictable routine. The Christmas tree was drying out and dropping needles, so he undressed it and put away the decorations, back under his bed—even tucked in the empty cigarette box they'd used in place of a crowning star—and dragged it out into the woods. Sweeping the floor took forever, and the needles gave off their disgusting, decomposed smell of cat urine instead of the fresh pine scent that had filled the cottage days before. He lay his new book of two-handed card games on the coffee table, and leaned Justin's refurbished tripod against one bookshelf-covered wall, to await his return.

He roasted chicken pieces atop a bed of potatoes, carrots, and plenty of garlic, all of it swimming in butter. It would feed him four times; twice if Justin returned. He'd have to make his trip into Parker Village middle of the following week; he needed a haircut, oatmeal, and silicone spray for the light's motor. He started a list and stuck it to the fridge with a magnet advertising a car lot that he had never found evidence of except an empty building with an ancient gas pump out front. The thing was so old the phone number only showed five digits.

He went to bed alone. Sent a text saying *Goodnight, see you soon?* which went unanswered in the few minutes he spent with his book before diving into velvety sleep.

Daniel passed two days in a manner that felt familiar but weirdly uncomfortable: attending to the light, playing with the dogs, making his meals for one, updating the logs no one ever followed up about, reading his books with his feet up on the coffee table. Call it Christmas vacation; he'd head into Parker on the morning of New Year's Eve, drop good wishes on whoever he met, fall back to the station. With every task he undertook, he felt vaguely condemned, his days shortly numbered, and he worked on a letter of protest to Parks, defending his light as much as his job, but it went in fits and starts—while writing it he felt righteous and passionate, but later rereading what he'd written it inevitably seemed overwrought and screechy, so he deleted and started again, over and over, and felt he'd never finish anything he was willing to actually send.

The snow melted quite a bit in a few days' worth of bright sunlight, revealing patches of the parking area and the gravel walkways, and a muddy swath of damp leaves at the edge of the woods. He stood out on the front step smoking, watching the crowd come and go at the bird feeder—a cardinal and some house sparrows, chickadees and one very determined but weirdly clumsy squirrel, who kept jumping down from above, swinging, falling, and then trying again.

Sunday morning he added apples and steel wool to his list, and at last heard from Justin.

TXT from Justin: Just leaving the grocery store. Bringing ice cream. Be there in 45 min.

Daniel texted back a smile and went to clean himself up and put on a fresh shirt.

"He'll be here soon," he assured Maggie, who was sitting curled in Justin's usual seat on the couch, saving it for him. She thumped her tail on the couch, probably in response to Daniel having directed attention to her rather than a more complex comprehension of his words, but to Daniel it felt like a betrayal. A minor one, but stinging nonetheless.

Running a comb through his damp hair, tilting his chin in every direction while he searched the bathroom mirror for white whiskers that might have appeared in his beard in the few days since Justin had last been there, Daniel wondered if he had enough of anything to put together lunch for them both; he'd been rationing his last few days' worth before his biweekly trip into the village. He was sliding cans around in a cabinet, looking for tuna, when Maggie leapt from the couch with her tail wagging an instant before Daniel heard the crunch of gravel under tires, and the efficient, quiet engine-hum of Justin's car.

Tugger had joined his sister near the door, awaiting Daniel's permission. "Out," he allowed, and the two shouldered past each other to get through the dog door, too impatient to greet a visitor to wait while Daniel turned the knob. By the time Daniel stepped outside, Justin was crouched by his open driver's door, receiving slobbery greetings from both dogs.

"I can't compete with that," Daniel called, shaking his head and spreading his palms in *oh well* fashion as he strode down the walk and through the open gate. "You may as well just turn around and go. That's the high point of your day."

Justin gave each dog a last pat on the side and gained his feet. "One way to find out if that's true," he smiled—he looked brighter than Daniel remembered, more upright and sturdier, and to his shame Daniel momentarily wondered if his therapist had adjusted his meds—and stepped around to his trunk, which was already popped open. Justin beckoned Daniel closer with a tilt of his head. "Come here and give it a try. I grade on a curve."

"Awesome; I suck at tests," Daniel smirked, and caught him hard around the waist, his whole being suddenly awake with a giddy need for him, a thrill at being with him, touching him, pulling him and making him stumble against Daniel's chest. Justin's arms wrapped hard around his back and they kissed around smiling mouths, laughing at their own and each other's adamant embraces. It had only been a few days. Daniel bit back an urge to ask why Justin hadn't been in touch more, hadn't called at night, texted during the day, maybe hadn't thought about Daniel or missed him all that much. Instead he gave his ass a rough, possessive squeeze and a sound smack, then let him go.

Justin lifted the trunk's lid and revealed several beige plastic bags full of groceries, some of Justin's usual garbage-food visible: bags of chips, boxes of mini-donuts, two six packs of middling beer and a slender paper bag that promised brown liquor. They each grabbed up as many handles as they could, and Daniel elbowed the trunk shut then followed Justin inside.

"We're cooking Sunday dinner," Justin announced, as they set all the bags down on the kitchen table and counters. "I got a roast beef and a little card that says how to cook it; potatoes; carrots and maple syrup; Parker House rolls." He tossed a small jar in the air, spun it, caught it in the same hand. "Gravy like Grandma used to make."

"Ice cream," Daniel confirmed, and slid two red half-gallon cartons into his freezer.

"And pie," Justin finished.

"My foster mom always did candied carrots with brown sugar," Daniel commented, as they continued to unpack.

"My grandmas did it with syrup, city boy. We can do half and half and see who wins."

"How long does it take to cook a roast?" Daniel wondered, trying not to stare too curiously at the surprisingly cheerful, well-rested man across from him.

"Couple hours," Justin said. "The lady at the meat counter gave me the smallest one they had, and the card with the instructions."

"I have cookbooks."

"What, *Beans and Rice for Lonely Lighthouse Keepers?*" Justin teased. "*Meals for One Plus Dogs?*"

"No, asshole. Regular cookbooks. There's a whole shelf of them." He motioned toward the parlor. "*Joy of Cooking*, that's a good one. Just normal cookbooks."

"Sorry, forgot you were normal." Justin's smile was full of light and mischief, teasing him. Daniel gathered up the bags and stuffed them inside each other, put them under the sink with some others to re-use or take with him when he went into Parker, to return to the store for recycling. Justin drew a shiny card from inside the pass-through pocket on his pullover hoodie, with an advertisement on one side for the same jarred gravy Justin had bought, and presumably the recipe for a beef roast on the other. He pulled out his chair and sprawled in it, and Daniel lit a pair of his cigarettes, passed Justin one.

"Is that beer cold?" Daniel asked.

"One is. The IPA."

"Have one?"

"You need to ask?" Justin had the cigarette clenched in the corner of his mouth, his face half-squinting like some rebel movie idol. Daniel felt like crushing him. He uncapped the bottles with the opener stuck to the side of the fridge and passed one to Justin, letting the caps rattle onto the table. "Hey," Justin said, and raised his bottle. "Good luck to us, here's to Sunday dinner."

"Candied carrots," Daniel agreed.

"With syrup."

"Whatever you say, you animal. Raised in the woods."

"You'll see." He held Daniel's gaze, and as he dragged on his cigarette, beckoned with a tip of his chin so that Daniel leaned close and their open mouths nearly-but-didn't touch as Justin exhaled and Daniel inhaled, shotgunning the smoke cooled by its journey through Justin's lungs, and they finished with a kiss. Daniel sat back, held the smoke, finally let it go in a tight, upward stream.

"Sexy fuck," Justin accused. "Whatcha been doing while I was gone?"

"Just wondering where the hell you were," Daniel replied with a shrug, grateful for the opportunity to scold him, but reminding himself to keep it in check.

Justin shrugged back, dragged his thumb across his lower lip. "Just the shit with my dad," he said. "Some stuff at the house."

"More roof leaks?" Daniel asked.

"Nah." Justin flicked the edge of the recipe card with his thumb. "Nothing that crucial. Just. Looking at the contract that lady sent. Getting rid of some stuff from the barn; took it to the Vets for the thrift store. Probably Lia will buy it all back." He laughed.

"And?" Daniel prompted, knowing Justin would pick up the meaning.

"I should tell her no and put her out of her misery, I guess."

"But you haven't."

Justin shook his head and stubbed out his cigarette butt in the ashtray, pushed it toward Daniel. "Nope."

"How come?"

"Just thinking," Justin said, not much in it, with another shrug. "Thinking, thinking." He stood and went to the fridge, took out the roast, bloody and marbled in plastic wrap on a white styrofoam tray. "One thing I can promise you is I'll make sure you don't get it when I die. You'll thank me."

"Hey. None of that." Daniel got up and washed his hands, motioned expectantly at Justin, who eventually caught on and joined him at the sink. Once they were through, they dried their hands on their shirtfronts and the thighs of their jeans—Justin by dragging his fingers through his hair—and Daniel said, "So let's cook Sunday dinner."

They agreed to grade the meal on a curve once they realized how much more complicated some of it would be than they had originally anticipated. The roast was already tied with twine, and the card told them that was right, so they left it even though neither of them remembered ever seeing such a thing before. The oven warmed up while they searched for all the proper pans, pots, and utensils. Daniel scrubbed potatoes and Justin chopped them into what they both agreed were about one-inch cubes ("how do you get cubes from a potato-shaped potato?" "hell if I know") and tossed them in a pot of water. They made a tent out of foil for the roast ("conspiracy theorist cow" "I want to believe") and Daniel felt a little triumphant just sliding the pan onto the oven rack and slapping the door shut behind it. Justin turned the light on inside the oven so he could check on it every other minute or so.

They built individual foil pans for their carrots, side by side in a roasting dish, and each found a recipe—in separate, normal cookbooks—that suited his taste. Daniel chided Justin for having bought pre-cut, finger-sized carrots rather than putting in the work of peeling and chopping, but Justin defended his time-saving measure on the basis that life was too short to peel carrots. Clearly it was, or Daniel would have peeled the potatoes. Daniel gnashed his teeth in the air beside Justin's cheek, threatening to bite him, but Justin only poked his ribs gently with a wooden spoon and went back to reading his candied carrot recipe from *Heavenly Tastes: Recipes from First Baptist Church, Meddybemps, Maine*, submitted by Melrene Murphy.

Once the potatoes were boiling and the carrots had been installed on the rack above the roast, they took a break to smoke, retreating to the parlor and settling into their usual seats.

"Your dad made it back OK?" Daniel finally remembered to ask.

"He texted me when he got to his place so I guess he finally did. I'm kissing that grand goodbye now, though, because there's no way he'll remember to go to his court date."

"You could plan to remind him. Take him down there? You should get the money back; that's bullshit."

Justin waved it away. "It's not until like April," he said with a shake of his head, and Daniel wasn't sure he thought that was so long in the future Justin himself would forget the date, or that April was so far in the future Justin wasn't willing to make plans. "Speaking of dates and trips to the big city. You're going to the hearing thing. About the light."

Daniel still couldn't imagine it, for several reasons, ranging from the impossibility of getting there and back in time for the light, to his reticence about so many unfamiliar people in an unfamiliar place, to his hopelessness about whatever he might have to say being persuasive enough to talk a federal agency out of something it had clearly already decided to do. He diverted instead. "I've been working on a letter to send." He dragged thoughtfully on his cigarette. "The deputy director sent me a list of job openings coming up. Field jobs, like this one."

"Are there any like this one, though?"

Daniel shook his head. "No. There's a beach in southern California. Run away with me and we can be surf bums."

"People talk so slow there. Always smiling." Justin sneered. "No winter."

"I think that's the only good thing," Daniel protested.

"You need winter as an excuse to hibernate," Justin told him. "And put on blubber." He grinned and patted his nearly-concave abdomen.

"I can see you've taken that one to heart," Daniel said sarcastically. After a minute or so, Justin got up and wandered over to the oven, where he steadied himself with one hand on the countertop to lean way over and peer in through the window in the door. The distance emboldened Daniel enough to say, "Maybe we should make a date to write our letters. I'll tell National Parks that if they automate the light they'll have to answer for the eventual suicide of *that Daniel Howard*, who you can be sure as shit will succumb to his PTSD if they take his job away; and you can write to the lady trying to buy your inn that the place is probably gonna have a curse on it if she makes you break a promise to your late husband, and he'll haunt the place forever."

Justin laughed a little. "The ghost-host with the most. Haunting it with blueberry French toast and too many charming stories to tell over too many caipirinhas."

"What are those?" Daniel's curiosity was caught.

"Trendy Brazilian mixed drinks. You wouldn't like them. No brown liquor. Speaking of." He found the bottle he'd brought—rye bourbon, middle shelf but better than what Daniel usually bought for himself—and rested his hand on the top, waiting for permission to break the seal.

"I'll have one," Daniel smiled at him. Justin nodded and twisted the cap.

Justin poured each of them two fingers of the whiskey, then added a little water to each glass. Keeping his back to Daniel, he asked, "Do you really think it will be that bad? Post-traumatic stress and all that?"

Daniel drew in a huge breath. "I don't know," was all he could think to say. He really didn't. "I don't know," he repeated, emphasizing a different part of the phrase, then one last time: "I don't know."

"You've been good for a pretty long time, though, right?" He brought the glasses, handed one to Daniel, and they tapped the rims together. "Cheers."

"Cheers. Pretty good, yeah," Daniel agreed. "But you saw me that night in the diner. And I know I put on a real show for the guy from Parks, and that city guy with the clipboard. I have a hard time imagining what else I'd do."

Justin had by then resumed his seat on the couch and rested one sock-clad foot on the edge of the coffee table. "Plenty of room at the inn," he said, then cracked a smile at the unintentional joke. "As the saying goes. This time of year."

Daniel didn't know what to say in reply, unsure if Justin was really proposing they make something official by living together, or if the discussion had merely activated the innate masculine tendency toward throwing out solutions to a problem regardless of their merits. Perhaps sensing Daniel's discomfort, Justin gave a quick shrug.

"I don't know. Just saying the only option isn't to move to Calais and get a job as a greeter at Shop-N-Go. You do all that tinkering. You could open a fix-it shop."

"Not a huge demand for that, even up here in the woods," Daniel chided gently.

"Well, then." Justin took a sip of bourbon that made him curl his upper lip to show his teeth. "You'll just have to make sure they don't force you out. You have to go to the hearing."

Daniel had an urge to ask Justin why he cared so much, but realized it was rhetorical.

"I'll think about it."

Justin grinned. "Good." He sat up and closed his eyes. "Damn that smells good; I think we might have done it right."

Two hours later they were sticking the last flakes of buttery pie crusts to the pads of their fingers, pressing them on their plates so they wouldn't miss even a tiny bit, depositing every last crumb onto their tongues. Their roast had turned out fine, and the jarred gravy was the same salty, gluey, over-sweet stuff they'd both appreciated in their youth. They called a draw on the carrots, as each liked his own recipe best but admitted the other was acceptable. Potatoes were hard to mess up—a ton of salt and butter and they were pretty much perfect, though Daniel had a little bit of cream cheese left in its silver foil in his fridge, so he mashed it in as well, and Justin seemed impressed. They'd put away a couple of beers each, and then made a fresh pot of coffee to go with the pie.

Daniel sat back and reached into his breast pocket for his smokes, gestured to offer one to Justin, who declined in favour of his own milder brand, lit up and shook the match he tossed into the ashtray. "Well that was fucking great," he said with smile.

Justin grinned back. "Pretty good idea, right?"

"Yup."

Justin looked pleased with himself, and under the table, Daniel used his shin to give Justin's calf an affectionate nudge.

"We'll do these dishes, read some," Justin suggested.

"The light."

"Right, go give your wife the light a goodnight kiss," Justin teased. "Then bring whatever you have left back to me."

"Side-action," Daniel smirked, puffing up his chest a bit in ain't-life-good fashion.

Justin gave a sarcastic nod and let it go. Fixing Daniel with a pointed look, he dropped his voice in both pitch and volume, and said, "Later share the shower? There's something else I want to eat."

Daniel's blood rushed and warmed him everywhere, a low growling that he knew would grow into a howl, once he'd finished digesting and put his kitchen back in order so that he could concentrate on what really mattered.

"You're a bad man," he said accusingly. "That's hours away. You like me to suffer?"

"Something to look forward to. Keep it in mind when you're out there with the missus." He tilted his head toward the tower.

"You're not really going to help clean up," Daniel said skeptically.

"I will. I totally will. You like to wash or dry?"

Daniel shook his head. "Well if this isn't going to go in my log as one of the most perfect days, I don't know what would."

"Who reads the log, anyways?" Justin wondered, and his expression was still devilish. "Will you include long descriptions of your man's tongue all over your ball-sack? Licking your asshole and opening you with his fingers?"

Daniel was aching. "*Fuck*, stop it, you prick-tease."

"I'm not teasing," Justin protested with a wide smile. He leaned over and gave Daniel a sound pat on the thigh, consoling him, then jumped to his feet and made for the sink. "Grab a dish towel," he ordered.

Not long after dark, and Daniel held back his own quivering thighs while his man did all he'd promised, and more besides, thoroughly and hungrily and sweetly and forever. A hot, strong tongue traced circles, first along the outer edge, then the inner, making Daniel choke a gasp and swipe his own tongue urgently over his palm to wind it around his prick, his strokes telegraphing through his hips, just barely rocking, and Justin nodded to keep himself centered, tongue-fucking, flicking, tickling, then gripping and pushing back on

Daniel's thigh to lift and steady him. He hummed a deep groan, and his lips were wet and nimble as he kissed, breathed warm and blew cold.

Daniel wanted to look, couldn't keep his eyes open, dropped his head back on a cranked-back neck and let out a rushing growl that sounded like a complaint. He licked then bit his lip, thought he could discern even the tiniest movements, the difference in sensation from one patch of skin to the next. A dismaying moment of disconnection, a slick-sounding pop, and then Justin's finger drawing a spiral around the rim. Daniel cried out.

"You taste good," Justin murmured against the inside of Daniel's thigh, and nuzzled in so that Daniel could feel his stubbly chin and jaw were wet with flowing saliva. Justin shifted his shoulder, rested his cheek against the sensitive skin next to Daniel's opening, and pressed his tongue in beside his finger, wetting it, then slid inside quick, twisted and crooked upward, slipping and stroking.

"Jeezus!" Daniel cursed, and licked his palm again, pulling his cock with long, twisting strokes. "More. *Fuck*. More," he begged, and Justin obliged, his tongue and lips making a delicious confusion with a second fingertip, then another sure inward slide, and Daniel saw flares of yellow-white behind his closed eyes. His thighs were taut, his calves straining, folded up practically beside his belly, and he could feel his toes splaying at the ends of his flexed feet. He stopped stroking, pinched the base of his cock. "I don't want to come yet," he huffed, and found the back of Justin's head with searching fingers, dug into his scalp a bit. Justin adjusted the angle of his fingers to take pressure off the spot inside him that made Daniel see stars, instead began to slip in and out, slow and soft at first, kissing and licking all around Daniel's hole as he went, gradually picking up pace and force, his breath hard and hot against Daniel's balls and the base of his cock. Justin started to moan as he fucked Daniel harder, as deep as he could go with two long, smooth fingers.

Daniel set his feet flat on the mattress, raised his hips, and they moved together, both grunting encouragement and sighing pleasure. Justin's voice was low and smooth, just *oh!. . .oh!. . .* with every stroke, and he slipped his shoulder up under Daniel's knee, made sure and sudden moves to rearrange himself between Daniel's thighs.

"I wanna fuck you," he whispered, and it sounded pleading. "Let me fuck you and make you come."

"Yeah."

"Can I?"

"Fuck yeah."

"Can I fuck you and make you come and come?"

"Sunny. . ."

Moments that never passed fast enough while Justin slicked his prick—Daniel raised his head off the pillow to watch, reached for the back of Justin's shoulder and pulled him down, lifted himself up, so they could kiss—and at last Justin settled his hips against Daniel's and sank into him—not slow—steady—deep—and Daniel sucked air like a man going under for the very last time, grabbed him at the waist, pulled him in.

As he found a sturdy, rolling wave to ride, Justin settled himself as close as he could get, tugged at the pillow behind Daniel's neck with one hand until they were close enough to kiss, muttered against Daniel's greedy, open mouth, "You feel so good. You feel. *So good*." Daniel's hand on Justin's ass rode the tide, gently squeezing and releasing in time. They kissed, licking damp onto each other's lips, dry from panting breaths. Daniel held the back of his hand up against Justin's belly, feeling the shift of his abdominal muscles as he shoved in and slid back.

"Love your cock," Daniel rumbled, out of his head, well beyond the point of filtering himself. His own cock was pressed against his body, between them, rough-rubbing up against his pubic hair, leaking fluid from the slit. On the crest of each thrust: "Fuck me. Fuck me. Fuck me. . ."

Justin rolled his shoulders, lifted up onto his palms, his hips finding a relentless roll of their own, each inward grind shoving Daniel's body up and back. Justin bared his neck, then dropped his head, and some primitive part of Daniel's brain recognized these as signs of submission, even as Justin pinned Daniel down with his belly exposed, even as he invaded him, staked his claim to Daniel's body, laid him low and helpless with pleasure Justin gave and controlled. It was a thrilling contrast, and Daniel whimpered aloud, and lifted his legs until his calves rested on Justin's shoulders, a claim of his own. Both were predators, both prey, using each other for their own needs, their own pleasure, ruining each other, reverent.

"You're gorgeous. Fuck me."

Justin growled and chewed his lips. His eyes were narrow, black, utterly afire.

"Harder."

He looked pleased with himself.

"Deeper. Fuck me."

He groaned, and both their bodies fell into the new rhythm.

"Yeah, hard."

Daniel willed himself open and shut, wide and tight, spread his thighs, gripped desperately.

"Fuck. Hard. Fuck. *Hard.*"

Justin's hips jutted quick, in, thrumming, thrusting, and his breathing turned to groans, and then to grunting.

"You gorgeous fuck. Gimme that cock. Fuck. *Fuck.*"

Daniel half-released him, grabbed his own aching, needy prick and pulsed his hand around it, up along it, quick and tight, pulling in time.

"Oh god. Oh fuck. Oh. Oh. *Oh. Oh!*"

"Jeezus you feel good inside, oh god, oh my god."

"Yes. *Yes.* Hard. Oh you're coming so hard. I can feel it. Feel you coming. Oh you fuck me so good."

"Oh my god."

"Yes."

"Oh my god."

"*Mmm.*"

Daniel pulled Justin close, kissed him, panted against his cheek and chin, licked his lips, kissed him more.

"You made me come and come," he whispered. "So good. I came and came, and came and came."

"Kiss me." Daniel kissed him. "Let me—" Justin drew away and sank down, hot belly skin against the hair of Daniel's thigh, a few sweet, open-mouthed kisses as he went, on Daniel's pec and nipple, over his rib. Justin's deft, pointed tongue, licking him clean, swiping up Daniel's already-cooling cum off his belly.

Daniel ran his fingers back through Justin's hair, slow, over and again, petting him as his breath slowed and Justin hummed a kiss against a spot just beside Daniel's navel, smoothed Daniel's pubic hair with the flats of his fingers.

"Up," Daniel softly commanded, slid his hand beneath Justin's whiskery chin and gently pulled. "Come up here." He opened his arms and Justin settled into them, half on and half beside him, dropping occasional kisses wherever he could reach. He sighed into Daniel's embrace, his temple against Daniel's lips, and Daniel went on scratching his scalp, combing fingertips through his waves of dark hair.

"Dear log," Justin said. "Today my man and I cooked a damn good meal and then he licked me and fucked me and now I forget my own name."

"I just may have," Daniel allowed. "But I know I've never written 'dear log'."

"Well, make sure you make it good, for whoever reads it. Say my dick is seven thick inches."

"Ouch."

They were quiet a few minutes, lazily running fingers and palms over the hairy and smooth surfaces of each other's bodies. Eventually, Justin stirred, stretching and rolling until he was on his way out of bed.

"Where you going?"

"Cigarettes. Get yours, too?"

"Thanks." Daniel rolled onto his side, propped up on his elbow, and he was suddenly and unceremoniously reminded of the consequences of bareback sex. "Towel, too?"

"Use a sock, like a man."

Justin winked at him and vanished, naked, into the parlor, where he let go an audible shivering breath. Soon enough, he returned, both packs of smokes in one hand and in the other, a washcloth Daniel recognized as one he'd wrung out and draped over the shower curtain rod not an hour earlier, after they'd shared the shower. It was damp, but cold, and he hissed a noise of his own as he reached down to clean himself.

Justin lit both cigarettes from the same match, shook it out, passed Daniel his smoke and brought the ashtray with him back to bed, pulling up the blankets to his waist. "You're going to hate this, but I have to leave in the morning."

"I do kind of hate that," Daniel agreed, and with the two fingers pinching his cigarette he traced a curlicue design onto Justin's belly, making him suck his breath, ticklish. "What for?"

"The usual. Headshrinker. Pharmacy run. Want to get some more stuff out of the barn and to the vets while I've got some momentum on it."

"Makes sense." Daniel rolled away onto his back, felt his shoulders melting down toward the mattress. Something occurred to him.

"Who *would* get the inn if you died?"

Justin, utterly unfazed by the morbid nature of the question, shrugged and replied. "Well, my will says Gabriel; we made them together when he was sick and I never re-did it. After him, my dad." Justin let out a scoffing laugh. "I should definitely change that."

Daniel only hummed, curiosity satisfied. Sleep was quickly closing in on him. He took a last shallow drag of his cigarette, lifted the ashtray off Justin's blanket-covered thigh, and stubbed it out.

"Dogs need to go out," he said, and started to stretch himself back to life. "Lock their door. Stir the stove."

"I'll do it."

"Nah." Daniel started upward. Justin caught him by the shoulder.

"It's cool; I'm not tired yet, and you are. Just stay and sleep. I'll button up the house."

Daniel allowed himself to collapse back into bed, even pulled the blankets around himself and closed his eyes. "Thanks, Sunny," he yawned. Justin kissed the blade of his cheek and Daniel kissed back, just the air, as Justin drifted away. Daniel heard him pulling on jeans and a sweatshirt, then the click of the lamp and the gentle tap of the door against the jamb, not quite closed.

"Come on, dogs. Out." Justin gave the command in just the way Daniel normally did, and the dogs' nails clicked against the floor on their way outside. Daniel heard the front door open, and Justin's low curse at the cold. But the door didn't close again right away, and after a second or two, the bedroom door swung open. "Hey," Justin said quietly. He sounded puzzled. "The light's out."

Daniel jolted upright. "What?"

"The light's out?" Justin repeated. "Don't freak."

"What the fuck."

"Don't freak."

Daniel jumped into his clothes, his heart thwacking in his chest, body thrumming beneath the skin, mouth dry, suddenly fully awake and hyper-alert.

"It's just *out?*" he demanded, pulling on socks and grabbing cigarettes and phone in one sweep of his hand.

"Just out," Justin told him, standing by looking helpless as Daniel hustled past him. The angles of shadow inside the cottage confirmed it. The dogs jogged around him, sensing Daniel's unease, seeking direction.

"Bed, dogs!" he snapped at them.

"What can I do to help?" Justin asked.

"I don't know. Nothing." Daniel stomped his feet into his boots, tied them with choppy efficiency, and grabbed his coat on his way out the door.

"Flashlight," Justin called after him, and after the few moments necessary to find the pair of flashlights stashed in the kitchen and get his boots and coat, he followed at a jog.

Daniel's mind raced through the possibilities, and he tried to call up the maritime schedules on his phone as he walked through the dark. Justin's flashlight beam bounced slightly ahead of them, their feet crunching over gravel gone icy-slick with melted—then refrozen—snow. Daniel was terrified—rage-filled—skirting full-blown panic; he had all but forgotten Justin, only a half-step behind him.

"Is that the generator? Listen."

Daniel turned his better ear toward the tower.

"Solar battery failed," Daniel said, mostly to himself. "Generator's sputtering."

"Low fuel?"

Given the noisy struggle of the generator, instead of heading straight up to the lantern room, Daniel circled the base of the tower to the generator's fenced-in home. Justin passed him the flashlight and lit another for himself, following Daniel's beam with his own.

The air around the tower carried a distinct smell of gasoline—much more than there should be—and their lights revealed a wet patch beneath the generator, soaking into its cement pad.

"Yeah, this thing's fucked," Daniel announced, and reached for the kill switch. "Dammit."

"So the battery died? Is that why the generator switched on?" Justin asked. Daniel found his presence irritating—yet another thing to take care of—and fought an urge to tell him to leave.

"Probably," Daniel grunted, and without inviting Justin to come along, he stomped up the stairs to the lantern room. Justin followed, wordless. Useless.

Daniel thought—as he trudged upward in a narrow, flashlit spiral—that had Justin not been there that night, he'd have noticed the problem while he washed his supper dishes, sat at his desk with the laptop, or read in his chair. They'd already been in bed over two hours; the light could have been out that long. And their shower together. Even longer.

Once at the first landing, Daniel swung into the watch room and fetched tools from the chest inside the door—only guessing at what he might need, far from certain he would even be able to identify what was wrong with the solar battery, let alone repair it. Beyond reattaching loose wires, he'd be lost and have to call a pro. Who knew how long that would take, whether the light would get any sort of priority. No one understood lighthouses anymore. No one would consider it an emergency.

Justin had gone up ahead of him to the lamp room, which was dreadfully silent. Daniel opened the motor's cover, then went out onto the catwalk to the metal box that sheltered the battery. A thick cable running to the solar array's battery on the south-facing side of the catwalk was protected inside a length of flexible PVC pipe that would require disassembly to get to the cable itself—not a job to be done in the dark of night, by flashlight, on a cramped walkway on the outside of the tower. Justin appeared, shining his flashlight toward the battery's box as Daniel unlatched it and swung it open.

He checked what he knew to check, which were basic connections, male and female plug parts, tugging each free and then pressing it back in, hoping for something to happen. He shined his light along the PVC tube seeking any obvious flaws—a tear or a cut—and followed it around, Justin trailing him, cursing the cold. A steady wind blew in off the sea, with force enough to steal the breath from Daniel's lungs. At last he shone his light at the base of the solar panel, slightly smaller than a door, horizontally mounted near the railing on the south-facing side of the tower. At the same moment Daniel saw the problem, Justin released a quick, hearty sigh of relief.

"Just unplugged."

Daniel was nowhere near the point of feeling reassured, and took a knee beside the panel, got hold of the dangling cable and swung it up into his other hand. He tucked the flashlight under his chin, against his shoulder, and examined the plug for damage. The cable's vinyl covering was marred by multiple small scratches, some cut through to slits, but the twisted bundle of wires looked intact where it met the plug. He ducked down to make sure the receptacle was free of debris, then scrubbed the plug with the cuff of his shirt, and plugged it back in. Daniel held his breath, heart hammering in his ears.

The lamp burst to life, the lens array whirring up a rotation around it. The vague hum of the motor could be heard through the windows.

"How the fuck did that happen?" Justin wondered, smiling. Daniel kept to his knee, not trusting either one to hold him if he tried to stand.

"I feel sick."

Justin's smile collapsed, but he gave Daniel's shoulder a gentle nudge with his fist. "Hey, it's all right. You fixed it."

"It shouldn't have gone out in the first place," Daniel snapped. Rather than subsiding now that all was set back to rights, Daniel's rising panic finally crashed and broke hard over his chest, and he wobbled, afraid he might pitch right over the railing. He sat back on the freezing metal slats of the catwalk, elbows on his knees, and pressed his face into his folded forearms.

He felt Justin lowering himself, laying his soft hand on the back of Daniel's neck.

"It's OK, man," he said softly. "What's up?"

Daniel's eyes were burning so he sank harder against his arms, gently rocking his face to dig in. It turned into shaking his head *No.*

Justin's arms closed around the back of his shoulders, and along the length of his crossed arms, and his mouth was close by Daniel's ear. "It's fine. It's OK."

Daniel snarled and shook him off. "It's not fucking fine!" He had an irrational desire to shove Justin away, instead pounded the sides of his closed fists onto the metal bars beside his hips, which hurt like hell, which helped. "In ten years I never once threw the switch even one minute late. And I sure as hell never let the light go out," he railed, his voice harsh and probably too loud. "This is the *one* thing I have to do. This is the one thing I *can* do." He was blathering, felt stupid and small, got to his feet and tried to step around Justin, to escape. Justin's face in the darkness, dim-lit by the flashlights each of them still held but didn't properly direct anywhere, was wide-eyed with puzzled shock. Daniel turned away.

"You fixed it. That's what you're here for," Justin said, trying to soothe him, but the confusion in his voice was obvious, wondering why Daniel was shorting out over it, as if what had just happened was not a catastrophe. As if Daniel had not just failed spectacularly at the only responsibility he could be trusted with, because instead of paying attention to the light, he'd been flat on his back in his bed, letting himself forget what he was meant for, losing track of what was important—for what?—for a fuck.

"If it wasn't for—" Daniel began, and bit down on every way the sentence could end. It wasn't Justin's fault; it was his own. He couldn't be relied on.

"Forget it. Come on." Daniel started toward the lantern room, stopped to look needlessly at the motor before closing its cover. He stared up at the slow spin of the optic, through the wood lattice, for as long as it took him to remind himself he was a fool to think he could take on more than the little life he'd managed to live since Abenaki. Justin stood by closed-mouthed, looking distinctly concerned, probably rethinking any decision he'd made to trust Daniel with what was left of his life. Daniel, burning with shame at his failure, at a cheap surrender to pleasure that had resulted in such utter disaster, started down the stairs, burning his hand as it slid along down the twisted metal rope that served as a handrail.

The dogs met them at the base of the light, and Daniel snapped at them that it was *home time*. Justin had given up trying to comfort him with words or by touching him; his last ditch effort was to extend his open pack of cigarettes. Daniel shook his head and went for his own instead, in the breast pocket of his shirt. They stopped walking long enough for Justin to offer him a light, both of their hands sheltering the match from the wind.

Back inside, they hung their coats and Justin stepped out of his boots. They took their usual spots in the parlor and Daniel checked in with his phone about the shipping schedules, trying to convince himself it told him the truth: that no ship had or would come within a hundred miles of North Hope Cove all that night. Jittery and exhausted as the adrenaline drained away, Daniel was left deflated and itchy beneath the skin. He suppressed a yawn.

Justin watched him. Daniel set his phone face down on the coffee table and pinched his cigarette from between his clamped teeth.

"No boats," he said.

"Good," Justin replied, and nodded. "That's a relief."

Daniel nodded, though of all the things he was feeling, relief was still not one.

"Do you want coffee? I can make some."

"Nah. Should go back to bed, get some sleep," Daniel said, knowing sleep was still miles out to sea and might not find the shore before dawn.

"Pie?" Justin asked then, and grinned a little in a way that elicited a breath of a laugh from Daniel, despite himself.

"Thanks. No."

Daniel dragged deeply on his cigarette, let his eyes close as he exhaled, and didn't reopen them.

"BJ?" Justin offered. "That's the last thing I can think of to suggest."

"Tempting," Daniel said, and smiled softly with his eyes still closed. "Just come to bed with me?"

"Whatever you want," Justin replied, and Daniel felt him lifting the butt of Daniel's cigarette from between his fingers, and after the time it took him to squash it out in the ashtray and then circle the cottage clicking off lights, latching the dog door, and stirring the stove, Justin took Daniel's hand to persuade him up and out of his armchair. Daniel left it until the very last second to open his eyes, allowed himself to be guided like a kid into his bedroom, and even let Justin persuade him down to sit on the edge of the bed.

"Come on—don't do that," Daniel protested when Justin knelt down to untie Daniel's boots, but Justin only shook his head, smiling up at him, and carried on with it. As the second one was tugged off, and Justin went under the cuffs of his jeans to peel his socks down, Daniel closed his eyes again and sighed, "I can't do this." He hated the words as soon as he said them, and wished he could suck them out of the air and back down his throat.

Justin didn't miss a beat, his voice calm as he replied, "You're doing it." Daniel could envision the shrug that went with it, implicit in the tone of Justin's voice.

"You need someone to rely on, and I'm not that guy. I can't—"

"I never asked you to," Justin said, and Daniel feared they were having two different conversations.

At last Daniel opened his eyes, looked down at Justin on his knees, both of Daniel's wooly socks in his hands, worrying them with his thumbs.

"I can't do both," Daniel said helplessly. "This is all I can handle. I barely can." He was stupid to have ever believed even Justin, a man risking so little—nothing to lose, resigned to his fate—could trust him. Abenaki had broken him so thoroughly, all that remained was a man who climbed stairs, flipped a switch, and fed his dogs. There was not enough of him left to take on even a dying man.

Justin set the socks on the floor beside his knee and leaned forward until his forehead rested on Daniel's thigh, turned and settled his cheek there. Daniel raised his hand, let it hover, and finally dropped his fingers into Justin's dark hair, slow-scratched and dragged. Justin stroked his calf with one hand, wrapped the other arm around the back of his waist and splayed his open palm against the small of Daniel's back.

Soon Daniel was shaking, shoulders collapsing, and though he squinted hard to hold them back, fat tears dripped onto Justin's bent head. Justin held him harder, dropped a kiss on the fabric of his jeans.

"I don't need anything," Justin whispered, and his voice was hoarse. Daniel sniffed hard, swallowed the muck. "The worst is over. We're already dead on the rocks."

Daniel felt it in his muscles, in his bones. Shattered. Beyond hope. Exhausted and bruised.

"It's not supposed to be like that," he argued, his voice small and edged with anger.

"That's how it is."

"I don't want to have to wonder if it could have been different," Daniel told him, resistant to saying it plain: If you do it, I'll blame myself; I'll spend the rest of my days hating myself for not saving you. Please just stay.

Justin rubbed his thigh with a cupped hand, comforting. "I know. I don't want you to." After a few moments he added, "There's time."

Daniel shook his head, though Justin couldn't see it.

"You need more," Daniel told him.

"No."

Seconds piled up in the silence between them.

"Time for bed," Justin said then, quiet and firm, and gathered himself up to his feet. "You wanted me to come with you."

Daniel nodded and grabbed for Justin's hand, pulled it to his mouth and kissed the back of it. His limbs were leaden as he undressed, and he let his clothes fall where they may, tangled with Justin's on the floor. In a few minutes they were under the weighty pile of quilts, Justin's narrow naked back nestled against his chest. The crook of Justin's knees the perfect cradle for his own. Justin's ribs under his arm rising and falling with his breath, and Justin's heart beating against the edge of his pinky where his hand lay curled against Justin's chest. His cock soft against Justin's backside. His lips and nose tickled by Justin's spill of hair on their shared pillow. In the dark—just cool skin and breath sounds—they were safe. But even before the sun rose the next morning—every morning—the whole chaotic world would roll in and crash against them. The dread of being drowned kept Daniel awake through the night.

Twenty

Once Justin's car had vanished from view, Daniel called the dogs over and threw balls for them, some on the road and some in the snow, which had melted down enough that they didn't mind running in it, and which was crunchy enough that in some places they didn't break through, only slid and slipped. Daniel tried not to laugh at them; they looked so affronted each time their paws flew out from under them.

He'd returned to Justin once the light was switched off, burrowed into bedding that smelled rank and sweet from their having spent the night in it, found Justin's sweat-salty, soft prick in the pitch dark and with gentle strokes of his tongue, wet brushes with his lips, brought Justin awake, pleased by his soft moans and caught breath, clasping an arm around his rolling hips to draw him nearer. Justin reached for him, skimming soft fingers over his shoulders and down the sides of his open throat, dragging the wrong way through his hair, clutching the bed sheets near his head, murmuring his pleasure.

Daniel swallowed, thick and bitter, a hot slide, and Justin dragged him up, took him in hand, kissed himself out of Daniel's mouth, praising him— *yes*—pleading—*yes*—wanting and needing him—*yes*—*yes*—*yes oh yes*—until Daniel shuddered a groan and held on to Justin's wrist. Held on.

As they lay together in the muzzy warmth of *after*, Daniel skimmed his fingers over and over Justin's slender bicep, their two faces only just far enough from each other to see clearly. Justin's eyes were closed, but his smile gave him away as awake.

"Last night," Daniel said, nearly a whisper because his panic was a light-sleeping beast and he feared he may wake it. "I was freaked out. I didn't mean it."

Justin whispered, "Yes you did," through still-smiling lips.

"I mean, it's hard. All this. But it's good, too."

Justin nodded, grinning agreement.

"Really good. I just got overwhelmed. I do sometimes feel like I can't do it, but I didn't mean let's not do it."

"I know," Justin assured him, and at last his brown eyes came open and fixed Daniel with a glinting gaze.

"It's good now."

"M-hm." Justin dipped forward, mouth-first, and Daniel closed his lips to catch the offered kiss. "It's good," Justin confirmed.

"OK?"

"OK."

Daniel's relief was a release of shocked breath upon emerging, naked and shouting, from the frigid ocean on a December morning—abrupt and consuming, a pleasant shock to the system. His momentary weakness and panicky blather had not ended them. They were good. They were OK. He let himself smile, then laugh, and when Justin demanded to know what was funny, Daniel grabbed for him, tickled his prominent ribs, invited him to wrestle until the two of them were grunting, breathless, exchanging roles as the one pinned-down and the one reared-up, back and forth until they collapsed against each other panting, laughing, and the dogs came and jumped on them, rousting them from the bed like gulls from the stone wall.

There were the usual teasing jokes over breakfast of scrambled eggs and toast, coffee gone bitter from having sat too long in the pot, but Justin looked unsure of him, averting all his questioning glances before Daniel felt truly compelled to answer. Daniel wanted to reach out and pull him back, but it was a selfish wish and he'd been selfish enough already, letting Justin float and sink, dragging him out too far. Daniel couldn't save him, and anyway Justin didn't want to be saved. And so in the end they were both going down. They kissed beside Justin's open driver's door, and Daniel pressed the thermos bottle of coffee into Justin's slender hand. Justin didn't smile, but kissed him once more.

By evening Daniel had gone through all his motions—put in a call to the solar equipment contractor, found the nearby nest of whatever bird had been plucking with its beak and talons at the cable until it had come loose and showed Daniel all his own nicked and scratched places. He'd pulled the nest from its tree and pulled it apart, assuring every straw and strip of grass blew away in a different direction—and as he buttoned up the house that night he found no need to sweep crumbs or replace lids, no rumpled, wet washcloths to wring out and drape over the rods, no green toothbrush to move from the sink's edge. No black wads of discarded clothing littered the floor of his bedroom. Justin had held him hard and kissed him goodbye, and taken everything as he went.

Coming back soon? Daniel texted. *I'll be in Parker on Wednesday. Lunch at the Coffee Pot?*

Sitting in the barber chair while John Senior trimmed his beard, Daniel kept his phone in his hand beneath the plastic cape, slowly turning it over again and again. Justin had not responded to his text Monday evening, or been in touch at all since he'd left the light station Monday morning, and it did not seem he would be meeting Daniel for lunch within the hour.

"Something on your mind, Danny?" John Senior's wife, Christine, asked. She sounded motherly but not a little nosy. "You're wound up. Everything all right out there at N'hope?"

Daniel pressed his phone against his thigh to still himself. "Fine, yeah. Well." He shrugged slightly. "They might reassign me. Gonna let a computer take a turn running the light, looks like."

She slapped her magazine down in her lap and exclaimed, "Oh! No!" She clucked her tongue. "Why would they—that light is as old as this town! Isn't it a historical landmark?"

"No historic designation," Daniel explained. "It's a national park, and the Parks department wants to save some money."

"What will happen to you, though? I'm gonna—you know what?—John, we need to call somebody. Who's our congressman? Danny, who can I call about this?"

Her honest distress over his fate if the light was automated touched Daniel's heart, then immediately set him on edge; he was being looked at too closely.

"No, I appreciate it, but I think it's kind of a done deal by now."

"Well that's just awful. What a disgrace. No one cares about old things anymore—trust me, I am one! Disgraceful."

"Modern world," John Senior put in, sounding resigned rather than outraged.

"Well the modern world is a disgrace," Christine said. "I'm sorry to hear that, Danny. You'll stay in Parker, though." She laid a hand on his forearm through the barber cape and Daniel tensed at her touch, even knowing it was meant nothing but kindly. The whole discussion was rubbing him raw, and he willed John Senior to finish in a hurry.

"I don't know," he replied, and the mental spill of explanations, possibilities—none of them satisfactory—overtopped the banks of his imagination in a hurry; he ground his back teeth together to keep from saying more. He didn't want a different Parks job. He couldn't live in town. If they were going to take the light station away from him, all Daniel wanted was to walk into the forest until even the dogs couldn't find him, build a lean-to, sit with a book until he grew roots, and eventually lie down in the soft wet mulch of fallen leaves and rotted logs, sink into it, and be done.

He pulled his phone out from under the cape, swiped its screen to life— a rude but obvious hint he wished no further engagement on the subject, why had he even brought it up?—and looked for a text he knew hadn't come, checked for missed calls, looked at his email in-box.

There came the jingle of a bell as the door opened and one of the local women came in, carrying a plastic car seat over one arm, and Christine stepped down from the chair to greet her client. She patted Daniel's shoulder as she passed. "You just tell me who to call," she offered.

"Yeah, thanks."

John Senior gave a few last snips beneath Daniel's chin and leaned back, peering over the top rim of his eyeglasses.

"Good enough," he said, and Daniel couldn't help but crack a smile.

"Couldn't ask for more," he said, and John Senior hummed a grumble of agreement as he began to brush the tiny, fallen hairs from Daniel's neck.

Daniel collected his mail from the post office, and his box of discarded books was pretty full, so he took it, deposited it all in the passenger seat of his truck. The dogs were grudging to give him room, exhausted from having ducked around each other to get the best view out the passenger window the whole way to town from the light station. He gave them each a scratch on the head before shutting the door, then crossed the street to the diner, thinking if Justin wasn't going to show up, he might take his lunch to go. Even the required minimum of small talk with the waitress and the regulars looked like too much to take on, from where Daniel stood pulling open the glass door, ringing a bell that blared his arrival to the whole world.

"You guys are going to help me retire early, buying up all the pie," Linda the waitress said with a smile. Daniel stood by the counter, not taking a seat on the stool.

"Us guys?"

"You and Justin Strongbow. Remember you two in here for supper one night, sitting over there, and didn't you take one to go? Now he's in here every week, and seeing how skinny he is I know he's not eating them all by himself!" She laughed. Daniel wondered what she imagined the relationship was between him and Justin; then wondered Justin's thoughts on the subject, given the stupid things Daniel had blurted, weepy with panic, crushed by the weight of his own incompetence.

He forced a small smile. "Can I get the turkey club and some tomato and bean soup, to take?"

"Sit down and stay a bit," she encouraged. "What's the rush?"

He played it off with a different smile and a helpless shrug. "Dogs are getting antsy about being in the truck. Time to head back."

"Dogs will run your life, won't they?" she agreed, then said over her shoulder, "Hey, Pat, you heard? Turkey club and soup of the day, to travel. I have a Yorkie at home who really thinks he's king of the castle. You want coffee, honey?"

"Sure. Thanks."

She fitted a cardboard sleeve around a paper cup and poured him one while he waited for his food.

"Has he been in here, the last couple days? Justin Strongbow?" Daniel heard himself ask.

"Not since the weekend, I don't think. I'm not here all the time, just feels like it." She smiled and set the cup in front of him.

"What do I owe you?"

"Ten-oh-nine." He passed her a ten and a five.

"Keep it."

"What? No, honey."

"Please."

"Well, thanks a bunch, then." She retrieved a brown paper bag, folded and stapled at the top, from the kitchen's pass-through window, and handed it to him. "No pie today?" She grinned as if she was teasing him, and though it was genuine—harmless and friendly—Daniel was inexplicably embarrassed.

"Not today. See you in a couple weeks." He gathered his bag and cup, couldn't wait to escape. "Take care."

"You too, honey. If I see Justin Strongbow I'll tell him you were asking for him."

"Thanks," he replied, already out the door. To himself he muttered, "Christ." His hands were shaking; he was coming apart. "Home time," he told the dogs as he swung himself into the driver's seat. They nosed around his lunch bag until he made a disapproving noise at them.

Heading back to the light. Are you home? Can I come out your way? He texted, so certain he would not get a reply that he didn't bother to wait for one, and didn't bother driving toward Six Rivers, instead only backed the truck out of the slanted parking space and headed for home.

Days passed with no messages from Justin. Daniel regretted having spilled his guts about how ill-equipped he was to deal with Justin's aftermath. Justin could assert all he wanted that the two of them had already fallen and crashed, with nothing left to worry about, but Daniel worried. Worried himself into sick, heart-pounding panics and sleepless nights and letting the light go out. A dying man deserved to be tended to and nursed, even if he wasn't to be saved, and Daniel was not the man for such a vital task. In the clutch, instead of cradling the defenseless or leveling the threat, he could only be counted on to knock himself out cold and then play dead until the worst was over.

No matter anyway; Justin had packed his things and driven away and gone silent, to punish Daniel or to more easily forget him. A clean break Daniel had never meant to make. Probably—though regrettably—for the best.

Mags loped around the parlor, stared at the sofa, stood on the middle cushion and looked accusingly at Daniel across the room.

"Nope, sorry girl, just us kids again."

She looked disgruntled, and took herself outside to walk it off. Daniel opened the file on his laptop containing his letter to Parks. He tried to envision himself reading it out at the public hearing to which he'd been repeatedly invited, in a small wood-trimmed meeting room, probably with tables arranged in a U-shape or a square. He imagined half-interested people staring across at each other while drawing doodles on legal pads, pretending to take notes on why it was important that Daniel Howard—yes, *that* Daniel Howard—be allowed to stay at North Hope Cove, a hermit and a slave to his routines, because it kept him sane, and kept him alive. The world assumed that as a man given a second chance Daniel ought to greet each dawn on his knees with gratitude, with grand plans to make every day his Best One Yet. Daniel only tried to make each day better than his worst one, which was not the day of the massacre, but the first day after the final memorial service, when Daniel—the lone survivor—was left without anyone to apologize to, with a headache and numb hands. He lay down on his bed behind locked doors and knew it was only a matter of time before the fuse lit on that awful day hissed its smoky, smelly path into his chest, and finally stopped his heart.

Daniel leaned back in the black plastic desk chair, rested his palms against closed eyes dry from staring at the screen. Five past noon. Time to feed himself.

Daniel's nights became restless, his sleep patchy and shallow. Long before dawn one early-January morning, he gave up hope of more sleep and let himself leave the bed to stoke the stove embers and start a pot of coffee. The dogs checked on him briefly, then went back to sleep. Daniel discovered a spot of crud on the stove top and scraped at it with his thumbnail, cigarette held between his first two fingers. He remembered Justin turning on the oven light to watch their roast as it cooked, and let out a laugh despite himself, slightly giddy with sleep deprivation. He sent a text even before pouring his coffee.

Come for Sunday dinner.

As he considered breakfast—eggs, toast, and meat; or oatmeal with yogurt and some frozen berries—Daniel's thoughts drifted to memories of that day Justin showed up smiling with armloads of groceries. How they'd stood close by each other as they peeled and chopped potatoes, nestled the roast into the pan, cracking wise and touching each other freely, exchanging chaste kisses across the table as they set it. Justin humming, singing under his breath, his face wide open and soft with smiles. It had been such a relief to see Justin feeling better.

But had Justin ever had a psychiatrist's appointment on a Monday morning before? Daniel couldn't remember; all his own days were the same, except that some were now days with Justin and others without. It was too much to ask that he pay close attention to Justin's calendar, especially early on. Four days had passed without word from him, which didn't make sense to Daniel, given how good their last time together had been. Unless.

Had it been the *last* time? A near perfect day, cooking and eating, reading side by side in the cozy parlor, soulful sex without bruises or cursing. Justin quick to assure him, in the dim light of morning on a shared pillow, that everything was good. A kiss goodbye that left Daniel smiling.

Fuck, was that you leaving me with a good memory of you? Like you do to your dad? Please text me back.

He waited perhaps ten seconds before he dialed; the call went straight to voicemail, which was full.

I know maybe it felt like I didn't want this anymore, but I do.
I still want you. I'm not ready for the end.
If you're alive, just please let me know.

Reminding himself of the ungodly early hour, and of Justin's propensity for long, deep sleep, Daniel carried his phone into the bedroom and left it on the side table, out of sight and mind while he went back to cook his breakfast. Eventually the dogs gave in to the smell of sausage patties frying and stretched themselves awake, shaking their coats and making their tags jingle. They reported to him for thumping pats on the sides, scratches beneath the chins, and he unlatched the dog door to let them out, though they hesitated. At last Maggie went out, but Tugboat elected to stay, making rounds of the cottage and eventually nosing up a half-stick of rawhide from behind the bathroom door.

Daniel ate his breakfast at his usual slow pace, though every gesture required determined restraint; he wanted to quick-kill the time until Justin replied. Three eggs, toast, sausage, and coffee. Dishes and skillet washed and set in the rack to dry. He managed to dress most of the way—flannel shirt left unbuttoned over his thermal one, socks but no boots—before he finally picked up his phone to check. Nothing.

If you're not alive, just please let me find you.

He bit his lips, thumb hovering, not wanting to send it. Daniel scolded his superstitious hesitation; he'd learned in the worst, most awful way that despite that old saw about speaking of the devil causing him to appear, the unthinkable could happen even completely unbidden, never even dreamed of. He felt it was not a matter of merely tempting fate, but of outright inviting it to gut-punch him. He braced for the blow, and sent the message. Then added another.

You promised.

Twenty-one

"Away to me, dogs. Go get'im."

Heavy-footed in the snow, Daniel trudged up the path to the cliff top, while the dogs picked their way through the rockfall with their noses in the air; he lost sight of them as the pines grew thicker around him. There were no obvious footprints on the path, but the recent non-pattern of sunny days and squalling snow made the snow's surface uneven. If someone had walked the trail days before, evidence of him had likely been blurred beyond recognition.

Long minutes later, panting softly due to his faster-than-usual pace, Daniel arrived at the cliff's apex—mostly flat—mostly rock. The sun had melted a lot of the accumulated snow so he walked easily, in a box-like pattern learned in a forest search-and-rescue course once upon a time. He scanned the ground, the crotches of trees, the thickest parts of shrubs—anywhere someone might leave an envelope, their phone, even the ground-out butt of a cigarette. The sea was roiling and the tide was in; the sky was overcast everywhere and downright dark a few miles west. Storm coming.

Daniel found he both wished for and dreaded something to find. He would not get close enough to the edge to see the whole rockfall; superstition and a sense of over-caution more than a fear of falling kept him away. Sometimes—if he got too close—he felt he might throw himself off, though when he stayed away from the edge such a thing never occurred to him. It was a panic reaction, a strange random idea that took up residence at the cliff's border with the sky. No sign of the dogs in the crescent of gravelly ground visible to him, and no sign of anything out of sorts. They hadn't barked, though with the sea roaring and the wind spiraling unpredictably around the cove, he may have missed it if they had.

Up top, there was nothing disturbed, nothing left behind. Daniel stood in what he figured was the center of the clearing, sheltered three matches from the breeze before he got his cigarette going, and turned a slow circle on the spot while he smoked it, making one last scan of the ground and the brush, even above him to the tops of the trees, just in case. He imagined a rope, corrected it to a leather belt. He imagined Justin's little orange car with the driver's seat reclined and a length of hose pinched in the window. The bed in his messy, dark gray guest room at the inn, and a pile of pills on the nightstand—easy enough to buy if he hadn't already been hoarding his own; teenagers and fishermen were often broke, always bored and in pain. Daniel imagined the TV left on, for company.

Once satisfied he hadn't missed anything—that there really was nothing to find at the top of the cliff—Daniel began hiking down, cigarette in the corner of his mouth, bare hands in the pockets of his coat. At the bottom of the trail, he turned toward the rockfall.

Tugger appeared behind a boulder, just his head visible, and he dipped down and scooted around it on his way to meet Daniel. He sat, tail wagging, looking expectant. Relaxed.

"Good boy," Daniel told him, and gave his head a scratch and pat, pulled softly at his ear. The dogs had followed the command to find someone among the rocks. Tugboat, at least, was sure it had only been for practice.

Mags let out a single bark, and Daniel moved toward it; a sourness gathering in his dry mouth he quickly attempted to smother in silvery cigarette smoke. Tugger trotted along beside him. Another bark from Maggie turned them south. Daniel came to a pinch point where two boulders faced off, and had to find a route around them. He called for Mags and she returned it with two quick yaps. His face tingled, not from the cold.

Around two more rocks the size of minvans he saw her, loping in a hesitant circle with her gaze fixed on the ground. There was no body, that much was clear, and Daniel let out a groan of relief. His gaze flicked reflexively, gratefully, up to the face of the cliff.

"Whatcha got, lady?" he asked, and stepping closer he saw what had alerted her: a soaked, rumpled glove that might have been Justin's, or anyone's, probably dropped that night they'd found the man in the blue parka. "Ah," he said, with yet more relief flooding into his shoulders, gently unknotting them. Daniel picked it up and flattened it in his hand. He brought it toward his face and sniffed. Just wet fleece. "Good get, Mags. Nice work."

He gave her praise and petting, and her tail went like a whip, pleased with her success.

Daniel resumed his full height and started back toward the cottage, both dogs at his heels. "Where's Justin?" he asked them, as if they might simply tell him the answer. They cocked their heads, probably wondering the same.

Once inside, he checked the time and the latest weather forecast; he'd seen dark clouds while on top of the cliff. It was a close cut, but if he put his foot down, he could make it back in time for the light, even if the storm landed before dusk. He tried calling Justin again, pulling together some road-food and loading it into a plastic grocery bag. There was no indication Justin's phone had rung, and the voicemail remained full.

I'm coming to Six Rivers. If you're alive, let me know and save me the trip.
Please.

Justin's car was not parked behind the inn, and it was Lia that let him in after he circled around from the sliding door at the back of the house, which was locked, to the front, where he paced on the granite stoop after ringing the bell.

"Donyell, *como vai? Entre.*" Her expression was inscrutable, but it was not relaxed.

Daniel stepped into the foyer while she shut the door behind them, and he blinked, letting his eyes adjust to the relative dim after an hour-long drive squinting at dirty-white snow and the gray-white sky. "Can't get ahold of Justin," he said. "Called and texted." His phone was in his hand so he shook it at her, knowing her English was minimal. "Do you know where he is?"

"Shustin is with you," she said, and her expression darkened.

"No," Daniel said. Lia put her hand to her heart, patted herself there. "Monday, he left." He pointed behind him with his thumb. "I haven't seen him, six days."

"Ay, Monday?"

Daniel interpreted that she had not seen him in the intervening time, either. That he had not been home.

"How did he seem when you last saw him?" Daniel asked, and he knew from Lia's frown she wasn't quite understanding his question. "He was happy? Sad?"

"Not sad, no," she told him, and shrugged. "With you, Shustin is happy. He say, buy dinner, go to Donyell."

"Yeah, he was with me Sunday, but he left Monday morning."

"If he come home, I did not see."

Daniel's hands were cold, sweating, and he wanted a cigarette even though he'd only just finished one in the car.

"Where else would he go?" Daniel asked, and found himself looking around for traces of Justin, for clues about where he might be.

"His father."

"No, not there. But. Do you have his father's phone number?" He held up his phone again.

"The father, no." She was wringing her hands in front of her waist, which did nothing to soothe Daniel's worry.

"Can I?" he gestured up the stairs. "Up to his room?"

"Yes. Yes."

"Maybe there's something up there with his dad's phone number on it," Daniel offered, and started climbing the stairs. The door was closed, but unlocked, and he paused with his hand on the knob before he pushed it open, bracing himself against images in his head of Justin pale and cold, naked, on the bed. Justin in a bathtub of tepid water and congealed blood. Justin hanging from the back of the bathroom door.

But no. Justin was not there, and it seemed he had not been. His bed was unmade but the trash can and ashtray were empty. The bathroom was clean. Daniel sifted through a pile of papers on the table beside the bed, thinking he might find something useful having to do with bonding Justin's dad out of jail on Christmas; there was nothing but junk mail, post-appointment printouts from Justin's psychiatrist listing his future appointments and his prescription dosages. Daniel's fingers were shaky and too thick as he dialed the office number. It was the answering service that picked up—of course, it was Saturday—and Daniel quickly explained he was concerned for the welfare of his friend Justin Strongbow and would appreciate the doctor calling him as soon as possible. He left his number and the woman read it back to him, her voice calm and reassuring that the doctor would return the call promptly.

He sat on the edge of the bed and muttered, "Where are you, where are you, where are you."

There came a soft knock on the open door, and Lia stood on the threshold with creases across her forehead. "I think, is Shustin in hospital?" she suggested. "Yesterday," she said, but gestured with her hand in a way that indicated she meant some other, more distant time in the past, "He no home, many days. Then he say he stay in hospital."

"Yeah, that's when we met. He left me and went to the hospital. University Hospital?" he asked, trying to remember what Justin had told him those months ago. "Or maybe Orono Med Center?"

"University," Lia replied with a firm nod.

Daniel did a web-search for the phone number.

"When I see him, he is happy," Lia said, sounding dismayed. "More happy. He is good with you."

"I thought so, too," Daniel said, as he tapped Call. "I thought he seemed better." He raised the phone to his ear and then berated himself under his breath. "Stupid."

"No," Lia crooned, and her face was full of pity for him.

"University Hospital, how may I direct your call?"

"I'm trying to find out if someone is a patient there. Is that something you could tell me?"

"Just the name. I can't tell you about a patient's condition. And if they have requested no one be told they are admitted, I would not be able to confirm. What's the name of the patient?"

"Justin Strongbow."

"Just a moment. Strongbow, S, T. . ." she spelled the name, then made Daniel repeat his first name before she said, "Yes, Justin Strongbow is currently admitted."

"Can you put me through to his room?" Daniel asked. He felt numb with shock; after so much failure to find any trace of Justin, it seemed too easy that all he'd done was say his name to finally be assured he wasn't dead.

"Yes, one mo—"

"He's not," Daniel blurted, and he heard the woman's hesitation as he cut her off. "He's admitted, he's not dead? Not in the morgue?"

"He's admitted. Not in the morgue. I'll put you through to his room. If there's no answer, hold on, and I'll come back and take a message for you, if you like."

"Yeah, thanks." Daniel had forgotten Lia, standing still and expectant before him. "He's at the hospital. He's OK."

"Ay, *graças a Deus.*" She slapped her palms together prayerfully. "Say he is bad, no call."

"I'll tell him," Daniel half-smiled at her and she went away, pulling the door mostly-closed behind her. He could hear the creak of the stairs as she descended, and then there was silence all around him and only the tinny buzz in his ear that indicated the phone was ringing in Justin's hospital room. Daniel tucked his lips between his teeth and bit down hard.

"Hello."

"Jeezus fuck I thought you were dead," Daniel gusted out. "I've been texting you. Calling."

"Hey," Justin said, quietly, maybe chagrined though his mood was hard to discern from two disconnected words. There was noise in the background, echoing voices and random electronics sounds. "Sorry. My phone died on the way here."

"Your voicemail's full," Daniel reported, needlessly.

"It always is. Messages from my husband. You know. Old ones."

"Yeah," Daniel said, and he let gravity lie him down on the bed, flat on his back with his feet still on the floor. He looked at the ceiling, though there was nothing to find there, either—an emerging theme for him—not even a crack or a cobweb in a corner.

"Sorry," Justin said again, sounding small.

"Christ, Sunny."

"Sorry."

"I looked for you in the rockfall. Sent the dogs out."

"I wouldn't."

Daniel hummed a little and they fell silent.

"I was halfway between the lighthouse and home, but I couldn't leave it like we did. I tried to make it a good few days, but then the light went out," Justin explained, near-whispering in Daniel's ear. "Your wife fucked me all up. I just drove here instead of driving off the road into a tree."

"I'm glad."

"Me, too. Well. Getting there."

"They're helping?" Daniel asked, feeling weirdly detached from the whole situation, up on the clean white ceiling looking down at himself lying on Justin's rank, unmade bed.

"I guess so. New meds. Talking to doctors. Group with a bunch of anorexic college girls."

After another too-long pause, Daniel said, "I should have seen it."

"Nah."

"I should have known. It took me almost a week to figure out what Sunday dinner was about."

"Don't forget a couple really good fucks," Justin joked weakly.

"I haven't," Daniel assured him, with half a smile. He closed his eyes. "Is it. . .did I do something? Hanging on too tight."

"It's nothing like that. It's my stupid brain. I know it's lying to me but it feels real. Trying for the millionth time to find the right recipe to trick it into acting normal for two seconds."

"I hope it works."

"Maybe for a while," Justin said, not sounding hopeful.

"Can I come see you?"

Justin didn't say anything, and Daniel took it for his answer.

"I'm at the inn," he redirected. "Lia wants me to tell you you're bad for not calling."

"Sorry," Justin repeated.

"I can bring you a phone charger," Daniel offered, as if he had not just been rebuffed.

"It's all right. They'll spring me in a couple days."

"OK."

The silence was enormous, and grew.

"I've been thinking I'll go to the hearing, after all. Read my thing instead of mailing it."

"Really? I think you should. Glad to hear it." Through the phone, Daniel heard a public address system summoning response to a Code Green in the ER.

"I don't know what else to say," Daniel admitted. "I'm relieved."

"Sorry again."

"Yeah."

"I have to go meet with a shrink. Not mine, another one. Old school; wants to talk about my parents instead of just writing me a scrip and waving goodbye."

"I'll let you go then," Daniel said.

"It's good to hear you," Justin said, and Daniel's throat thickened.

"You, too," Daniel told him. "Take care of yourself."

"I have to go."

"Right. OK. Bye, then."

"Bye."

The call disconnected and Daniel let his arm fall to the mattress, the phone loose in his fist, and opened his eyes toward the blank ceiling again. He'd failed Justin, failed them both, should have seen it coming, way out on the horizon. Instead it had crashed over both their heads while Daniel looked in the wrong direction. It had sucked Justin away while Daniel slammed face down in the gravel, sputtering and stupid with shock.

He heaved himself up onto his elbows, and then upright at the edge of the bed, feeling his shirt pockets for cigarettes before he remembered Lia's repeated admonishments that there was no smoking in the inn. He left without looking for her, without saying goodbye or thanking her for helping him find what there was to find, which was not a clue to Justin's intentions but Justin himself, in a place much safer for him than Daniel's dark bedroom had ever been. A failed experiment, its ending probably better for them both.

Daniel drove away from the inn with just enough time to get back for the light.

Twenty-two

TXT from Justin Strongbow: Just thought you'd want to know I'm out.
They wanted me to go inpatient but I'm good enough.
I might go to the beach.
Good luck at the hearing. Tell Mags and Tugger hey from me.

Daniel didn't reply to the texts; there was nothing much to say. Since he'd last talked to Justin, he'd settled back into his routines, cooking only enough for himself, sleeping between clean sheets, maintaining the light station, puttering around its grounds and buildings. Everything he did felt like he was buttoning the place up, the same way he did his little cottage every evening. Tying loose ends, settling things into place. He reorganized the back room of the shed, but didn't discard anything because he'd learned over the past year—even more so in the past few winter months—that one never knew what might be useful. A carved walking stick for a man who'd rolled his ankle. An old telescope stand to be turned into a camera tripod.

Justin had left it behind; the only thing of his that remained. Daniel studiously ignored it, propped in the corner of the parlor against the misaligned spines of books, until he no longer could. He returned it to its pre-holiday hiding place under his bed.

He still had no plan beyond his last day at North Hope Cove, whenever that day might be. He imagined perhaps the end of June, before the new fiscal year started. Where he went after that, he didn't know. Several times he'd sat down at his laptop with a mission to put in applications for transfer to open field positions. Not California, of course, but there was one on the upper Delaware river out in New York, and the Appalachian trail was still an option. His old job at Abenaki loomed large, challenging him to man up and walk back into the woods. The building where it had happened had been demolished, he knew; he wouldn't recognize the place, and maybe that would make it possible. He doubted it. He imagined the awkward phone call from the regional director or some other higher-up, asking if it was really what he wanted—after all this time away from it—to reopen old wounds. Joke was on them, though; Daniel's wounds were still fresh, and always would be. He'd go to his grave still bleeding.

The ocean was still an option, too, or a walk deep into the woods. The cliff. Daniel didn't allow himself the indulgence of thinking too much about it. Instead he focused on each day's work, and on reading the books he hadn't gotten to finish. The day after the light remained a blank calendar box in his mind, without even with a number or a day of the week assigned.

Day after day passed in similar fashion, only disrupted by an occasional snowfall or a troubling high tide. Daniel filled the bird feeder every few days, and once spotted the Canada lynx slinging sleek through the woods, loping shoulders in a figure-eight as it padded by, relaxed and confident. He thought about Justin—wondered about him—but reminded himself to let it go. More and more, he succeeded. The world was better off with Daniel on his little patch of ground, on his own, with nothing leaning on him for support he couldn't give.

Daniel dressed in his newest pair of work pants, which he'd been saving since the last time he'd washed them in the outdoor tub. He buttoned up a clean, muted-blue plaid shirt and tucked it in. His hair and beard were not so freshly trimmed as to make obvious his attempt to look normal and un-hermit-like. His letter was all he had to bring with him; he'd printed it at the public library in Parker, two copies, just in case. To get to the hearing and back in time for the light felt as impossible as staying a night in Portland, so for just the one day, he would leave the light on all day. Weather was forecasted to stay clear into the evening and overnight, so the light shouldn't require adjustment. He'd leave before dawn and be back mid-evening, the longest stretch he'd ever spent away from the station. When he thought too long about it, Daniel felt all wrong—disconnected and uncomfortable—so he reminded himself to focus on the most immediate things. Packing food for the road. Coffee in a thermos. His phone fully charged. His letter.

"All right, dogs. I'm going." He knelt to pet them both, and they walked him to the truck, obviously disappointed not to be invited inside. "Keep an eye on things. Back tonight." He checked again that he had all he needed; he'd dropped the plow off the truck the previous day, and gassed it up on his last trip into Parker. Patting his coat pockets for his keys, wallet, and smokes, Daniel tipped his chin toward the cottage. "Home time," he told the dogs, and they obediently returned to it as he started up the truck, took a great sigh of a breath, and started away in the pre-dawn dark.

Once he'd made it several miles inland, Daniel could get a few radio stations, first callers and hosts arguing about pro football, and later a replay of a college basketball game—Maine U versus Vermont Middleborough. By the time he stopped to gas up, use a men's room, and refill his thermos with coffee, he was able to get the classic rock station out of Bangor. In another hour, he'd pass through Old Portsmouth and then it was ninety minutes to Portland. He was making good time; he should arrive with an hour or so to kill before the hearing started, long enough to recover from the drive, not so long he'd be stewing in his own nervousness for too long. He'd practically memorized his letter by then, having read it several times a day even after he'd decided it no longer needed editing—had gone so far as to read it aloud a few times, while the dogs listened but offered no useful feedback.

Just past the truck stop, back out on Route 1, stood a billboard for Old Portsmouth Beach, A Great Maine Getaway Close To Home, featuring a photo of the big Ferris wheel, part of the beach, and a section of boardwalk. Daniel thought about how much trash they must have airbrushed out of the sand, how many sunburned tourists erased from the boardwalk in favor of a few bikini-clad teen girls and smiling families. Crowded beach, lines for the rides, music from the open front doors and windows of every restaurant, noise from the arcades. Wretched place. Just the idea of being in the thick of such a cacophony made Daniel feel pin-pricked and dizzy with the first flush of panic, so he drew in a quick breath and held it, cranked up the radio and began to sing along, refocusing his mind onto what was right in front of him: the steering wheel under his thumb, his elbow on his knee, the thermos of coffee balanced between his thighs. Traffic was growing thicker, though it was still nothing much, as he drove south. Between Old Portsmouth and Portland, it would thin again for a while.

Several miles and about twenty minutes later, another billboard for A Great Maine Getaway Close To Home, this time with three photos: a child with ice cream all around his mouth; a bright red, boiled lobster on a platter beside an ear of corn more yellow than any Daniel had ever encountered in real life; and a taffy-pulling machine at work on bright pink candy. Daniel thought about Justin's text from the previous week, implying he'd left the hospital prematurely, asserting that he might go to the beach, a place where he could be alone without feeling lonely, where the noise and hectic motion soothed him by taking him out of his own head. Daniel didn't know him well enough to know if that was an idle thought or if Justin really might venture there in the dead of winter, just to get away.

He checked the time; if he were at the light station he'd be throwing balls for the dogs, maybe about to start work on a project in the shed. Or quietly opening the bedroom door and laying a hand on Justin's shoulder to wake him. Or folding himself down beside him, finding the angles of his hip and elbow, and the warmth of his rough-whiskered neck. Later, they'd eat sandwiches and chips for lunch, and sit together reading. Walk out into the woods together. Justin would use the snow blower on the front walk and the path to the tower while Daniel plowed out their parking spaces, and up their road.

Jeezus, what was he doing? Driving six hours to talk about how North Hope Cove Light Station was important because it gave him—yes, *that Daniel Howard*, that failure of a man, that victim—a place to hide from the world. He'd embarrass himself. All those strangers, looking at him with pity while he read his stupid letter, poking at him split open and raw just so they could say we're sorry, there's nothing to be done. It was pointless. Meantime the only person he'd ever met who didn't look at him with pitying eyes was out there somewhere, thinking his life was over, and that he had to end it alone.

Daniel flicked his half-smoked cigarette out the window and went into his breast pocket for his phone, flicking his eyes back and forth between it and the near-empty highway ahead of him. He swiped his way to Justin's number and tapped *Call*. It didn't ring, and went straight to the full voicemail. Daniel cursed, killed the call, slowed and signaled as he moved right. There was no shoulder, only deep snow and a steep drop into pine forest. He dropped the phone onto the passenger seat, tried to figure how long it had been since the last off-ramp even as he kept his eyes open for a safe place to pull off the highway.

At last signs appeared for an exit, four miles up the road. A mile and a half. A mile. A half mile. Daniel was heavy-footed, in a hurry, hoping for no state trooper to appear between the trees to catch him doing 90 in a 65. If one did, Daniel would tell him it was life or death and ask for an escort, even though he wasn't sure where he was going. Wherever it was, two men would be saved there, but it could already be too late. Daniel couldn't imagine a life after the light—where he would live, what job he would do, where he would find peace and solace and now and then a cold-water shock to the system that reminded him he was still alive—but he could imagine a life keeping Justin's breakfast warm until he awoke.

"Dammit. *Dammit.*" He cursed at nothing, at the truck for not going any faster, at the road for not being any shorter, at himself for not being the kind of person who would try to text at ninety miles an hour. At last, the exit appeared, and he took his foot off the accelerator, eased down to a reasonable speed as he peeled right toward Old Portsmouth. Thirty seconds later he was in the parking lot of a donut shop with his foot on the brake.

I don't care about after. I want you now until the end.

Where are you? I need to find you.

He didn't wait for a reply, only clutched the phone in his hand as he backed the truck out of the lot and turned onto the state road, headed for the horrible boardwalk to find his lost man.

Daniel parked in a mostly empty lot at one end of the beach. With his silent phone in one hand and a lit cigarette in the other, coat zipped to his chin, he trudged up the boardwalk. Even in winter, there were crowds. Nothing like in summer, but the carnival rides ran year-round, and there was a casino at the other end of the beach. Vacationers bundled against the cold made their way between restaurants and shops, getting their money's worth of their off-season hotel specials.

Justin liked places that were noisy, full of people minding their own business, so Daniel skipped the more staid restaurants and focused on coffee shops, lunch places where the bar was likely more in demand than the food. He ducked inside door after door, looked quickly around, now and then asked a hostess or bartender if they'd seen a young guy, about this tall, long dark hair, dressed all in black? There was a bookstore, likely to be quieter than suited Justin's tastes, but it served coffee so Daniel went in and bought a cup to go, interrogating the girl behind the register while he waited for his name to be called.

Again and again, he found himself leaving a place full of chatter and background music having only had heads shaken at him, having only seen people who were not Justin. Daniel's shoulders were pulled up tight, and he took care not to brush up against anyone passing on the boardwalk; just walking among so many people made him feel abraded and raw, to touch one would be intolerable. A video game arcade seemed a likely spot, and he snaked his way through its dim light, upstairs and down, checking every face. A body of the right height and shape showed Daniel its back, hood pulled up, and he double-timed to reach it, only to find a kid in his late teens, with piercings in his face and a startled look in his eyes.

Another cigarette, more sidestepping to avoid having strangers touch him, or even see him—Daniel kept his eyes near the ground, knowing he could recognize Justin by his untied combat boots, only occasionally scanning far ahead for a familiar head of wavy hair in the distance. For the second time in a few hours, Daniel found himself wondering what the hell he was doing. What were the chances Justin was at the beach several days after an assertion he might go there, in the dead of winter, three hours from home? Daniel stopped to lean on the rail and looked out to sea, a view familiar enough to calm him slightly even as he berated his own stupidity. The hearing would go on without him, surely, while he made a pointless search in a place that made him want to crawl out of his own skin.

Still no reply to his texts. Justin could be anywhere. But Daniel had come to look, and he was three-quarters of the way down the boardwalk, so he may as well finish. Then he'd turn around and go back to the light—the day wasted, his nerves shot—to ponder his purposeless future.

Another coffee shop, and then a narrow bar populated by a handful of rough-looking characters—locals, fishermen newly ashore with money to gamble—where there stood a bottle of beer half-finished, a paperback book beside it, at the far end of the bar. No ashtrays nearby; the owner of the book had likely gone outside for a smoke. Something in the pit of Daniel's chest felt hot and tight, too big for the hollow space inside his ribs. There was a side door, propped open just a few inches, and Daniel strode to it and pushed it open, suddenly hesitant, not wanting to startle whoever was standing outside innocently enjoying a cigarette. Not wanting to be disappointed again.

The smell of the smoke was one Daniel recognized, but not his own brand. The man hunched in a black wool coat with the collar turned up leaned one shoulder against the brick wall of the bar, facing away.

Daniel heard himself murmur, "Hey, Sunny."

He turned, clearly startled, and his dark eyes were shadowed underneath but they went wide, and had a glitter in them, not the usual mischievous glint but one that gathered and which Justin had to blink away.

"I'm sorry." A raw-throated whisper, and as he stepped closer he threw away his cigarette and Daniel opened his arms to pull him in.

"You can stop apologizing," Daniel told him, turned to kiss his temple, held him hard. "Christ, I didn't think I'd find you." Only after the muscles in his arms began to tremble overexertion did Daniel at last release him, and

Justin half-stepped backward. Daniel searched his drawn, sallow face. "It's OK that I did?"

Justin nodded, slow at first, then more emphatically. "I hoped you would. I mean—" His expression pinched, realizing. "Isn't it the hearing today? What day is it?"

"Yeah. I'm missing it. I don't care." He really didn't. He clutched Justin by the wrist, would not let him go. Held on.

"But—"

"They'll do what they want, with or without me. Some things matter more. I needed to find you because I need to tell you." His throat was dry; he licked his lips and swallowed. He squeezed harder at Justin's wrist, probably too hard. "You don't have to be alone." A realization washed warm over him, that Justin was worth the risk of being relied upon. Justin was no burden. Justin could help him not to fail. Half to himself, Daniel added, "And neither do I."

Daniel didn't know what else to say, so shook his head, biting his lips. Justin gave him the smallest of smiles—he was beautiful and looked like hell—and he softened, a gentle settling of his shoulders and a smoothing of the stubbly skin around his mouth. Justin had walked away to spare Daniel a pain he himself knew too well—of being the one left behind after the heroic gave way to the merely comforting, then inevitably failed and fell apart. But as afraid as Daniel had been of another collapse in the face of catastrophe, he'd managed to stand up straighter in those few months than he had in the previous ten years. He could carry them through it. He could try.

Daniel's hand found the back of Justin's neck, warm inside the upturned collar of his coat, and pulled him close, kissed his smoky mouth. Justin grabbed Daniel's jacket-front and held on, pulling them together, fixing them both in place.

When they fell away, Justin said, "OK."

Daniel smiled.

"OK."

Twenty-three

All the paths and trails were overgrown, every shrub and tree exuberant with spring's sap-running warmth, and the brook through the woods ran high on its banks, babbling loudly. Justin thought Daniel, walking a few paces ahead with the carved wooden stick Justin still thought of as a wizard's staff, had never looked so hearty and handsome—so at home—as he did walking the land outside the house, his flannel sleeves rolled back to his elbows, his gold-beige hair a little out of place. A few dozen narrow metal stakes with ribbons of orange tape fluttering from their ends stuck out of the back pocket of Daniel's jeans, and every now and then he planted one, defining new boundaries.

They'd spent the morning indoors, awake nearly from first light, though Justin had made a valiant attempt to drag Daniel back to bed, licking his lips and pinning Daniel's wrists to the pillow over his head. Once the sun was up, there was not even a remote chance of denying it—no more burrowing in the cavelike dark of the cottage's bedroom—so in the end, all Justin had won was a few bites on the neck and shoulder, and a sound smack on the backside before Daniel had him upright and already working while the coffee dripped into the pot. Justin set books on shelves in the great room while Daniel opened the kitchen cabinets and arranged things in a familiar, efficient way Justin would never have had the patience to replicate.

Tugger and Mags bounded up to greet them as they circled around to their starting point between the back door and the three cords of firewood for the stove already stacked between two birch trees. Justin found a couple of sticks and hurled them one after the other, into the woods to keep the dogs happy, and Daniel caught him around the waist, crushed them together side by side with his strong arm, one hand possessively curved around Justin's hip. He steered Justin a quarter-turn to the right, and there in the distance, small but sturdy in their view, was the North Hope Cove lighthouse. It was the view of the light that had sold them both on the house, instantly, with no need for discussion. Isolated on top of its own hill, with a south-facing wall of windows to keep them both sunny, the house was nonetheless only fifteen minutes from Parker Village to the south, twenty from the university to the west, so Justin had access to distracting bustle when tempted to retreat into his own head. If their first few weeks were indicative, mostly they kept to themselves, establishing a routine that let Daniel sleep past dawn and stay awake long after dark, but also kept them companionably busy most of the day—in the house or the surrounding woods. Their list of summer projects would easily keep them working until October.

When the National Parks department announced its final decision to automate the lighthouse at North Hope, they'd offered Daniel his pick of jobs, but ultimately he elected to take the one offered by the three-person Parker Village Council: a newly created, one-man Department of Public Works and Forestry. Daniel had spent the early spring planting violets and pansies in the median along Main Street, and mowing the lawns in front of the elementary school and city hall; he'd filled in potholes created by winter's frost heaves and careless plowing of snow. His list of projects there, too, would keep him busy and earn his pay, which wasn't much, but enough to get him by.

Justin had invited the women who wanted to buy the Blue Moon Inn to stay a weekend so he could get to know them, and they could get to know what Gabriel loved about the house and the barn, the guests and the events he'd hosted, smiling and chatting, charming them with his easy smile and silky accent. Justin buried some of Gabriel's ashes in the dirt floor of the basement, as close to the foundation as he could dig, and more under a huge elm tree behind the barn. When he signed the papers and handed over the keys, it felt more like keeping a promise than betraying one, and though he wiped tears from his eyes the last time he drove away, letting go of the house was a sweet relief.

"Deb and Jessica are having a grand re-opening, Independence Day weekend," Justin reported, as they stood hip to hip at the edge of their woods, admiring the North Hope light from the still-unfamiliar perspective. "They want us to come."

"What, a party?"

"I won't make you stay long," Justin promised, though Daniel seemed surprisingly relaxed about the idea.

"I think it sounds good. Maybe we can sneak off and have sex in your old room," Daniel grinned, and turned to nose into the hair near Justin's ear, butting him like a pup looking for attention.

"It's a date," Justin assured him. Justin liked having things to look forward to; it helped. Lia would become a citizen in mid-June; when Justin sold the inn he'd wondered if she might go back to Brazil, but she'd met a man at church and they were pretty serious, so she rented an apartment over the barber's in Parker, and still shopped at the Vets' in Six Rivers every day. Then there'd be the party at the inn. Parker Village Old Home Days in August. He kept a list in his head, and kept his eyes and ears open for more events to add.

While they'd sat on their sofa that morning after breakfast, finishing their coffee and smoking one of the day's best cigarettes, Justin watched Daniel's hands, the easy way he moved. The creases around his eyes seemed softer than they had before, even in the sunlight that flooded the house, and warmed it so they had to open the doors to the deck, even in the chilly early morning. Justin looked forward every day to whenever the next time would be—that night, mid-morning, sometimes before supper—that he and Daniel would melt together softly, or clutch at each other with urgency, either way leaving marks to remind them they were alive, and that each belonged to the other. Even without a party or a village fair, there was always—always—something to look forward to.